DAVID DONACHIE was born in Edinburgh in 1944. He has always had an abiding interest in the naval history of the eighteenth and nineteenth centuries as well as the Roman Republic, and under the pen-name of Jack Ludlow, has published a number of historical adventure novels. David lives in Deal with his partner, the novelist Sarah Grazebrook.

The Perils of Command

DAVID DONACHIE

Allison & Busby Limited
12 Fitzroy Mews
London W1T 6DW
allisonandbusby.com

First published in Great Britain by Allison & Busby in 2015.
This paperback edition published by Allison & Busby in 2016.

A CIP catalogue record for this book is available from
the British Library.

10 9 8 7 6 5 4 3 2 1

ISBN 978-0-7490-1832-0

Typeset in 10.5/16 pt Adobe Garamond Pro by
Allison & Busby Ltd.

The paper used for this Allison & Busby publication
has been produced from trees that have been legally sourced
from well-managed and credibly certified forests.

Printed and bound by
CPI Group (UK) Ltd, Croydon, CR0 4YY

To Martin Cartwright for his generosity and his company,
both remarkable

CHAPTER ONE

Lieutenant John Pearce was luxuriating in the captain's cabin of HMS *Flirt*, albeit his tenure would be brief. The official occupant, Henry Digby, master and commander, was aboard one of the recently taken French merchantmen, in a convalescent state following the receipt of a bad wound in the recent action in the Gulf of Ambracia.

In a bout of despondency Digby had overexposed himself so his second in command, when he visited him, reckoned that if the man attending his superior had to look to corporeal repair, he had to work on the man's damaged spirit.

Pearce had good reason to be pleased with himself regardless of the sudden and temporary increase of space in which to work. The twin prizes the warship was now escorting represented a great deal of money, much needed to pursue his own private and legal affairs. With the sun well over its peak and with the brig sailing easy, he was in contemplation of that when the ship's master asked to be allowed to enter.

'Winds getting up, Mr Pearce, and I have in my mind that the sky does not seem as friendly this last hour.'

Matthew Dorling was young for his post but he was ten times the sailor of his titular superior. At sea since he was a nipper, Dorling had risen to the position of master by dint of hard work and application added to natural ability. He had also, in his years afloat, been exposed to observations on the weather both personally taken and related by older practitioners.

This constituted a body of knowledge and folklore that told him much about climate patterns, cloud formations and tidal flows that to an experienced sailing master were as plain as words on the page to a reading man and still something of a mystery to a man who had come by his rank in a sudden and unusual way.

It was not to question his judgement that John Pearce joined Dorling on deck, but to extend his own understanding. The master requested he harken to the singing of the wind in the rigging and note the slow but steady increase in the level of noise. Not that it was needed; the strengthening breeze could be felt on the skin and it was oddly warm in what was a Mediterranean midwinter. Next he was asked to examine the sky to the south-west, its present direction. That was looking what Dorling called 'very brassy'.

'I reckon there's a tempest behind that, of the kind thrown up by the desert.'

'Would I be intruding, sir?'

The question was posed by the marine lieutenant, Edward Grey, who had appeared behind the pair. Pearce turned to see a respectfully lifted hat and smiled; they were relatively new in acquaintance but he had come to respect Grey as a doughty fighter, amply proven in the recent action. In doing so he also observed that there were quite a few hands on deck looking towards the stern and it was clear they too were curious.

In the fighting line Pearce hoped they respected him and likewise Grey; when it came to surviving what the elements could throw at them, and at sea that could be anything and sudden, such faith would not apply. In those circumstances Dorling was their man.

'If it comes upon us and is as bad as I fear it will do so in darkness. I would wish to prepare for it while we can still see what we are about.'

'Sensible, Mr Dorling.'

'Happen it will pass us with no ill effects, mind.'

'I hope you know that when it comes to such matters you will scarce get an argument from me.'

That brought forth a jaundiced look from the brig's master, quickly masked. There had been more than one occasion since the pair had sailed from the Hampshire anchorage at Buckler's Hard when John Pearce had done precisely that and with perilous consequence.

'Are we expecting a hurricane?' Grey asked, softly.

'Taking precautions, Mr Grey, that's all,' was Dorling's reply. 'Mr Pearce, I have a mind to take us close to our two captures so you can have a word with the crews, given you are competent at their lingo. I will tell my master's mates what I want but it would be best if the men they must order about know what is required and are willing.'

It was not just the whistling rigging that indicated something troubling in the offing. Imperceptibly but noticeably the deck beneath their feet had canted slightly more from the pressure of wind on canvas and there was a discernible increase in the swell.

The sun, which had been sinking and would always finally do so in these waters as a red orb, was that colour already, which meant a higher level of dust in the air than normal, while the Southern Adriatic, across which they were sailing, was as prone as all other areas of the Western Mediterranean to sudden squalls and tempests.

Trapped between the southern deserts of North Africa and the massive mountain ranges to the north, sudden gales could come from any quarter, even Pearce knew that much. Given agreement Dorling quietly ordered the helmsman to alter course, first to close with *L'Elize*. Once alongside, Pearce, through a speaking trumpet, warned the French crew to prepare for the very worst, adding a reminder that they owed their very lives to the men aboard *Flirt*.

'What was the nature of that last request?' asked Grey. 'I heard you mention Mr Digby?'

'I asked that he be lashed in his cot and that made secure. The last thing he could survive is being cast out onto a hard deck. Also, that the man tending him stays by his side.'

Dorling was now instructing his master's mate, who had charge of the skeleton prize crew, to get rigged storm canvas, batten down the hatches and clear the decks of anything loose. As soon as he had done so the brig changed course once more to issue the same set of commands to the second merchantman, *Jeune Eugene*.

Matters were well in hand aboard *Flirt*, topgallants already struck down and the topmen bending on heavier canvas both aloft and on the bowsprit. Extra preventer stays were being rigged to the masts while the gunner, Sam Kempshall, was checking that his cannon were well lashed to the bulwarks, the round black balls in their plaited rings removed to be stored in the bowels of the ship.

These things happened naturally, almost without spoken orders. Pearce knew that below, men would be securing barrels with wedges and extra ropes, others adding straw to the manger to protect the livestock, bound to be tossed about on such a small vessel. It was ever thus on a well-run ship and HMS *Flirt* was such a vessel.

The crew were, almost to a man, volunteers and, despite some disagreements on the way from Corsica to the Gulf of Ambracia that had hinted at disharmony, John Pearce and Henry Digby had never allowed themselves to ignore the kind of duty that made such efficiency possible.

In the cabins – apart from the main, they were no more than cubicles screened off by canvas – the servants were likewise making safe their masters' possessions. A ship at sea was always a dangerous place but in severe weather anything loose could be deadly, so the work was carried out with care. A flying object was not choosy of the rank of its victim.

The wind was strong now and increasing; the final act for John Pearce, and he needed no advice from anyone about this, was to change the heading of the whole trio of ships. He reckoned he had plenty of sea room and that would allow him to run before the storm to mitigate some of its force. It would take him away from his intended destination but that mattered not at all since time was of little consequence.

The wall of water ran just ahead of the sun sinking into the western horizon, black and like some kind of celestial screen until any light was suddenly extinguished. It hit the deck to the sound of hard drumming to then disappear as strong jets through the scuttles. The hatches were shut and would remain so unless the sails needed to be adjusted, the only folk on deck being those who were needed to steer and a pair of steady hands in the chains with logs that would be continuously cast to try and calculate their speed.

Three men were on the wheel, one of them Dorling and including, for his strength, Pearce's friend and so-called servant Michael O'Hagan. The man in command, clad like the others in oilskins and a foul-weather hat, stood behind them swaying with easy grace on alternately giving knees, but that could not last.

When the full force of the wind hit the stern it would be time for that old and wise saw, 'One hand for the boat,' and in this case often two. The seamen in the chains were lashed off to avoid being cast overboard: danger would arise when it came to changing them; it was too exposed a position to be occupied for longer than a half a watch by the same souls.

Edward Grey had put two of his marines to guard the spirit room, with muskets and bayonets. Pearce was unsure if that was wise, given it sent out a message of distrust. Yet it was true that if a tempest evoked fear in those who could see and feel its strength, the effect was ten times worse for those confined below. Naval folklore abounded with tales of men made desperate by fear of drowning being determined to die in a state of total inebriation.

There was no quiet talking now, only shouts could carry. The waters around them boiled in that way particular to an inland sea, bringing high waves but with little trough between them, which presented much danger as the stern of the ship would have just ridden one before a second came thudding in to make holding a steady course close to impossible.

The brig, lifted and with its rudder exposed, would yaw and it took every hand on the wheel to steady the ship when it was once more submerged. In this, timing was crucial, it being doubly risky to overreact and swing a rudder while there was no force of water for it to act upon.

Given their stern lanterns were invisible, no one on deck knew how their sister vessels were faring. In theory, deeply laden merchantmen, larger by far than HMS *Flirt*, should handle such weather with greater ease. John Pearce could not avoid the thought that theory be damned; it depended on competence added to luck whether a ship survived. In such a sea a fluke combination of waves and wind could confound the most proficient helmsman.

Nor was the wind steady; it was gusting, which made the occasional diminution as equally treacherous as its full force as stretched canvas ceased to billow, that putting extra strain on the creaking masts. Not that it ever fully eased, but such a fluctuating gale put much stress on the falls holding in place the yards, causing them to tighten and loosen in a manner that could cause a break.

The moment when that fear became manifest was one to savour and take pride in, but only in retrospect. The line that snapped snaked across the deck and would have cut in half any human flesh it encountered so great was the force. The wind continued to act upon it to create a whip even when it lost its main threat, so it posed a continuing hazard.

The mainsail yard and the well-reefed sail upon it, released, began to swing one way then another so the way on the ship was now solely maintained by the straining jib sail. Added to this was the pressure of the waves, and since they were coming in at angles, the danger was close to mortal. It was John Pearce who went forward, driven along by the wind, holding on for dear life to the manropes rigged earlier, to call all hands on deck.

The men that rushed up from below walked into a near blinding downpour but that did nothing to impede what years of imbibed knowledge told them was necessary. The loose fall was taken in strong hands and bare feet were jammed into the soaking deck to hold steady the mainsail yard, this while their mates contrived a secure knot that would repair the break. That complete, the yard was once more hauled square and lashed off to a cleat.

John Pearce had witnessed this kind of behaviour before, but it never ceased to amaze him how well a British tar behaved in such circumstances, though he would be the first to concede that such skills were commonplace in men who made their living on the sea from whatever nation they came.

In calmer recollection it served to also remind him that his own skills, at least when it came to knots, were as good as those he commanded, albeit they were rusty given it seemed an interminable time since he had sailed before the mast as a pressed seaman and had received instruction in the art.

The night was long in these waters, a full fourteen hours and exhausting. The helmsmen could be changed but both captain and master must stay on deck and there was no relief until the light of day began to penetrate the thick overhead cloud, still dark and forbidding. Throughout the night the bells had been rung to tell all of the time and Dorling had dragged himself along the deck on the man ropes to enquire from those casting the logs what speed they were making, that marked on the slate below the binnacle.

Occasionally he would disappear into the tiny cubicle that contained his charts to make some calculations. In full daylight, and with a weary but worried face, he pressed his lips to John Pearce's ear to inform him that all that sea room they had enjoyed was fast diminishing. The gale was driving them towards the string of islands that dotted the coast of Dalmatia, while those same islands were surrounded by rocky shoals that would be near impossible to steer away from even if they could be spotted in time.

'You think it best to come about?'

'There's a rate of guesswork in my calculations.'

'But!' Pearce barked; this was no time for prevarication.

'Not at this moment, but if this is still gusting by the time we ring the first bells in the afternoon watch, then I reckon it to be necessary.'

The next voice in Pearce's ear was that of Michael O'Hagan, back on deck for his third stint at the wheel, who took the liberty of addressing the man he served in the familiar manner normally reserved for private conversation.

'How are we faring, John-boy?'

Pearce answered through salt-caked lips, while the Irishman's height required that he duck to make hearing possible. 'I daresay you have been praying for salvation?'

'Sure since I first put my hand on the wheel and spoke many an hour past.'

'Well don't give up on it.'

'Saints be praised,' came a mocking response, 'you've seen the light.'

'The only light I can see is from the sun and there's precious little of that, Michael.'

'Take my advice, John-boy. Before the water reaches your lips it is best to confess your sins.'

'There won't be time, Michael, for you or I, we are such transgressors.'

That joshing exchange cheered John Pearce; he and O'Hagan disagreed fundamentally about religion but kept their differences from ever becoming disputatious. To Pearce it was all superstition: Michael agreed with that but saw it as only proper that, while being Irish, his faith was of the Catholic persuasion and total. Sometimes it occurred to Pearce, and he assumed to O'Hagan as well, that they should not be friends at all.

There is a truism that a tempest will often blow itself out and in that case the point of maximum threat comes just before it begins to ease. It was hard to credit that the screaming in the rigging could become any louder but it did so, this as one of their merchant consorts came into view, the way it was being tossed about driving home just how much the sea was a torrid mass beneath their keel.

Like HMS *Flirt*, the *Jeune Eugene* was having its rudder exposed by the short troughs. Also like the brig she was safe as long as she could hold her course. The danger came from the head falling off so far that the waves began to strike beam on. This could drive it further abreast of the run so that a following crest would take the ship fully on its quarter, which would drive it over, and if that went too far before it could be corrected a capsize and destruction was inevitable.

It was a cruel necessity that had Pearce order a man aloft to see if, in the increasing daylight, he could catch sight of *L'Elize* and he watched the topman who climbed the shrouds with some trepidation. Was the fellow, young agile and arrogant, when he eschewed the lubber's hole and clambered past the mainmast cap, showing off in such conditions as if there was no wind to speak of?

16

That passed on he went up the narrowing rope ladder until he made the crosstrees where a swung leg and a strong arm kept him safe. The other arm shot out to indicate a sighting – there was no point at all in a shout that could never be heard – and John Pearce breathed a sigh of relief for he had hopes invested in those two ships that went beyond the mere desire that those who sailed them were unharmed.

There was also the comfort of knowing that Henry Digby was probably safe, for it would have been too cruel an irony that he should have survived a dangerous cutting out expedition to perish by drowning.

'I reckon it to be easing, Mr Pearce – not by much, I'll grant. but a bit has come off the last strong gust.'

The speed with which the tempest fell away was as swift as the manner in which it had come upon them. The sky cleared before it lost its full power and that alone was enough to lift the spirits, albeit it presented the men on the wheel with a deck covered in loose objects, mostly canvas and ropes. No amount of lashing off could survive such a blow.

A cartridge of powder was fetched aloft by the gunner, while his brother Brad Kempshall, the ship's carpenter, began an inspection of the damage. Part of the taffrail had been torn from its seating, a pair of gun port covers had carried away, but he was happy to report to the quarterdeck that they had suffered little, given the strength of the storm.

The signal gun was loaded and fired to call the attention of their consorts, and with all hands on deck and the topmen aloft and ready, HMS *Flirt* put up her helm and spun round to resume her original course, which was an order that the merchantmen should follow suit. The wind was easing by the ringing of each half-hour bell and soon the life of the ship could resume its normal progress under a full suit of sails.

Even if it was late in the day, the decks were swabbed and flogged dry while everywhere below from manger to captain's cabin was subjected to its daily cleaning with vinegar. The chicken coop was fetched on deck so that the sound of cackling could be added to the feeling that all was right with the world.

The cook had got his coppers lit as soon as it was safe to do so, and since it was a Sunday the whole crew were assembled to be read the Articles of War, which John Pearce related to them in lieu of a proper religious service, his reason for doing so being that he refused to act the hypocrite. Let those that believed pray to their own God – Papist, Anglican or Methodist.

As he closed the tract, which promised death for a whole raft of offences and a severe flogging for many more, he issued the order everyone had been waiting for.

'Mr Bird, please pipe the hands to dinner.'

CHAPTER TWO

When a British man-o'-war was sighted from the twin promontories that lay at the outer edge of the harbour of Brindisi, escorting two heavily laden merchant vessels, that in itself was enough to cause interest, being a rare event. When the locals could see the Union Flag set above the Tricolour, to denote the trading ships were captures, they flocked to the shoreline to catch a glimpse of the men who had effected such a coup, this observed by John Pearce from the crosstrees of HMS *Flirt* and through a telescope.

They had much time to assemble; with the wind coming off the shore, carrying with it the scent of warm, damp earth, it was necessary to beat up to the outer bay in a time-consuming manner. Added to that, Brindisi was a tricky port to enter, the passage to the inner roads being by a narrow channel into which it was only wise to first slot the two French merchantmen while he took a boat to confer with his superior.

'Henry, if you could look through a long glass as I have done you would see an amazing sight. The crowds are so dense I would not be surprised to find when we land a band will be assembled to play us ashore.'

The master and commander of HMS *Flirt* could only manage a wan smile as he tried to raise himself in response, an action checked by a gentle hand from a man who knew that one of the first tasks was to get Henry Digby ashore and into the hands of a proper physician. The man who had been treating him, French and a gentle soul, was competent, but only up to a point.

For all his palpable concern, Pearce was eager to get off the merchantmen and back to the brig. Given the crowds he had espied it would not surprise him to be in receipt of an official reception. He was still in his old working uniform so he would need to spruce up to make the right impression on any local dignitaries.

Brindisi lay within the Kingdom of Naples, allied to Britain in the war against the French Revolution. Being of such a size and importance the governor would be a person of some standing. For the naval and military he had spotted the upper poles of what looked to be a frigate in the inner roads, while the fortress that overlooked the city was formidable enough to warrant a decent-sized garrison under a high-ranking officer.

The salutes began while he was still in the cutter, fired from another fort set on an island in the wide bay, but that was of no concern; the reply from the brass signal gun was seen to by Matthew Dorling, left in charge until Pearce was rowed alongside to be enveloped in a cloud of smoke from the discharge.

There was a moment where he contemplated a quick dip in the sea but there was too little time and if he could see through a telescope what was awaiting them, those ashore and curious would likewise have many a glass trained on the British warship. Thankfully, Michael O'Hagan had drawn off some water from the barrels in the hold and that allowed him to strip off and wash, a hot bowl supplied with which to shave, all carried out to the sound of Lieutenant Edward Grey exercising his marines for whatever ceremony they might be required to perform.

'I am being hounded, John-boy, for what it is you are planning.'

The Irishman said this in a very soft voice, always careful to never let anyone hear him being overfamiliar with his officer and knowing the ability of his shipmates to hear through six inches of planking. In truth they were intimate enough for O'Hagan to tell Pearce when he thought he was being foolish, a trait all too common in the time since they had become acquainted.

'There's no plan, Michael, other than that we will not, if matters pan out right, be taking our captures back to Corsica. Added to that, Mr Digby needs to be ashore to recuperate and to recover his strength and that looks to me as if it will require time. I have suggested to him, and he agrees, that we will seek to sell our Frenchmen to the locals for the best price we can get.'

'Which even I know is not the right way.'

'The "right way", as you call it, would mean a voyage of a week or more and that argues a fair wind. So far our Frenchmen have been placid, but . . . ?'

'Sure it's no wonder. It was us that saved them from dancing on the devil's rope.'

'Gratitude fades, even for the gift of life. We are not well enough served with hands to provide full prize crews and properly carry our own ship through waters we both know to be dangerous.'

There was no need to elaborate on that point; HMS *Flirt* would be sailing across a sea that had led to the loss of a previous vessel on which they had sailed; to so deplete the crew in order to secure the captures would leave her too short of hands if it came to another serious contest. Chin smooth, Pearce slipped into a fresh linen shirt, soon to be followed by his white breeches.

'We have only got this far because our Frenchmen have done the sailing on their own ships and that tempest left them little choice but to do so willingly. What if such a mood fades? I have no mind to try to weather the south of Italy and beat my way back to San Fiorenzo Bay in such circumstances.'

'You reckon we'd lose them?'

'I reckon, Michael, that we face two possibilities – neither of them good. We have had trouble enough in the waters around Sicily. North of that and approaching the coast of their homeland there is a chance our Frenchmen will be tempted to take their ships back from us one dark night and make prisoners of our own men. If they split up we can only chase one and if they are lucky we could forfeit both, which will leave us with empty pockets and that I cannot countenance.'

'Am I at liberty to pass that on?'

'You may.' Pearce grinned as, black stock tied on, O'Hagan helped him into his deep-blue broadcloth coat. 'And you may tell those who have not already heard through eavesdropping that when the vessels are sold there will be an immediate distribution of the prize money.'

'While you say we could be here a while?'

'Not you, my friend, and it is for your own good. In funds and with me gone you would only get into trouble.'

O'Hagan pulled a face, but he did not dispute the point; he knew only too well his propensity to get blind drunk and seek to chastise anything warm-blooded and male within the range of his fists. At one time that had included John Pearce and he had connected once, although, apart from being fired up for battle, he was stone-cold sober and had acted to save his friend's life. It was, however, unknown to Pearce and Michael wanted it kept that way.

'No, the Pelicans are off to Naples, once the business is concluded, as my escort.'

'I smell convenience,' Michael responded, the look as suspicious as the tone of his voice, given Naples was at present home to Emily Barclay, his friend's paramour.

'I will not deny that the proposal meets my personal needs as well as those of the ship, though I hope you believe I would not put one in the way of the other. But I am sure we will have time to get there and back before Mr Digby is up and ambulant.'

'Holy Mary, I hope we get some liberty time there!'

'That I have to grant you, Michael.' The grin was accompanied by a pat on one large shoulder. 'It would be too cruel that I should enjoy the company of a woman while you are denied the chance to do likewise.'

'I will not be looking for a good woman as you will.'

'No, I daresay you will not.'

Coming up onto the deck Pearce found the marine lieutenant waiting and looking as spruce as was he. The lobsters Grey led were polished and properly blancoed so that their white belts stood out starkly from their scarlet uniforms and shiny blackened shoes.

The cutter was still in the water but the crew had set a flagstaff in the stern and hung from it a Union Flag, while the oarsmen, under the watchful eye of Tilley, Henry Digby's coxswain, had spent as much time as anyone prettying themselves. Each wore tarred sennit hats, their best checked shirt, a coloured bandana, while their pigtails had been seen to and decorated with ribbons.

'Mr Grey, you will of course accompany me?'

'Sir,' came the crisp reply as he indicated that four of his men should proceed into the cutter, doing service this day as a captain's barge. Grey followed and lastly John Pearce went through the gangway, this to the sound of a high-pitched pipe. 'You have your orders, Mr Dorling?'

'Aye aye, sir.'

Pearce took up his position at the stern, the oars were dipped as soon as the cutter was clear and, at a steady rhythm designed to produce the minimum spray, Pearce was rowed towards the narrow channel. The huzzahs, or whatever was the Italian equivalent, he could hear from a long way off and they only grew into a crescendo as they traversed its length. Pearce sat still and eyes forward: such cheers were not acknowledged as to do so would be, for a King's Officer, undignified.

Once through and into the inner roads, Tilley set the cutter's prow for a set of wide steps in the middle of the main part of the town on which stood a single classical column, one his passenger had seen in a pen and ink drawing. There had originally been two, for these steps were at the very end of the Appian Way that had run from Rome to Brundisium in antiquity and was reputed still to do so.

'I would not be surprised to see a Roman consul on yonder steps, Mr Grey,' Pearce said, having explained the significance.

'Clad in a toga with his *fasces* and axe?'

'It would be fitting, yes, when you think of the names that have departed from this very spot. Caesars from Julius to Hadrian and Trajan, even Pompey and quite likely Cleopatra came and went from here.'

What was waiting for them on the steps were not Roman proconsuls or Egyptian queens but their modern equivalents, the dignitaries Pearce had suspected would assemble. All were in somewhat gaudy uniforms, bright-yellow, stark-white and bottle-green combinations, in contrast to the simplicity of Royal Navy blue and Marine scarlet.

The fellow at the centre, his chest festooned with glittering stars, under a cocked hat decorated with ostrich feathers, wore on his shoulders the largest epaulettes Pearce had ever seen. It was an inadvertent but amusing thought that such platforms would be an excellent place to set down a goblet of wine when simultaneously trying to eat.

As he stepped ashore a band did indeed strike up, a rather tinny-sounding affair, but the tune was jolly in a martial sense. Pearce lifted his own naval scraper and introduce himself in French, the language of international diplomacy; it was a relief when the man greeting him, who turned out to be the governor, replied fluently in the same language.

The face fell when he was informed that he was not addressing the actual captain of the British warship, but his second in command, a countenance that went through several states of anxiety as the reasons were explained. The orders he subsequently issued were in Spanish, Naples being a Bourbon-ruled kingdom with an Iberian-born monarch.

The words eluded Pearce but were quickly related to him in French by an aide. The governor's own barge, wide, stable and comfortable, was given the task of fetching Henry Digby ashore, where the finest physicians would treat him at the expense of the kingdom.

'And now,' the aide added, 'His Excellency wishes to show the conquering hero to the multitude.'

And bask in the reflected glory, Pearce surmised, an aside whispered to Edward Grey who would accompany him, his marines left to guard the cutter and the crew. There was also the task of making sure the latter stayed with the boat, given the propensity of the British tar to wander off in a foreign port in search of pleasure.

What followed was a parade through crowded narrow streets to the gubernatorial palace where a banquet awaited, which impressed the guests, given there had been little time to prepare, and naturally Pearce was required to explain how the captures had come about.

When he mentioned Mehmet Pasha, the man with whom the crew of HMS *Flirt* had so recently done battle, the air turned blue with what he was sure were filthy Spanish epithets. Obviously the man who ruled for the Ottoman Empire on the Dalmatian coast was no stranger to those who lived on the shoreline of Apulia.

Details of the actual fight were demanded, to be greeted with equivalent bravoes, as was the sheer brio of the action itself. Drink flowed, strong local Salento wines, followed by a seemingly innocuous lemon liqueur that packed a hidden punch. Toasts were raised to both Kings Ferdinand and George, while the beasts of Paris and the French Revolution were reviled.

Grey had to be helped back to the cutter and it was an unsteady John Pearce who finally got away to visit Henry Digby, now in a comfortable chamber overlooking the harbour, with windows that admitted a cooling night-time breeze. Doctors had tended to his wound and he was now swathed in clean, well-bound bandages.

'I will seek out some people to trade with on the morrow and then I can report progress to you.'

'Not too early, John. By the way your words are coming out I reckon you need a couple of watches before you will be decent company.'

'Nonsense,' was the reply, the common one of someone drunk and unwilling to acknowledge he was slurring his speech. 'Decent night's sleep will set me up properly.'

The hangover with which John Pearce awoke gave a lie to that and not even a long dip in the sea, taken outside the harbour to avoid the effluent of the town, which seriously discoloured the water, was sufficient to alleviate his suffering.

'And here's you chastising me for my drinking,' was the caustic response from Michael O'Hagan when he came back on board to be towelled and groan. 'Best I fetch you some more coffee.'

The discussion regarding what to do with the merchant crews he had already held with Digby. Aboard the captured vessels the crews had been confined, but without any ferocity. While at anchor *Flirt* could spare as many men as were needed to ensure they did not try to get ashore prematurely. Once any trade had been completed they were to be given a choice: to offer their services to King George or to be put ashore with the aim of making their way by their own efforts back to France.

Neither John Pearce nor Henry Digby relished the thought of

taking them back to the main fleet as prisoners, even if in letting them go they were forfeiting the head money that would be paid out for their capture. *Flirt* was already a crowded vessel and the means of confinement that would not cause resentment simply did not exist. Added to that, such prisoners would be taken back to England and held in conditions in which not all would survive.

Brindisi being, outside Venice, the major trading port of the Adriatic, it enjoyed one major advantage for an officer of the King's Navy seeking to sell his captures. Such a busy entrepôt traded extensively with the Levant, so it had a small contingent of British traders permanently based in the town. These men were eager to offer their good offices, which would make the task of dealing with the locals that much easier.

What did not serve was the determination of these worthies to treat this officer to the very depth of their hospitality, which had him repeating the tale of the captures, while once more engaging in endless toasts in both port, wine and brandy. It was thus a staggering and silly-grinning officer who was rowed out to the sloop, needing to be aided to get back on board for a second night in succession.

'I swear I need to be away from here, Henry. My constitution can scarce bear it.'

'Are you saying I have an advantage for being laid up?'

There was jocularity in the enquiry and that, despite a thumping headache, cheered Pearce, given it hinted at a recovery of spirit from a man not much given to smiling. Not himself dedicated to a naval career that had come about by misfortune, just as rank had been gifted to him by luck, he understood that for Henry Digby it was his life. It was that being put in jeopardy that had encouraged him to act in a reckless fashion and to seek a hero's death.

From a middling background he was typical of the men who made up the service: loyal to their king, country and the thirty-nine articles of their Protestant faith. Men like Digby had entered their profession as boys with hopes of one day rising to both high rank and wealth; in short, there was not a midshipman born who did not dream of an admiral's flag and the prosperity that went with it, and such longings would not be abated by several years of service.

To prosper in the King's Navy required a degree of interest, the support of powerful patrons, as well as being seen as a client officer by a serving admiral. Even with that they were required to avoid multiple hazards along the way, those being human as well as practical. The latter was merely the dangers of an unpredictable element, the sea. Then there was sickness, which removed many more men than had ever been lost to the navy in battle.

Finally, there was that peril itself and the search for glory within its remit. The deck of a warship in a fight was as lethal a place as even Lucifer could dream of, with barely aimed round shot blasting around you which, if it did not cut a man in half, could smash through several feet of timber to send deadly splinters flying. These competed with musket fire from the enemy tops or slashing and crushing weapons from an adversary determined to board.

It had to be accepted, too, that a simple error of judgement or a misreading of an enemy's intentions could destroy the most illustrious career. Decisions had to be made well away from those who would approve or disapprove of the choice taken. Then there was politics, which could act to snuff out a promising career while the man suffering would be left with no idea why.

Pearce had to force himself to put such forbidding thoughts aside and return to the main business. 'Our fellow countrymen, traders all, have undertaken to see to the sale of our captures, but no agreement will be concluded of which you do not approve.'

'I would not wish it to be my sole decision, John.'

'Which will not, I am told, be immediate in any case. The doctors reckon you need several weeks to fully recover, perhaps a month, so I request your permission to absent myself. Mr Grey and Dorling are well able to care for matters without my needing to be present.'

'I have no need to ask where it is you intend to go.'

'I am hardly unaware that you disapprove, Henry.'

'Just as I am aware that if I sought to forbid it you would defy me.'

'It would pain me to do so.'

Digby closed his eyes, Pearce hoped to mask his desire to issue such an order. That John Pearce should be in a relationship with the wife of another man was bad enough to his pious mind. But in addition to that she was the wife of Ralph Barclay, a naval officer and a full post-captain and such a fact made matters ten times worse, given there could be consequences by mere association. Pearce had defied him before and his comment that he would do so again hinted that a relationship once fraught but then repaired might revert to tension once more.

'I think,' Digby finally said, his voice a near whisper, 'that I must let our Maker care for your soul, John, since you would not accept any such aid from me.'

'Then since I have bespoken a coach for the journey, I will depart on the morrow.'

'Money?'

'Our good friends here have advanced me a sum against the sale of our captures.'

That caused Digby to purse his lips; if his feelings were unspoken they were nevertheless far from a secret. It was as if he was wondering why John Pearce had bothered to ask his permission, since he plainly cared naught for the answer.

CHAPTER THREE

'Mr Burns, it seems to me that you are in want of confidence when it comes to dealing with the men of your division.'

There was not much Toby Burns could say to his captain in the face of such a palpable truth. It would do him no good to plead that many of the men he was in direct command of knew him of old, he having previously served as a midshipman aboard HMS *Brilliant*. It had been his first voyage as a young naval gentleman and had turned out to be a far from happy experience.

'And I am bound to add,' said Richard Taberly, 'that you seem shy of seeking chastisement when they show you disrespect.'

The sound of running feet were not allowed to distract from what was a wigging, nor were the commands that brought the ship round on another heading. The frigate was patrolling off Toulon, the task to keep an eye on the French fleet and to warn Admiral Sir William Hotham if they showed signs of wishing to come out. Alerted, he could sail his capital ships to bring about his heart's desire, one he shared with every other man in the fleet; a battle in which they were sure they would be victorious.

The disrespect Taberly was alluding to did not encompass half of what his acting lieutenant suffered. The whole crew identified him as a coward and a fabricator, either because they had been aboard when he took the credit for bravery and insight due to another or had heard the tale from those who were. It mattered not; all knew how to goad him without being too overt.

How many times did he hear the word Brittany in a sentence, or variations on the name of John Pearce, the man whose glory he had stolen? Near to drowning came up often, as well as allusions to what was possible on a dark and moonless night. In his heart he was sure there were men prepared to throw him overboard and the thought was a constant terror.

Not that his fears were confined to possible drowning; that merely stood in a long list of what Toby Burns was scared of, all the way up to and including the thought of being involved in a fleet action, or any combat for that matter, never mind the rewards that came with it. He was sure he was benighted by the malice of his superiors from the frigate's premier, a sandy-haired Scot called Glaister, through Captain Taberly to the very top and Admiral Sir William Hotham himself.

'Please take this as a warning, Mr Burns, that I will be watching you and marking your behaviour. I require to see improvement and, I might add, I would not wish to have to relate to our commanding officer that the faith he has so far placed in you was mistaken.'

The 'Aye aye, sir,' came out as a croak.

'Dismissed.'

With Burns gone Taberly sat in contemplation, for if the youngster was troubled he was not without his own concerns. Recently promoted to post rank, although yet to be confirmed by the Admiralty, he found his young acting-lieutenant to be a problem he was unsure how to handle.

Taberly was also wondering if it had been wise of Admiral Hotham to push the lad through the lieutenant's examination for he was clearly not fit for the rank. That too would need to be confirmed by London, his true station of this moment being that of a passed midshipman.

Hotham had hinted to Taberly that a touch of harsh treatment would not go amiss, yet in conversation with others the newly appointed captain had heard how cossetted the lad had been when he served aboard the flagship and the jealousies such favouritism had caused. Then there was his reputation as an acknowledged hero after some escapade in Brittany, which flew in the face of what appeared in the flesh.

Burns was not strong, he was weak; not brave, but shy; surely Hotham could discern that as easily as he? Yet he had been favoured with no end of opportunities to distinguish himself and had even survived a bout as a prisoner of the French just prior to his examination.

Hotham had mentioned Burns being engaged in questionable correspondence – what did that mean? Taberly was not a trusting sort of person with anyone and he naturally observed his superior officers through a jaundiced eye. Gnaw as he did on the words Admiral Hotham had employed, he could not be sure whether within them was set a snare into which he could himself stumble. He had a natural requirement to be careful of his commanding admiral. Did he also need to be cautious of how he treated Burns?

'Enter.'

The midshipman who obeyed was so small and seemingly childlike it was possible to wonder if he had been breached? Yet freckle-faced and full of wide-eyed innocence William Palliser was the very opposite of Burns. The grandson of a full admiral he was feisty, cheeky and adventurous, forever skylarking in the rigging despite strict orders to desist. Taberly had been obliged to have him kiss the gunner's daughter twice already and he had only been aboard *Brilliant* for a matter of weeks.

'Mr Glaister's compliments, sir, and the French are rigging their yards again.'

The temptation to yawn had to be fought; Taberly had no idea if the activity within the roadstead of Toulon presaged an attempt to get to sea, mere exercising of crews to work them up to a state of efficiency or a deliberate attempt to tease him and the other vessels of the inshore squadron.

The French had frigates at sea: that was known for they could come and go from Toulon in a manner denied to larger vessels. The line of battle ships were what mattered; they had been on bare poles for most of his time off the port and could not put to sea until they were properly rigged with yards and canvas. Ploughing to and fro, in sight of the enemy – and this they knew for they could see HMS *Brilliant* and her consorts as easily as he could espy them – he had observed them go about this farrago too many times to feel even a hint of excitement.

'We can do no more, Mr Palliser, than have our lookouts keep an eye on them. No doubt we will awake on the morrow to see bare poles again.'

'Mr Glaister required that I say the wind is in the north-west.'

That brought a frown to the face of a captain cursed by a temper. Glaister had been aboard the frigate for two years now and premier to two other captains. He felt and made little attempt to disguise that, in the appointment of his new superior, he had been passed over, the typical reaction of a fellow with no interest in the right places.

That thought was an unwelcome one; Taberly was not so well blessed with powerful patrons himself. Indeed, his elevation had come as a surprise given he had never before met Sir William Hotham. He had to assume it had come about through a shortage of officers within the Mediterranean Fleet and that was a tricky basis for confidence.

'Inform the first lieutenant that I am as aware of the wind as Mr Shakespeare's Hamlet.' Palliser's confusion was obvious; he had no idea what his captain was talking about, which had Taberly bark, 'Just pass on the message, boy!'

Thick planking did little to deaden the sound of that shout, nor did the skylight closed against the weather, which had the men working on the poop to blacken the cannon looking at each other. Blubber Booth spat a thumb in the direction of the glass, but not before he had allowed himself a good look round to make sure it was unobserved, an act which brought a smile from Martin Dent.

By careful movement both had heard what had gone on in the great cabin: like all tars they were adept at eavesdropping, so much so that it was taken as read they could hear a whisper through a wooden bulkhead. Both had witnessed the Burns interview, important given they were in his division. They despised him for the very reasons Taberly had seen fit to raise: he was useless, always uncertain, and if he was terrified of a fight he commanded men equally unhappy to be led by him.

'We did not draw a good straw when we got Taberly,' whispered Blubber.

Martin grinned at his well-larded companion – he was much given to such an expression – and gave a soft response. 'We got a straw out of the manger muck, mate, an' no error.'

It was ever thus in the King's Navy; you could be sailing sweet with a kindly soul one minute and then get a tartar of a captain the next. Taberly's predecessor had been a halfway house, intemperate one day and seeming kind the next, who had led Glaister, if anyone, a merry dance, but matters had gone downhill since he departed.

Glaister was known as the Skelton, this due to a face of scarce and pallid skin over prominent bones. The Scotsman they could live with: he was strict but fair and it had been expected one day he would get his step at least into a non-rated ship. The arrival of Taberly, and a right bastard as he had proved from day one, had turned a far from pleased Glaister into an equally harsh officer.

There had been floggings already, as Taberly set out to impose himself on the men he led, which had been rare under his predecessor. Deserved, no man objected to the punishment; it was only right if a man transgressed he should receive his due. But Taberly was too fond of it, his lashes too many for the offence, so that much blood had been drawn. HMS *Brilliant* was not a happy ship.

In San Fiorenzo Bay there was the usual cheer at the arrival of a packet from England. It carried despatches, of course, but also letters and newspapers to a set of men eager for news from home. For Admiral Sir William Hotham KB, the most important missive was confirmation from Earl Spencer, First Lord of the Admiralty, to say that Lord Hood would be relieved and that he was now de facto as well as the titular commander in the Mediterranean.

'Toomey, word to the captains. There will be revels this night.'

The clerk was unused to his employer being animated; Sir William was rarely given to excitement, indeed Toomey reckoned him too often vacillating, which made it a good job that he had a clever Irishman to counsel him. Now Hotham was calling to his steward to fetch up from his storeroom the finest wines he had in his private stock like a man favoured with a firstborn son.

'I take it, Sir William, you are in receipt of good tidings?'

That question was posed for form's sake alone; Toomey could too easily guess at what had engendered such a mood.

'The old devil has got his just deserts.'

'Lord Hood?'

'Who else, man. Thank the Almighty I shall not have to suffer his damned condescension ever again.'

There was real venom in that response; Hotham and Hood had been chalk and cheese. If outright dislike was tempered by manners it had been thin in both cases, never more so than when Hood sneered at whatever advice his second in command put forward. Now the old man was gone and Hotham could act as he wished.

'All we need now, Toomey, is for the French to oblige us with a contest.'

'May I be allowed to offer you my congratulations, sir?'

'Thank you Toomey, and now you are serving as clerk to a fleet commander you will enjoy a steep raise in your stipend, which I say is thoroughly deserved.'

'A trifle, Sir William, compared to your news.'

That was a lie; to the clerk, rising with his employer was as important to him as any other person's elevation. A man careful with his money – short arms and deep pockets were what others said of him – Toomey saved for a purpose. He aspired to nothing more than to accumulate enough for a life ashore with the means to take his pleasures. A good long spell as clerk to the C-in-C would secure that for him.

Hotham was taking his hat, preparatory to going on deck, for the fleet would find out his news quick enough. When the captain of HMS *Britannia* hauled down the white ensign that had indicated Vice Admiral Hood's command to replace it with the flag of William Hotham, Vice Admiral of the Blue Squadron, all would be revealed. He had not been long on deck when the signal gun boomed out to attract attention.

Captain Ralph Barclay was in his shirtsleeves, one empty part of the linen pinned up, when the cannon boomed out across the anchorage and he paid it little heed, given he was engaged in reading his own correspondence. A signal gun was a common enough occurrence and if it was not accompanied by the number of HMS *Semele* it could be ignored.

Whatever message was raised on *Britannia*'s halyards would be relayed to him by a messenger sent by the officer of the watch as a matter of course. There was no messenger this time but the lieutenant himself, eager-eyed and excited to say that Lord Hood's flag had been lowered. Given the arrival of that packet it did not require much thinking to guess what was about to occur.

'All hands, man the yards, and where in the name of Christ is my coat?'

Barclay was hauling himself out of his chair with his one good hand as beetle-browed Devenow hurried to help him dress. A brute of a man who could scarce cross a room without upsetting something, this was compounded by the fact that he was plainly drunk, a not unusual state in his case.

'Damn you, Devenow, you've been at the bottle,' was Barclay's response when he was exposed to a blast of foul breath.

'A tipple, Capt'n, no more.'

'Being a servant does not render you immune to the cat!'

'As if that would do any good.'

This opinion was a whispered one: Cornelius Gherson, Barclay's clerk and a man at permanent odds with Devenow, was sat in the small cabin that served as his workplace, close enough to overhear every word. His opinion was based on the very obvious fact that the so-called servant had been flogged dozens of times for the offence of drunkenness and it had made no difference at all.

HMS *Semele* had come alive. Men were running from all parts of the ship to get aloft to their far-from-familiar stations; it was a rare day, indeed, that any vessel manned the yards and for some, used to working as waisters, it meant no more than climbing a few feet up the shrouds while the more nimble topmen spread out aloft.

On deck Barclay surmised that he would have time to wait for the crew to properly assemble; Hotham would not do anything until he was sure he would receive the reception he thought he deserved and he was not the only captain to have reacted. All over the bay the ships had their nimble topmen slithering along the yards on the footropes with an occasional hand detached to ensure they had secure their tarred hats.

There was silence as William Hotham watched his flag being

bent on, the sailors turning to the captain of the ship, John Holloway, to await the command. And wait they did as the admiral savoured his moment. Finally he nodded, Holloway barked and the blue flag shot up the foremast. The joy was to watch all those white flags being struck and every vessel doing likewise.

There were three Neapolitan ships in the fleet, two 74s and a frigate. They had run up a signal to wish Hotham well, this as the sound broke out across the anchorage as every man in the British Fleet cheered their new commander, soon drowned out as he was afforded his due of a fifteen-gun salute from his own flagship cannon. It would have taken a keen eye to see that there was far from universal joy.

Sam Hood had been a popular C-in-C, a man who had fought in more than one successful fleet action and, to those he led, a proper sailor. He was the hero of the Battle of the Saintes, the man everyone in the navy reckoned deserved the credit for victory in that action instead of the rapacious sod George Rodney, who had been granted that honour.

If anyone had told William Hotham he was not loved he would not have cared; he had too much self-regard to be bothered. He could not help but look up at the blue flag, cornered by the ensign of the nation. It was forty-three years since he had first entered as a midshipman and now the dream he had harboured on that day was realised.

'Mr Holloway, we will need to send word to the inshore squadron to change their flags. Let the French see they have a new challenger to deal with.'

'Sir. And may I give you joy of your promotion.'

'You will be pleased to know, Holloway, that Admiral Parker is to return to us, so he will resume his post as Captain of the Fleet. Thus you will no longer be required to perform that duty.'

'A relief indeed, sir.'

'I think you may look forward to shifting to a frigate too, you have done enough service as a flag captain.'

The lie was smoothly delivered by Holloway. 'It would be a shame to relinquish *Britannia*, sir, and proximity to your flag.'

'A signal to all captains to repair aboard, if you please.'

The invitation to celebrate had to be extended to every captain and that included the Neapolitans, masters and commanders, lieutenants in charge of non-rated ships; sloops, brigs and bomb vessels. If many were welcome it was not all; too many of those coming aboard were Hood's men, none more so than Captain Horatio Nelson. To Hotham's way of thinking, Nelson was a man much overindulged by his predecessor; how many times had he been sent away on detached duties in place of men equally deserving?

Not that Nelson showed the slightest sign of disappointment, which in a way irritated Hotham. He was effusive in his praise, which the recipient took to be an attempt to crawl into his good books instead of genuine feeling. It would not wash; Hotham had his own client officers to care for, men like Ralph Barclay who would now be favoured with a chance to cruise independently and perhaps snap up a prize or two in the process.

There was a temptation to remove Nelson's blue commodore's pennant, given to him when he had commanded not only his own vessel but a trio of frigates; it was, after all, only a courtesy rank in the gift of Hood as C-in-C. He decided to let it rest for a while.

Nelson would find out soon enough how little favour he enjoyed in the great cabin of 'Old Ironsides', the sobriquet by which HMS *Britannia* was known throughout the fleet.

'Captain Barclay, I find you well?'

'Set up even better than normal, Sir William. No man deserves more what has come to you this day.'

Picked up by others, unavoidable it having been said in such a carrying voice, it engendered a whole host of salutations. The cabin rang with, 'Hear him, hear him!' and clinking goblets, any natural enthusiasm being fuelled by already copiously consumed wine. The less pleased were well versed in false zeal, it being a very necessary trait in the service to manufacture sentiments not truly held.

The bulkheads towards the stern were removed, to show a highly polished and long mahogany dining table, with all its leaves employed and set with crystal glass and silver cutlery, both gleaming due to the sunlight streaming through the casement windows.

The very best of Hotham's possessions had been laid out from which to eat and drink, in order to drive home that their host was already a wealthy man, to indicate that if God had answered his prayers, such good fortune would fall upon them too.

CHAPTER FOUR

The trip across Italy by the Pelicans was one taken in mixed circumstances. The Via Traiana, running straight and flat through endless olive groves of Apulia, had been built in the reign of Trajan to shorten the route to the Adriatic and was, as Michael O'Hagan observed when told of its age, in a far better state than many a road in England laid down in the intervening seventeen hundred years.

The benign weather that had greeted them at Brindisi did not last. Many times the Pearce party were caught in heavy rain, and in one case a ferocious storm that sent down bolts of lightning by the hundred, terrifying for the fact that there seemed no shelter for miles around; it was in the lap of providence that anyone or anything survived.

They saw an ancient olive tree split in two and set alight. Several cows and sheep were struck dead as the Pelicans cowered by the coach, with Michael O'Hagan wailing a prayer to the Virgin Mary for salvation, hardly audible against the fury of the wind and the regular claps of thunder.

Nor did they enjoy the comfort of a flat landscape for the whole journey. Seven leagues from Benevento the road rose into the Apennines, escalating continuously through snowcapped mountains while the passes through which they had to make their way were also of high elevation.

This necessitated that the passengers, wrapped up against the chill, walk alongside their conveyance so that it could breast the steep inclines, even being occasionally called upon to lend a shoulder so that the weary animals could make it to the next post house and rest, or to carry their own possessions – John Pearce's chest and the Pelicans ditty bags – for the same purpose.

Away from the ship and the hierarchy that imposed, the four men could act as equals in the manner they had on first acquaintance: for they had originally met each other as civilians in the Pelican Tavern, set on the banks of the Thames. That was an event much recalled, as was the arrival of the man who, it turned out, was running from a King's Bench warrant, most of these new acquaintances being in fear of a mere tipstaff.

In recollection, the name of Pearce's father Adam came up since he, according to Charlie Taverner, had been the cause of all of his son's problems. 'Don't you smoke it, John. If he had not been so keen on his levelling then you would not have had those King's Bench bastards on your tail and you would never have sought shelter.'

'You place a mighty burden on his old shoulders, Charlie. Happen if the likes of you had risen up in the same way as did the French, we would not have had anything to fear.'

'Excepting the loss of your head.'

This was imparted by Rufus Dommet in a manner that had become more common of late; the onetime tyro of the group, nervous and often silent, had grown up now and in doing so had acquired a serious mien as well as a handy pair of fists. Where Charlie, first met, had been a fly sort, not surprising given his background, Rufus had been a shy youth and on the run from the law for a broken bond of apprenticeship.

Handsome Charlie, with his winning ways, good looks and native cunning had been in the Thameside warren known as the Liberties of the Savoy for his way of life. He was a villain the tipstaffs would have dearly loved to collar for the way he had dunned the innocent out of their money.

This was done through the sale of glister not gold, forged lottery tickets and his dab pickpocketing hand. Trouble was, said bailiffs were barred from the Liberties by ancient statute and could not touch him within its bounds, and all were free to wander where they willed on Sundays.

In speaking of decapitation Rufus had alluded to something that had troubled John Pearce long before his own father had suffered the fate of so many. The mere mention brought back a horrible memory of the day in Revolutionary Paris that ardent tongue had finally been stilled. He had stood as witness to that terrible act in a jam-packed Place de la Revolution as the guillotine did its work.

Adam Pearce, the radical speaker and pamphleteer known as the Edinburgh Ranter, chased from his own country because his views were seen as seditious, had fallen foul of men who, spouting words of freedom, hated that he questioned their motives and actions which had descended into barbarism. In place of *Liberté*, *Egalité et Fraternité* there had come about a vengeful bloodbath.

No amount of threats would silence him until finally the vocal sermonising about their crimes led to Adam being incarcerated and proscribed as an enemy of the Revolution, which could have only one outcome in what had subsequently been dubbed the Terror. Sure that he was seriously ill, certain the hand of death was already upon him, Adam went to his fate in place of another, an aristocrat and family man who shared a cell with him in the fetid corridors of the Paris prison known as the Conciergerie.

Had he been right? Even before that dreadful day, son John had harboured doubts about his father's solutions to the ills of monarchy and government by the powerful driving down on the weak: while he agreed with the sentiment it was not so easy to see the reality. In a peripatetic life, touring the country with the man known for his forceful oratory, he had seen much of human nature which was compounded when the pair had experienced, thanks to a nervous British government, the hell of the Fleet Prison for a short spell.

The dregs of humanity resided there, and just as what had happened in France demonstrated the results of rapidly overturning the rule of law, that experience had shown John Pearce his fellow men and women in all their guises, and few of those, be they high born or low, could be described using a word like glorious.

The observation Rufus had made about losing your head was seen as unthinking by Michael O'Hagan, troubling to Pearce and that got the freckle-faced younger man a glare to tell him he had overstepped the mark, engendering an immediate mumbled apology, one brushed aside.

'My father was all for freedom of speech Rufus. He would not have had you hold your tongue, even if it was likely to cause upset.'

'Sure, John-boy, there's a way of saying things that's right and another that is not.'

'True.'

That brought to the Irishman's face a look that presaged a sally, a sure sign he was going to get great amusement from his own comment. 'Like a rebuke to me for the effects of drink when you come aboard two nights on the trot, three sheets to the wind an' scarce able to walk.'

'If I felt any shame for it, Michael, all I would have to do is recollect the night we met. You were blind drunk I recall and you sought to remove my head from my shoulders with those great fists of yours. Yet you have not behaved so since, so I must be content.'

The incident in that smoky tavern, prior to the invasion of a whole hoard of naval brutes, was a standing joke amongst the Pelicans, one of the few that could be drawn out as such from an occasion that lived in their minds as a calamity. Ralph Barclay had led his press gang into the Liberties, against both the law and custom, to take up for sea duty men not bred to it, which was another crime on its own.

Such a jocular response from John Pearce should have brought on shared laughter and repeated reminiscence, added to comments that it was a pity Michael's swinging hams had missed. That it did not confused him; indeed his companions, if anything, looked sheepish rather than pleased to be reminded.

'Have I said something untoward?'

'No,' replied Charlie, who for all his skill had a cast in his eye of false innocence.

'It has always pleased me that we are friends—'

'Not always, John.'

'True, Rufus, there are times when I have cursed you all. But deep down we share a regard and a history that binds us firm and makes us honest with each other, or so I believed till this very moment.'

'Don't get what you is driving at,' Charlie chipped in.

'I sense a secret shared by you and kept from me.'

'Imaginings,' opined Michael.

This only deepened the suspicions of Pearce, there being a deliberate attempt to avoid eye contact. He then reasoned that it had been a long time since they had been in a position such as they were now, free from the need to act as officer and common seamen, not since Leghorn and that had been brief. Had something occurred in the interval – his own behaviour being the most obvious – that was acting to stretch their bond? He could ask, but he doubted he would be afforded an honest answer and that was hurtful.

The cry from the coachman was a now familiar one – the need to disembark – yet it was no steep incline to overcome this time but a customs post, soon revealed as the crossing they must make from the Kingdom into the Papal States, fortunately as opposed to the French revolution as were Naples and Britain.

'This should make you happy, Michael. If the Catholic God has a corporeal presence anywhere it will be here as well as Rome. Happen you'll get a sight of where your Peter's pence is actually spent.'

If said in a jocose way there was an underlying mischievousness in the statement. Adam Pearce had lambasted the aristocracy for their blind cruelty to the poor, but he had even more vehemently cursed a church that called itself Christian yet acted as if Satan was more their master, and in this his son had entirely agreed.

How many times had John heard Adam ask in his stump speeches why an Archbishop of Canterbury required two palaces and an income of twenty-five thousand pounds a year, his inferior bishops just as well housed and just as suffused with personal greed, while minor clerics were often close to starvation and their parishioners rarely dined on meat?

He recalled telling Michael tales of the Catholic Church of France, stories he had heard in the salons of Paris after he and Adam had been forced to flee there and his father was still a feted visitor for his radical views.

Prior to the rise of the Jacobins, the city had been a delightful place in which to reside, free from the stench of monarchy and with a religious bloodsucker equally tamed. The Church in France had been broken. It no longer held vast swathes of property or was corrupt to an almost unimaginable degree.

Prior to the change, cardinals lived like princes, with retinues numbered in the hundreds, many armed, and incomes reckoned by the millions of livres. They and their bishops lived in sumptuous splendour, consorting openly with mistresses who made no attempt to hide their presence or the production of their illegitimate offspring. Adam had no great love for the notion of celibacy and neither did his son but both abhorred the blatant hypocrisy of a religion founded on the principles of poverty and simplicity.

'Never pay heed to that, John-boy,' had been Michael's response, and it was one that survived the sight of the numerous papal palaces and overdecorated churches of Benevento, a cool mountain retreat to divines in the summer months. 'The creatures who occupy these will have to answer for their sins on the Day of Judgement.'

'Then let us hope money plays no part in that assessment of worth,' had been John Pearce's jaundiced reply.

Soon they passed back into the Kingdom of Naples, making rapid progress downhill and on the flat, slowed every time they came to one of the hills between them and their destination, until atop one peak they finally spotted Vesuvius, or at least the column of sulphurous smoke that rose from its cone.

Nothing, not even a doubt about the strength of friendship that had troubled John Pearce, could dim the excitement he felt at being so close to his lover.

Emily Barclay had ceased to use the style of the husband she had come to despise, reverting to her maiden name of Raynesford, this being how she was known in Naples. She had sought to keep her residence discreet, a convenient cover as, even in such a lax environment, a married woman openly consorting with her lover was a cause of comment, but such sentiments were brushed aside by her hostess.

As Lady Hamilton had pointed out many times, marital fidelity in Naples was the exception not the norm, and too often for her own liking Emily found herself in an open coach with the wife of the British Ambassador, both hailed for their beauty by the populace as they passed through the crowded streets.

If Lady Hamilton was untroubled by such a liaison her guest was not. Emily had been brought up to respect her religion and the tenets by which women of her social class lived their lives and that did not encompass an acceptance of adultery. It was all very well for John Pearce to ridicule such sentiments, with his constant references to how life was lived in Paris and better for it, but Emily could not fully accept existing in such a state.

His presence alleviated that, obviously: she was in love with him and when he was by her side or shared her bed it was hard to feel guilty. His absences, however, brought back her feelings of doing wrong and the thought that the God in whom she firmly believed must be frowning at her behaviour, never mind her friends and family, if they knew, for she could not communicate with them to offer any explanation. This allowed guilt to triumph over any memory of pleasure.

She had tried to break their connection and return to England without him once already but that had been thwarted by circumstance. Yet the idea had not died; it was very much in her mind. As a guest of Sir William Hamilton and his wife she could not have asked for more in the way of comfort and with propinquity came a less harsh judgement of a lady with a very chequered past, a woman she had originally seen as somewhat spiteful.

Lady Hamilton had been branded a whore in the collective mind of the British upper classes, her husband pitied more than envied for first keeping her as a mistress and then marrying a woman of her background. Some of that, Emily realised, was brought on by jealousy, for Emma Hamilton had been a rare and stunning beauty in her younger years.

Often painted in classical poses by George Romney, Emma's looks were known to many in the *ton* who had never met her but were happy to traduce her from gossip alone. Such was her attraction to portraitists that the Palazzo Sessa was filled with paintings of her by any number of famous artists who has passed through Naples, and one Madame Vigée Le Brun was near to being another resident, so often was she calling. Emma's flaming hair was more muted now than hitherto and the purity of those looks had suffered a little from the consequences of time, but she was still a feast to a male eye and, Emily had discovered, accomplished in many ways.

Having been coached for a decade by a succession of tutors provided by her husband, she spoke Italian, French and German, played the harpsichord with some facility and was a confidante of the Queen of Naples, an Austrian princess and the real ruler of the kingdom, her husband being a man of severely limited mentality.

'If you really wish to take ship for home, Emily,' Lady Hamilton said, the subject once more raised, 'I would not do anything to stop you, though I will opine that my husband would be sorry to see you go.'

That made Emily blush and drop her head, for she too was a beauty but with none of the confidence in that estate as Emma Hamilton. Sir William, the Chevalier to his wife and friends, should have been, in his seventh decade, well past the age at which to engage in seductive verbal dalliance that bordered on the risqué, but he did so frequently.

Kindness dictated that his sallies be seen as mere raillery from a man whose manners came from a different age, for he was ever thoughtful, but much prone to the production of a blush. With his sallies he was forever causing a reddening of Emily's pale cheeks.

They were coaching through the city on the way to the English Garden, with Emma Hamilton acknowledging the cries of 'Madonna' by which she was frequently greeted, with Emily wondering whether to impart to her the reasons for her revived determination to return to England. She decided against it for it was not germane to what had become, if not a true friendship – Emma was not good at holding close female company – more than just acquaintance.

At least she had the blessing of not having to face John Pearce, but that was a parting reckoned not to be of long duration. He was on a mission to some place in Dalmatia and had sworn he would not be gone long. He would certainly call into Naples on his way back to the fleet, so if she was going to take passage, and there was more than one reason for haste, she knew she had to do so soon.

The afternoon walk in the English Garden was near to being a ritual for Emma Hamilton, only broken when she attended upon Queen Maria Carolina. She was popular in the royal palace for her ability to entertain the queen's children and it was said, not least by her husband, that the Maria Carolina paid more attention to Emma's advice than she did to his or that of her English First Minister, the courtier and military advisor, Sir John Acton.

It was pleasant on what was a calm and unseasonably warm day to promenade in such a place, personally designed and planted by the Chevalier. He had laid out flower beds, planted trees native to his homeland, now maturing to provide shade, and created arbours each with its own small classical temple, ideal for semi-secret trysts.

Yet there was too often an abiding risk and that came from the known presence in Naples of King Ferdinand, who had broken off from his annual hunting trip and was back resident in the Palazzo Reale, Ferdinand being a monarch with dull to non-existent wits and only two passions: hunting and copulation.

He had brought his poor queen to child sixteen times, the

most recent being not much more than a year past, this despite her constant attempts to divert his attentions elsewhere. The porcelain manufactory at Capodimonte was a happy hunting ground for the king, given the number of country girls brought in to decorate the pottery, but he was such a satyr even that was scarce enough.

The danger in the garden he often visited occurred when he encountered any woman to whom he was attracted, and his tastes were eclectic. Not only would he confront them, and this had happened to Emma Hamilton, he was given by way of invitation to exposing himself, impossible to ignore since he was extraordinarily well endowed and seemingly in a constant state of arousal.

John Pearce was fond of pointing out only partly as a joke, though not in the hearing of the Chevalier or Emma, that such behaviour was a standing argument against the hereditary principle.

The promenade passed off pleasantly and without incident, so it was one woman in a benevolent mood who returned to her home at the Palazzo Sessa, while her companion was plotting how to take passage and the dangers therein. Such a journey was a far from trouble-free voyage even in Italian waters, which Emily had already experienced, and it did not diminish once any vessel she was on cleared the narrows at Gibraltar. The sea between there and England was full of French privateers as eager to snap a prize as their British counterparts.

Deep in contemplation of that as the coach entered the gates of the Palazzo, it took some time for Emily to see that there was a small knot of men sat in the shade of a lemon tree, ditty bags at their feet, one of such a height and build even seated that identified him as Michael O'Hagan.

All three were known to her and they stood up quickly to doff their hats and smile, perhaps brought to wonder by the fact that a woman they saw as generous of spirit did not respond in a like manner. If they were here, so was John Pearce so it took a moment for Emily to react, while out of the portico that covered the doorway her man emerged, his grin as wide as the seas he sailed.

'My dear Emily,' said Emma Hamilton. 'I fear your plan to escape must be put on hold.'

John Pearce handed her down from the coach and made to kiss her, that avoided as she turned her head away. 'We are in a public place, John.'

'Behind closed gates and amongst friends,' he replied, unable to keep the irritation out of his voice. 'Surely I deserve a warmer welcome than that.'

'Let us go inside.'

'Not before you acknowledge my Pelicans.'

'Of course, not to do so would be remiss.'

'Lady Hamilton, I give you good day and hope you are well?'

'In full blossom, Lieutenant Pearce, despite the season and awaiting a bee or two to propagate my stamens.'

As always with this lady there was a look to accompany the response and one that annoyed every woman who knew her. Whatever Emma said it always seemed close to vulgarity. With it came an expression that hinted that a bit of flirtation would not be unwelcome. Having been exposed to it many times, Pearce merely beamed and, holding Emily's hand, took her over to greet his friends as the hostess went indoors.

Pleasantries were exchanged – they were happy to see her again and she feigned the same emotion, though her heart was in turmoil. Finally, Emily was led into the house and being they were lovers, obliged to lead Pearce to her private apartment. As ever, parting had made him impatient and when he was pushed away from a quick clinch the hurt was obvious.

'What in heaven's name is the matter?' he demanded as she put distance between them.

'You invoke the heavens, John? That is unusual.'

'Is it untoward that I have missed you?'

The 'No', was close to a whisper.

'And yet to rebuff my embrace.'

'I do so because I must part from you, John, even if it breaks my heart to do so.'

'What are you talking about, Emily?'

She spun to face him, her voice cracked. 'I am with child. Would you have me bring into the world a baby tainted with bastardy?'

'I fail to see how you could avoid it, unless—' The penny dropped and it was not a pleasant experience. 'Surely you cannot propose to go back to your husband?'

'Do I have a choice?'

CHAPTER FIVE

For Ralph Barclay the actions of his wife were like a running sore and had been for some time. He had manoeuvred to get himself and his ship sent to the Mediterranean knowing she was there, his intention to find her and bring her back to her proper estate. Yet since his arrival he had been stuck in San Fiorenzo Bay with no sign that he would be granted the independence of action required to pursue his goal.

Apart from the misery of rejection, he was sure the way Emily had run off affected him professionally as well as personally. Committed to his career in the navy and, fate notwithstanding, high enough on the captain's list to feel the time to him getting his own admiral's flag was on the horizon, any number of things could arise to check him and the state of his marriage fell into that category.

There was fear of then being beached of course: to suffer, even if he was given his flag, the ignominy of becoming a yellow admiral, having the rank but no meaningful employment. To avoid that fate, even with no reputational stains, required interest in high places and Ralph Barclay was poorly placed in that regard. It was also necessary to show no weaknesses, and an inability to hold onto his spouse looked very much like that; could a man who had failed to command one woman take charge of a fighting fleet?

In his favour was his reputation as a forceful sailor, for he had been lucky since the outbreak of the conflict. Even fighting a losing battle, badly outnumbered, against a pair of French frigates, counted in that; the Admiralty looked favourably on captains prepared to do battle when the odds were stacked against them and avoidance was impossible. Since then he had also taken several prizes as well as participating in a major fleet action, the Battle of the Glorious First of June, the first serious contest of the present war, which had produced rich rewards for the participating captains.

Apart from the blot on his marriage everything in his life had progressed well. From being an impecunious officer suffering five years on half pay he was now a fairly wealthy man, able to contemplate the option of buying the lease on a London residence or having, like many a successful naval officer, a home built for him on the Downs overlooking Portsmouth.

Yet the constant socialising of a fleet at anchor counted as torture. Hardly a day went by without an invitation to dine aboard another vessel, and there he would mingle with his fellow captains as well as specially invited lieutenants and midshipmen. No one ever alluded to the folly of a man like him marrying a mere girl half his age yet he was sure such comments were made behind the hand, for what had been a well-kept secret in England was not likely to be that in the Mediterranean.

Emily had fled with John Pearce to reside for a short period in Leghorn, the Tuscan port that was the revictualling centre for the fleet, and had been seen in his company, though he reckoned her gone from there now. The navy was as much a hotbed of gossip as any other profession and he had to assume it was now common knowledge that his wife had run off with another man, and a much younger fellow to boot.

Barclay needed to locate Emily and get her back by kidnap, if no other method presented itself, his frustration at being unable to do so compounded by his situation; as part of the Mediterranean Fleet he was not free to act as he wished, given his C-in-C was waiting for the French to poke their noses out of Toulon. In what amounted to naval indolence he had too much time to think and reflect and to gnaw on what had gone wrong.

He had not seen seventeen-year-old Emily Raynesford as hot-headed when he had first proposed the union to her parents – quite the opposite. She had seemed meek and dutiful, a perfect bride for a man proud of his rank and station, albeit one who had become adept at delaying bills and confounding bailiffs for half a decade. The prospect of war with France and command of a warship, plus full pay, had hastened his wooing and that had been laid upon Emily's father as much as her.

Ralph Barclay had a family entail on the house occupied by the Raynesford family, one he had subtly hinted he could enforce at will, which would render them homeless. Thus he had allies in both Emily's father and more particularly her mother, who had sung the virtues of her daughter marrying a full post-captain in the King's Navy, quite a catch for a girl who would struggle to match such good fortune in her home town of Frome.

Matters had proceeded to a wedding and it seemed as if Emily had happily accepted his proposal, there being no hint of hesitation in her taking of the vows. If the postnuptial congress had been full of awkwardness that was only to be expected, for he was not experienced in dealing with women.

His life in the navy, two and half decades of sea service and consorting with women of low breeding, were a poor preparation for a wedding night with a provincial virgin. Emily had no experience at all, which was only right and proper, and while he may have been a trifle rough, seen as necessary to overcome her maidenly reticence, from that point on matters had become settled as his young bride dutifully fulfilled her role.

Not that she was without faults, mainly follies brought on by her youth, like overspending on his stores and, when he was absent, making an exhibition of herself at a ball in Sheerness, being too exuberant in her dancing. Subsequently he had seen it as a requirement to educate Emily in the responsibilities incumbent upon his station as the man in command of the frigate HMS *Brilliant*.

Barclay realised now that he should have left Emily in Frome, where she could have been housed with his two sisters, yet he had feared extravagance from a trio of women who would overrate his position. Five years on the beach had left many bills to be settled and he needed time on full pay to repair his situation.

So to save money he had decided to take his new wife aboard his ship. Such an act was against the rules but it was also far from uncommon in a service where such matters were more often observed in the breach.

Ralph Barclay knew that all his problems had stemmed from

that decision. Naval life was harsh and he was determined to run a tight ship. Short-handed and ordered to set sail he had been obliged to venture out and press men to sea service, forced to show scant regard for the location from which they were taken or their fitness for the tasks they would be required to perform.

It had ever been thus at the outbreak of war; the navy needed men and the number of seamen never matched the requirements of the fleet. To compound his problems, Lord Hood, then the Senior Sea Lord of the Admiralty and no friend to Ralph Barclay, was holding a host of volunteers at the Tower for his own selfish ends. Of all the men he had pressed, the one that had brought him most grief was none other than John Pearce.

'Compliments of the officer of the watch, sir, your barge is in the water and manned.'

Barclay thanked the midshipman and rose from behind his desk, Devenow appearing for once, hat in hand, without having to be called and obviously stone-cold sober. The brute had a look of concern on his face, one that was habitual when dealing with his captain, who was never sure of the reason. Was it concern for his well-being or fear of his all-too-common wrath?

The call into Cornelius Gherson's cubbyhole was to collect the latest figures on the stores held within the holds of HMS *Semele*, these handed over with that infuriating air of superiority that his clerk could not seem to keep hidden. Such an expression was compounded by the man's looks; he was handsome, with a fair to girlish countenance and fine blonde hair. To a dark and brooding presence like Ralph Barclay it was a constant irritation.

'I have done my best, sir.'

'I damn well hope you have, Gherson.'

The growling response had no effect on his clerk, who was safe in the knowledge that as of this moment his captain depended on him. Barclay lacked the numerical skills to play ducks and drakes with the level of the warship's stores. Just like in his financial affairs he had come to depend on Gherson, though not with any degree of trust. It amused the clerk, even with that lack of faith, just how easy it was to hide from his employers how much was being siphoned off into his own pocket.

'I have had condemned as much as I could so we seem lower on victuals than we are in truth, but your real hope is us being so low on water that it needs proper hoys to replenish us.'

There was no need to tell Ralph Barclay that such a commodity was, unlike everything else the seventy-four carried, unquantifiable. They could top it up from the Corsican wells but not to the level that existed on paper, for it would have to be fetched from the shore in barrels, time-consuming and often less than a day's expenditure.

Water, or the lack of it would, the captain hoped, be the lever that would get him away from his present berth and at the very least to Leghorn where he could begin his search, mostly to find a clue as to where Emily had gone. Rowed across the bay, Barclay knew he would have to be subtle, for that which he planned carried a risk. Hotham was no fool and given it was he who had told of Emily's presence in Leghorn he would be quick to smoke Barclay's motives.

Against that Ralph Barclay was a client officer of the admiral, entitled to expect preferential treatment. In addition, he was fully aware of the machinations Hotham had engaged in, aided by his senior clerk Toomey, to rid himself of the menace of John Pearce – an intrigue of which Ralph Barclay thoroughly approved, albeit he had been careful to avoid personal involvement.

Piped aboard HMS *Britannia* he inspected the marines as was required before making himself known to Holloway, the flag captain – a necessary courtesy, Devenow dogging his heels to ensure that his one-armed master did not suffer a fall on a moving deck. Before he could enter the admiral's great cabin he encountered Toomey, from whom he could quietly enquire, with bowed head and a soft tone, if there was any news of John Pearce and HMS *Flirt*.

'No news is good news, Captain Barclay, is all I can reply.'

That came as a whisper. The clerk knew why he was being asked; the question was not one that could be put to William Hotham, even if he was the man ultimately responsible for what had been implemented. Commanding admirals saw the need to shield themselves from such matters.

'Let us hope that remains the case,' Toomey added.

'Quite. Can I proceed?'

'Sir William is awaiting you.'

'Did he ask why I requested an interview?'

'No, but I will say he is curious as to the reason you wish to see him alone.'

'A list of my stores, Toomey. You will see we are severely short on beef and pork, much of which has had to be condemned, and our water is critical.'

Toomey raised an eyebrow at that; he had been a naval clerk for many years and before that a purser. There was not a trick in the naval book of which he was not aware and, as the man who took in the daily reports on the fitness of the fleet to operate, even if he gave the perusal to his underlings, he could take a fair stab the ploy Barclay was seeking to execute.

Being close to his master, Toomey also knew why he was being handed the list, just as he knew that it provided, if accepted, an excuse for the admiral to grant HMS *Semele* permission to depart ahead of vessels more in need of revictualling. The two exchanged a non-committal look before Barclay proceeded past the marine sentry to the cabin door, opened for him by a second guard.

'Captain Barclay, you are most welcome even if your request intrigues me. I take it you will join me in a glass of this Tuscan wine, which I can assure you is more than a match for claret.'

Sir William Hotham was smaller than his visitor, slightly pink of face, the skin smooth, with none of the rough, red visage common to sailors. As much a courtier as a navy man he had come to his present position through the powerful patronage of the Duke of Portland, now a member of the Pitt administration, having split with his faction from his Whig colleagues to support the prosecution of the war.

There had never been any doubt in Ralph Barclay's mind that Hotham would settle with ease into his role as C-in-C Mediterranean. The man had worked for high and independent command all his life. To have achieved it would be, to his way of thinking, nothing but a rightful recognition of his abilities. In his manner and appearance, full uniform with flashing gold epaulettes and a newly powdered wig, he looked very much the part.

'Delighted to do so, sir. Any word on the French?'

'Supine, Barclay, supine. I worry that they so fear me they will never leave Toulon.'

It was typical of Hotham to make personal what was collective. The enemy would be in fear of the British Fleet, not its commander, but he let the hyperbole pass without even a raised eyebrow and moved more swiftly than was strictly polite to what he had come to say.

'While what I fear, sir, is to be so low on victuals and water that it will affect my ability to take part in a chase and an action should they do so.'

The frown was to be expected; how much it was performance and how much genuine Barclay did not know but it indicated a degree of discomfort. The two were very different; the man visiting knew that. For all they had gone to sea at the same age and suffered the rigours of being midshipmen, then lieutenants and finally very junior captains, their lives had taken a very different course.

Hotham had always enjoyed powerful connections and had been many times made welcome at court. Ralph Barclay did not, and had never even been close enough to King George to exchange a single word. He also depended on this man to help him prosper, albeit such a connection was a two-way affair.

That said, it never would do to fully trust an admiral and Ralph Barclay was no different from his peers in not doing so. He had only got his posting to join the Mediterranean Fleet due to his ability to possibly embarrass another even more senior flag officer, Black Dick Howe, who had led the Home Fleet to success against the French on the First of June.

Nor was he convinced that the actions Hotham had taken to get rid of John Pearce had been done in any respect as a favour to him. The admiral had his own reasons, not least the fact that it was he who had set up the court martial to try Ralph Barclay for illegal impressment.

That it was a conspiracy to acquit would never stand up to examination and nor would the fact that Hotham had made sure no hostile witnesses were present to testify. Pearce had been sent away on a voyage to the Bay of Biscay; with him had gone anyone who could have told the truth about that night in the Liberties of the Savoy: Lieutenant Henry Digby, Midshipman Richard Farmiloe and a trio of hands from the lower deck.

Only Toby Burns, Barclay's nephew by marriage, had been kept back and he, being the weakling he was, had been browbeaten into committing perjury. And there was the nub of it; Pearce had engaged a London lawyer to probe those very same people Hotham had sent away. If the likes of Digby and Farmiloe would be cautious, valuing as they did their careers, the same could not be said of Toby Burns, who would crack under pressure for certain.

There was one other problem not known to Hotham: John Pearce was not whistling in the dark as Hotham thought. He had a full transcript of the court martial, and if that ever saw the light of day in a civil court Hotham would be finished, it being small comfort that Barclay would go down with him.

The admiral, who had been lost in thought, raised his gaze from his red wine as Toomey entered the cabin, bearing in his hand a sheaf of papers. 'Well?'

'Captain Barclay is seriously low on water, sir. I would say that his need to replenish is acute. He is not well found in pork and beef either, due to the need to condemn.'

'Dammit, Barclay, how has this come about?'

'You know the dockyard as well as I do, sir. The provision of rotten stores is no rare event.'

'But to this extent?'

'I admit that carelessness on the behalf of some of my crew has made worse what was merely bad.'

'Which you let pass?'

'In no way, sir. You will see from my logs, if you care to examine them, that the miscreants have been punished.'

Men had been flogged, that was true; all Ralph Barclay had done was record the reasons as other than the truth, which was punishments for insubordination, drunkenness or gambling.

Hotham allowed himself a deep sigh as he indicated Toomey should depart and then he was back into his reverie, no doubt weighing up the pros and cons of what he was being asked for. He was no more to be fooled than his clerk and what he had to consider was how others, as much client officers to him as Ralph Barclay, would react to what would be seen as a blatant piece of favouritism.

'I have to say, Barclay, the temptation to issue a public reprimand is very strong. You may say there are men responsible for this, but—'

'I know, Sir William,' Barclay replied, with mock humility, the space being left for him to do so, 'that the responsibility lies with me as the captain.'

Looking directly into Hotham's rather weak blue eyes Ralph Barclay reckoned Hotham was working up to a refusal. He would do that by taking stores from other ships and employing the boats of the entire fleet for water, which brought matters to the crunch as far as he was concerned; he had to be granted the independence to cruise and Leghorn was only the first step. Barclay wanted to go to Naples and possibly Palermo. Time to muddy the waters.

'I wonder, Sir William, if there is any activity at all in our area of operations?'

'A certain amount of piracy and the odd roaming French frigate.'

'I believe our ambassador in Naples, Sir William Hamilton, has asked for a show of force in the Straits of Messina.'

'Which is a damned insult to our Neapolitan allies. The waters between Naples and Sicily are their bailiwick. We cannot just go sending in vessels without upsetting them.'

'I believe the excuse would be the delivery of despatches. Perhaps, instead of a sloop, a seventy-four would serve a dual purpose? Given permission to revictual in Leghorn, I could then sail south and show the flag, your flag.' The voice dropped to a low growl. 'It pains me to allude to the fact that we have a common interest but that is so, is it not?'

That made Hotham sit up as he suddenly realised he was being coerced; if the Pearce name was unmentioned it was as clear as Banquo's ghost. Ralph Barclay was engaged in a risky business; to upset this man could rebound badly. Would the admiral smoke that it was not only John Pearce and his doings that could sink him, nor Toby Burns? This captain before him was better placed than any to achieve that, even if he would likewise go down and might even hang, perjury – which he too had committed – being a capital crime.

Hotham knew all about his wife and it would be no mystery to him why this proposition was being advanced; the question was how he would respond to what was nothing less than a veiled threat. The mystery for the admiral would be how far Ralph Barclay was willing to go in seeking to find her.

'I suggest you return to HMS *Semele*, Captain Barclay, while I ponder on this.'

The tone of warmth had gone; if he was furious – and he might be – Hotham masked it well, his dignity being important to him and his courtier experience coming to his aid.

'As you wish, sir. About my need for stores?'

'That, too, must be considered, of course. Now I wish you good day.'

Hotham did not stand, which would have been a common act of civility. Ralph Barclay tried to read his features but there was nothing there to see; indeed, before he turned to depart Hotham had lowered his head to the papers on his desk in what was a clear dismissal. It would be necessary to have a word with Toomey on the way back to the entry port.

'I fear, Toomey, I have created a doubt in Sir William's mind regarding my loyalty to his flag.'

'Indeed?' replied the perplexed Irishman.

'I wish you to convey to him that which our respective ranks do not otherwise permit: I refer of course to the voyage of HMS *Flirt* and the reasons it was found to be necessary.'

Toomey looked as though he was in fear of losing his watch, so anxious was his expression, for he was as much in the steep tub when it came to John Pearce as anyone.

'I wish to stress that my need is great in my personal affairs and the only man able to grant me succour in my situation is just beyond yonder bulkhead. You will know I cannot make a direct request, but I have done so obliquely.'

'For what, Captain Barclay?'

'The right to cruise and perhaps bring back to the fleet a prize or two, given I have been lucky in the past.'

'You asked for this?'

'Hinted, Toomey, no more, while adding that despatches for Naples could be carried by *Semele*, but if you could see your way to easing my concerns, well . . .'

Toomey was even quicker than Hotham to see the point of that and just as quick to avoid commitment. 'All I can do, Captain Barclay, is give an honest opinion if asked. My position precludes anything else.'

'I see you as wise counsellor to Sir William. I seek that you act in that capacity.'

In other words, Ralph Barclay thought as he walked away, Devenow falling in close behind him, tell the sod which side his bread is buttered on. Tell him he needs to care for me in order that he will care for himself.

As he was rowed back to his ship he needed to breathe deeply; sailing close to the wind was one thing, a threat – however oblique – to a senior flag officer quite another. If Hotham declined, then he had forfeited his good opinion: if he acceded to the request there had still been made a serious breach in what had been a favourable relationship.

CHAPTER SIX

'I suspect you are now aware that your life has become more complicated? A child does that even to the wedded, I am told.'

Pacing on the terrace that overlooked the Bay of Naples, John Pearce had been ruminating on that very thought and he was far from welcoming to Lady Hamilton and her reference to his new-found dilemma. That was until he recalled Emily saying that her condition had been kept a secret.

'You know?'

'My mother is very experienced in such matters. As she manages the household and is often in places where not to overhear a woman regularly evacuating her innards of a morning is impossible.'

Pearce had met the lady in question, a woman with a rather formidable visage held in much fear by the rest of the palazzo servants. How she could eavesdrop without being detected he could not fathom, for she patrolled the corridors with a huge and rattling bunch of keys at her waist that sent a warning ahead of her approach.

Called Mrs Cadogan, though there was no sign or reference to a mister, she ran the establishment for the Chevalier in a way that occasioned from him much praise. Prior to her arrival as escort to Emma, he was open in his admission that those he employed to care for him had, since he had become a widower, run rings round his attempts at husbandry.

The temptation to snap at Emma Hamilton and berate her for stating the obvious had to be concealed; both he and Emily were still in her house and her debt for the level of hospitality they enjoyed. Added to that, Pearce was never going to accede to his lover going back to her husband and he might need the good offices of another woman to make his case.

'The law leaves us both in a parlous state.'

'It does indeed: paternity is no match for conjugal rights.'

The way that was imparted hinted at some past sadness, lacking as it did her usual ability to manufacture a double entendre. There was also no gainsaying what she had stated: it mattered not who was the actual father of Emily's child, Ralph Barclay had privileges that transcended bloodlines. As her wedded husband he could take the child from its mother and do with it what he wished, while in the process denying Emily bed, sustenance and a roof over her head.

Marriage was an estate that massively favoured the male. If a man managed to wed a wealthy woman, her money, unless special entails had been placed upon it in inheritance, became his to do with as he wished. The gossip of the town was replete with tales of seedy rakes gambling away a wife's fortune at the card table.

That it was a bad thing seemed beyond doubt yet, standing on this balcony now, it seemed absurd to recall that when his father had called for equality before the law regardless of gender and the denial of rights, much of the howling in protest came from the women he wished to help. Right of this moment it seemed he was faced with some of the same kind of stubbornness.

'I need to persuade her that what she proposes to do is folly.'

'While a woman carrying a baby is not always in a position to be wise.'

'You do agree, milady?'

'I did think we had progressed beyond such formality.'

That got a nod but no name; Pearce was cautious of being too intimate with this woman, who took pleasure in ensnaring men which she then displayed as trophies, though there was no more than that in his reluctance. Emily had been quite explicit: accounts of infidelity to the Chevalier, in a city where to indulge in extra liaisons would have been simple, were notable by their absence even as rumour.

For all her flirting and the attentions she received on a daily basis there was not even a hint of scandal attached to her name. It was something to be remarked upon that a woman with such a chequered reputation was by all accounts utterly faithful to her much older spouse.

'I need to formulate some plan to confound her intention.'

'Do you look forward to the birth of the child?'

'Who could not?'

'You will smoke why I ask the question?' A sad nod. 'There is a certain type of creature in a place like Naples who can facilitate a solution.'

'Something to which Emily would never agree. Neither, I think, could I seek to change her mind for my heart would scarce be in it.'

'Perhaps you could persuade her that a sea voyage risks harm to the child and may bring on that very result.'

'At such an early stage?'

The response was snappy. 'How ignorant you men are! That is the time at which a pregnant woman is most vulnerable. Coax her to wait on those grounds, which will give you time to perhaps change her mind.'

In his pacing Pearce had not been idle and that conclusion he had already arrived at. Emily was unaware that Ralph Barclay was in the Mediterranean, a fact he had deliberately kept from her so as to avoid her worrying that he might turn up in Naples. It could not be that he was in these waters by accident – the coincidence would be too acute – which meant that he could be present for the express purpose of searching for her.

Pearce had good cause to worry, as well. Ralph Barclay had proved already that he would stop at very little, possibly nothing, to get her back. There had been threats aplenty delivered by that slimy article Gherson, and there had even been criminality when the office of Emily's solicitor was broken into and all his papers stolen.

It took no great imagination to see what Barclay was after on that occasion: the copy of the transcript of his court martial, a list of damning perjuries that could ruin him. It was that document which had held him at bay, for he had the law on his side when it came to the forceful return of his wife.

John Pearce was then obliged to recall that Emily was not herself beyond subterfuge. The transcript should have been lost at sea and he had spent much time thinking it to be so, only to discover that she had stolen it from where it had been stored for safekeeping, this when the ship on which they were travelling back to England was engulfed in flames prior to being abandoned.

She had lodged it with her solicitor not to aid him – that came later – but to protect her from a man with whom she no longer wanted any truck. How, given such actions in the past, could she possibly consider going back to him now? How could he, who could not face that such an outcome could be allowed, stop her?

Admiral Sir William Hotham was reading the orders, composed by Toomey, that would send Ralph Barclay away from the fleet and he was far from happy at the contents. Such an act would have repercussions and he was searching his mind for some way to balance that which he reckoned he had to succumb to. He needed to find a way to remind Barclay that he was the C-in-C and not someone to be trifled with.

'Toomey,' he called towards the open cabin door, as enlightenment struck. 'Do you have the fleet muster rolls?'

'Of course, Sir William.'

'I seem to recall that HMS *Semele* is well found in the article of hands.'

The answer was delivered as Toomey entered the great cabin. 'Fresh from home, sir, she is bound to be.'

'While even *Britannia* is short.'

'Wear and tear, sir,' Toomey replied wearily, wondering where this was heading.

The fleet had been in the Mediterranean for coming up to two years and there had been the usual losses to attrition, added to those who had been either wounded or perished at the Siege of Toulon. Endless requests had been sent home for drafts of seamen to be sent out and all of them had been ignored, the Channel Fleet and an expedition to the West Indian Sugar Islands taking precedence. Hood had undertaken to press the case once back in England but so far nothing had come of it.

'Then I think we must strip Mr Barclay of his good fortune and balance it with the needs of the fleet as a whole.'

That still left Toomey in a state of wondering. First as to why Hotham was indulging Barclay, and then this, for he had not been privy to their private conversation and his employer had not enlightened him. That it had upset Hotham he knew, sensitive as he was to the admiral's moods, yet as of this moment the gloom seemed to have lifted.

'Write an order stripping out of HMS *Semele* one hundred and twenty men to be distributed throughout the fleet to those captains who plague me for their lack of hands. The lucky recipients we will grant twenty apiece, the flagship being first in line, which will please Mr Holloway.'

'You had in mind to shift him sir, I recall?'

'In time, Toomey, we must wait till Hyde Parker is back with us.'

The clerk hated to be in the dark and he justified his need to know as being essential to the well-being of his employer. There was a touch of the weathervane about the admiral and the Irishman was convinced he needed sound advice to act in his own best interests. It was a risk to ask for elucidation but one he felt he had to take.

'Can I ask, Sir William, what are your motives for acting to indulge Captain Barclay?'

The answer was a long time in coming and it was preceded by

a whole raft of emotions crossing the normally bland face, none of them kindly. 'He damn near threatened me, Toomey. Can you imagine that, after all I have done for him?'

'Threatened you, sir?'

Hotham glanced at the slightly open cabin door, aware that he had spoken too loudly. Toomey caught the look and went to close it, thinking of horses and stable doors. That remark might be all over the ship before eight bells so Hotham's next words were softly delivered.

'We made him too much aware of our plans for Pearce. He now feels he can make demands on me, which I must tell you, Toomey, I cannot abide.' The blue eyes were on the clerk now and positively flashing. 'I seem to recall it was your notion to confide in him.'

'He is committed to your flag, Sir William, he made a point of telling me so as he departed.'

'Did he, by damn?'

Being such a confidant and quicker of wit by far, it took no great leap of imagination to work out what had occurred. He had observed Barclay closely in the discussion regarding Pearce's mission and had seen in him a deep cove who knew when silence served a man best. Surely he had not been so foolish as to openly threaten Hotham? He came across as far too wily for that.

No, it would have been unspoken and left to the admiral's imagination. But that posed its own problem for an ambitious officer: to openly bait his commander was tantamount to professional suicide. Such speculation was as unsettling as ignorance so Toomey felt he needed a precise answer.

'Surely Captain Barclay was not overt, sir?'

'Oh no, it was all very subtle. He's off chasing his damned wife, of course. Be best if he found her and chucked her overboard tied to a cannonball.'

'Given the chance of never seeing John Pearce again, they may be reconciled.'

'I will do for Barclay, Toomey, mark my words. He had my good opinion but that is now forfeit. Write out the orders stripping out his crew. You know which vessels to send them to.'

'I do, sir.'

It would be the other client officers of Hotham who would benefit. Toomey was quick to reckon it as a ploy, something to mollify them when they saw HMS *Semele* weigh anchor.

The man who received the order later that day, along with another commanding him to sail for Leghorn, saw its purpose right off. He would write back and protest, of course, but he had no illusions it would do any good. It would, however, do no harm to accept Gherson's suggestion: to have a fair copy in his locker so that if his ship came to any mischief through lack of the men needed to sail and fight her, he would be able to shift the blame away from himself.

'Can I suggest, sir,' Gherson advised, 'that the copy should be sent over to the flagship for onward transmission to London on the next packet heading for home? It will thus be safe from any chance of destruction.'

'To whom would I send it?'

'To your prize agents, sir.'

'Is that not too obvious?'

'If it is in amongst other correspondence, crew letters and the like, it will not be noticed. And what can be suspicious about you writing to Ommaney and Druce? Their occupation is no mystery and nor, I suspect, is the fact that you are one of their most cosseted clients.'

As usual with Gherson, Ralph Barclay examined the suggestion for flaws, for he knew his clerk to be a slick fellow. Eventually he nodded and began to write, for this had to be a communication in his own hand. It could hardly be said to be good fortune that in losing an arm he had sacrificed his left, so at least he could still write and legibly.

'A word to the premier and fetch out the muster roll and any reports from divisional officers, while you study the logs. If we are required to strip out the ship let us make sure we transfer the dregs.'

Tempted to suggest Devenow, Gherson held his tongue. He was present to list the names as the least useful members of the crew were weeded out, added to them men who seemed to cause concern and in one case attract punishment, a quartet of ex-smugglers who were good seamen but troublesome and insubordinate shipmates. That had the captain looking at the list of vessels he was to ship them to.

'We can get those sods aboard *Britannia*,' Barclay snorted, which got him a very odd look from Mr Palmer, his first lieutenant.

'Send a signal to the various captains. They can carry them in their own boats and once they are off my deck prepare to get to sea.'

'Am I allowed to say, Captain Barclay, that this leaves us seriously short-handed?'

'According to Admiral Hotham, Mr Palmer, it merely makes us equal with every other line of battle ship in the fleet.'

When HMS *Britannia*'s boat came alongside, Cornelius Gherson, under a single seal, slipped two letters addressed to Ommaney and Druce in to the hands of the midshipman in charge: the one discussed with Barclay and also his own communication. If he dealt with his captain's affairs in relation to his investments he also operated for the prize agents to ensure that the way they handled the Barclay monies was not too closely examined, which allowed them to speculate more than was strictly prudent.

Such a transfer of personnel could not be accomplished without attracting attention, not least from those vessels whose number had not been raised on HMS *Semele*, the same ships not being in receipt of this gift.

On the deck of HMS *Agamemnon* Horatio Nelson was standing with Dick Farmiloe, his officer of the watch and now risen to the position of fourth lieutenant. It did not take too long to get the sense of what was happening.

'I smoke a touch of favouritism, sir. Nothing seems to be coming our way.'

'I daresay you are right, Mr Farmiloe, but do not let it make you gloomy.'

Nelson produced a large handkerchief, for he was suffering from a cold; indeed when not in such a state he seemed to be prone to afflictions of one sort or another. Only activity cured him and being stuck in San Fiorenzo Bay was not efficacious.

It was far from a secret that he was not Hotham's favourite subordinate, being a client officer of Lord Hood and much cherished by him in the past. How many times had the fleet watched as *Agamemnon* weighed to depart on some cruise, one in which Nelson was free to seek opportunities?

'We are as short on hands as anyone.'

'True,' Nelson replied, smiling through a loud sniff. 'But would we want men who are not Agamemnons? Are we not like King Hal's happy few at Agincourt, not wishing for any to share our glory? We will do very well as we are.'

If the transfer of hands was a cause for grumbling, the sight of HMS *Semele* hauling herself over her anchor multiplied that on many a quarterdeck, the most vocal that same HMS *Agamemnon*, for she had been listed as the next vessel to revictual.

If one or more captains were upset, Ralph Barclay was not. As soon as he cleared Cape Corse, well out of sight of his peers, he gave orders to his master to set a course for Naples, which obliged the premier to ask for confirmation. That got him a cold look from his captain.

'Please understand, Mr Palmer, that I enjoy the confidence of Admiral Hotham or we would not be at sea at all. Now we want sharp eyes in the tops, do we not, for it would be a damn shame to let opportunity go begging.'

'Why did you forbear to tell me of this before, John?'

'I did not wish you to worry and it was something I felt I could deal with on my return.'

'My husband is close by—'

'Hardly that, Emily, he is in a Corsican bay and likely to be stuck there.'

'How can you know that?'

'The purpose of the fleet demands it. They are there to fight the French, not to pursue private affairs, and that applies to your husband's ship as much as anyone.'

'And you do not see it as coincidence that he is in the Mediterranean?'

'I would admit to you one thing, my wonder as to how he has achieved it, but that serves little. He has, and if you agree to my suggestion then I would say his being so close is fortuitous. With the Chevalier's aid I can be with the fleet in a matter of days, wind permitting and, once there – well you know what might be possible.'

'You cannot believe he will simply allow himself to be persuaded, John. If he has come this far he will scarce desist in his pursuit of me.'

'I have the means to put pressure on him.'

'Those court martial papers,' she sighed. 'How I now regret stealing them.'

'How can you say that when they have kept you safe?'

She exploded then. 'I am not safe and I never will be as long as I am with you.'

'That, I am bound to protest, is cruel.'

Emily's shoulders slumped then and Pearce knew, even if he could not see them, the tears had begun to flow. He closed with her and took her in his arms, to sob on his shoulder while he uttered what he thought were meaningless platitudes. Should he tell her that it was not only the court martial papers that might make Barclay hesitate? John Pearce had good grounds to believe he had been party to the conspiracy that had sent him and Henry Digby into such danger on the coast of Dalmatia.

That accepted, Ralph Barclay was a minor player. The real culprit in the matter was Hotham and he intended to put pressure on that sod to ensure that HMS *Semele* never got close to the Bay of Naples. As Emma Hamilton had said, given time he might dissuade Emily from what he considered an act of pure madness. If he could guarantee she was safe here it would give him a basis with which to argue.

'All I ask,' he said, after a while, 'is to be allowed to try. If I fail, well . . .'

'Divorce requires an Act of Parliament.'

Thankfully she was not looking at Pearce when she said that for she would have seen him suddenly discomfited. If he had not actually lied when he intimated that as a way out of their dilemma, Pearce had no illusions as to the possibility of getting a bill of divorce even before the legislature. Besides the sheer amount of effort required there was the cost, which he could not hope to meet.

'I will not say it will be easy. All I will say is that I will bend my best efforts to it, for it is a case of my heart being broken or kept whole.'

'And if you fail?'

'Then I shall seek for some occupation in Frome so that I can be close to you and our child.'

'Even if I would not wish it so?'

'You have made it plain how hard it is to command you, Emily. Believe me when I say I will be ten times more tenacious.'

CHAPTER SEVEN

Cole Peabody was far from happy – not that many would have known, given he had been miserable for months now – before he had even been brought aboard HMS *Semele* as a pressed hand. Prior to coming a cropper he and his mates had enjoyed what they saw as an enviable life.

When in the Low Countries' port of Gravelines they had money to spend on pleasure, and did so lavishly. Time at sea, while dangerous given they were engaged in cross-Channel smuggling and the excise-used cannons and muskets, tended to be of short duration; once their illicit goods were landed and sold it was home to Ramsgate where Cole was treated as a man of parts.

Life had not been all roses; working for the Tolland brothers, who owned the ship on which they carried their contraband, had never been easy. The older brother Jahleel had a temper to make Old Nick cautious. If his younger sibling Franklin had seemed more sensible he was yet a fellow of whom to be wary. Not that he held either in regard now: the pair had abandoned Cole and his mates to the press, no doubt buying themselves off HMS *York*, a receiving hulk into which John Pearce had dumped them all.

'Can't be worse than what we had, Cole.'

'Who knows, Cephas? You was flogged on a whim by that sod Barclay and who's to say where we's going won't be worse?'

Over the months since they had been sent from the hulk, Peabody had come to exert a semblance of control over his equally unfortunate mates. Cephas Danvers, Fred Brewer and Dan Holder were, like him, ruffians and they looked and acted it. They had held themselves apart from the rest of the crew of *Semele* as being of a different stamp to men they saw as dupes. What fool would sign up for the King and a pittance when they could be free spirits and rake in money by running smuggled goods?

Even men forced to serve, and there were a number aboard the seventy-four, they disdained as too low to consort with. Only a chump would allow himself to be taken up by the press, a fact known to the whole quartet, who had spent their lives either avoiding such gangs or when they could not do so, fighting them to a standstill with knives and clubs to remain free.

They knew themselves to be hard bargains and behaved like it. They would have been pleased to know that the men watching them over the side were glad to see their backs, for they had been nothing but trouble to the lower deck as long as they had slung their hammocks there. Their divisional officer was likewise relieved; it would have been hard to admit the truth to anyone, but he had been cautious of men he reckoned were no strangers to dark deeds and he knew he should have been harder on them.

'That ship we're headed to has an admiral's flag aloft, Cole, do you note that?'

'So it has, Fred,' Cole replied looking up, before calling to one of the oarsmen. 'What's the name of the barky, mate?'

'*Britannia*,' came the whispered reply as the mid in charge of the cutter, young and fresh-faced, loudly called for them to be silent.

'Happen that nipper might need a midnight swim,' opined Danvers.

'Belay that talking there or your first sight of the flagship will be a grating.'

'Beggin' your indulgence, young sir,' Cole called, 'we's new to your ways.'

'By damn you'll learn soon enough.'

'And so might you, baby face,' Cole whispered to himself.

A lieutenant was waiting to list them in the muster book and to assign them to individual mess tables but that did not hold. A word here and there, plus the odd threat, soon got them messing together as a group. Their table was hard by the lower deck 32-pounder cannon that they would work in battle. Following on from that, the next task was to so intimidate the other members who shared their mess as to ensure that most of the mundane duties required to be carried out fell on them.

A ship of the line that had been at sea for two years was a settled place; the wardroom officers knew their compatriots' foibles and had learnt to live with those they found annoying. On the lower decks there had been jockeying when first assembled, sometimes coming to blows but those too had long been resolved; a new draft revived old problems and none more than a quartet so clannish and determined.

'There's one or two eyeing us up to put us in our place.'

Cephas said that to three lowered heads as the four conversed in undertones. What he was relating they expected; a first rate, supposed to have an eight hundred strong crew, had its hierarchy on the lower deck and some of them would not take kindly to the notion of the ex-smugglers muscling in.

There were two ways to deal with such a problem: by handing out a good hiding to the top dogs or, and this Cole favoured, by never upsetting them and pointing out that they were prepared to fight their corner, so harmony served everyone best, for bloodshed was certain.

'Had words with some,' added Brewer. 'No chance of coin in this bugger lest we bring John Crapaud's fleet to a contest.'

'You might get more'n coin if that occurs, Fred, you might get a bit of round shot up your arse.'

'Only happen if he was running away, Cole.'

'Which, Cephas, we must set our mind to do first chance presented. This is a new berth and they knows us not well. Word is we goes regular to Leghorn for victuals.'

'Where in the name of Christ is Leghorn?' Dan Holder asked.

'How would I know?'

'We's a long way from home, of that I is certain.'

'Its land, mate. Put my feet on good earth and I'll find a way to my hearth, even if we 'as a rate of miles to cover.'

That did not produce much in the way of enthusiasm, even if it had been a constant theme ever since their misfortune at Buckler's Hard, where Pearce had outfoxed the Tollands and taken them prisoner. They had vowed to desert at the first opportunity, only such a thing never occurred. Ralph Barclay had been a mean sod with liberty even to those he trusted, and they were few. The chances of these four ever getting ashore on leave had been nil.

Added to that they had missed out on the prize money paid out for the First of June battle, which had lined the purse of every man on the seventy-four from the great cabin to the meanest nipper, and that rankled. Fate was a cruel mistress, as Cole Peabody had seen the need to constantly remind them.

'An' she has set us on the ship with not a pot to piss in.'

That led to talk of bloody revenge on the Tolland brothers for dragging them into this situation in the first place and then leaving them to their fate, braggadocio and distance allowing them to forget that they had lived in mortal fear of Jahleel. Even that paled when the name John Pearce was mentioned; if the Tollands would shed his blood, these men intended – should they ever meet Pearce again – to skin him alive and then burn what was still breathing.

'Pity, seems to me,' Cole would remind them, hissing through lips lacking in teeth. 'There's as much chance of coming across that bastard as a pig flying to the masthead on its own fart.'

'They says God provides, Cole.'

'Not any one we worship, Dan.'

There being a constant stream of coastal traffic between Naples and the other ports of Italy, finding a vessel to take him to Leghorn posed no problem for John Pearce. From there he could get aboard any of the ships sent for revictualling and thus on their return back to San Fiorenzo Bay. The tiny cabin he got on the trader was filthy, which annoyed him, he now being accustomed to the cleanliness of a British warship, but he comforted himself that it would not be a journey of long duration.

Like all ships it creaked and groaned as timbers moved and ropes stretched, perhaps being old and poorly cared for more than most, especially when changing course. Carried out with none of the efficiency of a king's ship, this tended to be a noisy and shouty affair – certainly enough to wake him from his slumbers and to wonder why what he was hearing seemed to have a note of alarm about it.

In a stilted conversation with the master the following morning he learnt that, under a clear sky and near full moon, a large warship had been spotted sailing south under full sail. Fearing it to be French and afraid to risk being taken as a prize, the course had been rapidly altered to close with the land but the vessel had shown no interest in the small trader and had sailed on without itself altering course.

'Probably Neapolitan,' was John Pearce's opinion, which once it had been understood got him a shrug.

The drill on board HMS *Semele* was that set by the standing orders. The crew were roused out before dawn to man the guns, which were loaded and run out. Ralph Barclay was on deck as the sky lightened to range around the seascape with a telescope resting on a midshipman's shoulder. He was not alone; every officer on the ship was likewise alert, for this was ever seen as a time of vulnerability in hostile waters.

Sure that no enemy had snuck up on them in the hours of darkness – the moon state made no difference – he waited till he could, as the mantra had it, 'See a grey goose at a quarter mile'.

There being nothing in sight but the odd fishing boat he could give the order to Mr Palmer to carry on, which began the job of worming and housing the cannon, then swabbing the decks before they were flogged dry.

If Ralph Barclay saw the looks directed at him in his time on deck, or as he departed, none of them friendly, he paid them no heed. He had no desire to be loved by the crew: he wished to be obeyed and promptly, with the requisite punishments available to those who failed to meet his exacting standards.

In his absence the great cabin had been cleaned with watered-down vinegar, as it was every day, and the odour of that stung Barclay's nostrils as he sat with a cup of strong coffee and contemplated what lay ahead, this as the hands were now piped to breakfast.

Opposite him sat Cornelius Gherson, a man who had been roped more than once into the affair of his captain's troubled marriage. His solution to the problem of Emily Barclay and her desertion – hinted at, if never stated, but understood nonetheless – was that to seek to repair the union was a waste of time; a permanent end to the problem was the only viable answer.

'It won't wash,' Barclay said, when it was once more alluded to. 'If the whole fleet does not know what I am about then they soon will, for Hotham will have some explaining to do and I don't see him being shy in letting on my motives.'

'Irate captains?'

'As I would be myself if the shoe was on the other foot.'

Gherson looked over his employer's shoulder then, out of the salt-caked casements to the startling blue of the sea, his mind on the man's wife. She was a beauty and would still be that, not yet twenty years old with long auburn hair, fair skin, a delectable figure and a very becoming countenance enhanced by light freckles. What she also had was a waspish tongue and he had been lashed by that more than once.

On initial acquaintance he had made it known that she was, to him, an alluring prospect. Being vain, Gherson had fully expected the woman to be equally attracted to his person – after all, he had enjoyed great success in such matters before – though he was then obliged to recall that his previous dalliance with another man's wife had come perilously close to getting him killed.

Emily Barclay had rebuffed him in the most vicious and to him unwarranted way, not once but repeatedly, which had turned attraction into dislike and through his own anger into hate. Her husband was being weak in the head to think a woman like that would come back to him, twice her age and not much to look at either, with his heavy dark jowl and ruddy-red cheeks.

'The task, Gherson, if we find she is in Naples, is to get her aboard the ship. Once I have her confined well, I shall make her see sense.'

'Indeed, sir,' came the sceptical reply; Barclay had tried to make her see sense before and failed miserably.

'And in order to do that you must come ashore with me and put out feelers, for I cannot be seen to do so. Duty demands that I call upon our ambassador but you can act the free agent.'

'I will be in a place where I lack the tongue of the natives.'

'I know you will need an interpreter, Gherson, but when you charge me for his services have a care not to try and dun me as you have in the past.'

'Money will be required to loosen tongues as well.'

'Some of which your sticky fingers will be reluctant to part with, I daresay.'

Gherson made no protest at this growling accusation; he had long given up trying to persuade Ralph Barclay that he was careful with his money because he had never been believed. That the man had the right of it induced no guilt, yet such a response underlined what he had come to realise quite quickly in their relationship: his employer did not trust him one little bit. This was a fact not to be taken personally for the man was a stranger to dependence, his attitude being, after a life in the King's Navy, that anyone who could would steal from him and, as long as it was within reasonable bounds, he could let it pass. He was not beyond the odd bit of peculation himself, of the kind that even sharp-eyed Admiralty clerks would fail to spot. It was easy to despise Ralph Barclay, especially for a man who applied the same to most people he met. Gherson was adroit with figures and no more honest than his employer, able to so construct accounts in a way that hid well the minor felonies while diverting some for his own purse. To be insulted, as he regularly was by the man before him, he would abide since he was a source of income that was decent now and could grow to a much more lucrative one if he ever became an admiral and a fleet commander.

Certainly in his daydreams Gherson looked forward to the day when he could tell Barclay what he really thought of him, but such a dawn was a long way off. That accepted it was common for him to ponder on things that might go some way to redress the imbalance between them and such a possibility occurred to him now.

If he found Emily Barclay in Naples, perhaps the chance would arise to take from her that which she would not surrender willingly, a thought that had him wriggling uncomfortably in his chair. Barely aware of the shouts aloft and the sound of running feet, he was brought to the cause of the commotion as a midshipman knocked and entered.

'Mr Palmer's compliments, sir, but two sail have been spotted on the horizon and the lookout reckons them to be warships by their canvas.'

'Nationality?'

'Not yet established, sir, all we have is a sight of their topgallants.'

The yawn from the captain was both studied and deliberately theatrical and if it impressed the midshipman as a sign of sangfroid it failed to fool Gherson. 'Ask Mr Palmer to alter course to close and please let me know when that has been established.'

'We know they cannot be ours, sir, given there are none of our vessels in these waters.'

Gherson saw Barclay swell up. But before he could issue a sharp reprimand to the cheeky youngster the lad was gone, with the captain saying, 'Pound to a penny they are out from Naples.'

It took a whole glass of sand to disabuse Ralph Barclay and take him onto the quarterdeck with Devenow right beside him, for there was a fair swell and he risked a fall while using a telescope. The sightings were hull up now and many an eye was ranging over them.

He had aboard men who had served a long time in the navy and they knew the lines of the vessels they had spotted. They were French by design and, having identified HMS *Semele* as British, if not by name, they soon put up their helm and ran for safety, having seen her flags and reckoned on her size and armament.

Duty demanded he give chase. He commanded a well-found vessel and one that could be said to be fast for a seventy-four, being very fresh of the stocks and he commanded a crew that had already tasted prize money and were eager enough for more. If frigates, which they were, could normally outsail a ship of the line, luck might come to their aid and carry away something on an enemy vessel, canvas or a spar, perhaps one in panic bearing too much aloft.

Added to that they were running from safety; there was no harbour or bay outside of the southern French coast where they could anchor and not be vulnerable. The meanest tactical mind had to reckon that they would seek to come about and reverse the course in the hours of darkness and that, with luck and the right course, might put the seventy-four within long range of their decks.

'An opinion, Mr Palmer?'

That made the premier blink; his captain was not one to seek the views of others.

'We have no notion of their qualities, sir.'

That required no further explanation: were they well manned, for the French Navy had suffered much from the Revolution, most tellingly in its upper ranks? Many vessels seemed now to be commanded by men who had not previously been ships' captains. How long had they been at sea and where had they sailed to, for warm Mediterranean waters were faster to foul a hull than the cold Atlantic?

If HMS *Semele* could get close enough by a well-worked chase, would a pair of frigates reckon that to fight gave them a chance of glory – not in terms of gunnery but by being able to manoeuvre more quickly and sting a larger opponent?

'I think we know the calibre of our enemies, Mr Palmer. They are inclined to avoid battle are they not, which we can see before our very eyes?'

'True sir.'

'I think we must pass on what would be a fruitless chase that might take days. We shall raise Naples before we lose daylight, so let us resume our course and rue the fact that we did not come upon yonder fellows close to and at first light.'

The feeling of anticlimax was palpable and even an insensitive soul like Ralph Barclay could feel it, which had him step before the binnacle and glare along the deck as if to challenge anyone to speak or even scowl. That he held while the orders were being given to resume their original course, the sails hauled round and sheeted home, no one willing to catch his eye.

The smirk on Gherson's face as he passed his tiny cubicle infuriated Ralph Barclay, but the reprimand died on his lips; with what he was about he needed this man too much to chastise him now.

John Pearce was landing at Leghorn by the time HMS *Semele* raised the channel running between the Isla Procida and the promontory of Bacoli, the sun sinking to the west, which meant any attempt to land would have to wait till morning. Such a vessel could not come close to Naples without it caused excitement and long before she dropped anchor in the wide bay word had been sent to the British Ambassador to tell him that a capital ship of his nation's navy was in the offing.

'Emma, my dear, we must prepare to receive the man in command.'

'Do we know of him?'

'How could we?'

'A stranger, then. Let us hope that he is of the entertaining variety. Too many of these naval fellows are dullards.'

The Chevalier smiled. 'I have known you to find one or two entertaining, my dear.'

'One or two, yes, but no more than that.'

CHAPTER EIGHT

It was a wary, rather than a weary traveller who landed at Leghorn; given the trouble he had previously encountered in the Tuscan port that was to be expected. There was a strong naval presence to support the commissary needs of the fleet but at present no warships in the roadstead, which was a disappointment and led him first to the *pensione* in which he and Emily had previously stayed to leave there his sea chest.

Pearce's reasons for caution centred on redcoats not blue, soldiers not sailors, for he had encountered much grief from contacts with army men here, though there seemed little evidence of their presence now. Enquiries at the office of the Navy Board, and the Captain Urquhart who oversaw their work, provided no information as to when he could expect a ship, while he had to be circumspect as to how he had come to be there without one.

Obliged to identify himself he dare not mention HMS *Flirt* or the mission on which she had been engaged, while the excuses he provided, hastily conjured up since he had not previously thought of the need – that he had become separated from his vessel by ill health – sounded feeble to his ears and judging by the expression that greeted his explanation was scarce believed.

'Well,' the captain said, his manner decidedly unfriendly, that being enhanced by a dour and heavy Scots delivery, 'your name is known, sir, in these parts and not in a good way.'

'I am at a loss to know why that should be particular to Leghorn.'

'Come, sir. You are by common consent not qualified for your rank. Even monarchs make errors. Do not deny that you induced a near riot in the port – one that, fortunately, did not end in fatalities, though it sailed damn close.'

Pearce declined to protest, for the first accusation was something fruitless to respond to, while the other left him genuinely confused. 'I have no idea what you are talking about.'

'Come, sir, do you really expect me to believe such a plea? The bullocks you set your men upon made sure the whole town knew who to blame.'

'For what, sir?'

The tone John Pearce used then, one of rising anger, met with even less approval than his name. Urquhart flushed angrily and his response was spat out with real venom, a hand slapping down on his desk.

'It pains me to mention, and I would scarce want to allude to it, but I find I must do so: the way you embarrassed the service by your behaviour in a duel. That the mere engagement is reprehensible and forbidden is a matter of fact, sir, but much worse is that you chose a low trick to end matters in your favour. Not content with that you then had the very man you fought and his companions set upon, assaulted by every midshipman and liberty man then in the harbour.'

'Captain Urquhart, I will acknowledge the former charge and I am not happy at the memory, though I will add that when a fellow sets out not to merely draw blood for satisfaction but to kill you, the rules by which gentlemen engage in such pursuits go by the board.'

Urquhart was not listening; judging by his breathing he was struggling to contain himself, close to an outburst that would pass the bounds of acceptance.

'You do not seem to observe that I have work before me, which you are preventing me from getting on with. Because of that, Lieutenant, I must bid you good day.'

Once outside the building, standing under the fluttering Union Flag, John Pearce was at a loss to make sense of what he had heard and damned annoyed at the way he had been dismissed. Passing through to get to the street he had been eyed with deep suspicion by Urquhart's underlings, men who must have overheard the exchange in the captain's office. Tempted to enquire of them, their expressions did nothing to invite questioning, which left him at a loss as to how to proceed.

That, he felt he must do: some deed was being attached to his name and it was even more annoying to have no notion of what he was accused of, while in a port full of Italians layered with Austrians there was a shortage of places to go where he could seek enlightenment.

Walking along the quay, a possible alternative presented itself.

Leghorn, as well as being the revictualling port for the fleet, was home to a fair few privateers, many of them English, given letters of marque by the British Crown to pursue and harass the trade of the enemy for personal gain.

They were a rum bunch held in contempt by their naval contemporaries, which was hypocrisy of the first order. King's officers chased after prizes with a zeal that matched that of the men they termed predatory wolves. Their objection centred on the freedom privateers had to act at will, their obvious successes adding to the fact that their captures meant fewer opportunities for their naval rivals.

The letters of marque occupied their own part of the port, a small harbour they shared with the larger local fishing boats, well away from the naval dockyard on the far side of the old castle that had at one time protected the anchorage. It was an area into which naval ratings were discouraged from going, and that was with only the most reliable hands allowed ashore.

Leghorn posed a danger that did not apply to many other ports and for that reason some warships never let a soul below a warrant on to dry land. Privateers required sailors as much as the navy and had a strong preference for their own countrymen, for if they suffered casualties – inevitable when they generally had to fight to take their seizures – they found it hard to procure replacements, which made the proximity of a fleet tempting.

Added to the bounty they might offer to recruit a King's sailor they were adept at keeping them too, able with a change of name to provide the kind of exemptions from naval service that protected their own crews from impressment; if they were forged, and the navy was sure it was so, it was done with such skill as to be impossible to gainsay. If the stream of recruits was low, men still managed to make the transfer for it mattered not what was put in place to prevent desertion: a few always found a way round it.

Leghorn had been a fortified port since Roman times, laid out with new fortifications in the style of Vauban the previous century, with a star-shaped bastion surrounded by moats and canals, and that forced anyone seeking to capture the new citadel into approaches that could be easily defended. Such features forced Pearce into a long detour and in making it he was aware that he was being eyed by small knots of folk that seemed to have time to lounge on corners.

Such creatures might just be innocent locals yet it was known the navy had set men in place to prevent their crews from disappearing, paid crimps whose task it was to spot a wandering sailor and prevent him from passing through to the privateers' part of the city, by persuasion if it could be achieved, by violence if not.

Coming upon the privateers' basin John Pearce eyed the berthed vessels with something approaching professional appreciation. Sizes and shapes varied but all the ships were sleek, well maintained, armed with sufficient weaponry and looked to be fast on a bowline. Yet there was no profit in being tied up to a quayside; the making of money was done at sea.

So he had to assume that if their captains and crews were in port it was due to success not idleness, spending what they had gained by their licensed piracy, a truth brought home when, passing under a painted board that named the establishment as the Golden Hind, he entered a tavern that in its layout – low-beamed ceiling and smoke-stained walls – could have existed in the London docks.

The babble of talk died as he came through the door; naval

officers were rare in such places and not welcome, judging by the reaction, for they were generally in pursuit of deserters. He returned their stares, some being glares, with a set face, before finding a rough wooden table at which he could sit.

A serving wench was by his side immediately to place on his board a pitcher of wine, a bowl of olives and some bread. The notion of coming to this place had not fashioned a way to proceed, which left him at a stand, especially when those present chose to ignore him and go back to their own murmured exchanges.

John Pearce had been a solitary presence in a strange setting many times in his life. Had he not entered the Pelican Tavern in much the same manner as he had come to this place, albeit on a foul night? Having been on the wing more than once in his life gave him a steadiness in such an impasse that few could match, as well as a devil-may-care way of acting when no other method presented itself.

'My name is Lieutenant John Pearce. Is that known to any of you?'

The loud question stilled the voices for a second time and this lasted longer as he was carefully examined. Finally, one fellow stood up and, picking up his own cup of wine, came to sit opposite him. Examining this new companion Pearce was wont to think him a caricature for he matched in almost every way the depictions often seen in the London playhouses of old buccaneers like Henry Morgan and Edward Teach.

His black hair was oiled and arranged in ringlets, some of the lower curls decorated with ribbons. He had a thin but substantial moustache and sharp features though he was far from ugly, quite the reverse, and that handsomeness was enhanced when he smiled.

Indeed Pearce thought he was a fellow who would not struggle at all with the fair sex.

'So you are the infamous Pearce. Have you come to join yonder merry band?'

'Why would I wish to do that, sir?'

'Come, sir, your credentials are perfect.'

'You have my name, but I lack—'

The head tipped a fraction, to which was added a wry smile. 'Oliver Senyard, at your service.'

'Owner of one of the vessels I passed?'

'Lord no, sir, I am a trader. I cannot abide the sea, which apart from rendering me sick as soon as I leave harbour has a strong inclination to remove me from this life when on water and that is before you come across some cove who would dearly like to slit your gullet. Let others take such a risk, I am the fellow who trades their captures, quite a quantity of it sold to your own service.'

'You deal with Captain Urquhart?'

'I have that misfortune, yes, but the navy pays well for stores seized from privateer successes.'

'Can I say your appearance does not match your occupation?'

Senyard grinned. 'In a piratical setting, sir, it serves to look the part.'

'If I were to indulge you with some more wine, sir, perhaps you will tell me why my name is so well known and even more to the point, why you use a word like infamous?'

'Come, sir, that needs no words from me.'

'I fear it does, Mr Senyard, for I am at a true stand.'

* * *

Ralph Barclay was rowed ashore wearing his best blue coat and hat to be much impressed by what lay before him. The Bay of Naples was famous throughout the world for its beauty as well as the ever-present menace of Vesuvius with its cone smoking to the south, benign-looking at present but with no one knowing when that would alter and it would suddenly erupt.

At a distance the shoreline properties, including the royal palace, looked very fine, while a military eye naturally took in the forts that protected the town and the various harbours dotted along the shoreline: one for the Neapolitan Navy, another for trading vessels and any number of tiny moles to protect the fishing fleet from the sudden squalls common in the Tyrrhenian Sea.

Such an idyll did not survive proximity; close to the buildings, the Palazzo Reale apart, showed much wear and tear, many bordering on neglect, while the smell – not an unusual one for a port, made up of rotting fish and vegetation, added to human waste – seemed to have more power than most. Yet there were occasional wafts of something sweeter, for there was a mass of colourful flora both on the balconies and in the hills behind.

Dropping his gaze Barclay cast an eye over the crew of his barge. Being wealthy he had outfitted them in a manner he thought appropriate to his dignity. Every oarsman had a hat with a bright-red ribbon, a short blue jacket with brass buttons, this over a cambric shirt. All wore matching bright-red bandanas, clean white ducks, and by their feet as they worked the sticks a pair of patent leather shoes to be put on as they accompanied him ashore. There were two marines along and they would guard the barge while it was tied up.

The saluting had taken place at first light, HMS *Semele* acknowledging the royal standard and the locals replying to his own flags, not least that of Vice Admiral Hotham. His departure from the ship had been noted so there were dignitaries on the quay waiting to welcome him, which they did as soon as Devenow, leaping on to the solid surface first, reached down a hand to aid Barclay up the short ladder.

'Be quick about your business, Gherson,' were the last words the captain said as he ascended.

The clerk ignored an injunction made too many times already. He had a decent purse in his coat pocket and that he padded to reassure himself, which occasioned a discreet smile for he reckoned not to disburse it but to keep the contents. Gherson hoped Ralph Barclay had shown his naïvety when he had handed it over.

What good would it do to seek an interpreter and question Italians regarding Emily Barclay? If she was in Naples the people who would be aware of her presence would be English and there had to be a rate of his countrymen in such a busy trading port.

It was also common knowledge that many a rich traveller from home landed up here, usually in search of antiquities from Pompeii and Herculaneum with which to return home and decorate their mansions and country piles. Having been an avid reader of popular journals in London – wishing himself to be rich he was eager to hear of the exploits of those he intended to emulate – Gherson knew of Ambassador Hamilton.

And he had seen him once, he was sure, at an exhibition held at the Duke of Richmond's gallery in Whitehall, where those in possession of ancient artefacts had been persuaded to display their trophies, Hamilton being but one of many. But he was more than that, and his position gave him a unique ability to indulge his interest.

The man was an avid seeker of antiquities and he was known to regularly dig at the appropriate sites. Hamilton had unearthed so many treasures that he could show off his own finds at the Royal Academy and fill the space provided, to be greeted with much acclaim and not a little envy, but the real point was different. He would be called upon by other collectors visiting Naples, and people who looked for beauty in ancient art would likely not miss it in a comely young woman.

Watching as pleasantries were exchanged with the Neapolitan naval officers, Gherson's eye was taken by a striking-looking woman, a redhead under a parasol, in the background. Standing with her was a tall, slim man, older but with the air of a natural patrician, who stepped forward once the official greetings were completed to introduce himself. Having seen him sketched in those journals the clerk had little doubt as to their identity.

'Allow me to welcome you as our nation's ambassador to the Kingdom of Naples. Sir William Hamilton, at your service.'

The ambassador executed a slight bow as Barclay replied, and in doing so exposed to an even clearer view the notorious lady who must be his wife. Painted many times by Romney, hers was an image known to him as well. She was striking enough still to hold his gaze but why did she react so to the words she then overheard?

'Captain Ralph Barclay, Sir William, of His Britannic Majesty's Third Rate HMS *Semele*. I bear for you letters from my commanding admiral, Sir William Hotham.'

'No longer Lord Hood?'

'No sir, Admiral Hotham has the honour to now hold the command.'

'Then I must send my congratulations to a man I consider an old acquaintance.'

Lady Hamilton stepped forward, her expression concerned, to tug at her husband's sleeve and whisper in his ear as he canted his head to listen. Fixated, Gherson looked for a reaction from the old man but his face remained a mask, immobile if you excluded an occasional minimal nod, until finally he looked at Ralph Barclay and smiled.

'You are, of course, invited to be my guest at the Palazzo Sessa.' If Emma Hamilton was agitated before she was even more so now as her spouse continued in his even tone. 'Naturally, my wife will go ahead to prepare while you and I take a turn round some of the more entertaining sights.'

'At your service, sir,' Barclay replied.

He said this before catching sight of Gherson. He had looked at the buildings lining the quay, none of them warranting the description of entertaining. The glare he aimed at his clerk was one to ask what the devil he was still doing standing there.

'The churches are particularly fine,' the ambassador added. 'The remaining Norman examples make one feel perfectly at home.'

As he moved away Gherson heard Barclay's response and, knowing him as well as he did, recognised the manufactured quality of his enthusiasm; he was not a man for places of worship but manners left him no option but to oblige.

'And as we walk, sir, you can tell me of Admiral Hotham, whom I have met at a royal levee but only when he held the rank of captain, so it is some time past.'

'A fine officer, sir, and the very best produced by the service.'

'As has always been said of him.'

Emma Hamilton was gone, moving towards her open coach at what seemed a rather forced pace, one observed by Gherson but not Ralph Barclay. The temptation to tell his employer what he surmised was strong, but then a few hours of ignorance would do Barclay no harm and him some good. To be ashore was a blessing in itself; to have coin to freely spend was even better and Naples must be blessed with some very fine houses of pleasure, manna to a fellow who had been too long at sea for his own comfort.

There was a comical element to the way the barge crew, now fully shod, fell in behind the ambassador, their captain and the ever-watchful Devenow, spruced up like them for the occasion. They were unused to marching and even more discomfited by the leisurely pace of the pair they were now escorting.

Barclay, with his back to them, could not see it and he would have had an apoplexy if he had; far from enhancing his dignity their swaying gait and stumbling walk was attracting smiles and laughs from the locals.

John Pearce listened to Oliver Senyard with increasing incredulity; what he was being told would certainly be justified in blackening his name if it were true. But it was utterly false, which left him wondering: if he was not at fault, who was? There had certainly been a serious breach of the peace and, by the account he was hearing, great physical harm done.

He cast his mind back to the last time he had been in Leghorn, not to rehash any of the unfortunate events he had experienced but for a more general appreciation of what had been happening in the port at the time. The ships that had been present included HMS *Leander*, in which Henry Digby had been second lieutenant, with that piece of ordure Taberly as his premier.

According to Digby, Taberly was the person who really ran the ship for both served under an indolent captain. He was certainly a man to only allow shore leave to officers and warrants, keeping hands on the ship and letting the pleasures of the port come out to them. The other line of battle ship present had been *Agamemnon*, accompanied by a trio of frigates and that as a case was chalk and cheese.

Nelson was known throughout the fleet, and condemned by some as being too soft, too indulgent of his whole crew, none more so than his midshipmen. He was strong on the notion that granting shore leave was a good thing, easy for him to advance with a wholly volunteer crew raised in the main from his home county of Norfolk, the rest being old hands who had served under him previously.

Not that such knowledge provided any clues. Meanwhile he had this privateer factotum sat opposite him clearly not prepared, any more than Urquhart had been, to buy his claims of ignorance. The sounds of cannon fire turned both their heads to the doorway and Pearce recognised what had now become familiar: signal guns wasting powder as a vessel coming in saluted the port and the old bastion on the shoreline replied.

'Mr Senyard, I thank you for your company and the way you have enlightened me.'

That got a jaundiced look as the man replied. 'If you're ever stuck for a berth seek me out, Mr Pearce. Those I deal with can always use a man aboard who knows how to sail a ship and is not afraid to act the brigand and will pay a bounty for enrolment.'

Wanting to tell him where to stick such an offer, Pearce just forced out a smile, lifted his hat and walked out of the door, aware that every eye was once more upon him. He was on the quay when he recognised the vessel coming in as HMS *Agamemnon*.

CHAPTER NINE

If Emily Barclay was all frozen shock, then her hostess was the exact opposite. Emma Hamilton was good in a crisis; so, normally, was her guest but not one of this kind.

'My husband, here?'

'I've sent to the servants' quarters for those fellows Mr Pearce left behind and I have ordered a shay to carry you to a small beach residence my husband keeps for his sea bathing. That will not serve for long but it will do so in an emergency. Now, Emily, I suggest you pack some clothing for a brief stay there.'

'Do you believe in fate?'

'I believe, Emily, I have a duty to protect you.'

'There is not just me,' Emily replied, a hand going to her still flat belly.

'You are with child, I know.'

'How do you know?'

'I am, like you, a woman and what's more one who has borne a child. I am no stranger to the signs.'

'You have had a child?'

'In another life!' Emma Hamilton snapped as Michael O'Hagan appeared at the door of the suite of rooms Emily had occupied. The swift explanation of what had occurred and the proposed solution had the Irishman crossing himself and getting a less than wholeheartedly pious response from the ambassador's wife.

'Prayer will not serve our needs, haste will. The Chevalier is at present keeping Captain Barclay amused by visiting churches and the like, but he will then bring him to the palazzo. None of you must be here, for the mere sight will tell him all.'

'Perhaps I should stay and face him,' Emily interjected softly.

'In God's name why, when you have spent so much time running away?'

'I told John of my intention to return to him, for the sake of the child. If my husband will accept it as his own it will not be tainted for life.'

'Holy mother of Christ,' came from O'Hagan, more of a sigh than an exclamation.

'Which the man who *is* the father is seeking to alter.' Seeing the reaction forced Emma Hamilton to own up to the conversation they had prior to his departure.

'He seems to have told you, Lady Hamilton, a great deal regarding our affairs.'

There was no escaping the tone of pique, nor was there any doubt of Emily's annoyance for it was evident on her pinched face and sharply dilated nostrils.

'He confided in me his concerns, yes, and why? Because he wishes to rescue you from a life of misery.'

'He cannot be certain it will be so.'

Emily hesitated then; did she really want to state her reasoning: that with a husband serving in the navy she might not be burdened much with his presence? There was a very distinct possibility of his being at sea more than he was at home, some commissions lasting years, even in peacetime. That in Frome she would be surrounded by her own family and friends, which would serve to make what could be intolerable bearable. That an occasional submission to her brutish husband's needs was a small price to pay to avoid the taint of bastardy for her child.

Lady Hamilton gave up on Emily and addressed the Irishman, still in the doorway and hat in hand. 'Your name is Michael, I recall; can you reason with her?'

'Only to say, Mrs Barclay, that you stand to break John-boy's heart. That I do know. He came from the other side of Italy for he could not wait to see you, when he might be sailing by this place in a couple of weeks. Sure, that speaks of something more than fondness.'

'While I would hazard,' their hostess added forcefully, 'that he will not give you up easily.'

That hit home and had Emily biting her lip; it brought back to her the words of her lover, the promise that he would no more let her be than Ralph Barclay. A vision of his stalking her in the streets of her hometown made her shudder.

'Sure, it would please me,' Michael added, 'if you was to consider for a bit.'

That led to silence and Emily considered her options until

finally she spoke. 'I will go with you, Michael, to where Lady Hamilton has directed us. But, milady, I do ask this: that should I wish to confront my husband in order to make up my mind, it will be in your presence.'

'You have my word. Now pack. I told our coachman to be tardy in returning to the city but that leaves little time.'

The shay was not large enough to accommodate Emily and all the Pelicans, which had Charlie Taverner and Rufus Dommet, as well as one of the Hamilton servants to give directions, jogging alongside her and Michael, with the observation that the poor creature hauling them would have preferred a lighter carcase to bear.

What was called the Bathing House sat on the shore beyond the promontory, in a wide and arcing bay that lay to the west of the Palazzo Sessa. If Emma Hamilton had described it as small it was because she had never been accommodated aboard a ship of war. If it was plain it was also, on two floors, as spacious as a small London house of the artisan type.

The Chevalier obviously took his sea dipping seriously. There was a large cistern on the roof to collect rainwater, that to feed not just the needs of the house but also a plunge pool by which he could wash off the salt after bathing. Added to that he could rest here if he wished, with a comfortable first-floor room for him with a day bed as well as a shelf of books, a functioning kitchen and accommodation for any servants he fetched along with him.

The party, despite the fears of their hostess, had been afforded much time to get clear for Naples was blessed with numerous churches as well as the Cathedral of San Gennaro. Ralph Barclay found himself ushered into one after another, to be shown painted panels, arched roofs replete with heavenly visions, magnificent stained-glass windows and enough statuary to fill the Horse Guards' drilling ground, but only after he had been obliged to admire the exterior stonework and carvings.

None of this impressed very much a man who preferred a plain English country building with weathered blocks of grey stone and whitewashed walls inside, lacking any embellishments bar the odd crucifix and a carved pulpit. Indeed, he was bored and finding it hard to disguise the fact, glad when finally the Chevalier led him back to the quayside and his waiting coach.

'If you wish to fetch along your barge crew, Captain Barclay, I have no objection, though they are scarce necessary. We will, of course, accommodate you tonight and if you wish to name a time, your boat can come for you on the morrow.'

About to agree, Barclay hesitated. 'I have one request, sir. I have given my clerk a certain task to carry out and I need to know if he has been as zealous as he is required to be. I ask that he be allowed to call upon me at your residence prior to going back aboard.'

'Of course.'

'Then, if you will furnish him with directions, my man Devenow will await his return to the quay and tell him to come on to . . . ?'

'The Palazzo Sessa in Posillipo. If your man engages a hack and requests to be taken to the home of the Madonna *Inglese* he will not need directions.' To a raised Barclay eyebrow, the ambassador added, 'It is the name with which the locals favour my wife.'

As a sea officer, Barclay lacked the diplomatic skills of his companion; he could not keep off his face the confusion such an appellation created. How someone called a whore by many in

England could be termed a maternal virgin here escaped him and his response thus lacked any conviction at all.

'Fully deserved, I'm sure. Now, if you will excuse me I will tell my man of the duty he needs to perform.'

On the journey the Chevalier was the main instigator of conversation, asking about the loss of the captain's arm and then, Toulon having been mentioned, for his impressions of that event and the subsequent siege. Barclay was quite vehement about it having all been an error and too preoccupied to note the slight surprise that he should say so.

'Captain Nelson stated it was the most perfect thing.'

'But Admiral Hotham, a much wiser fellow than Nelson, was dead against it, sir, and he was right to be so. Sadly, Lord Hood ignored him.'

That said the Chevalier fell into a contemplative silence, not broken by a companion who failed to spot there should be a reason, which was of short duration given they were soon at the palazzo.

'Well?' Emma demanded, as she faced her husband prior to joining Ralph Barclay on the veranda, where he had been left to sip a cooling glass of lemon water and admire the view.

'I fear he is as coarse as many of his breed, my dear. I doubt you will take to him. Also, he has sent a man to enquire around in Naples, you can guess what for?'

That had Emma biting her lip; how many times had Emily Barclay shared her open coach these last months and been hailed almost as much as she herself for her beauty? Anyone enquiring would soon be told of her presence as well as the company she kept.

'He may not find out that she was accommodated with us.'

That got a very severe look and what was tantamount to a command. 'If he asks after his wife, Emma, we cannot lie to him.'

John Pearce had been welcomed aboard *Agamemnon* like a long-lost brother: it was not a mood that lasted. Horatio Nelson had no sooner had brought to his table the wine they would consume, as usual delivered by his surly servant, than his guest demanded to be told if the Agamemnons had had any hand in the affair of which he was being accused.

Nelson looked so embarrassed it precluded any attempt at denial.

'Our C-in-C severely castigated me about the affair. I fear Admiral Hotham found my excuse of overenthusiasm and mere high spirits did not answer. The only thing I could do to mitigate his anger was to take the blame for my ship and leave out the fact that we had a trio of frigates with us.'

'Your midshipmen have a reputation, sir.'

'I know, but my liberty men were just as involved as *Agamemnon*'s young gentlemen, which goes some way to explaining the level of violence visited on those bullocks. Their injuries were inflicted by hardened tars.'

'Then I need to know how my name came to be associated with the actions of your men?'

'While I must tell you, Mr Pearce, that I have no idea. I would, however, point out, and you cannot gainsay this, that one of the number assaulted, indeed the fellow who brought it to the attention of our commanding officer, had, prior to the event, literally crossed swords with you.'

Nelson gave him a look then, head canted and eyebrows lowered that invited Pearce to relate the details of a fight he had no desire to describe. Nor, and for the same reasons of a degree of shame, did he wish to admit that the bullocks in question had deliberately insulted Emily, then left him with no route to achieve recourse. He took refuge in an untruth that could not be challenged.

'Yes, and the matter ended there.'

'That, Mr Pearce, is plainly not the case.'

'If your men took on these bullocks it was not on my behalf, was it? Outside yourself and Mr Farmiloe I would scarce recognise one of your young gentlemen to speak with and I certainly do not have any acquaintances on your lower deck. Why, in that case, would they take up cudgels on my behalf?'

'I am at a loss to know how to satisfy you.'

'I must ask if you enquired into the affair with your men and you must forgive me for the temerity.'

'I read them the Riot Act, or emphasised the relevant Articles of War at Sunday Service to be precise, but I doubt it made anyone feel remorse. We engage men to be fighters, Mr Pearce, and if they get into such scrapes while off the ship I do not see how it can be stopped. I was a tad more severe with my young gentlemen, of course, than the hands. As budding officers they should know better.'

Nelson smiled, which lit up what had been a rather severe countenance.

'Threatened them with all sorts, the gunner's daughter and endless mast headings, but I fear they know me too well to take seriously such exhortations.'

'I ask to be allowed to question them.' That had Nelson sitting back and it was clear he was far from keen. 'I need to know, sir, for it is my name and my reputation that is on the line.'

'Mr Pearce . . .' The hands spread and the expression was sad; it was obvious, without being stated, that his visitor was a man under a cloud by his very rank and existence.

'I know that it is not good in the cabins and wardrooms of the navy, sir, but I would not have it blackened further by base rumour. If you will favour me in this I will be forever in your debt.'

'One I would be most reluctant to call in. Lepée, send for the midshipmen.'

'All of them?' was the growled and less than respectful reply.

'Aye, they have questions to answer.'

'Being born would serve to damn most of them.'

'Just do as I ask,' Nelson sighed. As the servant departed he gave Pearce a look of tolerance well overstretched. 'Everyone wonders why I keep him, Mr Pearce. Tell me, how can I dismiss a man who, however badly he behaves, once saved my life?'

There being no answer to that both sat sipping wine in silence until the 'young gentlemen' appeared, half a dozen youngsters of varying ages. John Pearce had seen many a group of midshipmen gathered, yet it was clear that none of these had become the kind of creature who would ever be stuck in the gun room, thirty years old and rising. Nothing could surely be more depressing than to never have any prospect of making lieutenant but such long-serving souls were a far from uncommon sight.

The questions Pearce asked had them shuffling their feet, until their commander quietly insisted they respond. What came out lacked clarity to an alarming degree and that forced their inquisitor to be more direct, until a young fellow called Hoste, well into puberty by the spots on his cheeks, chose to answer.

'We could not abide the insults, sir.'

'What insults?'

Josiah Nisbet was the one to respond. 'Made against my stepfather, sir.'

Pearce had seen Nisbet before, on an occasion when Nelson had acted in a far from respectable manner in this very port, drooling over an overripe opera singer at a ball and clearly the worse for wear with drink. He was, of course, known to be lightheaded when it came to wine and no more chaste than any of his peers. Yet to behave badly in front of his wife's son was risky in the extreme.

'They had been calling into question his qualities in a very offensive way. Said he was a burden at Calvi for seeking to do what was best done by redcoats.'

'We were told so, were we not, Josiah?'

'Told so, Mr Hoste?' Pearce asked.

'That and a lot more besides, downright insults of a most personal nature.'

'What kind of insults?' Nelson demanded, an interruption which irritated Pearce, though he could not say so.

'That you lacked height, ran a filthy ship, were born out of wedlock, greedy and that no boy was safe in your company.'

'What!'

That shouted outburst of fury produced a strange reaction, very close to a veiled smile. It was almost as if the lad was enjoying the discomfiture his words had caused. Nelson was shaking his head, clearly upset and did not observe the look, which allowed Pearce to continue.

'Told? You did not hear these insults delivered yourselves, is that what you are saying?'

'No, Mr Pearce,' Hoste responded, before realising he was causing confusion. 'I mean to say, yes. They were related to us by a couple of hands from another ship.'

'A swab I got hold of by the throat,' Nisbet added, with a face screwed up to indicate the level of his recollected fury. The questioning look had him continue, his snarl designed to show resolution. 'Thought the sod was the one making the accusations. When I got hold of him he soon told me the truth of it. That it was the bullocks. They had been goin' round the whole town slighting *Agamemnon* and our captain.'

'They paid the price,' Hoste added. 'Be a rate of time afore they insult anyone in a blue coat again.'

'Which ship did these fellows come from?'

'No idea, sir. We didn't ask and they didn't say.'

'There were three of them, one being a lad who had never dipped his wick,' Hoste added, with a sly grin, 'which was put paid to by a collection. Had to be carried to his doom and came back all grins.'

'Freckles damn near fell off,' Nisbet said, with a chuckle. 'There was another of the trio, a brute of a Paddy, hands like hams and a real bruiser by the look, well drunk he was, too, dancing and singing with some of the hands from the frigates, they being Irishmen likewise.'

'Didn't get the name of the one that related to us what these bullocks from the 65th Foot had been saying. But he told us where they rested and so off we went to teach them some manners.'

The sinking feeling in John Pearce's gut was acute and he had to fight hard to keep his voice even. 'A description might help.'

'Sandy hair, comely look about him and a silvery tongue for sure.'

'And they accompanied you?'

'No,' Hoste replied, 'which seems strange now. Didn't remark on it at the time. Never saw hide nor hair after we went looking for the bullocks.'

'Well, gentlemen, I thank you.' Never comfortable with blatant lies Pearce had to force himself to say the next words in a like tone. 'I don't feel much enlightened by what you have related to me, nor can I tell why my name is associated with what happened. But it is and I will be at a stand to find a way to correct it.'

'Be assured, sir,' Hoste added, 'we will put the word about that you had no part.'

'Thank you, Mr Hoste.'

'Best be about your duties,' Nelson ordered, which had them nodding and exiting his cabin, he not speaking till they were gone. 'I cannot see what further aid I can give you, sir.'

'Neither can I, sir, though I would request that when you set out to return to San Fiorenzo Bay I can come along as a passenger. I have a need to see Admiral Hotham.'

The name got a raised eyebrow but no request for an explanation. 'Most certainly. It will be a matter of a day or two, but how many I will not know until I have spoken with Captain Urquhart. You may berth aboard till then, if you wish.'

'Most kind.'

Nelson stood up. 'Let me see you to your boat.'

'Uncommonly civil of you, sir.'

They came out onto a busy deck, with derricks being rigged to take in stores and many a shout from below as what they had left was being shifted to make space for what was already being piled up on the quay.

'Odd that *Semele* is not here,' Nelson said idly, looking across the anchorage.

'That being Captain Barclay's ship,' Pearce responded unnecessarily; who had what was no secret.

'Aye. She departed Corsica two days before we did, though it was our turn to revictual ahead of her. If she's not here she will be cruising. I daresay our C-in-C was keen to indulge Barclay, given they are close. He will be out there somewhere seeking to line his already bulging purse.'

Captain Urquhart was unhappy to see Pearce again, but not enough to refuse to answer the question posed, even if he did so with ill-grace.

No, he had not seen any sign of HMS *Semele*.

CHAPTER TEN

'Lady Hamilton, it is an almost unmeasurable pleasure to meet with you.'

'How very gracious, Captain Barclay.'

Had the woman addressed known of the thoughts coursing through his mind she would not have smiled at such a greeting. He was thinking of how he could relate to others that he had actually encountered this Jezebel. His listeners would be avid to hear of it, to be told if the signs of her known debaucheries were plain to the eye or hidden from view. And was her husband the old booby he was supposed to be, hoodwinked into marrying a woman whose reputation was so tainted that he had apparently forfeited the good opinion of society and his childhood friend King George?

'No words can do justice to your beauty, milady, which is famed throughout the land.'

Two deep lines appeared at either side of the top of Emma Hamilton's nose, which told Ralph Barclay he had overcooked his compliments; her beauty might be what he had said, but it was not that for which she was best known and in terms of bloom it was past its peak. That said she was too experienced to let on.

'It is always a pleasure to have officers of our country's wooden walls as a guest, sir, though too infrequent as my husband will tell you. And sir, I beg you to resume your seat.'

Manners had Barclay wait until she had herself taken a chair. The point made by his wife was taken up by the ambassador. 'I cannot seem to persuade your seniors of the dangers under which Naples labours.'

'While I admit to ignorance.'

'Really?' came the surprised response. 'The monarchy hereabouts is shaky, Captain Barclay. There is a deal of republican sentiment—'

'Harshly dealt with, I trust,' Barclay interrupted, which earned him a frown.

'I have made representations to Lord Hood on more than one occasion that the sight of a British ship of the line in the Bay of Naples would do much to temper the more fervent elements seduced by the scoundrels of Paris.'

'And he declined to respond?'

'From what I have been told he could not do so, his responsibilities elsewhere being so great. But Captain Nelson—'

Now it was his wife who interrupted to say, 'Our good friend Captain Nelson,' though it was received with a graceful nod from her husband.

'Quite. He has written to us many times to say that he reminds Lord Hood of the need, though of course that must now be aimed at his successor.'

Pigs might fly, Ralph Barclay thought; Hotham would not listen to Nelson, quite the reverse.

'This city,' Hamilton continued, 'is also across the main shipping routes from the Levant to the Atlantic and it is much pestered by piracy. That, I have suggested, would be solved by a pair of frigates and I need hardly point out to you, Captain Barclay, that such a service in such an area against such people could prove to be very profitable.'

'I fear that Admiral Hotham can no more oblige you than Lord Hood. The task at hand is to beat the French fleet, sir, and he would say nothing may distract from that. Believe me when I assure you, I know his mind.'

'No doubt he feels he must compete with Lord Howe for the affection of the nation.'

Said with a wry tone it was Barclay's turn to be offended. Even if he was far from a partisan of Black Dick Howe – in fact the very reverse was true – he felt the need to defend him against what was a scurrilous opinion.

'Whom I was privileged to serve under on the Glorious First, Sir William!'

'Were you, by damn.'

'Perhaps,' Emma Hamilton interjected, 'you will relate to us the events of that over dinner for it is bound to be an enthralling tale. Now, enough of this talk of ships and battles, sir, you are fresh from home, I believe, and you will thus be aware of the talk of the *ton*. We're in receipt of news out here but gossip, the true story of what is happening, does not often come this way.'

Ralph Barclay was only misled by that for a moment; he soon realised what he suspected to be the truth. Emma Hamilton was uncomfortable in conversation of which she was not the centre.

'Then I will make for a poor fountain of news. I rarely mix with the people who engage in tittle-tattle, milady.'

It was incumbent on the ambassador and his wife to be good hosts and they were, but without what Barclay called tittle-tattle it soon became a struggle as the subjects on which they could converse began to dry up. Despite what their visitor thought, Emma Hamilton let the men talk; she was too occupied in assessing the man before her and for the life of her she could not fathom how a striking and sweet-natured creature like Emily could have ever become involved with him.

She was prepared to acknowledge that questions of the same nature circled around her marriage but a mere look satisfied those. Even with his greater years her husband was a man of the world, urbane and witty, well read and still studious. And he was yet handsome, tall and slim. He kept a good figure by his activities, overseeing digs in search of ancient artefacts as well as regular swims, while his mind was kept alert through the complexities of his mission to the Kingdom of Naples.

Ralph Barclay looked coarse and was, as her husband had said, that very thing. His face was red from being at sea, but under that it had a saturnine quality that went with the stiff and dark hair, peppered with a touch of grey. And he was bad at eye contact, which laid a suspicion of a manner less than entirely honest. Certainly Barclay was being polite, but since he was not looking at her Emma could see the effort he put into appearing polished.

If he sought not to reveal his thoughts, Barclay failed under such an acute examination. He was a man who found it hard not to show his true opinions on his features, despite rapid attempts at disguise. Mention of Lord Hood clouded his face as did the frequent mention her husband made of Horatio Nelson. Hotham got equal approbation and his praise of the man bordered on outright sycophancy.

Hints from Emily Barclay told of a conjugal tyrant and his hostess was sure she could observe he would lack gentility. She also opined that he had courted and married his young wife not from any deep love but because it made him appear good; in short Emily was like a medal to be worn to demonstrate prowess. She finally decided he was both a trimmer and a self-serving climber long before a servant appeared to announce that his clerk was at the door.

'The sun is dipping, Captain Barclay,' the Chevalier said. 'You will wish to prepare for dinner and so must we, while I dare say you would want to converse with your man in private.'

'I would indeed, sir.'

'Then we will go about our occasions and a servant will call you in an hour or so.'

The two men raised themselves as Emma Hamilton stood, aiming a smile at Barclay and wondering if he noted the lack of depth within it. The couple were inside and parted from their guest before she spoke again.

'You were right, Husband. I cannot say I like your Captain Barclay.'

'Quite apart from the fact, my dear, that he is decidedly not *my* Captain Barclay, I rather fear dinner, which was going to be trying anyway, might be much worse than that.'

'His clerk?'

'Can only have come here because he has information

to impart. Mrs Barclay has hardly been a discreet presence in Naples and being seen with you would make her doubly remarked upon.'

The Chevalier was correct. Gherson had the very news that his employer wanted, but in receipt of it he was far from content. As usual he took his ire out on the nearest target, for Gherson had the smell of wine on his breath and it took no great leap of imagination to suppose that had been the least of his indulgences. Having vented his spleen he finally came round to the true culprits of his anger: the Hamiltons.

'Give me a plain-speaking sailor every time, Gherson, to these hair-splitters who call themselves diplomats. And his wife, well, falsifiers would be a better tag!'

Kettles, pots and black bottoms came to Gherson's mind but only as a somewhat slimy smile. He was in a state of utter bliss, his belly full and having spent the afternoon with a pair of truly athletic whores, beautiful women and fully Latin in every way.

'Well, if they think I am going to be their guest they can kiss my arse.'

'Do not be hasty, sir.'

'Hasty,' Barclay growled, and not in a soft way, with his clerk putting a finger at his lips and casting an eye towards the closed door. 'I've half a mind to slap Hamilton's cheek, and as for his trollop of a wife she is fit for a pigsty not a palazzo.'

Gherson was wondering, for what had to be the hundredth time, how the man he worked for could be so stupid. It was also the case that explaining to him what he should do was far from easy, given his irascible nature and dislike of being counselled, which he took as being condescended to.

'What if the Hamiltons know why you are here?'

'How could they?'

'Would it be beyond the bounds of possibility that your wife might have told them?'

'I dislike your tone, Gherson.'

'I merely wish you to consider that if she has, they have set out to protect her. There is no doubt, given what I have been told, that she is here in this very place or was until news of your arrival was brought to her. It is common knowledge in Naples that she is their guest. I observed Lady Hamilton—'

'She is no damn lady!'

'I beg you to be calm, circumspect and quiet, sir.'

That got Gherson a 'damn you' look, which he ignored, being too accustomed to pay it heed.

'As soon as she heard your name she whispered in her husband's ear. He then took you off on a diversion to those churches. Why? To give Lady Hamilton time to get your wife out of the ambassadorial residence and away to somewhere else.'

'But where?' Barclay wailed, throwing his arms wide to indicate either the density of Naples or the size of Italy.

'That has to be established, but until it is you must play a long game.' Barclay threw himself into a chair with a look of near despair. 'It is the only way, sir.'

'I cannot dine with them.'

'On the contrary, sir, you must.' Seeing the objection rising in a breath-filling chest Gherson was quick to continue. 'You need to convince them that your sole object is to talk with your wife and seek to persuade her of the falsity of her position.'

'Falsity you call it. Cuckoldry, I say. Sitting with your so-called

Lady Hamilton I would be bound to wonder who offends most in that area, she or Emily?'

'If I could advise you of the tone to adopt?'

The cheeks blew out to be followed by a long exhale. 'Go on.'

'You must admit to past errors and be open as to why you are in Naples.'

'What!'

'Captain, keep your voice down, I beg you. You must create in their mind a genuine desire for reconciliation as well as a sense of your contrition for past mistakes.' Seeing another explosion coming, Gherson had to speak quickly to cut it off. 'They have Mrs Barclay's side of the story, not yours. But if you can counter that by being reasonable then . . .'

'I do not like this.'

'You will like it more, sir, than if, by belligerence, you underline to them what they may have been told about you. Better to imply you have been misunderstood. Play the man wounded as much by his own actions as hers. You have been at sea since you were a mere child, a life that ill prepared you for marriage to such a gentle creature.'

'She is far from that, Gherson. Little did I know I wed a vixen.'

'I agree. Messalina would be shamed in her company.'

'Who in the name of the Lord is Messalina?'

God these tars were so ignorant. 'A Roman empress, much given to wickedness.' A fulsome nod was the response to that. 'You must say that you seek to make amends, to act in the future with more consideration.'

'So she can deceive me again?'

'So they will produce her, and if not, time will be granted to us.

First ask to meet with her, to be given a chance to make your case and, it is hoped, amends. To that they might agree and while they are considering I will seek the required information.'

'While taking your pleasures in the process?'

'I know it will try your justified anger, but it forms a wise way to proceed, for if you accuse the ambassador of what he has plainly become engaged in he will only defend Mrs Barclay's right to choose for herself where she resides and who she lives with.'

'Exactly? What about Pearce? If she is here they likely know of him too.'

'I would reckon the less said about that swine the better.'

Gherson, who hated Pearce as much as his employer but for different reasons, wondered why Barclay smiled then. Even more curious was that it had that quality of a man trying to convey to his clerk that he did not know everything.

'If there is something pertaining to Pearce which impinges on what I'm suggesting, sir, it would be best I know.'

'No, Gherson. Suffice to say he may no longer be a factor in this. By the way, where's Devenow?'

'Back aboard ship, sir. I feared to leave him loose in Naples.'

'Wise, very wise.'

John Pearce was toiling like a navvy, in his shirt sleeves, helping *Agamemnon* to get in her stores, exhorting the men on the derricks to haul away in a manner that got him black looks, even darker when he tugged personally on a rope. His offer was taken as a kindness by the ship's officers, for they were under pressure to load and get back to sea. As Nelson had insisted when they took dinner together, there was scant profit to be found sitting in a harbour.

It was the very opposite of kindness: with HMS *Semele* at sea he had to get back to Naples and he reckoned there was no point in that lest he had a direct command from Hotham that Barclay should return to the fleet and at no time while under his command should he accommodate his wife on board. The notion of making an immediate return journey had been considered and put aside. Barclay commanded a ship of the line and a crew numbered in the hundreds who would do his bidding, even in ignorance of his true purpose.

If he was engaged in skulduggery, and that was his way of behaving, then he and the Pelicans lacked the means to stop him. The order he wanted would tell Barclay that whatever schemes he was engaged in would not remain hidden and he was prepared to accuse Hotham of conspiracy on his own quarterdeck to get what he needed.

He could not harbour any doubt that Naples would be Barclay's first port of call. Gnawing at him as he worked was the knowledge of those last words he had exchanged with Emily. The mere arrival of her husband might fix her intention to return to him and that brought on feelings of near despair.

He was a tired man when darkness brought the work to an end and even if not in the mood to take a supper of dried ham and fruit in the wardroom he felt obliged to do so, though he welcomed the crisp white wine that had been chilled with Apennine ice. Nelson had obliged Pearce by sending Mr Hoste ashore to fetch his dunnage from the *pensione* in which it had been left so he was able to change into decent clothes.

Dick Farmiloe was present and if the first exchanges were guarded the fourth lieutenant knew Pearce to be non-judgemental regarding his part in the act of pressing men from the Liberties of the Savoy and he soon relaxed in what were convivial surroundings.

They had sailed to the Bay of Biscay and back together, a curious combination until, on their return to Toulon, Pearce had found out why; like himself, Farmiloe had been got out of the way while Hotham arranged to get Barclay off the hook. Even sharing an anchorage they had not met to talk since, this far from avoidance but due to mere circumstance.

'I wonder, Mr Farmiloe, if you would take a turn round the deck with me?'

That raised eyebrows around the wardroom table and did not sit too comfortably with the person at which it was aimed. Yet that left Farmiloe in a bind for a refusal would require an explanation, if not now then on some future occasion, and given he had a good idea what it was about might lead to embarrassing disclosures.

At anchor and on a cool night, with Leghorn well lit on the shoreline and lanterns rigged above their heads, they had the deck to themselves and Pearce started to reminisce about that voyage to Biscay and the result. Farmiloe was not a brusque young man, far from it, but he was having nothing of what he clearly saw as a softening up.

'I replied to the letter from London, John, if I may avoid formality.'

'I am grateful you address me so.'

'"Sir" seems inappropriate, given our history. As to rank, we are not that far apart in seniority and besides I am as amazed at my own elevation as yours.'

'I daresay there are those in your wardroom not best pleased if my name is mentioned, let alone tolerating my presence.'

'If they are they say nothing to me for I have told them I know and esteem you. Besides, they take their cue from our captain and there is no man less given to harsh judgement than Nelson.'

'I also have to thank you for your honesty, Dick. My lawyer told me of it.'

'What other way could I behave?'

'Would it were enough.'

Even in the glim Pearce could see the slight surprise on Farmiloe's face, which forced explanation regarding the necessity of having several witnesses, adding that the Pelicans were too close to him personally to carry much weight, that compounded by what would be a disinclination to believe men from the lower deck.

'So it requires men who are not that. Digby hedged for the sake of his career but I am happy to say may now repudiate his earlier communication.'

'But surely you have Toby Burns?'

Now it was Pearce's turn to show surprise. 'He wrote, if not a pack of lies, then a set of circumstances very close to it, or that is how it reads to me and I must say my lawyer felt the same.'

'I advised him to tell the truth, John, and he assured me he would, on the good grounds that only by doing so could he save himself from condemnation.'

'If the matter ever came before a judge, that is?'

'He was coerced into his lies, he came close to admitting as much. That places the blame squarely on the shoulders of Barclay. I know Toby to be weak but even he saw the sense of what I was saying.'

'Whatever he told you he would do was not what turned up at my lawyer's chambers. If I had the letter with me I would show you and perhaps you would see that which occurred both to myself and Henry Digby. It seemed too competently composed for someone of his age.'

'Do you suspect someone dictated to him what he should say?'

'A likely scenario and the mind does not have to search too far for whom that might be.'

'Not Ralph Barclay, he was fighting with Lord Howe.'

John Pearce stopped suddenly and looked into the invisible rigging. Forced to do likewise Farmiloe was looking at him, his expression full of curiosity, waiting for his companion to speak.

'I owe you a great deal, Dick, for I think you have just seen through a mist that I should have penetrated a long time past.'

CHAPTER ELEVEN

For Ralph Barclay the dinner with the Hamiltons was torture; typically he never considered that they equally took little pleasure in the occasion. Also, being obsessed with his own explanations he did not once observe that his mea culpas regarding the state of his marriage were being taken with large doses of salt which had surfaced from his early admission of why he had come to Naples.

'I have sound reasons to believe she may be here; indeed I must be open and admit that I know it to be the case.'

The name of her lover hung in the air but if it was not politic for Barclay to mention it the stricture applied equally to the Hamiltons. Waiting for them to be forthcoming with the truth, their silence forced Barclay to continue.

'I cannot begin to explain to you the depth of regard I have for my wife. All I can hope for is that it is evident by my being here at your table and in receipt of your kindness.'

'That, sir, is both an obligation and a pleasure,' the Chevalier replied, his well-honed urbanity hiding a patent falsehood.

'My information tells me that you extended the same to her. It has been made known to me that Emily has been your guest.'

'Indeed she was, Captain,' Emma replied. 'It could hardly be otherwise, a woman on her own in such a place, which for all its beauty can be unsafe.'

'That renders me doubly in your debt. I can appreciate your desire to protect her, for I would want to do that myself.'

'My duty as an ambassador obliges me to care for the needs of my fellow countrymen and women who find themselves in distress. Your wife needed a safe place to lay her head, we provided it here.'

'And I would go so far,' Emma Hamilton responded, 'to say it had been no burden. Your wife has become my friend.'

'It pleases me that you no longer hide her residence under your roof.'

The Chevalier was quick to jump on that, though he evinced no anger. 'Had you asked, Captain Barclay, I do assure you we would have been open on the matter. It is not in our nature to indulge in fabrications.'

The word 'liar' was on Barclay's tongue but that was where it stayed. He steadied his thoughts with the notion that if he could deal with admirals like Hotham, Hood and Howe, he could also deal with William Hamilton. It was an absurd aside to conjure up at that moment a singular fact and one never before registered: they all had the same letter at the beginning of their surname.

'Would it surprise you to know that I feared to drive you to a falsehood, sir?'

'Your consideration overwhelms me.'

Completely missing the irony, Barclay ploughed on – his dear wife was an innocent, led astray, but he could not absolve himself of being partly the cause – as he employed wholesale the wording provided by Gherson.

'A life at sea scarce prepares a man for the marital chamber at all, but with one of such surpassing innocence I fear my manner had my wife see me in a light to which I do not wish to be held. I have made mistakes. All I want is an opportunity to make amends.'

'You wish to meet with her?'

'Yes, Lady Hamilton.'

'Assuming that can be arranged, what will happen if your wife declines a reconciliation?'

'Then I must sail away with a broken heart, milady.'

'You will abide by her decision?'

'What choice do I have?'

'It is not within our gift to grant you that, Captain Barclay, but we can pass on the request.'

'Most kind. Can I ask when that will be put to her?'

It was the ambassador who responded. 'In the morning, Captain. Now I suggest you attend to your plate.'

A raised female finger had Barclay's wine glass filled, his hostess smiling at him, with a sort of twinkle in her eye that could mean anything from dalliance to mockery, which forced him to hide a grimace of irritation behind the rim, given he would welcome neither.

Barclay took solace in the drink that was freely provided so was in a far from sober mood when he parted from the Hamiltons to find Gherson snoring atop the bed he had expected to occupy, which had him employing his one good hand to drag him off and onto the floor.

'Damn you for sleeping when I have had to endure abasement. I would rather be flogged round the fleet than go through such a humiliation again.'

'I deduced we could do nothing till morning.'

'As stated by the ambassador. Were you listening at the door?'

Wishing to say it was common sense, Gherson kept that observation to himself, only to have his employer state another fact he had come to because he thought it so obvious.

'I have good grounds to believe she is no longer here in the palazzo.'

'But?'

'I have been promised that she will be asked to attend a meeting with me, possibly on the morrow, which implies wherever she is cannot be far off.'

'Will she agree, sir?'

'It makes no odds, man, don't you see? If she is accommodated elsewhere someone must be sent to request she return and that, I hazard, is no task for a servant. I would not be surprised if Jezebel herself must carry the proposal. I can't see the ambassador stooping to such an errand, he's too much the nabob.'

Still slightly befuddled with sleep Gherson, as he got up from his knees to stand upright, was uncommonly slow to pick up the drift.

'All we need to do is follow her.' The clerk was not fooled by the 'we'; Barclay meant him. 'With no idea at what hour she might set off we must be outside waiting for her.'

'You do not anticipate success, surely, sir? Past efforts point to a refusal to even meet with you.'

Barclay started pacing, a habit when he was both angry and

thinking. The wine affected his balance and occasionally he needed to grab a chair or a more solid piece of furniture.

'You have the right of it, of course. I have no mind to pin my hopes on my wife believing I am contrite, for nothing I heard tonight leads me to suspect that will be the case. The Hamiltons, God rot them, should be promising me her return as a matter of duty. Even the one-time whore knows the rights a husband has over his wife. But they are her partisans and for all I know they extend the same to Pearce. If they do arrange what has been suggested it will be mere window dressing. No more lazing about and snoring your head off, Gherson. You must be out of the palazzo at cock's crow, as soon as whoever holds the keys undoes the locks. And for the love of God make sure you are not spotted.'

John Pearce had encountered trouble getting to sleep even though he was extremely tired from the day's labours, the time he took marked by the regular ringing of the bells. It was ever thus when the object of castigation was his own being. How could he have been so blind as not to see that Hotham had as much of a need to coerce Toby Burns as Ralph Barclay?

If he had no idea how it had been done he was sure of the act. As Dick Farmiloe had suggested, his response to the lawyer's letter from London, seeking details of where he had been the night the Pelicans were pressed, would probably have been dictated to Burns, a creature so malleable as to be without a spine.

The admiral would not stoop to that himself, of course; his creature Toomey stood as the most likely culprit. And the same fellow had played a major role in the sending of HMS *Flirt* to the Gulf of Ambracia: indeed the more he gnawed on it and recalled the Irishman's involvement, he had to reckon him as the progenitor of the whole shameful scheme, for in Pearce's reckoning it was beyond the wit of his employer.

If there was a positive to be taken from the whole conspiracy it was that Sir William Hotham greatly feared him, so much so that he was prepared to countenance sending Pearce himself, Henry Digby and the Pelicans into a situation in which they might all conveniently perish.

When he drifted away, he was locked in a mental argument with his father, who had always abhorred that man should be hanged for a crime instead of redeemed. His son had agreed with him, but not now; some people were so evil that the rope was the only remedy to their actions and a trio of swinging bodies meant he fell into deep slumber with a smile.

The naval day began before that of any household and being at anchor made no odds. If the guns could stay housed, the decks still required to be swabbed while the ship's 'tween decks were cleaned from end to end, the heads scrubbed out and the straw in the manger changed. In a hot climate the shore parties started early too, so after a hurried breakfast Pearce had the need of overseeing the loading of stores to take his mind off his concerns.

Accustomed to a willing and efficient crew himself – *Flirt* was manned by the very same fellows who had set out with him from Buckler's Hard – he could yet appreciate the same qualities in the Agamemnons, quite unaware that they felt he was more of a hindrance than a help.

'If the wind stays in the east, my men will have dinner at sea, Mr Pearce,' Nelson opined as he passed his volunteer. 'And having had only one night for the liberty of Leghorn, I cannot see they will be entirely grateful for your efforts.'

Even if he knew that his contribution meant little in the scheme of things Pearce answered with grim humour. 'Given their previous exploits, that makes me content.'

As predicted by Ralph Barclay, it was Emma Hamilton who set out in the early morning to go to his wife. Gherson, having been outside since the palazzo servants rose to prepare for the day, was not one to run to keep up with her. He had found a fellow willing to rent him a donkey, an arrangement that had taken a long time to conclude, given mutual incomprehension, but the flash of a few coins sealed the bargain and that allowed him to proceed at a trot and keep his quarry in sight.

Cresting the final rise he observed the coach pulled up outside a two-storey dwelling practically on the actual beach of a deep bay. Being silhouetted against the skyline he was quick to dismount and find a bush with which to tether the animal, and was back on the ridge in time to see the person who had come out to greet the ambassador's wife.

'O'Hagan,' he hissed under his breath.

This only served to remind him of how dry his mouth was, added to how the tang of stale wine made what he could taste bitter. The Irishman helped Emma Hamilton to descend and the pair went into the building, leaving Gherson to wonder if there was any purpose in his remaining.

If Emily Barclay agreed to meet her husband she would return in the coach; if her hostess came out alone then she would have declined and so informing his employer of her whereabouts became paramount. Next they would need to get a party ashore to effect the proposed abduction, which led to the thought that it would be unwise for Barclay to carry out such an act himself, he being too obvious in what could be construed as a crime.

This was not England and he had no idea what the laws were in this part of the world. Certainly the Hamiltons would see it as such and no doubt bend their efforts to prevent him getting her aboard *Semele* – for once there, Barclay would be in control – by, if necessary, calling on the local gendarmerie.

Back astride his donkey that thought was at the top of his ruminations; whom could the captain entrust to lead the men necessary to effect what needed to be done – someone who could overcome any objections from a crew who did not know Emily Barclay from Eve? He and Devenow were the only options and the so-called servant was a dolt, though with O'Hagan present his fists would come in handy.

Was O'Hagan alone? Gherson doubted John Pearce was there; even if he despised the man he knew him to be a person who would do nothing to avoid Ralph Barclay. Quite the opposite: he would do his utmost to seek him out as he had before to challenge him to defend himself.

Gherson then recalled his captain was a one-winged bird. Pearce was such a sanctimonious sod he would probably decline to take advantage of a man so afflicted. Such thoughts were idle speculation; Barclay had evinced a certainty that Pearce was elsewhere.

A shoreline dotted with fishing boats and tiny moles was also home to the kind of rough taverns that served such folk. With a tongue now akin to leather, Gherson felt the need to stop and seek a flagon of wine and, being unbreakfasted, some bread and olives too, as well as to time in which he could think and plan.

He could not believe Emily Barclay would agree to return to the marital fold, while her spouse was fooling himself to think that abduction was a solution. Barclay could not seem to accept that if she had become embroiled with John Pearce – and everything about that pointed to her having been intimate with him – the problems Barclay had now would not disappear but increase.

She had been a witness at the gimcrack court martial. The law said she could not testify against him but would that still her tongue? If he could confine her on board ship that could not last forever. Gherson could imagine any number of places where she could freely gossip, because logic dictated that at some time she would be back in England and, if he was at sea, granted a large degree of liberty.

As usual Ralph Barclay was seeing only that which lay before him, a fine attribute in a naval officer, perhaps, though Gherson was uncertain if even that were true. He was failing to extrapolate to where matters would proceed and the very least of that would be even more strenuous efforts by John Pearce to bring his employer to justice in order to win her back.

Given Emily Barclay had aided such efforts in the past, as an unwilling returnee she would continue to do so in the future and Gherson could see no way to prevent that. It had always been his opinion that Ralph Barclay should put the problems of his ill-advised union behind him and expend his energies concentrating on his career, yet he had done the very opposite.

How much good capital in high places had the fool expended just to get out of the Mediterranean? What damage had he done in his relationship with Hotham? How much more was he prepared to endure to avoid losing face?

'End it now, and for ever, would be best,' he said out loud, almost as if rehearsing words that would be required in the future. 'An accident, of course, and what a tragedy in one so young and pretty.'

It was necessary that Gherson reimagine the lubricious thoughts he had experienced in the great cabin of HMS *Semele*, to ensure it was not those that were leading his meditations. Much as he was prey to desire, he reassured himself that what he sought was a solution not personal gratification. Of course if the two could be combined . . .

Back on his donkey, swaying on its back, Cornelius Gherson was untroubled by his thinking. He had been on the wrong side of virtue ever since he could remember, not that he would have deigned to describe it as such. Like most entirely selfish people he found it easy to attach blame for his weaknesses to others as well as an unkind fate.

His own father had thrown him out of the family home and his mother had done nothing to prevent it when he was still close to being a child. Cast onto the streets and his own wits it was only by the superior employment of those, added to his being unscrupulous in every way, that he had survived, with a particular predilection for soft-hearted women.

His good looks had helped and his sharp brain and skills did the rest until that night on London Bridge when a powerful man he had cuckolded sought extreme revenge. If it had not been for that boat passing under the arches . . . Gherson shuddered at the memory and even on a warm morning shivered at the recollection of the shock when he hit the icy water of the River Thames.

The wine was so awful he reckoned his palate had been less nasty before it was consumed. His problem was that when he rejoined Ralph Barclay the smell of that was the first thing the captain picked up, which led to another of his irascible reprimands.

'I take it you breakfasted well, sir,' was Gherson's sardonic and ignored response before he informed Barclay of the presence of O'Hagan, though from what he could see no others.

'Pearce would have passed this way.' Gherson sought by an enquiring look some enlightenment as to how he knew that; Barclay ignored him. 'He must have left the Irish bruiser as protection for her and Pearce rarely moves without those other creatures he esteems, so we would be best to assume them present. What instructions did you give to Devenow yesterday?'

'To return to the quayside at first light.'

'Right. Get down there now and both of you get aboard *Semele*. I want you to tell Mr Palmer that I have discovered, thanks to the ambassador, rumours of a nest of deserters hiding out in Naples. We need a party suitably equipped to take them up if it proves to be the case, and no brass buttons or bright bandanas either. We can always say it proved false if my wife agrees to acquiesce.'

'Who is to lead it? Sir, you dare not give the task to an officer or even a midshipman, and you surely know it would be dangerous for you to participate yourself.'

'In God's name why?'

'Things could go awry. O'Hagan is there and we know what a fighter he is.'

'A marlin spike will see to that,' Barclay scoffed. 'And remember

I took the bastard up once before, though I seem to recall he was drunk.'

'If your wife will not come willingly that implies force will have to be employed, will it not?' A shrug; the notion of employing physical violence to recover her seemed to Barclay a matter of little concern, which had Gherson pleading. 'It would serve you best if you were not part of that and can you entrust it to Devenow?'

'No, he is faithful but lacks acumen,' came a rather weak protest.

'If I am along I can ensure matters proceed as they should.'

'Are you volunteering, Gherson?' Barclay asked, his look suspicious.

'Is it so strange?'

'You're not the type for such behaviour, very much the opposite I would hazard.'

The clerk put as much feeling into his reply as he thought it would bear and having been something of a player on people's emotions in his past life that came to no small amount.

'Would it satisfy you, sir, if I say I wish this matter concluded?'

'I still do not see why I cannot carry out this task myself?'

'You, sir, leading a party of armed seamen through the streets of Naples. You might as well run up a signal on the ship to outline your intentions. No, sir, you must act the distraction, for such an attempt must have occurred to the Hamiltons or why remove her from here? Ask to be presented to their Neapolitan majesties, a request the ambassador can hardly decline. With every eye upon you, others can act with freedom.'

The knock at the door of the apartments had Barclay hold up a hand to still Gherson's pleading. Opened, it revealed a servant with a note, which told the captain that his wife had agreed to meet with him and would arrive at the palazzo after midday.

'Perhaps there will be a solution after all, Gherson,' he crowed.

'If there is, you are to be congratulated, sir,' he said, with faux enthusiasm. 'The order to Mr Palmer?'

'That can wait.'

CHAPTER TWELVE

Being at sea and with no duties to perform allowed John Pearce to gnaw on how he was going to proceed once HMS *Agamemnon* raised San Fiorenzo Bay, thoughts that seemed impossible below in a busy wardroom, easier when pacing a small section of the quarterdeck and with an ample supply of the fresh air which was driving the sixty-four along at a fair lick. Nelson was proud of her as a fast sailing vessel; what he could see if he looked over at the bow wave only confirmed he was right.

The notion of bearding Hotham, his original thought, might backfire; a commanding admiral could pretty much do as he pleased within his own area of responsibilities and the man who wished to accuse him of conspiracy singularly lacked allies with the fleet. Even Nelson, seemingly well disposed towards him, would be wary of taking sides and even if he did the effect would be minimal.

There was also a need to be careful in what he divulged

regarding that court martial and possible witnesses; to let on that Henry Digby would support his efforts or that Dick Farmiloe had already related the truth of deliberate and illegal impressment in his reply to London would do no good. To do so would only put both individuals in jeopardy.

As for the mission on which he and Digby had been despatched, Hotham, or more likely Toomey, had been cunning. The actual written orders had not been composed by either; that had been delegated to John Holloway, the captain of *Britannia* acting as temporary executive officer pending the return of the man who had held the appointment of Captain of the Fleet, Admiral Sir Hyde Parker.

There was thus no evidence on paper of any involvement by the pair who had cooked up the shameful plan and Holloway, as was common on a flagship, a quite junior post-captain, was not going to risk the wrath of a vice admiral in order to support a lieutenant of whom he very likely had a very low opinion. The conclusion was stark: brute behaviour would not serve. In order to achieve his object and get back to Naples subtlety must be employed.

Easy to deduce but not that in execution. Lacking a court to try him, and that had to be a civil one, Hotham seemed proof against anything Pearce could chuck at him. He had high-level partisan support and an institution, the King's Navy, that would rally round to protect him even if in person many disliked him. Lord Hood, too, would do all in his power to ensure the service was not brought into disrepute.

The key had to be Toomey. Pearce reckoned Hotham was the type who would sacrifice anyone to protect himself. Did that leave his chief clerk exposed? It mattered not if he was, as long as he thought he might be. Pearce recalled the soft words the Irishman had used to seduce him into accompanying Digby, the almost throwaway mention of despatches for Naples.

How foolish he had been not to spot that ploy and the implication, to not fully realise his relationship to Emily Barclay had been key to drawing him in. There was, too, the crew he had commanded aboard the armed cutter, now without a ship. He had requested they be transferred as a body and that had been acceded to, unprecedented as a step in a service wont to treat the lower deck as chattels.

Toomey must have been central to the whole enterprise, while the supposition reached, that he had dictated the reply Toby Burns sent to London, might well put him in commission of a deliberate crime. Pearce, after much thought and not a few imagined irate conversations reckoned that to be his best line of attack. The mere fact that he had survived an attempt to be rid of him would, on its own, serve to induce disquiet.

'Mr Pearce, sir.' Turning he saw a dwarf midshipman lifting his hat. 'The captain wishes me to inform you that we are going to practise clearing for action and that a position on the poop might best serve as a place of safety.'

'Meaning the position least likely to allow me to be a nuisance?'

The lad grinned in response to the demeanour of cheerful acceptance displayed before him. 'Weren't put like that, sir.'

He was up the companionway in a flash to take up a position between the mizzenmast and the poop fore rail, for Nelson had come on deck and already had his watch in his hand. The officers were all assembled, which was to be expected given such an order would only be issued when a known threat was in the offing. Even the hands were alert to the need and happy to rehearse that which might make them more effective in a real battle.

Pearce had no idea how often other navies practised their drills but the Royal Navy, unless they were at anchor, never ceased to do so on a daily basis. From sword drill to battle drill it was a common occurrence and the one that gave British warships the advantage they always enjoyed against an enemy; they simply did that which was necessary at a greater lick than their enemies.

'Clear for action,' was the quiet command from Nelson to his premier.

To say *Agamemnon* came alive was an understatement. The continuous drum roll began, nets being rigged immediately to protect the heads of those on deck from falling debris, while felt 'fearnought' screens were rigged and hammered home across the companionways that led to the lower deck.

Below, wooden bulkheads and canvas screens would be disappearing as all the furniture was struck into the holds, to leave the gun decks clear from bow to stern, this while the gun ports yawed open, the cannon behind them being loosed and drawn in below the mess tables that had hastily been triced up to the overhead beams.

The galley fire being doused sent a column of thick steam up the chimney, this as the fighting decks were being sanded and water buckets, as well as swabs and tourniquets, were laid in precise locations. The hands working the cannon were now shirtless. A musket, splinter or case shot wound was made a thousand times more difficult to treat if they took a wad of dirty cloth into the skin.

The gunners, with silk bands round their heads, would be

hauling in the heavy cannon to load and then run them out, with the gunners' mates fixing flintlocks and powder monkeys distributing cartridges of gunpowder to the gun captains. A steady stream of messages came to tell the captain that each division was in place and ready, that the carpenter and his mates were below to plug any leaks, the last to report the surgeon who had taken up his station on the orlop deck with his saws and knives.

'Six and a half minutes, gentlemen,' Nelson announced when the last of the reports came in and that had him examining his watch again. 'We have mislaid thirty seconds somewhere, which I would see recovered on our next drill. I wish you to consider that such a thing might take place under the eye of an admiral and with a French fleet in sight. It would not be fitting that we should grant another vessel any advantage, even one of our own.'

What ensued was apologetic murmurs; his officers felt they had let him down.

'Well, let us pretty the old girl up.'

If the pace of return to normality was slower, HMS *Agamemnon* was back to a proper state in very short order.

Both Emily and Ralph Barclay were at a loss as to how to greet each other, more like a couple first introduced in a parental match than a pair married. As much to do with time spent apart as their differences, neither wished to be the first to speak and when her husband did so it was not to refer to Emily but to object to the presence of Michael O'Hagan, stood by the door to the salon, his eyes fixed on a point above his onetime captain's head.

'I refuse to be embarrassed before a creature from the lower deck. While Lady Hamilton is here at your request, and I respect that, I have some concern for my dignity, Emily.'

'I am obliged to reply that he is my friend and besides, his being here is an insurance against any acts of violence.'

'You think I would resort to that?'

'Past behaviour indicates the risk does exist.'

'I have wronged you, I know, but allow me to plead that I was a man ill prepared for the life I needed to live.'

The excuses were trotted out, the very same he had related to the Hamiltons; life at sea was no preparation for domesticity, the service hard for a fellow not much above a boy, only getting more so as he progressed. If repetition made it easier to get the words out Ralph Barclay lacked the manner to make it sound truly convincing.

'What I am saying, Emily, is this. I have erred in my treatment of you in the past but I will bend every effort to do better in the future.'

'Do you really think we have that?'

'You are my wife until, in the words of the service, death do us part. I am obliged by my vows to provide for you, care for you and cherish you and it is that that I wish you to accept will now be my mode of behaviour.'

Barclay looked at Michael O'Hagan and scowled, which was more in character than his less than sincere supplications. 'There are matters I would blush to discuss with you in private, Emily, let alone . . .'

He could not bring himself to refer to O'Hagan by name or rank and even Emma Hamilton got a despairing look.

'If you refer to the brute treatment you meted out to me in the cabin we shared aboard HMS *Brilliant*, Husband, then your behaviour is not much of a mystery.'

Dark-skinned it was hard to see the face flush but suffused with blood it was. 'You have discussed intimate details of our relations with that fellow!'

'For someone raised in the service you show a disturbing lack of knowledge of the obvious fact that there are no secrets aboard ship. Do you think our relationship, or rather the way it deteriorated, was not remarked upon by your crew?'

'I would have dared any man to refer to it.'

'What is it about the navy that it supposes it can flog opinion?'

'I will not try to justify the practice to you since you so obviously abhor it, but I will say that the navy would be at a loss to be effective without it. Anyway, that is beside the point. I have come to Naples, and have done so at some risk to my prospects, to try and effect a reconciliation. I am not fool enough to think such a thing does not come with strings attached, which I assume relate to the way I will behave in future. You will have conditions and I assume you have agreed to meet with me to lay those out. I ask that you do so now.'

'While I am bound to wonder if you can change, for mere words will scarce serve to reassure me.'

'What do I have but words and my own sincere desire?'

'Is it to protect what you call your prospects, Husband?'

'I will not deny it has a bearing. No man enjoys being subjected to behind-the-hand denigration and nor will a troubled private life be entirely lacking in any consideration of future employment. But that is, I assure you, secondary so I reiterate, madam, lay out your terms and let me see if I can meet them.'

'I will not embarrass you by open explanation,' Emily said, coming close for the first time.

Emma Hamilton, watching closely, saw Ralph Barclay's nostrils twitch as he picked up the scent of Emily's body. His reaction was all-consuming to her, for she knew what was being demanded of him, the points raised between the two women in the coach, imparted in low tones to not include the Irishman stood on the back.

They were laid out in the knowledge that he was now a wealthy man and could afford a style of life that would never have pertained when they were first wed. The looks such conditions received were instructive and it was a good game to try and guess which brought the most awkward response: a slight nod, a seriously deep frown or a look of surprise that what was being asked for should be part of the arrangement.

But it was the final requirement that was most eagerly awaited. Emily had to tell her husband she was carrying another man's child, one he would be required to acknowledge as his own, to be raised without equivocation in that manner. In consideration of the hurt that might cause immediately, and the continuing anguish to come, she would do her best to provide him with a child or children of his own.

The shock induced by what had to be the first admission was enough to induce a degree of sympathy even for a man Emma Hamilton held in scant regard. The eyes opened wide, the eyebrows nearly hit the hairline and Ralph Barclay took on the appearance of a man who had just seen a ghost. He might have been aware of being cuckolded, if not he was a fool, but this revelation was of a very different order of magnitude.

His head dropped and a hand went to his eyes. Unable to see Emily's face it was natural to wonder if that might display a degree of compassion, for she had no doubt of the seriousness of what she wanted. When his head came up she was still talking to him quietly, no doubt reiterating her own promises.

The push was violent enough to have Michael O'Hagan quickly move forward, his first task to catch Emily Barclay and ensure she did not fall. Once she was steady he closed the gap between himself and a furious post-captain, a man whose face was suffused with deep and angry passion.

'Don't come near me, you Irish shit.'

'Sure that would be no way to calm things now, sir, would it?'

The passionless tone in which Michael said that seemed to enrage Barclay even more.

'Remember your place. Lay a hand on me and I see you swing.'

'I'll lay no hand on you lest you seek to lay one on your wife.'

'Wife!'

The shout was so loud it must have been heard throughout the Palazzo Sessa, which rendered Emma grateful that the Chevalier was at the Royal Palace to confer with Sir John Acton. She had no desire to involve her husband in this.

'Sir, I beg you, control your passions.'

'You dare to ask *me* that, when you—?' Emma flushed herself but Ralph Barclay was not looking at her. His glare was directed at Emily now stood head bowed as if ashamed. 'You make a fine pair of whores.'

'Captain Barclay, I demand you recall who I am.'

'Fear not, I know you only too well and the stench of your reputation does not inspire me. As for you, madam, for I will no longer refer to you by your given name, you have shamed your family and what is more important you have shamed me.

Raise another man's bastard, what do you take me for?'

'It is necessary you know the truth.'

'I should have known it before I ever allowed myself to be seduced into marrying you.'

That brought up Emily's head and instead of looking abashed, which her previous spoken words had indicated, her green eyes were flashing and now it was her voice that would carry beyond the closed door, this as he moved to one side of Michael O'Hagan.

'You seduced, sir! Never. You went about acquiring me as your wife with the same lack of honesty that is your abiding trait by implying a threat to my parents that they would be rendered homeless.'

'Which they will be forthwith, I assure you. As for you, the gutter will serve for I will deny you bed and board. As for your bastard, I will take it from you, as is my right, and dump it in the first workhouse I encounter. With luck, disease and deprivation will serve to wash clean the stain you have put upon my good name.'

'Which is one of the things you singularly lack, sir, along with kindness, compassion and any notion of how a real man should behave.'

The spittle flew then. 'Don't tell me who you consider to be a real man, I can guess, though I will no more name him than you. God grant that I should get him at a grating a second time.'

'Your answer to all your faults, cruelty.'

Barclay was looking at O'Hagan, his eyes full of hate. 'You! I will certainly flog you should the chance present itself – that is, if I don't grant you a rope.'

It was the wrong thing to say to such a man. Michael stepped forward at a speed Barclay had not anticipated and grabbed him by his stock, to physically lift him from the floor, the Irishman's threat softly issued but more deadly for that.

'I'll break your neck if you try and long before any hand can stay mine.'

The man he was holding was having trouble breathing, for Michael had twisted the stock into a tourniquet. With an elbow in Barclay's chest and a forearm on his ribs the captain's feet were dancing in thin air.

'Put him down, Michael,' Emma Hamilton, 'for his corpse in our residence would be hard to explain.'

'For you, milady,' came the reply as, let go, Ralph Barclay fell to the floor from where, after a short series of inhalations to recover his breath he looked up at his assailant.

'Touch a King's Officer, would you, cur? Now you will most certainly swing.'

'Did you see him touched, Emily? It is my impression he slipped.'

'Not far enough for me, Lady Hamilton. The only fit place for such a creature to slip into is the public latrine.'

'Sir, I request you vacate my house, forthwith, while I assure you a report of your insulting remarks made to me will be reported to my husband and by him to those in authority. As for any alleged assault, it will be denied that it ever occurred.'

Ralph Barclay looked from one face to another and worked hard to compose his features into indifference, but it was to Emma Hamilton he responded.

'Insulted? You? For that I would anticipate the gratitude of decent society even if I am as obvious a dupe as your husband.'

Then he picked up his hat from a small table where it had been laid, and for all his attempts at evenness as he addressed Emily, the strain in his voice was obvious.

'As for you, I never wish to see you again. I will have your bastard, make no mistake, for the only thing I now wish to give to you is a future full of grief.'

The hat was jammed on and, forced to walk round O'Hagan, he made his way out. Emily waited till his footsteps faded on the marble floors before she allowed herself a tear.

CHAPTER THIRTEEN

The journey between Leghorn and San Fiorenzo Bay was not one of long duration if the wind was fair, which meant that HMS *Agamemnon* was taking its anchor station before the sun went down, not that Nelson could hang about. It was a requirement of any captain that he report to the flag officer immediately on joining, even if he had only been absent for a period of days, and there was a pennant with *Agamemnon*'s number at the masthead of the flagship. With Nelson went his logs and reports on both the vessel's condition as well as her stores and water.

It often seemed to John Pearce that the King's Navy ran on the use of the quill more than guns or cutlasses. Everything was recorded: course, speed, what sails had been set to achieve that and any sightings made on the journey, however trivial. Food in the barrel used by the cook, each with its own unique identification, as well as peas and duff had to be set down as having been used and its condition, as well as the precise level of wastage or condemnation for being unfit to consume.

Minutely recorded were the quantities of small beer and rum allotted to the crew. The master kept his logs, the purser a set of his own, while the warrant officers reported on their areas of responsibility on an equally regular basis. The gunner was required to account for his powder, shot and slow match, both used and in hand, the carpenter for the state of the hull and decks as well as his level of timber held in reserve.

Canvas had to be accounted for as did masts and spars, cordage especially, since it was at the mercy of wind, weather and poor usage and difficult to quantify. It was also valuable; there were ever masters of merchant vessels eager to buy it, even if it had an identifying red thread running through it to say it came from the royal rope works. A coat of tar soon disguised that and few naval officers had ever been had up for selling it.

If a hand was to be shifted or promoted that had to be noted so that his pay warrants were for the correct grade, added to the names and punishments issued to transgressors, from stopping grog, stapling to the deck or a flogging, the number of strokes administered included. The ship's surgeon, if they had one, was obliged to list the names and ailments of those he treated, the venereals especially, since he was allowed to charge for the service of treating that particular affliction. He was a busy man after a stay in port.

Each report went through the ship's captain, on to the executive officer of the fleet – passed to his clerks, of course – to be subsequently available to the commanding officer so he could assess the state of his fighting vessels. Finally these logs, along with his assessments, were despatched to the Admiralty itself where the minions there, better paid than most sailors and by reputation notoriously indolent, scrutinised them for discrepancies.

Anything seen not to add up was passed back down the chain. Much of a captain's time was taken up accounting for matters long in the past and that could only be achieved because he had a copy of everything that had ever been written. In theory it was impossible to cheat or to hide various misfortunes from the Navy Office. That it happened, and frequently, was a credit to naval ingenuity. If a rising officer learnt to sail and fight a ship of war, he also in his progress was tutored in the very necessary skill of how to muddy the handwritten waters.

Horatio Nelson had his barge in the water before the ship was secured, John Pearce with him and they were soon rowing towards *Britannia* at speed. It mattered not how many times he had been in a cutter, barge or even a small jolly boat, Pearce found himself impressed by the skill and strength of the oarsmen. With expressionless faces they employed their heavily muscled arms to propel with seeming ease a craft made of heavy timber that took several dozen men and the employment of the capstan to get it in and out of the water.

Their strokes were even so no orders were required to be issued until they approached their destination, on this occasion the gangway that led to the entry port in the side of the flagship. Quietly instructed by Nelson's coxswain, the barge swung in a smooth arc to come to rest right by the sea-level platform, John Pearce pulling his hat low to ensure no one looking over the bulwarks would spot an arrival in which he hoped to employ the element of surprise.

Nelson came out of the barge briskly, he being a man who did anything that could be observed by his peers or superiors at pace. It was therefore odd that he stopped on the stairway and turned to face his passenger with a look of deep curiosity, his countenance made pink by the setting sun.

'It occurs to me, Mr Pearce, that I never got round to asking you how you came to be in Leghorn. Admiral Hotham is bound to enquire and I would look foolish if stuck for a reply.'

'You intend to mention my name?'

'I fear I must, if only to offset some of the opprobrium that arose from our last visit there.'

'Is that not a subject rendered dead by the passage of time?'

'Most certainly not. My crew labour under the shadow of what occurred, Mr Pearce, and it is my duty to see that thinned if not shifted. Indeed I may ask that you be brought in to explain yourself what took place and to be more honest with Sir William than you have hitherto been with me.'

'Sir?'

'Come, Mr Pearce. I was watching you when my youngsters were explaining matters to you. Something they said, and I reckon it comes down to descriptions, triggered a response in your features which means there are facts you know but have not shared. I am sure our C-in-C will be as eager to hear from your lips what they are, just as am I.'

'Then I beg you take note of Sir William's expression when you mention my name.'

'Why are you grinning, sir?' Nelson asked, slightly piqued.

'I think you'll find it can be noted as unusual.'

Someone banged an object against the interior scantlings to

advise Nelson that he was keeping waiting the reception party and that had him moving, to be greeted by the required bosun's call and the stamp of marine boots in a ritual that was replicated a dozen times a day or more as ranking officers came to visit their commander. Pearce reckoned it to be, like the endless gunfire salutes, nothing more than flummery.

'Captain Nelson, sir, welcome aboard.'

As he nodded to the premier – no mere officer of the watch would suffice for a senior post-captain – Nelson raised his hat to the invisible quarterdeck and the flag that hung on the mizzen mast. Below their feet the men on the lower deck had raised their heads as the marine shoes landed with a collective thud, some to wonder who was coming aboard now, others to curse the noise.

Cole Peabody was one of the latter; he hated anything that smacked of order. That was doubly so when it was naval and he was not shy of saying so and less guarded on the ship than the previous one. In the short time he and his mates had been aboard *Britannia* it had become clear that Captain Holloway was not Captain Barclay. Not that the flagship was slack, but there was none of the tension of mistrust that had existed aboard HMS *Semele* and hung between the lower decks like a miasma.

The way Ralph Barclay ran his ship ensured that few trusted any other and most granted that to no one at all. The lieutenants ran their division competitively, always seeking approval from the quarterdeck and in doing so they bore down on the hands, more on those who could not be counted amongst their favourites, and Barclay kept them at odds with each other to ensure efficiency.

'Flag's been at anchor, Cole, who's to say Holloway won't be a right tartar once we is at sea?'

'If we ever raise sail,' moaned Dan Holder. 'We're stuck here in a mess of our own shit.'

'Suits me,' Cole responded, his voice as usual rendered hiss-like through the lack of teeth. 'Can't think why any bugger would be at a rush to get into a fight for some other sod's glory.'

'Winnin' lines the poke, Cole. We never heard the end of how much the swabs aboard *Semele* made under Black Dick Howe.'

'Pennies, when you might get your head blown off. Not for me, mates – if I is going to risk my person it will be for a decent reward like we used to get.'

A hoot came from Cephas Danvers. 'Then find where the admiral keeps his coffer, for that will be stuffed with gold, fer certain.'

The marines dispersing were as noisy as they were assembling, which had Cole Peabody lifting his head and swearing, as Fred Brewer enquired as to who it might be coming on board.

'It will make no odds to us, mates, so best not hark to it.'

John Pearce had received a look from the premier, one he had come to recognise on the face of many of his fellow officers. It spoke of an attempt to mask with a carapace of good manners the disdain they felt for his person and the way he had acquired his rank without going through the rigours of years at sea and the hard-to-pass examinations.

There were others who were less troubled by the fact that King George had jumped him from midshipman to lieutenant by royal dispensation as a reward for an act of outstanding bravery. Pearce had saved a ship of the line, albeit a small one, from certain capture and they were fair-minded enough to rate his elevation deserved. Yet in a service rife with competiveness they were in a minority and the object of most folk's contempt had learnt to ignore both opinions.

Nelson was striding towards the great cabin with Pearce at his heels, hunched in an attempt to stay unremarked behind the much smaller captain. If his efforts failed with one lieutenant they passed, it kept it from anyone dead ahead, which allowed him to get close to the cubbyhole Toomey used as an office without the clerk being forewarned.

Toomey greeted Nelson by half rising from his seat and informed him that he could go right in for the admiral was awaiting. Pearce had half turned to look down the main deck as the clerk did so to remain mysterious.

'You will wish to leave me your logs, of course, sir.'

The thud as the heavy ledgers were dropped on the clerk's desk was very obvious as he heard Nelson acknowledge Toomey's instruction. As soon as the marine sentry came to attention he turned to face the admiral's senior clerk and spoke in a clear and carrying voice.

'Mr Toomey, I bid you good evening.'

The head shot up; clearly he recognised the voice and his face suffered a complete loss of blood as what he had hoped was an error turned out to be fact.

'I daresay you are surprised to see me?'

Toomey had not got to his present position without ability and that extended beyond numeracy and the skill to compose clear orders. If his shock was palpable even in the glim of a pair of lanterns it was swiftly masked to be replaced by a rictus-like smile.

'Surprised and delighted, Mr Pearce,' he croaked. 'To see you here implies what? That the mission on which you set out was aborted, perhaps?'

'On the contrary, Mr Toomey, it was carried through to a conclusion and was an outstanding success and led, I have to say, by a most gallant officer.'

'Mr Digby is . . . ?'

That was prevarication; Toomey did not want to hear about any successes.

'Recovering from a wound that with an inch of difference might have killed him. But he will soon be whole again and therefore not be a burden to your conscience.'

The few moments of talk had allowed Toomey to recover some of his poise and that came out as a skill at deflection. He puffed his chest out to protest. 'I cannot imagine why such a thing should be implied, sir.'

'Do not seek to avoid your misdemeanours, sir, and I might add the chicanery of the swine you serve. You have been cunning, I will grant, but there is not a shred of doubt in my mind that you contrived with Hotham to dispose of both Digby and myself, while the fate of the whole crew of HMS *Flirt* was a matter of utter indifference to you both.'

Was it genuine anger or fear that had Toomey come near to an explosion? Pearce did not know and nor did he care.

'How dare you, sir! I will not sit here and listen to such base and wayward accusations. I rate you as mad, sir, and I have a mind to call for a file of marines to confine you.'

'There is one by the admiral's door who can hear every word. It will make for a fine tale once he is back at his mess table. Prepare yourself to be confined, Mr Toomey, but only for a brief spell until you are led to Tyburn and your just deserts.'

Pearce pointed to the cabin door and played what he reckoned to be his best card. 'Do not doubt that somewhere on those orders we received is your imprimatur, while I seriously doubt that Hotham's part could be so easily discovered, and even if it were he would deny it.'

The face lost blood again.

'Nor, I suspect, do you have a moment's doubt of this. That if his position is threatened then yours will be forfeit. I would reckon the mere sight of me, Mr Toomey, renders you a threat to your admiral even greater than the transcript I have of Captain Barclay's court martial and the blatant perjuries it contains.'

'Transcript?' Toomey demanded, obviously confused; so, for a moment, was John Pearce until enlightenment surfaced, the realisation Barclay must have kept that bit of information to himself.

'Now, here is me reckoning Hotham and Barclay to be two cheeks on the same arse. But by your reaction I am led to suspect that the good captain has not informed you of that which I have in my possession.'

'Transcript?' Toomey asked again, albeit in a fearful whisper.

Pearce put his fists on the table and rested his weight upon them. 'Every word said at Barclay's trumped-up court martial, and that is before we come to the forgery of certain correspondence supposedly from Midshipman Toby Burns.'

A hand went to Toomey's brow, to be run across it, making truth of what had been no more than a guess.

'What a tangle you have become engaged in, sir. It is one that will most certainly be taken amiss by the two gentlemen who sent me out with letters to Lord Hood. I refer to the First Lord of the Treasury, Mr William Pitt and my fellow Scotsman and Minister for War, Henry Dundas.'

The door to the cabin opened and Hotham stood framed within it, his stocky body silhouetted by the stronger light. That was so dominant that his face, and thus his expression, was in shadow. There was no way to tell what he was thinking by sight, only by supposition. The vision was brief; the door was slammed shut.

'The cat is amongst the pigeons, Mr Toomey,' Pearce hooted, with manufactured glee. 'Your admiral is at a stand, sir, and I have no doubt where that places you. Shall I enter and tell him that his client officer has kept from him just how threatened he truly is, that as soon as I get hold of Toby Burns and intimidate him with the prospect of the rope the game is over?'

'You shall not enter, sir,' Toomey spat, indicating the marine sentry with his head. 'And that fellow there will prevent it on my command that he do so.'

'It matters not. Hotham will see me or see himself damned.'

'He will not!'

'We shall soon discover who has the right of it, Mr Toomey. Meanwhile I will take a turn around the deck while you contemplate the less-than-rosy future that awaits you.' The pause was well timed for effect. 'Or is that no future at all?'

Well before he reached the companionway leading to the upper deck John Pearce was almost purring with satisfaction. He was sure he had played his hand well, while the exposure of that transcript had proved explosive, merely by its existence but also because quite clearly Barclay had not let it be known. The old saw about there being no honour amongst thieves came to mind and in his reflections he played out an ever-increasing number of pleasurable scenarios as the men he considered responsible for that mission to the Gulf of Ambracia sought to deflect blame away from their own actions.

Lost in such thoughts he paid no attention to the seaman passing by on his way back from the heads, even when the man stopped for a split second to stare at him. By the time Pearce responded the man was moving again, making for the companionway that would take him below, so he was just a figure and a receding one at that.

Fred Brewer hurried to his mess table, beginning with a cold glare that shifted two of his messmates he did not consider should hear what he had to say. If they moved slowly they were soon out of earshot and an eager look and a crooked finger from Brewer soon got the heads of his fellow smugglers close to his own.

'You is never goin' to believe what my eyes have just seen, mates.'

'You havin' been to the heads, Fred, we might not want to.'

'You're wrong, Cole, well wrong, for on my way back I spied an officer on deck.'

'Christ, a miracle.'

'Scoff you might, all of you, but you will not when I tell you his name.'

'Cut the shallying, Fred. If you got anything to impart get on with it.'

Fred was determined to enjoy his moment. 'Tall fellow, well set and good to look at if you like that sort of caper. Looking well pleased with hisself an' smiling away as I passed him by.'

'I can feel my fist a'twitchin', Fred,' growled Cephas Danvers.

'It will do a rate more'n that, Cephas, when I tell you what I clapped eyes on.'

'I'll poke the buggers out if you don't speak out.'

'There I was a-crossing the deck, breathing a bit of fresh by coming that route and the cove I espied was none other than that snake in the grass John Pearce.'

CHAPTER FOURTEEN

Cornelius Gherson knew the interview had not gone well just by the expression on Ralph Barclay's face. That said he was surprised to be viciously barked at when he enquired as to the details. His employer did not see him pout, not that he would have cared that the man felt slighted; had he not been a vital part of the whole affair ever since Emily Barclay had enforced the original separation?

He had guided the captain with good advice, even if much of it had either been scoffed at or ignored. Stomping along behind him as they made their way from the village of Posillipo towards the centre of Naples he reprised with bitter resentment the acts he had undertaken, more than one of which had put him at serious risk and left him questioning why he allowed himself to become so engaged.

He needed to hang on to Barclay's coat-tails in order to prosper, but prior to drawing that conclusion he had been motivated by the way Emily Barclay had treated him, as he acted as her husband's messenger, with a degree of contempt that had made Gherson want to slap her hard. His approach having gone wrong and with her husband desperate to recover the court martial papers, he had acceded to Barclay's request and engaged the services of some of his old acquaintances from his past criminal life.

Naval service might reckoned a rough trade but it was milk and honey compared to the underbelly of London, where a man's life would count for no more than the possession of a soiled linen handkerchief. To exist in such a milieu required guile, wits and sometimes sheer braggadocio of the kind that gave opponents pause.

Gherson had gone from childhood to manhood in the face of an almost permanent danger from a community that saw murdered bodies daily dragged from the River Thames to be sold – if they remained unidentified, and they rarely were – to the surgeons at St Bartholomew's for dissection without much being cared for in the way in which these victims had met their end.

To help Barclay – really for his own sake, though he would not admit to it – Gherson had engaged the services of one of the most villainous sods in a world peopled by such creatures. Jonathan Codge was such a conniving bastard not even Satan would have been able to collar him. Gherson himself had come close to being one of the numerous poor dupes Codge dobbed in to the Bow Street Runners in order to save his own skin.

'Sir,' he gasped, for Barclay was setting a pace that matched his mood. 'I hazard you are going to ask me to once more advise you. How can I do that when I have no idea of the outcome of your meeting?'

The captain stopped so abruptly Gherson had to halt swiftly to avoid a collision. 'I need no advice, hear me. I require action not words and, by damn, if Devenow is not by the quayside when we get there he will find that any flogging he has had till this day was as a kiss from a buttercup.'

The response that surfaced, to say the allusion was quite poetic, as well as something he would welcome, given his loathing of Devenow, had to be bitten back. Besides, Barclay was moving again and still venting his spleen, forcing his clerk to hurry to keep up.

'I want that harlot aboard my ship before the sun goes down and if it lacks gentility to get her there, so be it. I have a good mind to confine her to the cable tier as well. I doubt she would much like the rats nibbling at her toes, though they might decline to contaminate themselves, for even rats must have—'

The word Barclay was seeking would not come to him, which had him cursing in a near incomprehensible manner, while his more knowledgeable clerk thought it unwise to advise a choice. From what the captain was saying things had gone from bad to worse, leaving an abduction his preferred option. Having seen the building she occupied, indeed if she had returned there, Gherson set his mind to planning how to get to it and fulfil such a task which would include ten minutes alone with the victim.

A full hour of trudging left Barclay's blue coat rendered near grey with dust and Gherson exhausted. The captain's face was that, too, only the streaks of running sweat creating any sight of the red and furious countenance below. The diatribe had shifted from bile to self-pity and had included for Gherson some acknowledgment, grudging but profound, that his advice in the past had been sound. If Barclay did not go so far, alas, to cast himself as a fool for ignoring it, he did label himself that for ever becoming wedded to such an ingrate.

Devenow was sat on a bollard and behind and below him was the barge, fully crewed by men inured to waiting and to refusing, even if it was reluctantly, the invitations from the local whores who had gathered to tease them into stepping ashore for a bout of pleasure. The servant standing stopped the oarsmen crouching and his bellow sent the trollops away.

Their captain was approaching and he would have them smart even if his mood was a good one. Devenow was the first to realise it was as black as the pit of hell and a sharp word to look lively rendered the barge crew rigid. The man might be despised, and he returned their feelings in full measure but if the captain's mood were so dire he felt the need to let on, then it must be dark indeed.

'Don't just stand there, oaf, get aboard.'

'Look at the state of your coat, Your Honour,' Devenow protested; if he was useless as a servant that did not dent his attempts to appear as one.

The glare that got had the brute moving at catlike speed and he jumped into the boat with such disregard the coxswain swore at him for near capsizing them, a complaint that received a raised single finger in response, while the words Barclay spoke to Gherson were quietly delivered once Devenow was out of hearing.

'I wish to look at the place you found this morning, so will row to the Hamilton residence, then along the coastline.'

'Sir.'

Barclay dropped down with an equal disregard for the safety of the cutter, his good arm taken by Devenow, but that occasioned no rebuke. The coxswain glared at Gherson to warn him to be careful, which was stupid; surely he knew the clerk to be excessively cautious of his person.

Barclay growled his commands as soon as the oarsmen could dip their sticks and the cutter fairly raced away from the quayside only to veer sharply right once they were clear of the anchored shipping. All aboard were curious but inured to naval life and the vagaries of officers too wise to even hint at their wonder. They stared blank-faced as they hauled and lifted, an attitude maintained when they were ordered to ease off.

The route from the Palazzo Sessa touched the shoreline at several points and Barclay sat in silence studying it until they opened the bay in which lay the place occupied by Emily. Gherson was wise enough to whisper to his employer, indicating what he should be looking at, the small house and the adjoining countryside examined in a long silence that had the clerk worried.

He was looking at Barclay's face and the range of emotions that swept across it, which spoke of anger, disappointment and most of all self-pity, none of which was of much use. He employed a slight cough to break the spell.

Barclay did not respond for several seconds, then came a nod and the sharp command. 'Coxswain, HMS *Semele*.'

The order was obeyed instantly, the cutter fairly racing towards the seventy-four. There, the ship's officers and marines were lined up to receive their commanding officer with all due ceremony, only to find themselves ignored. Barclay ran up the gangway and right past the receiving line without so much as a nod, Devenow forced to trot to keep up.

In the cabin he tried to remove the dust-covered coat with

gentility as Barclay did his best to fling it off and he made his way to his desk, demanding quill and paper. Once that was delivered by Gherson, whatever was intended was quickly composed before being untidily sanded and handed to his clerk, who in the meantime had fetched wax, a seal and a lantern with a lit candle.

That applied, Barclay handed it over. 'Take this to Hamilton.'

'Am I allowed to enquire what it contains, sir?'

'It is a demand that he send my wife aboard immediately and I have reminded him, not that he requires it, that the laws of our country oblige him to respond in the correct manner.'

If Barclay was grinding his teeth as he spoke, and still clearly in a foul state of mind, Gherson was all crafty consideration, he having a very shrewd idea of what Barclay planned to do. 'He will not take kindly to such a tone, sir.'

'Do you think I give a damn about that?'

'You may do as you wish, sir, but I am obliged to say that alerting the ambassador to your continued intention to have your wife join you, which this note will achieve, is a bad idea and it may lead to her being moved to somewhere other than that beach residence, out of your reach and unknown to us. I take it that you are determined that when you sail from Naples she will be on board?'

'Bound and gagged if need be. The ungrateful sow will be lucky if she does not feel the whip.'

It had always been a struggle to get Ralph Barclay to think clearly when he was angry, and as a man too often in that state, doubly so. He could fight his ship and command his crew with seeming ease and mental clarity, yet a single female and her refusal to obey rendered him partially blind.

'If it were me, sir—'

'Damn your presumption, Gherson!'

'I would sail away and make a very public display of doing so.'

'Without her?'

The notion was so shocking to him it quieted his mood and that allowed Gherson to continue. 'The Hamiltons and your wife might be on their guard for some kind of response, even perhaps a violent one, but if we sail away—'

'That will be lowered,' Barclay interjected.

'It may be that your wife will return to the Palazzo Sessa because she feels safe; perhaps she will choose to remain in that seashore residence until she is certain that you have departed, for she has no idea we have knowledge of it. If my thinking is correct, sir, you have already discerned that the strand on which that residence sits is highly suitable for the landing from one of our ship's boats of a party of seamen.'

'True, Gherson, and if Hamilton declines his duty that is something I now look forward to leading personally, even if it ends up in that damned Palazzo.'

'That, perhaps, would also be unwise,' Gherson protested as the dream he had been harbouring came under threat.

'I cannot see why, man, there will no longer be a requirement for subterfuge.'

'The ship's officers, sir?'

'I will employ the gambit I proposed earlier, regarding a party of deserters so that the men I lead will have no idea of the real purpose.'

Barclay had gone from bile through bemusement to a sense of purpose and now his face, still streaked with the dust of Naples, was close to being animate with enthusiasm. Gherson saw beyond what he had just said to a fact his employer would be reluctant to acknowledge. His mode of command required that he construct an excuse; there would be no body of hands aboard willing, out of loyalty, to aid him if they knew the truth.

'Then I can only wish you joy, sir,' Gherson lied.

'You can do more than that, Gherson, you can come along. Why would I deprive you of the opportunity you were so keen previously to undertake?'

There was no relating the real reason but Gherson felt somewhat more secure now that Barclay had calmed down, enough to re-ask the question to which he had not received an answer. Barclay fell silent, his chin dropping onto his chest and he thought about the reply.

'I tell you this because it will be nigh on impossible to keep hidden over time, but relate this to anyone else without it has already become obvious and it will not be threats that I issue, but a scarring so profound you will never forget it.'

Said quietly, Gherson took that warning much more seriously than the bellicose raging to which he was accustomed. 'Sir.'

'Pearce has got her with child.'

The captain sat in silent contemplation while his clerk reflected on that, mentally damning John Pearce for taking something Gherson had set his mind on.

'But I see your suggestion as a sound one. Now send for Mr Palmer so that I can give him orders to weigh.'

The departure of HMS *Semele* was carried out with the accustomed banging of signal guns, the sound and smoke of which were observed from the balcony of the Palazzo Sessa.

'Well, Emily, it seems you have prevailed.'

'Have I? Why, then, do I not feel content?'

'I know you are troubled but it may be I can advise you, for I have been where you are now.'

Emma Hamilton took her arm and led her back inside, away from the sight of her husband's ship crowding on sail to leave behind it the Bay of Naples. Once seated, Emily listened as she was told the tale of a girl, young, foolish and besotted, left with a child by a lover who declined to accept he was the father.

'You do not face that, for which you should be very grateful.'

'You had the child?'

'I did and left it with my grandmother.'

'Who raised no objections?' Emily asked.

'I suspect you think your family would not do likewise?'

'I am near to certain the disgrace would come close to killing my parents.'

'Which only goes to establish how different are our backgrounds. Though it is never openly spoken of, no one in my home village of Ness will have any doubts as to who is the mother. But as to disgrace? Let us say it is too common to be scandalous.'

'And you care for her?'

'Sir William's nephew took responsibility for the monies required for raising her and her education.'

'That was kind.'

'Not entirely, but it was generous.' Emma Hamilton had never cast down her eyes in Emily's presence but she did so now. 'He did it because he thought himself the father.'

Emily did not dare state the obvious; if he thought that he must have had grounds. Perhaps all those rumours had some foundation, perhaps Emma Hamilton had been a— Emily checked herself; she would not allow the word 'whore' to be attached to someone who had been so sympathetic.

'I am sorry.'

'You will move back to the Palazzo,' her hostess said, firmly.

'In a day or two, if you do not mind. I find the seashore peaceful and it aids me in contemplation, which, with what has happened today, I am much in need of.'

'As you wish, but I would ask you to vacate it if the Chevalier wishes to go sea bathing.'

By the time Emily got back to the residence the sun was sinking in the west, while the sails of HMS *Semele* were no longer visible even from the hill behind the house. With a profound sense of relief mixed with confusion Emily went for an evening stroll along the strand, for the dilemma of what to do had not been resolved, the only option now removed that she should make up with her husband.

His outburst had shocked her. Emily had not been naïve enough to think that he was going to take the news calmly; she expected fury and if she put herself in her husband's place that mood was justified. There had been a brief thought that he might relent from his first reaction but that was now laid to rest.

He had set sail but she could not believe the matter would end there. The man she had married was not of that stamp. If she ever set foot in England he would claim the child and there was nothing she could do to stop him, while she was equally sure her family would disown her and decline to offer support.

So where would it all end? It was rumoured that Emma Hamilton had begun life as a roadside coal seller, or at least she had been that as a child. It was a sobering thought that having been born into better circumstances their roles might be reversed. Where Emma had risen, Emily might sink.

'It's getting dark, ma'am, perhaps best to go indoors.'

The quiet voice surprised Emily, so deep in contemplation she had no idea the Irishman was close by. 'You followed me, Michael, even although I did not ask you?'

'John-boy set me to look after you, and sure that I will do.'

'The others?'

'Charlie and Rufus have gone into the city.'

There was no requirement to ask what for and Emily did not do so; they would likely not return before the morning but she felt the need to acknowledge that Michael had done the right thing. Being stuck out here with her had not been an unalloyed joy.

'I think we are safe now. You saw my husband's ship sail off, did you not? If you too wish to go to Naples I cannot see how I could object.'

'That ship is captained by the man who took me up from the Pelican Tavern, and John-boy with me. The sight of its sails disappearing might assure you, but I beg you will forgive me if it leaves me less at ease, so happen I will wait for another night.'

Emily hooked her arm into his. 'You're a good man, Michael.'

That got a grin from the huge Irishman. 'Holy Mary, there's not many would agree with that.'

'It is possible for the whole world to be wrong.'

'Then I pray you will pay them no mind in the matter which troubles you.'

'How I wish it could be so.'

'Best step out or, like the wise men, we'll need starlight to find the doorway.'

Aboard HMS *Semele* the party Ralph Barclay required was assembled. Palmer, as well as his other officers, had fallen for the story of naval deserters occupying a seaside house in the bay along from the ambassadorial residence, the tale embellished with the fact that Sir William Hamilton had let news of their presence slip out while being unaware of the consequences.

'And, gentlemen, we have a duty, do we not, to redress this?'

The assent was unanimous; desertion was a crime to set every wearer of a blue coat on edge. It was frequent and dangerous enough to threaten – as was mutiny – the whole fabric of the fleet in which they served. Not one of their senior officers would forgive that every effort was not bent on recapture. Had not the navy sent a frigate all the way to the South Seas to fetch back for punishment the *Bounty* mutineers?

Excited faces seemed less animated when their captain told them he would personally lead the raid; they were not to be included, for it promised to be ferocious.

'But I wish you to pick for me the hands I will take along. No milksops or men who will have sympathy. I want only those to whom what these swabs have done is hateful.'

In that there was no shortage; deserters were no more loved 'tween decks than they were on the quarterdeck, so Barclay was sure the men he would lead were willing and ready to employ violence.

'You know, Gherson, I have not engaged in this since that night you were fished out of the Thames.'

'Not for me a happy memory, sir.'

'I daresay not. You know what I will miss? The presence of the swine Pearce. You cannot imagine how much I would love to break his skull.'

CHAPTER FIFTEEN

'Afore you go breaking Pearce's crown or chucking him overboard, have a think on it, lads.'

'What, Cole? You was hard for it afore I spotted him. Is it cold feet you're getting?'

'It will be a cold body you will have, Fred Brewer, if you don't have a care. What I is saying is this. It ain't as easy as you are now getting worked up for. There be considerations.'

'Like us being stuck aboard this barky,' said Cephas Danvers.

'Hit the spot, Cephas. Old Ironsides might be short on her due but she is still home to more'n seven hundred souls and where is the place where mischief can be done without some swab catching sight?'

'It don't answer either, Cole, for it leaves us aboard and there might be blood staining the deck, not handy with a bluecoat missing.'

That was responded to with a sly smile. 'But what if we could use Pearce to get redress?'

'Don't follow,' whispered Dan Holder.

'Nowt new in that Dan, you bein' the slow one.'

'Let's hear yer thinkin', Cephas insisted.

'Say we could get him to order up a boat crewed by us? Need a knife close to his vitals, mind.'

'To get to where?' Brewer complained, scouring the faces. 'You'se has asked around as have I. The nearest spot is an island.'

'So the place we goes to revictual is the only hope.'

'An' not much of one,' Brewer protested.

It had been depressing for them all to hear where Italy lay. Never having been real deep sea sailors the wide oceans were a mystery. From fishing they had graduated to cross-Channel smuggling. They knew the waters between the Low Countries and Kent like the back of their hands, every shoal and sandbar; beyond that were dragons, even if it was common knowledge that places like America were a six-week sail away at best and sometimes a three-month voyage if the winds failed.

'Let's reckon we can do no better than this Leghorn place.'

'And then?' Cephas asked.

'We do what we has to in order to eat.'

That did not need much expanding on; they would need to steal and maybe more to survive.

'I want to get home,' Dan Holder wailed, his round, pale face with its button for a nose and innocent-looking eyes making him look childlike.

'Forget that,' Cole spat, 'as I heard tell, it's as good as the moon fer us.'

'Did they say how far?' Holder whined.

'Came up with a number that made no sense to me, so it would be a waste on you.'

Cephas Danvers knocked on the mess table. 'Then best forgotten, but that is hard.'

'When was it ever going to be easy?'

'Never, Cole, but you has a notion, so what's your plan?'

'The barky has to go in to revictual and word is we are close to being in need. Anchored off Leghorn we take Pearce by surprise and get him to order up a means of getting ashore. No one is goin' to query an officer needing a boat, are they?'

'An' if he lets on?'

'Then he will bleed to death by the gangway, for I will knife him, for sure.' Peabody leant forward and spoke eagerly. 'We needs to convince him the only way he'll live to tell the tale is to aid us.'

Dan Holder tapped the table his time, his eyes filled with hope. 'Happen we could convince him we is not to blame for what the Tollands tried to do. Can we say we went along with them out of fear and we bear him no grudge personal?'

'A point, Dan, an' a good one. Might be you're not so slow, truly.'

The talk went on and round but there was one fact that stood out starkly. They had no way of getting off the flagship without they had help of some sort and there was no one but John Pearce who could provide it.

Toby Burns hated being the sole lieutenant on the quarterdeck but that was ten times worse on the middle watch when it was dark anyway, made worse on this night by heavy overhead cloud and a wind that was coming in from the north-west, one to favour a ship departing Toulon.

He had been instructed to be on special guard, given the enemy ships of the line had come out en masse, two days previously, sixteen sail, to anchor in the great bight that formed the outer roads of Toulon, and they had their yards crossed too, meaning they could weigh when they felt they had the right wind.

The information had already been sent by pinnace to Admiral Hotham, though it was as likely to be a feint as an attempt by the French fleet to get to sea, one that had been employed previously. What worried Burns was that in this Stygian darkness they could raise anchor and sail right past HMS *Brilliant* and he would have no knowledge of it. There were lookouts in place, as was customary, but their ears would be of more good at present than eyes.

The obvious fact that he could do nothing to stop them if they did sail out was not a point to raise Burns' gloom: Taberly would skin him regardless, a thought which had him reprising the several schemes, all of them truly desperate, to get himself shifted to a commander more benign, not that he had any idea who that would be.

Nelson had the right reputation but the man was mad, always seeking a fight and ready to put both himself and his men in a position of maximum danger. Toby had been burdened with that before, first at Bastia, where Nelson had manned cannon so close to the walls that they stood as invites for the French to bombard. He had been just as hare-brained at Calvi, where a stupid scheme of a sortie had seen him captured and locked up in the citadel. The accommodation had been far from comfortable but it had been safe; the part occupied by captured enemies of the French was immune to cannon fire.

Such thoughts were the bane of his life at a time like this, when little happened unless they were called upon to reverse course, the creaking of the timbers only broken by the ringing of the half-hour bells, the calls of one man casting the log for speed, another for the depth under the keel, and the scrape of the chalk on the slate as these figures, along with the course and the time, were recorded.

He would be relieved at four of the morning when it was still dark and the ship silent, so he could get some sleep, though that depended on the snores of the men who shared the wardroom, particularly the marine officer, whose trumpeting seemed to reverberate through the whole frigate due to his endemic overconsumption of wine.

'Caught a sound, Mr Burns, hard off the larboard quarter.'

That soft call obliged Toby to move forward and cock an ear, while staring ahead into a vision of light spots dancing before his eyes.

'Creaking timbers,' the lookout hissed, 'can you hear it, Your Honour?'

'I can,' Toby lied, for he could hear nothing.

The dilemma? Whether to rouse out Taberly who, if it turned out to be nothing, would flay him alive. Dare he send up a blue light without alerting the captain? That would tell him if what the man beside him claimed to hear was true or false. And what did creaking mean? It could be one ship and not a large one, or the precursor of the whole French fleet coming out, and their progress discovered, how would they react?

He had a vision then, of a whole triple row of run-out cannon on a hundred gunner, all of them pointing at him and the thought made him shudder, only to be made more terrifying when he recalled there were sixteen capital ships in the French fleet. One salvo from such a body of gunnery could reduce a frigate like

Brilliant to matchwood and anyone on deck would stand little chance of survival.

'There it goes again, Your Honour do you harken to it?'

Was that a note of impatience in the lookout's tone, as if he was wondering why this bluecoat was delaying and getting shirty because of it? Toby Burns was unsure, but he did know that if such a thing was suspected he should issue a reprimand. The fact that it might be imagined meant nothing; as a King's Officer he was expected to behave in that fashion. Being wrong was better than being challenged.

'I think I must call the captain,' he said, which removed the obligation for a rebuke. 'Keep those ears of yours pitched for more sounds.'

It was not the correct procedure that he wake the captain himself; there was a midshipman on watch with him whom he should despatch as a messenger. The marine sentry snapped to attention and shouldered his musket but he did not automatically open the door to the captain's cabin.

'Mr Taberly is abed, sir,' he said.

'Then rouse out one of his servants to wake him, he must be advised that we may be in proximity to some activity. I will wait till he has vacated his cot.'

Again that was not quite proper, but Burns was happier off the quarterdeck than on it. HMS *Brilliant* was not the only possessor of flares; the French had them, too, and if they knew the British frigate was close they might send one up as a precursor to a broadside; it was safer here.

It took time to rouse out Taberly, he being no slouch with the bottle himself. Eventually a knock from within signalled that the sentry could open the door and Burns was admitted to find his captain bleary-eyed and in his nightgown. He made his report, including the fact that he was unsure he heard anything, only to see the face close up.

'You did not see fit to send up a light?'

'No, sir.'

'Or rouse out the hands?'

Toby felt his heart physically shrink for he suspected that, had he done either of those things independently, Taberly would be just as likely to roast him. As it was the captain brushed past him with scant courtesy plus a small shove to go on deck, where, with his gloomy lieutenant on his heels, he made for the lookout bent over the hammock nettings, a hand cupped to his ear.

'Speak to me, man,' he barked.

'Faint sounds, Capt'n, but regular. I reckon we is not a cable's length from some'at.'

Taberly hoicked up his nightgown and levered himself up likewise and put a cupped hand to an ear, a position he held for some time. Something, and it had to be a sound, made him jerk.

'All hands, Mr Burns, but quiet as a mouse. Prepare a blue light, which will be fired as soon as we are cleared for action. And send someone to fetch my coat and breeches.'

For a drill normally carried out with excessive noise it was credit to the men aboard the frigate that they prepared for battle with a minimum of noise, which naturally took double the time. Taberly showed no patience for the need to be quiet and growled at all and sundry. By the time the last report was delivered he was fully dressed and in position. He had the master remove the right number of men from the guns to be ready to bring HMS

Brilliant round on a reverse course as soon as the flare exploded.

The fuse was lit on the rocket and it fizzed for half a minute until it ignited the main powder, to send the canister shooting into the sky where, within a second, it burst to bathe the seascape in its ghostly light.

'All hands to man the falls,' Taberly yelled, as before him lay a string of leviathans slowly sailing out of the Toulon bight. One of them was within that cable's length the lookout had reckoned and soon its gun ports began to yaw open, which brought from Toby Burns an anguished cry. 'For the love of Christ get us out of here.'

'I believe, Mr Burns, your station is with the main deck cannon.'

'Sir,' the youngster acknowledged before hurrying off.

Taberly had inherited a good crew and for all his faults he was an efficient sea officer. The helm was down, the falls released and the frigate was coming round in a few grains of sand, being at the point of maximum danger when beam-on to the enemy. Toby Burns, behind the main deck battery, could not breathe. If he could not fully see the threat his imagination was enough to magnify what was already perilous.

It would not have aided him to know that every officer aboard, from Taberly down, was similarly afflicted. At such a range against such weight of shot the frigate was in mortal danger and once the falls were again sheeted home a silence fell as the crew who could observe awaited what they knew must come.

It did not; the nearest ship of the line sailed on, identified as the *Ca Ira*, its ports still open but with no cannon emerging and that held as the blue light faded and died, to leave them once more in pitch darkness. Taberly croaked a second change of course that would lay them parallel to the enemy, though with a widening gap.

'We must wait till daylight, gentlemen,' he said, to no one in particular, 'and if what we have seen is confirmed we must make all sail for San Fiorenzo Bay and alert the fleet.'

HMS *Brilliant* was not alone on the station; there were other frigates and they would have seen the flare and perhaps even the upper sails of the enemy. They would shadow the French and send off messages to Admiral Hotham regarding their course and speed while Taberly would be first to say they were definitely at sea and thus anticipate being the messenger carrying the kind of welcome news that was enhancing to a career.

If Admiral Sir William Hotham was troubled by the appearance of John Pearce he was obliged to put it to the back of his mind, for matters more pressing impinged. He had the news sent by pinnace from Toulon: the French had engaged in bluff before but would they finally actually weigh to tempt him to the battle he so desired? It was near time for HMS *Britannia* to make up her stores and he feared to be caught at that if they came out, so having checked with Hyde Parker he issued orders that the fleet should weigh for Leghorn in its entirety.

Pearce, having been given, though with scant grace, a berth in the wardroom, was sound asleep and dreaming of Emily, himself and a scampering babe outside a rose-covered cottage bathed in warm sunlight. The sound of the ship stirring put an end to that as the decks were scrubbed with sand and holystoned prior to being washed and flogged dry.

He was still lying flat when he realised what he was hearing was stamp and go. The flagship was in the process of raising anchor and by the time he was dressed and made the deck, Old Ironsides was taking up her position in the centre of the line, while the van under Sir Samuel Goodall was already heading out to the open sea.

Stood amidships he saw Hotham was on deck, as was only fitting; he stared at him hoping for some eye contact, which was not forthcoming. Pearce was unaware that he too was under scrutiny by a quartet of men set to tidying the falls, coiling the loose ropes into neat loops.

'Word is Leghorn,' Cole Peabody hissed.

'Then when we has a chance, we has to take it, for we'll scarce get another.'

'Fair,' said Cephas. 'But I wonder if yonder fellow will know our faces?'

Dan Holder was scathing. 'How can he, seeing he only spied us proper once?'

'Well I is going to get close so he can see me,' Cole insisted, 'and we must all do the like. If the sod can put a time and place to any one of us it will need a damned hard bit of thinking to get round it.'

It was a magnificent sight, the only difference to the paintings Pearce had seen being that the sails were dun-coloured from exposure not the near white employed by artists. An enquiry brought the information that the destination was Leghorn, which suited Pearce. He needed to beard Hotham, of course, but from the Tuscan port he could get a ship to Naples. Had Barclay got there and if he had what had occurred? There was little point in gnawing on that, he was too far off to affect matters but the image of raging Ralph Barclay did keep coming to mind.

'Where in the name of the devil is Barclay?'

It was not John Pearce shouting that but the admiral; if his information was correct, then the enemy had been reinforced, at least six sail having come from Brest to even up the contest, and he needed *Semele* to be sure of parity. Their appearance had sent him into a near apoplexy for not only had they passed Gibraltar without being intercepted, they had sailed on past the Spanish Fleet anchored at Minorca. It was a blessing that Admiral Sir Hyde Parker had arrived with several vessels to augment his own forces.

'One day, if God wills it, we will end this farrago of being allied to the Dons and go back to what we should be doing, fighting them and stealing their plate ships.'

'I hesitate to raise it, sir, but you do know that Lieutenant Pearce is here on board?'

'He could be on the moon for me, Toomey.'

'I can appreciate that present circumstances are not conducive to that particular problem . . .'

'I have waited my whole life for this.'

'And the whole fleet is sure of a victory that will raise you in the eyes of the country.' It was the right thing to say; Hotham's eyes positively gleamed at the words spoken. 'But.'

'But what?' came the query, this after a long pause.

'I fear that Captain Barclay has been less than honest with us.'

'Go on.'

'It seems that John Pearce has a copy of the transcript of his court martial and it is on that he intends to bring a case against him.'

The admiral looked as if he had been slapped and hard. He sat up straight, his features rigid, and Toomey knew that there was no need for further elucidation; Hotham got the drift and the ramifications without them being explained. Then he suddenly relaxed and smiled.

'If we thump the French, Toomey, Pearce can go to hell.'

CHAPTER SIXTEEN

Ralph Barclay was not fool enough to think HMS *Semele* would escape observation from the shoreline; to achieve that would require he be so far out to sea as to preclude his aim. Instead, Mr Palmer would, once they parted company, sail in a circle for a rendezvous the following day while he and his 'press gang' were rowed to their destination at a distance that would allow a return in good time.

The great unsaid was left unspoken: what would happen if his wife was not at the house on the strand, for that would mean her being once more ensconced in the Palazzo Sessa? Gherson did consider posing the question but since he had wriggled out of going along he felt he would be wasting his breath.

Not that he failed to consider the consequences. Barclay was in such a passion that he might well invade the ambassador's private residence and the repercussions of that did not bear thinking about. Hamilton might be in bad odour in high places for his marriage but he was the representative of His Majesty King George at a foreign court and thus not a man to be trifled with.

These thoughts were rattling around his mind as the seventy-four heaved to and hauled in the cutter. First thing was to have it fitted with a stepped mast that would allow it to progress while not depending entirely on human muscle. Getting a one-armed captain into the boat was solved with the use of a whip from the yard and a chair, lowered with gentility. Gherson, watching, wondered how many men on the rope considered the option of letting go as Barclay was in the air and over water.

'You have your orders, Mr Palmer.'

'I have sir, and may I wish you good hunting.'

'A worthy quarry, Mr Palmer, I do assure you.'

That brought a look of curiosity to the premier's face but no words as the chair was lowered till the captain was safe in the boat and seated in the thwarts. The triangular sail was raised, the boom hauled round to take the wind with the cutter heeling and moving forward as it felt the force. Before the captain's gaze there lay a sea of faces, those of the men chosen to accompany him; a less pleasant prospect could hardly be imagined.

He had checked with Devenow to ensure no milksops had been included and been reassured, but it was doubly certain under scrutiny; they were without doubt an assortment of real hard bargains, a dozen in number and collectively one of the ugliest groups of specimens he had ever clapped eyes on: scarred, many toothless and none given to smiling or a hint of humorous exchange.

With little to do, Ralph Barclay could continue his contemplation of what would happen if he was successful. His initial reaction had been, he had finally realised, intemperate. Not that he wished to retract a single word but he knew that to behave in that fashion with his wife would not serve for several reasons.

If she stayed with him aboard HMS *Semele*, and he had no guarantee Hotham would approve of such an arrangement, she was with child and that would excite comment. How far was she gone he had no idea and lacked any of the kind of knowledge of domestic matters that would enlighten him. But he had observed her figure to be unchanged, so the pregnancy could not be of long duration.

If she was got ashore a few months before the birth, to have the child, he could time the announcement so that his fellow officers would reasonably assume him to be the father. But that was months away and much as he would have loved to have chained her up in the cable tier that could not happen either.

In days the whole fleet would know and with her burgeoning figure he might as well run up a signal on the mainmast to say he had been cuckolded and the child was not his own. The best solution might be to send her home, but that too was fraught with problems: if she had run off once then she might do so again, while his career needs precluded that he accompany her.

He could always fain illness, of course, yet was it wise to leave an area of conflict, and one in which he might be allowed to participate in a second fleet action, when it would soon become common knowledge that his wife had produced a child? That would appear soft and not allow him to be seen as he desired, as a hard-driving officer and a competent one.

At the seat of his concerns was the loss of face and the dent to his dignity. He needed to get his wedded wife back to the family home and he could not go with her. There she could go to term, with his friends, neighbours and both families in a joyous state of an impending confinement, blind, he hoped, to the fact that he was not the father and that depended on her acquiescence in the deception. To get that far would require he behave in an exemplary fashion.

What happened subsequently would depend on how she behaved both before the birth and in the future, which presented a whole raft of possible situations but of one fact he was certain: Pearce's bastard would not enjoy a happy existence regardless of what Emily wanted. He was the man of the house and his rights would be enforced.

He had been sitting, head tilted forward in contemplation, and when he raised his gaze it provided no comfort for there was no one along in whom he could confide. It gave him scant joy to think that even on board he only had one person with whom to discuss the scenarios running through his mind and that was Gherson. The feeling of loneliness was acute, but then he had lived with that ever since he had first commanded a ship of war.

The approach to land had been timed for dusk to avoid the risk of being spotted before they could get close to their destination, where it was assumed all would be abed. Once they had beached and got the cutter out of the water to sit on the sand, Barclay ordered that lanterns be lit by which they could illuminate their way. Two men were left as guards, both with loaded pistols that would act as a signal as well as a deterrent, and with Devenow on his left side, Barclay led his men inland, glad to be out of the boat and his gloomy ruminations. How much better to be active.

On the step outside the Hamilton bathing house Emily Barclay had placed a chair and was, under the stars, deep in contemplations that unknown to her in some way mirrored those of her husband. The servant sent along by Emma Hamilton had fed her and Michael O'Hagan, which, given there was little to do was, for the Irishman, a precursor to sleep.

In her lap lay a book and on the table at her side a candle but attempts to read were constantly interrupted by her thoughts. These centred on a letter she might possibly send to her spouse. Various levels of apology were examined, some too grovelling for her to truly contemplate, yet Emily felt certain that at some time she must make an effort at a reconciliation.

Having never considered herself maternal, the advent of her pregnancy altered everything. She was no stranger to babies: in the company of her mother she had visited the poor when they were sick to offer comfort and had held in her arms many a grubby infant to dose them with the palliatives that had been fetched along. That was the duty of every right-thinking family of the standing of the Raynesfords, to not only give succour but to be seen to do so as an act of Christian charity.

Now her entire concentration was on that which she was carrying in her womb, even if the baby had yet to make itself felt with a first kick. There was terror as well as joyful anticipation; from those same visitations Emily knew childbirth to be fraught with risk but she sought to overcome that by her confidence in her own strength and health. As to survival once born, the good Lord would see to that.

There was a clock in the parlour that struck regularly to note the passage of time, little heeded until it struck ten chimes. Looking at the book told Emily how little she had managed to read and the candle was beginning to gutter from being low as well as from an evening breeze. It was time for her to sleep even if she doubted that would come easily.

As she stood up, her eye was caught by a blink of light from along the strand. It was not a steady one of the kind that could be seen in various dwellings along the shore and something stirred inside her, perhaps the foetus, enough to make her concentrate. What appeared the second time was not one light but several, soon extinguished, and they dipped behind a hill. Blowing out her own candle Emily made her way through the lamplit parlour and up to the first level, to a window facing north-west.

It did not appear immediately but eventually there it was. A string of moving lights that could only be carried lanterns, given the unsteady way they flashed. The words of mistrust Michael O'Hagan had uttered regarding her husband rose to her mind and she dashed into the room he occupied to shake him awake.

As a man who had slept in hedgerows and under bridges in places far from refined he was one to come alert quickly. Following a whispered instruction he trailed Emily to the window to have pointed out to him that which she had observed, much closer now and without doubt heading in their direction.

'My billy club will see to it,' the Irishman said making to leave the room.

'No!' The firmness of the reply stopped O'Hagan in his tracks and he searched for a clue to embellish it on a face very much in shadow. 'If that is my husband, then I beg you count the lanterns.'

'Sure I have taken on numbers before.'

'I see a dozen, Michael, or near it and if it is who we fear they have come for me, not you.'

'To do murder, happen.'

'You, possibly, if you seek to defend me, myself I reckon not.'

'Holy Mary, that is not a wager I would take.'

'It is I who must calculate and I will not have you killed to protect me when the odds mean it is impossible. If my husband has brought a party to take me up they will not be gentle types.'

'You know I cannot leave you.'

'You must. I want you to go to the Chevalier and tell him what has occurred, if indeed it does.'

'It's my turn to say no.'

'Michael, my husband will have you slain without a thought and to no purpose.'

'I was given a task by a man I hold dear and that I have to fulfil.'

The bobbing lights were very obvious now, so the time in which Michael could get clear was rapidly diminishing, while the glow from one lantern was adding flesh to a companion and two things were clear. The rolling gait by which they moved, which indicated sailors, added to the odd sight of the kind of coloured bandana common to the British tar, made doubt near impossible. Finally, the fact that the man at their head had only one arm engendered an ever more desperate tone to Emily's pleading.

'That Hamilton servant needs to up and away too. He is at risk as well, for merely witnessing. See Hamilton and then get to John and tell him that I have been taken. Only he can alter that, and Michael, I think you know I am uncertain if I wish it to be so. But at least he will know what has happened.'

'You seem sure he will not harm you, which I am not.'

The voice that replied lost all passion or urgency; if anything it was deflated.

206

'Allow that I know the man to whom I am married. He will not be tempted to murder for the very simple reason that would deprive him of the chance to humiliate me at his pleasure.'

The sense of determination resurfaced quickly. 'Now get going, Michael, and if John asks you may tell him that you did so at my express wish and that your departure suits my purpose. I no longer want or need your protection, but do say our child might. He will know the meaning.'

'I have said before you will break his heart.'

'That a person can live with, but a broken head can be an ending. I will not have you on my conscience.'

The Hamilton servant was a harder creature to rouse out than Michael O'Hagan, so woozy from sleep that it took an age to get him out of the door and running. A quick glance showed those lanterns so close it was hard to think he himself could do likewise. The Hamilton retainer was a slight fellow, and local he was not; his size alone would alert Barclay to his flight. Perhaps it would end in a chase and one he could not be sure of winning.

In the jumble of thoughts running through the Irishman's mind, many of them deeply troubling, there was one that was paramount, for even he had come to reason that if he fought such odds he would lose. He had to get to Pearce. Barclay must know he was here and it mattered not as of now how he had found out that his wife was too. They might not kill him but the very best he could hope for was a beating, to then be taken aboard Barclay's ship and that was a far from comforting thought on its own.

There could be no doubt that what Michael was seeing was like a press gang. It had all the hallmarks to a man who, like many folk who shared his islands, had been raised to see the signs. His last words to Emily were that he intended to hide and he ran for the stairs, taking them three at a time while she walked out through the doorway to confront a body she could now hear talking, more growling really, in that way men do when bent on violence.

Michael O'Hagan was on the roof and able to hear the first words uttered by Ralph Barclay, a shout to halt the progress of his party and a demand that his wife, framed in the doorway by the oil lamps behind her, give herself up. The roof was flat, the only object upon it the rain cistern that the Chevalier used as a douche, which made the next remark by Barclay one to be concerned about.

'I am told that Pearce's Irish brute is with you.'

'Not as we speak.'

'He would not leave you.'

Emily managed a laugh. 'Is he not a man, and are the fleshpots of Naples not within walking distance? I sent the servant lent to me by Lady Hamilton off as soon as I saw the lanterns. I am here alone now.'

'I intend that you should come with me.'

'How can I refuse such a kind invitation?'

Emily had adopted the wrong tone and she awaited the blast of fury that would follow her temerity; it did not come, instead he spoke softly.

'I have no wish to harm you.'

'I had no notion that you would.' If it was less than the full truth, Emily thought it a better response than her previous one, not humble but not point scoring either. 'Am I to be allowed to collect my possessions?'

'Of course, and you will need stout shoes in which to walk.' As she turned to re-enter the parlour, Barclay added, 'Devenow, search the place and see if you can find that for which we came.'

Devenow indicated a couple should follow him and he squeezed past his captain's wife. Barclay hoped for all three of Pearce's stupidly named Pelicans – they stuck together like glue – which would justify the expedition in the eyes of others. What they would think of taking up a woman who was clearly his wife he declined to consider, for it could not be avoided.

Emily turned to go and pack, only to find her husband hurrying close to whisper, 'It would pain me if you mention your condition.'

'Never fear, Husband, if I do not know what you are about I can guess there are things best kept undisclosed.'

That was rewarded with something close to a smile; he had seen it for what it was, a definite olive branch, and he followed that with a slow hand to indicate she should carry on. From inside he heard Devenow crashing about and wondered if he should stop him, only to reckon it made no odds; Hamilton would guess what had occurred and he could go to hell for all Barclay cared.

Up on the roof Michael was in a bind; he too could hear the banging and crashing as furniture was moved and doors to cupboards hauled open at speed, lest lurking behind them lay someone armed and dangerous, and the sounds were getting closer.

The water, when he lowered himself into it, made him gasp, for if it was not cold in these parts neither was it summer. Off came his hat to be placed under his leg so it would not float and he sat with the water up to his neck and his head resting against the rim of the cistern, listening for the sound that might precede discovery; heavy footsteps on the stairs.

They came eventually, which had him take in as much air as his lungs would hold and when he judged them about to exit onto the roof he lowered himself gingerly into the cistern until his head was underwater. Would a diligent body have found him? He did not know for he could neither see nor hear. Eyes closed he sat still, unable to release any air given that would cause a bubble, until he could do so no longer.

Michael came up as slowly as he had submerged, ready to leap out and fight if that was the only recourse. The roof was empty but sense told him to stay put and he sat in the water shivering until he heard the sounds of the party leaving. He had no need to see if Emily was with them after he had searched the now empty house. Barclay had what he had come for.

CHAPTER SEVENTEEN

Heads were close together once more at the ex-smugglers' mess table and if Cole Peabody was hissing his words low enough not to be heard outside his circle, they were still full of irritation.

'What narks me is that you don't think things through.'

'What's to think on, Cole? We do as you say and put a knife into Pearce's ribs. He does what we ask or he dies.'

Cephas Danvers imparted this with conviction, a feeling shared by the other two judging by their vigorous nods, which got a snorted response from Peabody.

'Simple as kiss my hand, eh?'

'Can't see what can go wrong,' opined Dan Holder.

'Well, if you don't reckon that flawed there's nowt for you but the rope. We is goin' to get to the entry port with a knife showing, a bluecoat with shit in his smalls and the watch officers is just goin' to wave us by.'

'Knife would be hidden,' Holder protested.

'So, Pearce says to the watch officer that he's facing bein' sliced and what happens then with a set of marines hard by?' That produced no immediate response so Peabody carried on, his tone now full of ridicule. 'The swine dies and we swing, is that the plan?'

None would catch his eye now, their heads were down and the eyes were examining the rough wood of their board. Fred Brewer was tracing circles with his forefinger on that surface too, a clear indication that he, like the others, had no alternative to offer.

'Well, it's a damn good job there's one bugger with a sight of things at this table.' The heads lifted slowly to engage with Peabody's stare and to wonder at the sly smile on his face. 'Do you recall what happened when we was bested by Pearce?'

'Humbugged us good and proper,' Cephas nodded.

'But then what did he do?'

'You know that as well as we, for the love of Christ.'

'I do, Dan, I do an' what I want you to think on is this. Given it were t'other way round, what would we have done? Say we'd caught him and his mates as intended.'

'Cut their throats, that's what.'

'Aye. But we ended up where we is now, which tells you that Pearce ain't got the guts for the cold kill.'

Fred Brewer shook his head. 'It would be a caution to test out that one.'

Now it was Cole Peabody's finger on the mess table, the point tapping hard. 'The man is soft, that's what I am saying. He should have seen to us all for good, that being the only safe way, but he does not, he chooses a path that gets rid but not forever. So that makes him spineless an' to me there lies the way to get him to act as we wish.'

Dan Holder was shaking his head, which if it was sizable did not, on the reckoning of his mates, have much with which to fill it and nor was his normally glaucous expression likely to alter that opinion, his words even less so.

'I reckon to be well lost on where you is headed.'

'But say he has a reason to keep his mouth shut an' do as we bid?'

'Stop playing us, Cole,' Cephas Danvers growled, his dark brown eyes flashing. 'If you has a way then tell us so we can look it over.'

'He's soft, right, not a'feart of blood in the right place, happen, but killing casual is not his way. So say we has in our grasp another, whose throat we reckon to cut if he does not get us off the barky. In my reckoning, Pearce is the sort to care for the life of another even if he has no kin cause.'

'If you are wrong, mate!'

'I reckon he'll no more hand us to the rope than see blood spilt so his skin stays whole. Now I sense you don't see it as I do, so think on that day outside Buckler's Hard and what has occurred since. I reckon if you do that you will see what I see, an' that is a man who reckons himself as wily as a fox. He had a chance to finish us an' he shirked it. What we has to do is put him in the same boat now.'

'As long as it ain't this one,' Fred Brewer sallied, his grin anticipating laughs from his mates; all he got was groans.

'This be no time for joshing,' was the heavy hiss from the toothless Peabody.

'A mid?' asked Danvers. 'A young un' will burden his mind.'

'Never. Might catch one that's set to be a hero, seeing they all

213

want to be admirals one day. But the thinkin' is sound, Cephas, a younker could serve well. I reckon on a nipper might do the trick. There's one or two forever scampering about and annoying all with their japes. Shouldn't be too hard to catch hold of one of the nippers and . . .'

There was no need to say more and Cole Peabody sat upright to make that point. 'Are we settled on it?' Two nods and an 'aye' settled the matter. 'Then we best be about our game. We's set to raise Leghorn this very day.'

Pearce knew Hotham would have to summon him and was content to wait, though frustration entered into things when bell after bell was rung, watches were changed and still he was mainly left to sit in contemplation in the wardroom, avoiding polite enquiries as to his presence and from whence he had come, or the odd malicious stare from those who resented him.

An odd turn around the deck showed a fleet sailing in its three components but not in line ahead. Instead it was stretched out somewhat to cover a larger amount of sea, with lookouts in the tops hoping for the sight of a French topsail, while the mood below them among the officers was one of keen anticipation for they had been at anchor too long.

He was on deck when Toomey approached and demanded a written report of the mission to the Gulf of Ambracia, something Pearce declined to supply. The Irishman was told in no uncertain terms that any report he made would be verbal and if Hotham had any sense, his clerk too, they would see that in acceding they would be protecting themselves. His obduracy worked and he was eventually informed his presence was required in the great cabin, which he entered to find a stony-faced admiral awaiting him and standing for once.

'I will keep Toomey by us to make a record of this conversation, Pearce.'

'A record of your previous conversations would interest me, yet I suspect there are none.'

It always shocked such a senior officer to be addressed so, as if he was of no account. They were accustomed to obsequious acceptance of their natural superiority and Pearce watched as Hotham worked himself up to a rebuke. It never came.

'Since you refuse to submit a written account, what Toomey writes will serve in its place.'

'I do believe I would be usurping the privileges of Mr Digby if I were to put in writing what occurred. The glory for such an astounding outcome should go to the man who led the expedition, don't you think? I do assure you, when it is read there will be a clamour to reward him.'

'Clamour, Pearce?' Hotham sniffed. 'I rate you're overpraising.'

'Since you were not present, except in your malice, I care not a whit what you think.'

Hotham was not given to blushing but he reddened now and it was not from embarrassment but fury. 'I cannot abide this, Toomey, call for a marine officer to remove Pearce. He can go to the cable tier until he learns some manners.'

'I wonder how your marine officer will react when he hears we took possession of two fat French merchantmen and the man who brought the news and is partially responsible is to be confined. And will the wardroom not wonder what this is all about?'

'You took prizes?' Hotham demanded, a hand held up to delay his clerk.

'We did – Levanters – and they are now in the process of being sold in Brindisi. Fully laden they were, so they will fetch a good price. As for Mehmet Pasha, thanks to our recent exploits, I doubt he will trouble you for some time to come.'

Was it curiosity or greed that stayed the order that Pearce be arrested; it mattered not. Hotham wanted to hear what had happened, to find out why his machinations had gone so badly awry as much as anything else, Pearce reckoned. The admiral knew he was beyond censure for that: the precautions taken in having another write out the orders for the mission insulated him from harm.

Then, of course, there was the fair copy of the court martial record sitting in London. Had he been told about that or had Toomey supressed what must be a surprising bit of news? So far unmentioned it was impossible to tell, Hotham being no slouch at dissembling. Pearce knew he must temper his impudence too; continuing to rile the admiral would not get him what he sought.

Neither man opposed to him could know there was an element of guilt in John Pearce's approach, given he was about to use what had happened in the Gulf of Ambracia to pursue a private matter, not, as he had indicated to Henry Digby, a combined assault to make Hotham pay for his actions.

Only desperation would make him act so: he needed a vessel of some kind – even a pinnace would do – and he needed orders to stay the hand of Ralph Barclay, and right now nothing mattered more.

'Selling prizes in a foreign port!' Hotham said eventually. 'I could court martial Digby for that.'

'Why bother, you will get your eighth.'

'You think that is of interest to me, Pearce? I command a fleet and I would have the laws of the navy obeyed to the letter. Such principles are more important than money.'

The temptation to call him a liar had to be suppressed. Money was the subject closest to the hearts of all the King's sailors, and admirals were the most avaricious of the lot.

'Can I suggest, sir,' Toomey interrupted, 'that we hear what Mr Pearce has to tell us and then move on to how you react to what is a clear breach of standing orders.'

Hotham could not accede to that immediately; his dignity required that he appear to give it some thought, which had his chin resting near his chest for several seconds.

'Very well, Toomey, but do not let the lieutenant depart without we come back to it.'

In the time of waiting, Pearce had fretted on his approach, the temptation to outline in clear detail what Hotham had hoped would happen, and his manoeuvres to bring it about, very strong. Emily Barclay and his need to get back to her obviated that. So it was with a degree of circumlocution that he made plain he knew precisely how the conspiracy had been laid out and what was its nefarious objective.

In terms of reaction he might as well have been talking to a wall. He was aware that Toomey's quill might be moving at certain points but there was no accompanying sound of the nib scratching. The clerk was filleting out anything even loosely incriminating while recording that which would reflect well on his employer.

To the details of the action, Hotham kept his expression bland, as though such acts of heroism were commonplace. Pearce naturally played down his own contribution while emphasising the bravery and ability of others, not just Henry Digby but Edward Grey and his marines, as well as the ship handling of Matthew Dorling and the bravery of the crew.

'So we have partially broken up a nest of piracy and perhaps Mehmet Pasha will curtail his activities. If not, a ship of the line should be sent to persuade him.'

'You will oblige me, Pearce, by leaving such matters to those who have the responsibility for them. Now, the sale of these prizes.'

Pearce outlined the reasoning in the same way as he had explained it to Michael O'Hagan, receiving a distinct impression that Hotham saw the sense. Not that the admiral's attitude to him softened; if he looked upon him at all it was with clear distaste.

'And now I have a request to make.'

'Indeed?'

'I have been circumspect, Admiral Hotham, in my account, and I note that what I have said has been carefully filtered by Toomey—'

'Nonsense,' was the clerk's shocked response; he had never suspected his actions would be noticed.

'I am prepared to let that be for a consideration of that which I require.'

The word 'require' saw blood in the admiral's face once more, yet given he suppressed a verbal response gave Pearce a strong feeling that he had the man worried and that meant Toomey had passed on what had been revealed.

'I have no desire to shout from the rooftops that I was duped and played for a chump.'

That elicited a thin smile from Hotham. 'Your *amour propre* means much to you, I surmise.'

'You will know by now, for you will have been told by Captain Nelson, that there was no sign of HMS *Semele* in Leghorn Roads.' No response from either man: neither an acknowledgement nor a denial. 'I doubt his whereabouts are much of a mystery regarding the purpose on which he is engaged.'

That was fishing; Pearce had no certain knowledge that Hotham knew of the tangle of the Barclay marriage, yet he had, according to Nelson, information regarding that duel in Leghorn. Added to which, in their conspiring, he and Toomey had dangled a despatch for Naples as temptation to get him to accept the mission with Digby. It was left to Toomey to prevaricate.

'It is the admiral's habit to grant his officers a degree of licence in the execution of their duties.'

'Does that include him being in search of his wife?'

'I have no idea.'

'I suggest that you do and it is not as simple as you may suppose. His previous actions lead me to state without equivocation that Captain Barclay is not beyond violence in that pursuit. You mentioned my care for my *amour propre*. I think you know there are few people who care more for how they are perceived by others than Ralph Barclay.'

'It is a private matter and none of my concern,' Hotham said.

'And if he harms his own wife, will you stand by and just exonerate him because he is a client officer?'

The admiral tried not to allow himself to react to that but he failed. Involuntary it might have been, but the way the cheeks tightened he could not hide. That was when Pearce knew for certain that Toomey had told him of the court martial papers and the way it had been kept hidden. Whatever standing Barclay had enjoyed in this cabin was no longer as high as it had previously been.

'I would also point out, though it should not be necessary that I do so, a captain using a vessel of the King's Navy for private purpose is highly irregular and should anything untoward occur the repercussions could be hard to contain. I would most certainly have no reason for silence and that applies to everything previously discussed and actions in the past.'

'What do you want, Pearce?'

'A vessel and explicit orders to Captain Barclay to return to the fleet directly and a cessation to his purpose. I leave it to you to decide if you wish to mention his wife by name.'

'Your mistress!' Hotham spat.

'If you reckon that to embarrass me, sir, I cannot tell you how far you are from being correct. I am proud of my association with the lady.'

'Which tells me you have the morals of a snake.'

Again Pearce had to bite back the words that came to mind; how dare this devious bastard, who had done his very best to get not only him killed but others too, refer to morality in his presence? It was hard to do and Pearce was glad of an interruption that obviated the need to speak.

'Captain Holloway's compliments, sir, but we are in sight of the coastal fort of Leghorn.'

'Thank you, I will be on deck presently.'

Hotham's chin was back on his chest as soon as the messenger departed and it was clear he was wresting with a conundrum. He would hate to give in to Pearce, that was obvious, but then what he had been told bore within it a grain of inescapable truth. Barclay was not prize hunting and hard as he would try to disguise it, his logs might not stand up to scrutiny if, in some way, a scandal came about that related to his wife.

'I am told you have in your possession, Pearce, certain papers that might be of interest to me.'

Another knock at the door and a more flustered messenger this time, his features not eased by the glare he got from the admiral. 'HMS *Brilliant* has departed the Inshore Squadron, sir, and is making for Leghorn, which Captain Holloway surmises may presage some good news regarding the enemy.'

'Indeed. Please thank Mr Holloway.'

'Sir,' came the reply as the head disappeared.

John Pearce was never to know that in such a piece of information lay the reasons for his request being granted. It pertained to Ralph Barclay, of course, and the court martial papers possessed by Pearce he had singularly failed to reveal. But the real reason was not that: Toby Burns was on *Brilliant* and the notion of him and John Pearce being in the same place was anathema, for if they met and the boy blabbed both he and Barclay could be sunk.

Hotham could not sail immediately and nor did he see the requirement to; he needed a day or two to make up his stores and that with a possible battle imminent would be extended to the fleet. If the French were out it would be advantageous if they felt themselves unthreatened, and how much better it would be to lead men against the enemy who had enjoyed a short break in port. For a man whose calm was legendary – many thought it to be natural indolence – Hotham was decisive.

'I will not agree to your request, Mr Pearce, for the reasons you outline. But you will have a boat and a despatch for Captain Barclay and that is for him to rejoin with all haste, at his peril. If the French are out I need every ship I possess to fight and beat them and that puts your private concern in the shade. Mr Toomey will write out your orders and designate a craft for you to employ. Now be so good as to vacate my cabin.'

Granted his wish, Pearce was not about to question the reasons; it was enough that he could hopefully prevent Barclay from getting anywhere near Emily. He was on deck as the saluting guns banged out in their usual wasteful chorus, still there when HMS *Britannia* anchored, aware that with the duty performed the crew had been stood down.

'Pearce it is, by God!'

The abrupt demand for his attention made him turn to face a toothless fellow with a scarred face and a broken nose, dressed as a member of the lower deck and clearly of no rank. Not over-fussy about his own, he was nevertheless annoyed to be addressed so by a common seaman.

'Don't know my face, do ye?'

'Why would I?' Pearce demanded, adding, 'And I think the proper form of address is "sir".'

'High and mighty, eh?'

'Are you looking for a flogging, man?'

'Justice more like. Name's Cole Peabody, not that it will ring with you, but if I was to refer to a certain road down to a place termed Buckler's Hard and a get-together you did not expect it might jog. Then there is a receiving hulk off Haslar called HMS *York*. Put together, happen you might guess where we met afore.'

Given what had just happened, the Pearce mind had been elsewhere; it took time for him to make the connection. 'Are you one of Tolland's brutes?'

Cole Peabody laughed. 'Was a time when that was true, but thanks to you I am stuck in this barky.'

Pearce was stunned; the coincidence was almost impossible to accept, yet it had to be true: those few words from this fellow established that. It also presaged danger, if not from this man, from those for whom he had one time done his smuggling, a pair of villainous brothers who had sworn to skin him alive.

'What of the Tollands?'

'Never fear for them, Pearce—'

The shout from the quarterdeck stopped the smuggler, as the officer of the watch demanded to know what was going on.

'An old shipmate, Lieutenant. Just catching up.'

'Well, I hope you know, sir, what you are about is unseemly.'

'Walk towards the companionway,' Pearce insisted as he slowly moved, the smuggler keeping pace, this as the previous question regarding the Tolland brothers was repeated, to be responded to with real bile.

'Looked after themselves, they did, the bastards. Must have had gold hidden to pay their way out, but none for their shipmates, which left us nowt but the navy.'

'Us?'

'Four.'

Tempted to commiserate, Pearce suddenly realised how stupid that would be. If he had not been a leader of the gang that had set out to murder him, this wretch had been part of it so he was just as deadly.

'But that's set to change, Pearce. Me and my mates has a plan to get off this here barky and we are looking to you to aid us.'

'Why would I do that?'

'Out of the kindness of your heart.'

'I fear I must disappoint you, as I have neither the time, and I certainly lack the inclination, to do anything to aid you. You sought a rough bed, lie on it.'

'I reckon you can do better, for if you do not then another will pay the price.'

They were off the deck now on the companionway and Pearce was about to turn and go back on deck, where he expected Toomey would bring him his orders. But he could hardly part company without asking an obvious question. 'Who?'

'We reckon you're not one to see another pay fer your errors. There's a knife at this minute to a nipper's throat and that will be employed if you just walk away. He'll be through the gun port in a trice to mix with the shit of this Leghorn place and us with nothing to fear. Eleven summers the brat says he has, pity him if he don't see no more 'cause of you.'

CHAPTER EIGHTEEN

There was little choice but to follow Peabody; if the threat was true Pearce had no doubt there was a life at stake. The type of ruffian employed by the Tolland brothers were not the kind to shy from killing: men who were could never last in the smuggling game, where the only way out, if the excise or a rival got onto their tail, was to spill blood without a care for the consequences.

On the occasions he had been close to the brothers who had led the gang – a pair also convinced he had stolen their boat and cargo – there had been no doubt about their intention to kill him, but only after they had sought to extract information he did not have and that was a prospect to make him shudder, given he could imagine the methods they would have employed.

If the fleet was at anchor and awaiting stores there was no actual activity yet. It was known from previous visits and a lament in the wardroom that no amount of badgering would shift Captain Urquhart to move swiftly. There was a way of doing things and that could not be altered, regardless of the fact that there might be an enemy at sea. Even the water hoys were on other duties and not available, so the crew had a free day to frolic and that they were now doing.

The sea state being flat calm the gun ports had been opened on both sides, yet the noise under the low beams was deafening Fiddlers and flute players always came out in the bumboats long before the vessels anchored: the location – Portsmouth or Leghorn – made little difference. In addition, there were castrato singers, acrobats, traders in everything from clothing, gaudy cloth and gimcrack baubles to playful monkeys that screeched either to get attention or out of distress.

The first customers would be the liberty men prettying themselves to go ashore for a night of debauchery, few in comparison to the complement of the ship. HMS *Britannia* would have aboard a high number of seamen not trusted to come back if they ever touched dry land, some pressed, certainly. Yet such behaviour was also true of volunteers who, inexplicably, given they had taken the bounty, would run for reasons too numerous to reflect upon: a grievance, a sudden desperation to see home, a woman or just sheer devilment brought on by too much drink.

The last thing Hotham would want, when he was already short-handed, given the fleet was hoping to sail into battle, was that he should lose men to the whim of chance or a desire to join with the Leghorn privateers. Marines were placed at intervals along the deck, though their presence was a commonplace, for in addition to preventing attempts to desert they had the task of ensuring no drink got aboard. It did, and in decent quantities:

sailors were adept at deception, added to which a blind eye could be bought if there was no officer about.

Women came out too, selling their services to needy sailors, John Holloway being the kind of captain to allow the local trollops on board. Those same marines had to ensure that when the time came they were off the ship prior to sailing, or in this case by nightfall, that too a hope never quite realised. On the larger rates of warship women sought to stay on board and once again the reasons were numerous.

For such creatures life ashore could not be comfortable; indeed it was very often the complete opposite, given they were likely never to be far from starvation or male violence. Hiding was difficult but not impossible and sailors would often aid them, thereby gaining themselves a companion, and as long as it did not get out of hand by their being too numerous, many captains let it pass.

As Pearce progressed through the happy throng the looks he got were far from respectful; in port an officer below was an unwelcome presence, the fear being that he would interfere with long sought-after pleasures: illicit drink, but most notably those of a carnal nature.

As he was sighted through the throng, Peabody's mates looked at him in anticipation but that soon switched to the taller man alongside him, changing to one filled with malice. No words were spoken, clearly none were needed, as a bit of tarpaulin under the mess table was pulled back slightly to reveal a gagged, terrified and grimy young face while at the same time one of the ex-smugglers crouched down, a blade in his hand catching the light from the lanterns.

There was no need for Pearce to wonder if that was sharp or

to see the victim in his entirety and discern if he could move: ex-smugglers were experienced seamen and much valued by the navy for that reason. They knew how to whet a knife and whatever knots they had employed to bind him would do their job. It was also true that with what was going on all over the lower decks the proposed victim would not be missed, for no one was where they would have been at sea.

If he had mates, and the lad must, they would reckon him away seeking to enjoy himself or find something to steal, for nippers were rarely saints. Often the illegitimate offspring of serving sailors or port ragamuffins, many sought out the navy as a way to stay with a parent or hide from the law and a life of pilfering or sleeping in doorways.

They were a valued part of the crew, for all their mischief, having vital tasks to perform that required small hands and agility, nipping the anchor cable as it was brought in board when berthing and acting as powder monkeys, running to and fro from the gunner's magazine to keep the cannon firing in battle.

The sight was not of long duration and in a blink all eyes were back on him, searching to sense his reaction. Pearce just spun round and glared at Peabody, then jerked his head to say he should follow as he strode off, his coat clearing a path. He declined to look back to see if he was being obeyed, instead searching for a spot where the noise would abate somewhat and being less crowded he could talk.

'What is it you want?'

Peabody looked around to see who was paying heed but they were few. A bluecoat in deep conversation with a lower deckhand was a far from common sight and none would want to come close to authority, so they were subjected to no more than fleeting and curious glances. Satisfied that none were nearby enough to hear, Peabody started speaking softly but insistently, repeating his demand for a boat. To the suggestion that Pearce could just go aloft and tell whatever officer he found on the quarterdeck what was afoot, Peabody just shrugged.

'The lad will expire and afore a marine lays a hand on any one of us, an' I swear so will you. Might be none of us sees old England again but that's better than this hellhole.'

Was that bluff? It was impossible to tell, so Pearce tried another gambit. 'Do you have any notion of where you are? We are a thousand miles from the coast of England and that is by a direct route across a country full of Frenchmen. Add half as much again to avoid meeting them.'

'That's as maybe and to be thought on after. We knows of now we are on a barky that will not be goin' close to home, and we would never be allowed off even if she did. You want to see that nipper alive you get a boat and us crewing it.'

'Do you think the watch officer is that stupid? I ask for one of the ship's boats, not one of which is sitting idle, very much the opposite, and gaily row off with a quartet of pressed men? The notion he will agree to that is mad.'

'It's mad you make me, Pearce, with your shallying.'

'So much so you are prepared to kill an innocent?' Peabody did not even bother to nod; he did not have to, his eyes provided the positive response. 'If I swear to aid you, will you let him go?'

'Think we'd take your word, a man who thieved our ship from under our noses and stole our cargo to enjoy the worth of it while we scraped for a crust?'

If the former was true, albeit Pearce could make excuses as to how it had come about, the latter part of that statement was not. He had no more profited from the cargo than had they or the men for whom they worked. At the same time as he was thinking on that he was also searching for a way out of what was an intractable dilemma and it made no difference if what Peabody wanted made little sense.

Having been once a pressed seaman himself he had a clear appreciation of the kind of desperation that would make a man resort to any hare-brained scheme that could be contrived to get free; had he not once sought to swim from ship to shore and in the process risked drowning? Men taken up by violence were wedded to the navy for the duration and would only be granted their freedom once hostilities ceased, and that could be years away.

'And don't you go thinkin' we're not canny, Pearce,' Peabody added, tapping his head. 'If his body is found, who's going to think a British tar would harm a nipper? But with all these here local folk aboard, and some right evil-eyed ones amongst 'em, then one being found with a bloodstained knife in his bag . . . ? The lad will die if the sun goes down and we is still at that mess table, but we won't pay the price.'

With eyes locked Pearce was thinking hard. There was no way to get one of *Britannia's* boats; every single one was either shipping liberty men or officers ashore to come back laden with the private purchases for the very bluecoats they were transporting. Added to that one would be in use by the marines, to patrol the waters between ship and shore to counter the possibility of deserters. But an idea did present itself that might serve and he reached for and produced the pouch that contained the remains of the monies he had been advanced in Brindisi.

'You can't buy us off, Pearce,' Peabody snarled as he looked down at the coins being poured into a hand.

'I'm not trying to. This is for you to purchase disguises.'

Looking hard at the man, Pearce could sense his confusion; he could not comprehend what was being suggested, which marked him out as slow-witted for all his swagger. It was as well to remember that as a smuggler he had been a follower not a leader.

'Buy clothing from the traders on board, of the sort that will make you look like a native, but not everything from the same one. Darken your skin, too, for at least one of you is too fair of face to pass for a Tuscan. I will go ashore and procure a boat and bring it to your gun port at dusk, when the locals will be departing the ship. Disguised, you can slip out, though I reckon you must distract any marine that is nearby.'

'You?'

'I will be in the boat.'

'You'd best be 'cause—'

'There's no need to tell me, Peabody!' Pearce had barked that and turned heads because of it and he needed to drop his voice to continue. 'But without my coat to aid you, you will be apprehended and I reckon the punishment to be a flogging round the fleet.'

Even in the glim Pearce saw Peabody pale at the threat of that; such an outcome was as fatal as the rope but a thousand times more prolonged and painful, as the victim was taken from ship to ship to be flogged in turn by the Master at Arms of every one, so that those tempted to likewise transgress should be brought to consider the consequences.

'There's no requirement that you tell me how much you mistrust me.'

'Never was it so,' Peabody responded with a mocking tone. 'You passed on the chance to see off the Tolland brothers for good and me and my mates with them. Man like that I reckon I can put faith in, if the stakes be right, an' they are.'

Pearce walked away without replying; there was no need to say any more and time was not on his side, nor was there any doubt that he would be required to act. The notion that anyone should pay with their life for something he was purported to have done he could not abide. It was on the companionway stairs that the added fact of Emily's pregnancy surfaced. What if she was carrying his son? The mental replacement of the grubby boy under that mess table for his own flesh and blood could not be wiped from his mind.

'Mr Dinsdale, is it not?'

He was the officer who had the quarterdeck and Pearce now found himself face-to-face with one of the members of the wardroom who had declined to speak with him on his previous visits to the flagship. Dinsdale and his ilk took their cue from the premier who ruled the roost and always looked upon Pearce as if he had just crawled out of the gutter. Normally he would have avoided the man but this was not a situation that allowed for private feelings.

'All my dunnage is on HMS *Agamemnon* and I wish to go ashore. It will lead to a great loss of time if I have to go via Captain Nelson's ship.' Pearce tried a winning grin; by the blank reaction it was a dead loss. 'The streets of Leghorn are not always safe.'

The man would not look at him. 'From what I am told, you would know of this more than most.'

'Perhaps, but I wonder if I may borrow a cutlass and the strap to carry it. I have to attend upon Admiral Hotham on the morrow, so it will be returned. I will, of course, take the opportunity to mention to Sir William the aid you afforded me.'

Did this fellow know how much he was hated by Hotham? It was unlikely, the admiral being too elevated and by nature not one to confide his feelings in lesser beings. The name and the possible praise did the trick and Dinsdale, still unsmiling, produced the key to unlock the chain that kept such weapons secure. The carrying strap was no more than a leather over the shoulder band with a slot for the weapon and it was unwieldy as well as sharp.

'Have a care you don't cut yourself, Mr Pearce,' Dinsdale said, in a tone that indicated he wished for the precise opposite.

For him there was no trouble in getting a boat: he was an officer and entitled, duty notwithstanding, to go ashore as he pleased on any still making the journey, and that was everything the flagship possessed. The anchorage was crowded with such craft going in all directions, every one possessed by the fleet employed in some errand or other, they massively outnumbered by the local wherries hired by those officers and higher-value tradesmen who would brook no delay, which added to his hope that he could pull off that which was required.

Back on dry land he strode down the canals, heading for the small harbour that was home to the privateers. He could only hope the Senyard fellow he met would be still in the tavern; if not it would leave him hoping for a like-minded soul. In the fug of smoke from dozens of pipes it was near impossible to see anyone and that left him standing in the doorway for some time as he examined the room. It was Senyard who came to him, pushing his way through a crowd and grinning.

'Have you come to enlist with one of my fellows, sir?'

'Tempted as I might be, I am on another mission. I need a boat and men to row it. For the favour I will grant you a quartet of prime seamen, ex-smugglers and bloodthirsty sods, who are exactly the kind of hands your fellows need.'

'Generous.'

'I cannot tell you how far from the truth that is.'

'I think I require more of an explanation, Mr Pearce, for the men with whom I trade are not given to kindnesses and with so many naval boats in the harbour, not to mention their warships, it might be a risky thing to venture out on such a day. The navy is not beyond the snatch, even of men with exemptions.'

'Then I suggest they arm themselves.'

Pearce's mind was racing and it was the thought of the Pelicans, brought on again by the dimensions of this tavern and the atmosphere engendered, that came to his rescue; how many times had he gone out on a limb to rescue Michael, Charlie and Rufus? And when he spoke it was easy to be convincing, for he was telling the truth, albeit in a partial way.

'These men were pressed into the navy by my actions and I am determined to get them free. I must employ my rank to bring it about in the hope that no marine will dare challenge an officer going ashore.'

'Smugglers, you say.'

'Running from Gravelines into the Kent coast. I suspect I do not have to relate to you how dangerous that can be and the kind of men needed to ensure it is profitable.'

'On which vessel?'

'*Britannia*.' That got a raised eyebrow. 'It is my aim to remove them as the sun goes down and the traders and entertainers are sent packing, which they will be so that the vessels can get ready to take in their stores. The women will be removed as well, and it is my hope they will scream, which will be good for distraction.'

Senyard pondered for a moment in a very deliberate manner before speaking again. 'It may be that I can personally oblige you, but I must warn you, sir, that if this is some subterfuge there will be a price to pay and a high one.'

Pearce was wondering what Senyard would want with four seamen, until it dawned on him that such men, prime hands, were as much a commodity as pork in the barrel. He would find for them a captain willing to pay a bounty for their recruitment and no doubt it was he who would provide false exemption certificates.

'I am not fool enough to think it otherwise.'

'Then I bid you wait, sir. Will you take some wine while I arrange to meet your needs?'

'No, but I thank you. This needs a clear head, but if you can oblige me with an unopened bottle I would be grateful.'

As Pearce reached to pay for it, Senyard held up a hand. 'Allow me to treat you, sir.'

'I would have the cork removed and jammed back in, if I may.'

That got a look of deep curiosity that Pearce did nothing to satisfy.

CHAPTER NINETEEN

Never gifted with much in the way of patience, Pearce was doubly troubled by the time Senyard took to sort out what was needed: the sun was dipping fast at this time of year and there was scant time left to act. Finally he appeared with two strongly built men, with heads that melded into necks with no discernible join, so scarred and brutish in appearance they made Peabody and his lot look like saints. Both were armed with heavy-handled short swords and had a pair of pistols stuck in their belts, though Pearce reckoned them not to be loaded and more for show than use.

The names were proffered but at such a distance and in such a clamour of talk, echoing off the walls and low ceiling of the tavern, Pearce did not catch them; not that he cared, they were sailors by their garb and just what he required. Senyard led them all out of the Golden Hind along one of the quays to where a boat was tied up to the painter of a sleek-looking barque. One of his villains stretched out to haul it in before indicating that Pearce should board, an offer declined given he wanted his rowers in place first. A shrug met that suggestion and the pair obliged.

'I think you will observe, Mr Pearce, that my associates are not the type to be trifled with. They are adept at the use of the weapons they carry and ruthless in their execution.'

Pearce, now in the boat, did not reply immediately, removing his borrowed cutlass as well as the holder and placing them at his feet, the bottle he was carrying now clasped between his knees. 'As you can see, sir, I am now entirely at their mercy.'

That got a wolfish grin from the trader. 'Not a position I would wish to share.'

'What have you told them?'

'The bare bones.'

'That is enough. I can instruct them in whatever might arise.'

'That will not be easy, given they have no English, though you might surprise me by saying you have their tongue.'

'Which is?'

'Bulgar, though they respond to the argot of the Turk.'

Almost as if he wished to brag of the facility, Senyard addressed them in what Pearce reckoned to be the latter tongue, which got a bit of a grunt in response.

'And if I wish to direct them?'

'I suggest you point.'

As soon as they were clear Pearce dipped the tiller and the boat headed out of the harbour into the wide anchorage. He did indeed point but most of the steering was down to him and they headed past the first of the ships of the line, the side of which was a mass of boats of all shapes and sizes, while from out of the gun ports came the sound of much music and merriment.

Looking at the pair as they dipped the oars he observed eyes that had a dead quality. That lack of expression applied to the broad faces too, and did not alter as he tried a smile. He had a sudden feeling that he might have jumped out of a frying pan into the fire, given he hardly knew Senyard and the man might, despite his protestations and explanations, suspect him of seeking to play a trick regardless of the outcome.

To make a point he reached down and raised his cutlass, examining the blade for sharpness before replacing it, adding the bottle, which he jammed under the thwart, to then reconnect with his eyes and a steady stare: there was still no expression in response that would hint at feelings.

The sun was not yet where it needed to be so a hand waved up and down slowed the pace as Pearce pondered on what he had to accomplish. The time window was tight; in the Mediterranean it went from dusk to full nightfall very quickly and he had no desire to be within easy sight of the flagship before making his approach, albeit he could see her clearly.

At single anchor *Britannia* had swung on the falling tide, small as that was, so that the route to get Peabody and his lot out and into a boat was going to be near invisible to the marine piquet cutter. That was rowing back and forth between the flagship and the quayside, so he employed the tiller to give it a wide berth. Another factor with timing was the fear that the smugglers would think he had not fulfilled his promise and they might resort to murder out of frustration.

Watching the sun dip into the west he waved furiously as the rim hit the horizon and was rewarded with a pleasing reaction as the rate of rowing really picked up, for these two brutes were well muscled. With tiller and pointing hand he was approaching the side of *Britannia* at a lick, counting the larboard gun ports so that he could come alongside the right one.

That was a hope made difficult for, as he had anticipated, the traders, singers, fiddlers and whores were being chucked off the ship, their boats crowding the side as well as the waters in between, which meant Pearce had to gesticulate much and work the tiller hard to avoid a collision for he dare not shout too loud, even if there seemed to be plenty of noise to cover it. Drawing attention to himself was not a good idea.

Peabody was half leaning out of his gun port, which effectively precluded it being used by anyone else, and even at fifty yards Pearce could see the anxious expression on his face, one that was swift to evaporate. He took a risk and lifted and waved his hat high in the air to draw the ex-smuggler's attention, a clenched fist in response assuring him it had been seen. Then Peabody disappeared.

In a babble of noisy Italian, or whatever local dialect the Tuscans spoke, Pearce had his Bulgars get alongside. Their oars having been shipped, he was obliged to use his hands on the rough planking to edge the boat along till he could himself lean through the right port. There he saw the quartet hastily donning various gaudy pieces of cloth, none of which went to a full garment.

As he had hoped and expected, the women were being removed – and that was being carried out forcibly, with much yelling, cursing and the odd high-pitched scream. The marines being now fully occupied in that task it would be possible to get his party out unobserved, but no one was going anywhere until he knew that nipper was safe and he told them so.

'You'se in no position to make demands, Pearce,' Peabody spat.

'And you are going nowhere until I see him alive.'

It was one of his companions that urged Peabody to comply, indeed he did not wait for a response but directed the other two to haul off the canvas and fetch the lad out. Pearce ducked back and used his hat to cover the lower half of his face, not very visible anyway, he suspected, as it was now getting dark outside.

The still terrified youngster was on his feet now, the gag and the knots binding him being undone. Faintly he could hear Peabody issuing dire threats of retribution should he speak of his ordeal, those repeated by his companions until the lad was finally released to run as fast as he could away from his tormentors. If he blabbed, and he might, it was hoped they would be well clear before anyone reacted.

The smugglers did not delay, yet Pearce was still barking at them to move, for the wailing of the trollops was diminishing, a sound they would cease to utter once they were in a boat and it was pointless. Pearce had to hold the boat steady to the side of the warship to allow it to be boarded, without the pressure creating a dangerous gap. With panic-driven swiftness and any number of curses at the scrapes endured, he soon had the smugglers aboard and was able to signal to the Bulgars to fend off and row.

The problem now was from above; as they came out of the protection of the ship's tumblehome anyone on deck would be able to look down and see them and as yet it was not dark enough to make them invisible. Sat with his back to *Britannia*, Pearce hunched his shoulders having a real feeling of eyes boring into his back, for if it went awry now one cutlass was going to be of scant use.

Slowly, for he signalled his oarsmen to row steady, the boat pulled away from the ship, Pearce using the tiller to get in amongst the locals' bumboats and barges wherein he would be hard to spot. Now his problem was that marine cutter, which had a man standing upright to direct the local boats to pass close to him so he could see who was aboard, this being a good time for desertion.

Pearce steered a sideways course, he having no desire to encounter the man who might be an officer from the flagship and who could know his face from wardroom intimacy. More importantly, he would be well aware that he was not on the flagship's muster. His act on the tiller got a suspicious comment from Peabody.

'It is time you shut up, man,' came the sharp reply. 'I am carrying out my part of your devilish bargain and I would remind you that without my being in this boat it will be stopped by the first piquet cutter we approach.'

'And we knows you can dish us, too.'

'If I thought I could easily explain what I am about I would be tempted. But what is keeping you safe now is no threat of yours. It is another bargain I have had to make and one that it would be foolish of me to ignore.'

It was close to dark by the time he waved to his Bulgars and employed the tiller and oars to set the boat on course for the shore, and given the time that took they were now separated from any other craft. Pearce issued a demand that the smugglers sing, though what emerged was so feeble one of the Bulgars grinned, showing the gaps in his teeth, which brought from Pearce a furious demand that Peabody and his ilk act as if they were drunk. He nagged them until they were bellowing out their song, a raucous and bawdy sea shanty.

He grabbed the bottle from under the thwart and hauled out the cork with his teeth, tipping it over the side so that half the contents spilt. He then put it to his lips and allowed enough of a trickle to enter his throat to make him smell of having consumed. This was in case they got so close to the marines he was required to breathe on them. That done he began to sing too and deliberately well off key.

'Ahoy there, who goes?'

The last of the dusk required a lantern be held aloft, while underneath that light was the scarlet coat and white waistcoat of a marine. Pearce paid close attention to the details and was able to see that this was no officer – it was not a duty such men relished. He surmised instead a corporal or sergeant and that was to the good. The next positive was that in coming from a different direction it would be a piquet from a vessel other than *Britannia*.

'Lieutenant Barclay,' he yelled, seeking to sound very inebriated, 'off Old Ironsides, don't ye know.' Then he growled for the noise had diminished. 'Keep singing, damn you.'

'Ironsides? Where in the name of Christ are you headed, sir?'

'Ashore man, to take my pleasures. And I would ask you to attend to your manners and belay the blasphemy. Whom am I addressing?'

'Corporal Needham, sir, off *St George*.'

'I come from *Illustrious*.'

'Then how come you are dining aboard, sir?'

They were getting close and Pearce had to hiss to the smugglers to slow the oarsmen. 'I suspect an unsteady hand on the tiller, Corporal, and can blame no one other than myself.'

'I would be obliged, sir, if you would come to where I can see you.'

'Certainly, my man, and if I come close enough you may take a drop from this very fine bottle of wine I have. It saddens me there will scarce be enough for you all. How many men do you command?'

'Eight plus myself, sir.'

'Not a pleasant duty, what?'

'Necessary, sir, as you will know.'

Pearce had been holding the tiller and crouching. Now he stood so that was held by his shins and raised the bottle, wondering if his coat and the flagon could be seen for they were on the very edge of the pool of light. The corporal was in plain view under the held-up lantern and Pearce released the breath he found himself holding as the man got into a confused state. He was obliged to pass the lantern, thus lowering it, so he could put a hand to his tricorne hat in a form of salute. He had seen Pearce's blue coat and white breeches but that lowered lantern put the rest of the party out of sight.

That was when Pearce appeared to fall over, a howl of pain emerging to be followed by a stream of curses aimed at the crew of the boat, the next words threats of dire punishment for their inability to hold the boat steady.

'Haul away, damn you, and row proper or I'll have your hides.' The bottle was raised high again and Pearce shouted out. 'I bid you good evening, Corporal.'

'Sir, I—'

He never got the words out. Pearce issued a loud and repeated order to row and put your backs into it, there being a fine filly waiting for him in the nearest bawdy house. Would Needham insist he stop? That was the risk, and despite the differing ranks

Pearce would be obliged to obey him for his task was one with authority. His next shout was to confuse the man.

'You have done your duty, Corporal, and I will make it my business to let your captain know the next time I dine in his company. And may God grant that you get your just reward for your Spanish captures.'

The hope was that such a thought would be enough to distract him and his men. He hoped to turn their thoughts to the rewards that would come their way once the value of the Spanish plate ship captured by *St George* two years previously was granted, as every sailor thought it should be.

The navy was adamant that Admiral Gell, his flag captain and crew, were due the prize money and that the Spanish captures were not Droits of the Crown, as claimed by a greedy government. Said to be worth close to a million pounds in specie, it had been the talk of every wardroom ever since the news came of the capture, eyes going glossy at the prospect of such a windfall.

Pearce was back on the tiller, making sure the boat stayed on the very edge of the circle of light, holding his breath again as they passed the stern of the marine cutter. He was now signing with as much gusto as he could muster, this from a throat so dry he could feel the rasp and that had to be maintained until they were well clear and he could set the tiller for the lights he knew to be those around the privateer's harbour.

Out of easy earshot he took his cutlass in his hand and there was now a bit of moon and enough starlight to allow the waved blade to flash. He intended to talk and the only thing to ease his throat was the remainder of the wine, the bottle laid back by his feet as soon as it was finished, for that too was a potential weapon.

'I am now going to tell you a tale.'

'Spare us, Pearce, and don't think that cutlass will stand against four, for we have cause to take our due for what you stole out of Gravelines.'

'And so say we all,' another voice concurred.

'Well said, Cephas,' Peabody retorted.

The response was delivered with a jauntiness Pearce did not feel. 'I always had me down to be skewered when this was done but I reckon I could see to a pair of you afore you got close, so who is it going to be?'

That was greeted with silence. 'What is certain is that in this boat you would be pressed to come more than one at a time, so I am going to talk and you are going to have to listen.'

He was as good as his word, going back to that theft and how it had come about as well as the outcome for him and his friends. He did not expect to be believed but it was the truth and one day it might come to be seen as that. It was a precaution: if these four wanted revenge they were not alone and he feared another coincidence that would put him in harm's way in the future, not least with the men who used to employ them.

'Let's get onto dry land, for the sake of Christ,' said the one called Cephas. 'That's a tale for a feeble mind.'

'Even if I am minded to do you a favour?'

'What favour could we want or take from you?'

'We are headed to the port used by the Leghorn privateers. You may have heard tell of them, as well as the fact that many of them are English.'

Silence again; perhaps they were ignorant of the fact just imparted.

'I have no notion if licensed piracy is more or less profitable than smuggling but it will serve you better than being pressed men.'

'Happen the navy will come fer us.'

'There are people there who will forge for you certificates of exemption.'

'Why you doin' this, Pearce?' That was Peabody's voice.

'Maybe because I was once a pressed seaman myself.'

'Don't believe it.'

'I am going to hand you over to those who will employ you and it is my fond wish that the first time you are engaged in a capture you get your gullet slit. Before I came ashore I told the officer of the watch, Lieutenant Dinsdale – a particular friend of mine by the way – to look into a certain place if I did not return and he got my drift.'

The curses were soft but obvious, which was to the good; they had taken the point.

'Harm me and there will be King's sailors by the hundred raiding this part of the port. I have also made sure the possibility is known to those with whom you will serve and the consequences of any action you take. I can assure you that if Admiral Hotham takes the opportunity to close down what he considers a nest of vipers, you will wish for your gullets to be cut so your end is quick.'

'The devil resides in you,' Peabody spat.

'The devil does not exist but I do, and know this. I will be fully armed if I am ever in Leghorn again and should I see one of your faces it will be the death of you.'

'You ain't got the guts.'

'To see you swing for desertion, I think I have. All I have to do is call out your name for you to be taken up and once you are back aboard *Britannia*, whoever has command of you will swear to your true status.'

The boat was close to the privateer's quay now and Pearce was on his feet to tell them so.

'Make your minds up now.' Their lack of any response was all he needed. 'I will get off the boat first and depart. There is a tavern yonder called the Golden Hind. Go to it and ask for Mr Senyard and may it be my fate never to clap eyes on any of you ever again.'

CHAPTER TWENTY

Michael O'Hagan did not go looking for Charlie Taverner and Rufus Dommet; they would return to the bathing house once their carousals were over and besides, what could they do that he could not? Instead he called at the Palazzo Sessa only to discover that the ambassador and his wife were attending another house and were not expected to return till late. Already familiar with the kitchens he went there to sit and wait and that was where Mrs Cadogan found him.

'Best sleep,' was her opinion, once the tale had been related to her, 'there's not much that can be done afore first light and I suspect little then.'

It was a truth Michael was reluctant to accept and quick compliance was not required. The lady might be titled the housekeeper but she was Emma's mother and was thus able to offer Michael a drink to ease his mind, not that he was to be allowed to consume that alone; Mrs Cadogan filled two goblets, not one.

Naturally they talked for there was nothing standoffish about the lady, so she heard of a rural upbringing in Ireland with too many mouths to feed off poor soil – which drove Michael to seek his future elsewhere – and of roads travelled and much earth shovelled to turn them from potholed winter mud tracks full of ruts into profitable turnpikes laid with Mr McAdam's black bitumen. In time such roads brought him to London.

'The Great Wen,' Mrs Cadogan sighed. 'All roads lead to there and not just for the Irish.'

'Would I be seen as probing if I enquired from where you hail, lady?'

'Lady, is it,' she said with a soft laugh. 'Not many have termed me that for long years past. I hailed from a village near Chester, which if you do not know it—'

'Forgive me, I do not.'

'Sufficient to say it is a long way from London, Michael.'

'Sure, it pleases me you know my name.'

'Have you not smoked that I am one to know what goes on around me? If I did not, the Chevalier would be a poorer man by many a dubloon.'

'I dug ditches for the foundations of houses for the rich, Mrs Cadogan. I doubt you came to London for the same purpose.'

'You would be right there. You have seen my daughter and I am sure noted her beauty. Would it surprise you to know that I was once considered as one such too?'

It would have been easy to say yes; the skin was heavily wrinkled and if there had been beauty there it had long faded; easy, but not polite.

'You have not lost the trace.'

'You manage untruths easily, do you not?'

There was no rancour in her tone, more amusement but then her face clouded and she began to speak of a life where a woman had little more than her charms by which to make her way. Michael knew that she was talking about her daughter as much as herself. That changed when she returned to the subject of Emily Barclay and how John Pearce would act when he heard what had happened.

'Holy Mary, he will kill for her.'

'Then he will hang for her too. Some rise to a better life, Michael, and some sink further by far than I have. I would say to Mr Pearce's lady to forget him and make what life she can, for I sense Captain Barclay is not a poor man and love does not fill a belly.'

'She is carrying John-boy's child.'

'I know,' came the reply, delivered with an air that implied superior knowledge of the ways of the world than her Irish acquaintance, only to soften immediately. 'A bairn fills a belly, that is sure, but is it right to let that child rule your life, eh?'

Michael knew she was talking of herself, not Emily Barclay.

'Sleep, Michael. My Emma rises early and if anything can be done she will contrive it.'

It was the Chevalier who spoke on it, not his wife and he was adamant, though sympathetic, that there was nothing he or she could do. Emily was the captain's wedded wife and the law was certain on the point of her duty to her husband, while he had the right to disown her if he wished and could stand the scandal.

'I am obliged to enquire what you will do now.'

'I thought on that, Your Honour, and it seems to me we would be best, my companions and I, to return to our ship, only . . .'

Michael had to hesitate and the Chevalier picked up on why immediately. 'You lack the means.'

'Mr Pearce left us provided for and Mrs Barclay likewise. But that has gone with her and I reckon my two companions will have given to Naples what they had in their pokes last night.'

'I will supply the money you require to travel to Brindisi.'

'Sure you're a kind soul, Your Honour.'

'I am put upon by people less deserving than you.'

Michael had the funds when he returned to the bathing house, to find Charlie and Rufus sound asleep and in total ignorance of what had happened, which was remarkable given Barclay's men had not been gentle in their search. The two had rolled into their cots and ignored the furniture thrown about and it was with sore heads they were appraised, accompanied by much castigation.

'How was we to know?' came the constant refrain from a pair suffering much.

'Well you knows now, so first we worry about putting the Chevalier's house to rights, and then it's back on the road.'

'What about Mrs Barclay?'

'Jesus, we can do nothing there, boyos, except pray. God knows I hope she is being treated as she should be.'

Emily Barclay had been accommodated in one-third of what was a very spacious cabin, for the navy looked after its commanders well. So far her husband had said little; the journey overland precluded talking and even in the boat as they rowed out to sea he had been silent, perhaps fearing to talk too much when he could be overheard. HMS *Semele* had made her dawn rendezvous and he was piped aboard with due ceremony, albeit it was again in a chair secured by a rope used subsequently by Emily.

If her coming on board occasioned any comment it was not vouchsafed to her or her husband. The faces of the officers who greeted him were rigid in their expressions and none would look at her for fear that their curiosity would be manifest. Only that oily creature Gherson even looked her in the eye, to favour her with a sycophantic smile. She had been escorted to her present location by the brute Devenow and left to her own devices, food and the ability to wash and change her clothing notwithstanding.

Having unpacked her books there was nothing to do but sit on the casement cushions and read by the strong sunlight pouring in. That became increasingly hard as her thoughts turned to John Pearce and their combined troubles, a position altered as the locked door opened and her husband entered, his face set in what she assumed he thought to be indifference; with his dark countenance he could not carry it off.

'You and I are required to talk, madam.'

Emily knew she had to get onto the front foot quickly; he could not be allowed to dominate her for his very nature ensured that would be his common mode of behaviour if it were ever established. So she sat rigidly upright in her seat and she replied, keeping her tone devoid of emotion.

'We are required to come to an accommodation, sir, and one that meets my needs as much as it meets your own.'

Much as he tried to disguise it he was thrown; Barclay had come for an argument and he was not getting that which he expected. The fact made him hesitate long enough for Emily to continue.

'I made you an offer in the company of Lady Hamilton—'

'And that big Paddy, I recall,' he interrupted, his anger evident even as he sought to supress it.

'His being there is by the by. I want to know if you are wedded to the outrageous threats that you issued to harm my child.'

'Not my child, so why should I care?'

'You know that and so do I. I will undertake to ensure that it remains a secret to those on whose good opinion you rely, namely my own family, as well as your sisters, neighbours and naval acquaintances. I know I can trust you to maintain a fiction.'

'What are you after, Emily?'

'Security, Husband, which only you can offer me.'

'Not Pearce?'

'He would do so were you not my husband.'

'Do you intend to disregard his existence?'

'I will not deny a fond memory, but I undertake not to mention his name again.'

'I cannot believe you can hold to that. He must be in your thoughts.'

'And there he will remain.'

'Even when—' Barclay stopped; he could not say what he wanted in a manner that would fit the requirements. His high-and-mighty tone was thus much diminished when he continued. 'I intend to demand my rights, madam.'

'While I intend to succumb to them.'

'Succumb?'

'I wish you to understand, sir, that while your attentions will not be in any way welcome, I know it my duty to satisfy what I see as your primeval needs.'

'And in return?'

'The child I bear is to be raised as your own flesh and blood and in the manner in which it would be if it were so. In short, Husband, I will save your face in order to protect my child.'

'And if I demur?'

'Then prepare for your cuckoldry to be shouted from the rooftops.'

'You see yourself on land, do you?' he hissed.

Emily was wondering why he did not shout – he was much given to the raised voice – only to realise he could not, even in his own cabin. This was not HMS *Brilliant*, on which she had come to know the officers, midshipmen and crew both in the normal course of sailing the frigate, as well as below decks as a nurse aiding the surgeon, Heinrich Lutyens, and finally as a visitor when they were in captivity.

She would know no one on this ship, Gherson and Devenow apart, and they would probably have been sworn to silence. How had he explained her presence to his officers and who she was? Had he even condescended to, for none of such creatures would dare ask? She knew enough about naval vessels to be sure that the whole ship would be abuzz with conjecture if he had offered no explanation.

'Do I detect a threat, sir?'

'You would do well to consider it possible.'

'But it is not,' she insisted, her voice taking on a hard edge. 'You have passed the point at which you dare do me harm. If you had intended that it would have happened already when you came to abduct me. If I am not known to the crew of this vessel they know me to be alive and someone of enough standing to occupy part of your cabin. Harm me now and you will pay a felon's price.'

Emily stood and began to pace, not far in each direction for her part of the accommodation was constrained.

'If I repeat myself, indulge me, for there are conditions attached to whatever agreement we make and I will hold you to them. Not only will you raise and provide for *our* child, you will treat me in my public life as a wife should be. I will demand and receive your open respect and I will also require a set of my own rooms in whichever house we occupy.'

'Now you are purchasing property.'

'I find your tone of sarcasm unbecoming and that is what I fear in public. Contain it, sir. As I say, my own set of rooms and when you require to visit them for' – a waved hand was used to cover conjugal rights – 'I will require ample notice and I wish to have the right to agree or decline, though I undertake not to do so with unbecoming frequency.'

'Anything else?'

'Yes. I require that you grant my parents full title to the house they occupy.'

Emily could not know that Ralph Barclay wanted to smite her fatally there and then for, as a man of much passion, he was holding himself very much in check. He was also thinking that she could demand the moon now and he would agree but in time they would be back in England and that was when any rules would be laid down and not by her.

'Naturally, as I am with child now, I expect my person to be respected for the very obvious reason that any conjugal activity might do it harm.'

'The Lord forfend,' he whispered.

'When do you anticipate that we shall join with the fleet?'

'Two days. The wind at present is not favourable.'

'I suppose I will be obliged to meet with your fellow captains and, of course, Admiral Hotham?'

'Only if you behave.'

'There you have it, Husband. It is in that crucible I will be tested and in such surroundings in which I will satisfy you that the commitments I have made will be held to.'

'Go back to your book, madam. I have a ship to command.'

He was gone; only the voice of Devenow, standing by to help him on the swell, could be heard. The key was turned in the lock and Emily sat down again, the facade she had presented collapsing immediately for she suspected a life of misery and constant battle lay in her future. Ralph Barclay was not one to easily accept her demands; they would have to be fought for to be maintained.

The tears welled up as she said to herself, 'Forgive me, John, for the love of God forgive me.'

Hotham was not about to favour John Pearce with anything approaching comfort and besides, he required every vessel he had for the coming battle. A pinnace was provided and four men with which to sail her, as well as rations and water for a week, which meant there was not much room aboard. Inured to the whims of their superiors the seamen took to the task with no more ill grace than they would any other duty, and in one, Tucker, they had a man who knew how to hand, reef and steer. He knew the boat and how to get the best out of her.

Dressed in foul-weather gear – the sea spray was a constant on such a compact vessel – John Pearce looked less the officer than usual and this on a vessel rarely commanded by anything higher than a midshipman. A cause of curiosity for sure, the question was never even hinted at. They were carrying despatches for HMS *Semele* and that was an end to it, and when Pearce introduced himself there was no evident animosity, a possibility since the pinnace came from the flagship and at a time when it would have been fully employed in its normal duties of ferrying stores.

Quite naturally, Hotham had declined to personally pass to Pearce the oilskin pouch he now carried in his uniform coat pocket. That had been handed over by one of Toomey's under clerks, not even the Irishman willing to face the humiliation of compliance with the request of one so troublesome. The problem was they were sealed and since the under clerk had not written them Pearce had no idea what they said. He could only hope that his threats were so potent Hotham dare not play ducks and drakes.

Yet the possibility existed that Barclay would have orders to act against him and not do as Pearce required. Could he open the orders and read them first? Not with the men he now commanded so close by. There was nowhere to gain privacy, either, even when basic needs came upon them – it was over the side or not at all.

At least they were making good speed, and with the pressure of the wind it was sometimes necessary to take up positions on the gunwales to keep the pinnace sailing stiff. The boat fairly raced along sending up a pleasing bow wave and bringing smiles to all five faces aboard. It was necessary to reduce sail as night fell, with a pair asleep and a pair awake, with Pearce doing his best to be fair and keep his eyes open.

Breakfast was biscuit – thankfully fresh baked from Leghorn – and cold duff washed down with water. That consumed the sail was set to draw once more and since the wind had held overnight they were soon creaming along on a blue sea that reflected a clear sky, leaving behind a startlingly white wake.

'What was that?' the senior hand Tucker asked, standing to hold on to a brace and pointing ahead. 'Topgallant, by the shape of it.'

They had seen the odd sail and even the occasional hull-up merchantman the previous day, but it was not a type of canvas they bore aloft. Topgallants were naval and soon Pearce too was on his feet, the telescope that he had brought along employed, ready to catch sight of what Tucker had seen on the next rise of the boat. What he could not know was that aboard HMS *Semele* the same question was being asked and answered.

'Frigate, sir, very like one of the pair we espied on the way to Naples.'

'I will be on deck presently.'

And he was, to find that his lookouts had spotted not one frigate but three and it eventually became evident that they were making no effort to avoid him, holding their heading instead of running, as they had done previously.

'They might be bluffing, Mr Palmer. We will maintain our course. Let us see what game they want to play.'

It would be a fine balance of force if it came to a fight, Ralph Barclay knew that. He had the heavier weight of shot but they had numbers and manoeuvrability so it came down to will. If they wanted a fight he had little choice but to oblige them if he wished to return to join Hotham, for they held the weather gage. In addition they enjoyed a greater turn of speed than *Semele*. Against that he was sure of his ship and confident that if they could not emerge unscathed, they could do so victorious and perhaps a trophy to take back to the fleet.

'I suggest an early dinner for the hands, Mr Palmer, and a double tot of grog immediately after.'

'And then, sir?'

'Then? If these fellows are still coming on, we must clear for action.'

CHAPTER TWENTY-ONE

Pearce and the crew of his pinnace were much slower to rate the odds in what looked to be the makings of a contest; all four vessels were closing in on each other, though it was, as ever at sea, painfully slow. Low in the water, it had taken much time to observe the enemy numbers and for the man in command even more time to reason that he lacked the knowledge to work out where the advantage lay.

He had been in a sea fight when still rated as a midshipman – indeed it was that action that had got him his promotion to lieutenant – but that had in essence been one capital ship against another. This was different in too many respects, while his rank prevented the men he had with him from speculation, which was frustrating, given he reckoned they might have a better appreciation than he. There was one obvious fact; they had no part other than that of observer in whatever was about to happen.

'I think it would be wise to shorten sail.' That got a nod from Tucker, but before he could move to obey Pearce took the opportunity to seek to break the previous silence. 'And if any of you have words to say, pay no attention to my rank.'

It was like the breaking of a dam; Pearce was obliged to order them to stop babbling and jumping about lest they affect the boat and to speak in turn, but the conclusions were of a piece. HMS *Semele* was new built by the standards of the fleet and the French were no match for the Wooden Walls of Old England, even if they did have numbers.

All knew that she had already taken part in the Glorious First, which spoke of a crew who would enter a fight with relish as well as a captain who knew his business. It was only as the speculation was taking place that John Pearce was brought to wonder what Ralph Barclay was doing on this patch of water and to question his northward course.

He had never thought it possible to beard him before he reached Naples. At worst, in terms of distance, he might find him between there and Palermo. Yet now he was on a heading taking him away from both. Was he just prize hunting, in which case he had a chance of a sterling success? Or was he on his way back to the fleet, which could mean any number of things?

'Frigates splitting apart,' Tucker called, he having granted himself the task of observer, 'and there is steam rising from *Semele's* chimney.'

'Galley fires doused,' commented another of the sailors, 'they are certain to fight now.'

'Which John Crapaud will see as easy as can I, mate,' said another, 'so they will know what to guard against.'

The man looked at Pearce to see what he thought but received no response for he was subject to mixed emotions; for Ralph

Barclay to lose a battle could not but be welcome to Pearce. But he commanded hundreds of men for whom he held no grudge and in a fight there would be no respect for rank. Even as the least patriotic of men – he found such sentiments facile – he had to be on the side of his fellow countrymen, for no other reason, if he needed one, than because they were contesting with the bestiality of a French Revolution he had come to despise.

Pearce had shortened sail but he was not going to be content if he could not observe what was unfolding, though he had no notion to get even close to an arc of danger from falling shot, so he steered as near as he thought he dared before taking down the sail to leave the pinnace bobbing in the waves. Nor did he wish those frigates to know of his nationality, which had him take in the small flag that had been raised on the masthead – an act, judging by the looks he got, that found little favour.

To be so close to the water was frustrating; things would occur of which he could only get a partial sight, but that did not apply to the masts of the enemy, now a mass of changing flags as whoever commanded the squadron deployed his force. *Semele*, further off, appeared no larger in sight than the closer French frigate. Only on the very odd rise of a larger wave could he get anything like a plain sight.

Nor was Emily Barclay sure of what was happening. She knew by the commotion that it was serious, not least when the wedges were knocked from the bulkheads that formed her cabin to be swung up and attached to the catches on the overhead deck beams. As she grabbed a shawl she looked right along a deck on which cannon were being loosed and the objects normally stowed out of the way being taken down for use.

As the sailors who had dealt with her walls cleared away the furniture, Cornelius Gherson appeared with a look on his face that, in the way it changed in a blink, defied analysis. Standing still while a mass of activity took place around him he started by licking his lips and examining her as if she were a fine meal, though Emily thought she recognised his look as filled with lust.

The change in those corn-blue orbs as he spoke, which surfaced only to disappear, was more telling, given it indicated deep loathing. 'You are to go to the cable tier.'

'From what I can see this is no exercise.' That got a shrug. 'If it is not, then my place is on the orlop deck with the surgeon.'

'I am happy to take you to the cable tier.' The lips were wetted again. 'And perhaps I might stay there with you.'

'Get back to your grubbing, Gherson, it is all you are fit for.'

'What a pleasure it would be to teach you a lesson and grant you pleasure at the same time.'

'You teach me something every time I clap eyes on you and it troubles my Christian beliefs. I learn that there are indeed people in the world with no redeeming features at all.'

The single four-letter expletive summed up where his interest lay. If he had hoped to shock her he failed: Emily had spent too much time on ships of war and overheard too much to be in ignorance of filthy blasphemy.

'Take this woman to the cable tier,' he shouted.

If the men close by stopped, it was telling he was not obeyed and indeed one responded, 'Who are you ordering about, quill scratcher?'

'Do as you're told.'

'Bugger off, savin' your presence, lady.'

Gherson's features now showed a degree of petulance, mirrored in the hurt look and the screech that followed. 'It is a direct order from the captain and you ignore it at your peril. Take hold of her and drag her to the cable tier if need be.'

'And I am the captain's wife,' Emily spat as the hands reluctantly moved to obey. The words stopped them dead for there had been much speculation on her status since the supposed press gang outing and Barclay returned with only her. 'Lay a hand on me and I think you know what my husband can be trusted to do.'

More likely to flog me than you, she thought, but they hesitated and that allowed her enough time to continue. 'I intend to go to the aid of the surgeon and it is my fond hope that I do not see you in that place.'

The imperious way she moved kept them still, and despite the yelping of Gherson, they let her pass. They had duties to perform and the clerk was left standing in frustrated impotence as Emily disappeared down the companionway, still unsure of what the ship faced.

That did not apply on the deck of a 74-gun third rate now cleared for action. *Semele* was reduced to topsails, main and forecourse raised and the netting rigged to catch falling debris: Ralph Barclay could very easily see what the enemy was about, though he had little choice but to let them do as they pleased if he declined to reverse his course and enforce a chase.

He had been tacking and wearing into the breeze all morning but that had to be abandoned in favour of a fixed course. Short of hands, he would require everyone on the guns and that left too few men to work the sails in a way that would permit manoeuvre, difficult in any case with a contrary wind.

'Ensure that this is entered in the log, Mr Palmer. That our commander has left us short of the men needed to both sail and fight the ship.'

The premier looked set to speak, the head movement noticed by Barclay out of the corner of his eye. But the man decided to remain silent. What he might wish to say was no mystery, for the very fact alluded to seriously affected HMS *Semele*. Did he wish to advise caution, perhaps even flight?

'Gunnery will decide this, Mr Palmer, and there we ever have the advantage.'

That was not true and Barclay knew it as well as every officer aboard. If the enemy manoeuvred with skill, *Semele* would have to fight both sides simultaneously and that brought risks that some cannon would not be as well employed as they should be, for'tween decks in a battle was no place for a choreographed switch from one weapon to another.

There would be confusion and gun crews long accustomed to working with each other would become mixed. Again, being short of twenty per cent of their complement mattered. Over a hundred men down on the needs of the ship, they could not man all the cannon in the way proper tactics demanded.

As they had closed on the enemy frigates, two had been definitely identified, for like all warships they had features as familiar to anyone who had seen them as those on the face of a friend; individual figureheads, the lines of their design and how they were decorated with carvings in certain places. *Alceste* 32 was the smallest and a surprise, for she had been given to the Sardinians by Lord Hood after the fall of Toulon. Clearly she had been retaken, which given the efficiency of the Sardinian Navy was not too much of a shock.

The outlines of the 30-gun *Vestale* were well known, she having been sunk by the Royal Navy during the American War only to be refloated and sold back to them with the peace, but not before being drawn in many a pamphlet. It was the third and largest frigate that caused the most curiosity and speculation, though few could doubt her name for she had been on the stocks in Toulon when Lord Hood had agreed to the takeover of the French naval base on behalf of the legitimate monarchy.

'Has to be *Minerve*,' Ralph Barclay opined, for he had been there as a prisoner before and had seen her being built, carving and painting included. 'Forty guns and she will be stiff.'

'*Alceste* has altered course to leeward, sir.'

The information, from the man in charge of the forecastle division, had Ralph Barclay shift the midshipman's shoulder on which he was resting his telescope. It counted that the information was true; it mattered just as much that two other frigates were staying to windward. Whoever had command was offering the middling fighting ship as a tempting target and inviting him to a slight alteration of course to engage her.

'Clever, my friend, but I decline to bite. Hold her steady, Quartermaster.'

'It would be instructive to know who has command of the enemy, sir.'

If the question was posed quietly, the answer was loud enough to be overheard by many. Barclay knew that the remark was prompted by a feeling of disquiet; that had to be countered with an expression of confidence.

'I think not, Mr Palmer. Since the fall of the Bastille they have been a rum bunch I have found, men promoted above their abilities. As to their crewing, they will have had to scrape the barrel for that and with so little time at sea – recall we keep them bottled up most of the time – they cannot be as well worked up as we are.'

The voice rose to an inspiring shout. 'Work your guns as well as I know you can and we will see one, if not two of these fellows, with our flag above their damned tricolour.' Ralph Barclay reckoned the response to be feeble and felt he was required to add more. 'I have lined your purses once and I will do so again.'

Still no more than a ragged cheer followed but he was not concerned by that; his men would fight not for the love of him or their country but for their own lives and the possibility of a monetary reward.

'Your wife refused your order, sir.'

Barclay spun to hiss at Gherson as everyone else in earshot went rigid, even if they did nothing to avoid eavesdropping. 'Keep your voice down.'

The reply lacked courtesy as well as discretion: Gherson had been wounded not only by Emily but by the response of the crew, men he rarely addressed and never considered worthy of an opinion. They had treated him as of no account.

'There would be no point, sir, given she has told the entire lower deck her name and status.'

'Where is she now?'

'Gone to the orlop with the pious intent of aiding the surgeon.'

Intended to diminish her, Barclay sought to use it for praise and raised his voice slightly to do so. 'My wife, indeed, gentlemen.

Aiding the surgeon, which shows her sterling qualities.'

If Gherson intended to respond, the first boom of a firing cannon stopped him as *Alceste* was wreathed in smoke. Anyone watching would have seen him visibly shrink, his shoulders hunching into his body. He was a man who suspected every weapon fired by an enemy was aimed personally at him and reacted accordingly.

'Stay where you are, Gherson, and for the love of Christ stand up straight.'

Barclay said this in a conversational tone and not without a note of humour; he knew his clerk to be a coward and delighted in exposing him to at least the same danger as himself, even if his presence was superfluous. It helped to keep the man in his place. The captain now had Devenow on one shoulder and Gherson on another, the brutish bully indifferent and the clerk resentful enough to wish his employer dead and not peacefully so.

The salvo from *Alceste* had been a ranging one from her 18-pounders, the balls falling short into the sea, which sent up great plumes visible to the crew of Pearce's pinnace, which told them they had done no harm. Barclay gave the order to reply from his upper deck 28-pounders which, with the greater range plus elevation peppered the sea around the French frigate.

'You have marked the time, Mr Palmer?'

'Aye aye, sir.'

'There is always a moment of relief, is there not, when the waiting is over and the game is afoot?' That got another affirmative reply as the quickly reloaded 28-pounders spoke again, at exactly the same time as those from the frigate to larboard. 'And that tells us our differing rates of fire, does it not. Let us see what the lower deck cannon can do.'

Orders were called down to the lower gun deck and when that broadside was fired it reverberated through the whole ship, shaking timbers and knocking some of the surgeon's instruments off the one-time door on which he would treat the wounded. Emily picked them up and replaced them, smiling at a fellow clearly nervous of what he was about to face.

It was all very well signing up for naval service, his expression seemed to imply; as he then explained to her, the pay was adequate and drowning apart, the risk small, but he had been in a sea fight before and knew that if blood was spilt it would be very messy.

'If you think you will find that hard to bear, it might be best to avoid the sight.'

'Fear not, sir, I too have been in battle before.'

If he was tempted to enquire that was stopped by another broadside.

Ralph Barclay had turned his attention to *Minerve* and *Vestale*, noting that the former had shortened sail less than her consort, which would bring her, in time, to lay off the larboard quarter where she would hope that the 74-gunner would be so reduced by her companions as to get across *Semele*'s stern and seek to deliver a killing blow through the casement deadlights.

Alceste was closing, risking destruction as she fired bar shot at the rigging. That was only alleviated by Barclay needing to shift gun crews from larboard to starboard and engage the other two, who had now opened up at a cable's length with round shot. Soon all three vessels were shrouded in smoke as the cannon fire steadied to salvo after salvo, the rate from the British vessel faster by far.

If *Semele* suffered, and she did, the 74, with her superior firepower, was inflicting great damage to the enemy scantlings. In the moments when the smoke cleared enough to give sight to those on board, they could see the shattered woodwork and the rigging hanging loose. Yet that was replicated on *Semele*. The mainmast was wounded, the stays and shrouds in tatters, while the deck was littered with what had been dislodged from aloft, especially heavy wooden blocks. They had fallen with enough weight and pace to slice through the netting.

All battles resulted in a sense of chaos, but that was the apogee of naval captaincy. Ralph Barclay stood, with his two supporters either side, as if he was on a peaceful heath enjoying the fresh air, issuing orders only when necessary, exuding the required calm. Nothing about his presence hinted at the danger of being on a deck enfiladed by shot from a trio of enemy vessels.

What commands he did give out were shouted, certainly, but the midshipmen he instructed carried them out, even if they had to be in terror of that which was going on around them, and did so with aplomb. The cannon were being well worked, even if some were idle, and the rate of fire from his ship was being maintained.

A salvo of bar shot, fired from *Alceste*, now within musket range, sliced through the upper rigging and shredded the topsails as well as the falls that held it. Men had to withdraw from the guns to reset it, for should he wish to come about lacking working sails he would struggle to do so. In holding his course he had very nearly got to the position he had long sought and orders went below that saw sweating men haul out of the sail locker a new bit of canvas for his intended manoeuvre.

To bend a new topsail on in the midst of a fight was hard but not impossible, and Barclay knew that *Semele* would suffer as it was carried it out. But he had passed his enemies by and if he could come about he would have stolen the weather gage, which would allow him to close with any one of the three. Once upon them he could ensure their utter destruction as a fighting entity by concentrating all his fire temporarily on a single foe.

Success might provide the chance to engage another in the same manner, though he suspected the consorts, seeing the loss of one of their number, would break off the action and seek to put blue water between him and themselves. He shouted to Palmer, for the noise made it essential. He had been a coming-and-going presence throughout the battle, as he did what was required to shore up his inferior officers struggling to carry out their duties.

'We are coming upon the moment of truth, Mr Palmer. In ten minutes from now I want the gun crews sent to other duties. I sense a prize waiting to fall like an overripe plum into our hands.'

Palmer's face was filthy from the smoke-blown black powder, which made more obvious his smile, for he too knew the value of confidence. That was applied to Barclay as well as Devenow, who was holding his captain's good arm in one hand and his telescope in the other. Palmer had to bend his head to extend it to Gherson, who was hunched up and sobbing at the mayhem around him.

The bar shot took off Palmer's hat and he was unsure if he still had the top of his crown. When he raised his eyes with some trepidation he realised his captain did not; Ralph Barclay was no more than a pair of shoulders bereft of a head, a figure that seemed able to remain upright as if nothing had occurred to dent his abilities. That did not last, with Devenow yelling and a blood-soaked Gherson screaming like a terrified girl; the legs folded and the trunk sank to the deck.

'Get that body below,' Palmer shouted, as inured naval discipline immediately took over.

It was necessary to slap Devenow's head to get him to respond and then the premier obviously had a thought that made him hesitate, but only for a second or two.

'To his cabin, not to the orlop deck. The man's wife cannot be allowed to see this.'

CHAPTER TWENTY-TWO

Ralph Barclay had not shared his tactical intentions with Palmer, holding it to himself and that left his first lieutenant, now in command, at a loss as to what to do next. His sole aim thus became survival, a gunnery duel in which he pitched *Semele* against the trio of French frigates who now seemed collectively intent on disabling the 74. There was little round shot slamming into the hull now: it was chain and bar shot of the kind that had decapitated his captain and it was shredding the rigging.

News of Barclay's demise spread rapidly even in what was a maelstrom of furious action, and if there had been little love lost between commander and crew his demise dented the morale of those he had led. The captain of a ship of war, any vessel for that matter, carried with him an aura of authority that was hard to quantify; all anyone knew was that it existed and that it counted.

Semele was firing on both sides now with every man, officers included, working as many cannon as possible, especially the 32-pounders that would do the most damage. But it had long ceased to be broadsides: now it was ragged firing at will or as soon as a weapon was loaded, and in that method aim came second to discharge. The red-painted decks had plenty of blood shining on the planking, albeit the number of fatalities was small; it took more than a 28-pound cannonball to smash through several feet of stout oak; vulnerability lay at the open gun ports.

The youngest powder monkeys were dashing to each gun team with cartridges, those slightly older fetching balls from the depths of the holds while others wetted the cannon with buckets of seawater to cool what was becoming metal hot enough to burn skin. At a distance it was black smoke shot through with the orange flash of the exploding powder, each salvo cheered by the men in the pinnace, Pearce excluded, till they were hoarse from their shouting.

An occasional increase in the strength of the wind showed the damage done to *Semele* and Pearce wondered how long it could go on. Every bit of canvas was now in tatters and if he could not see the detail he knew that would apply to the rigging, for it was the French habit to seek to disable an enemy and prevent them from being able to sail clear of the action.

In what had been the great cabin, Devenow was kneeling over the remains of the man he had faithfully served while Gherson, crouching and choking from the smoke, was huddled by a casement trembling like a leaf. Below on the orlop deck the surgeon worked on the wounded with knife, saw, needle and thread, with the three limbs he had been forced to sever at his feet.

Emily, still in ignorance of what had happened on deck, was assisting, bathing and bandaging, on one occasion employing only words of comfort aimed at the terrified eyes of a young topman on the verge of passing away, this while the ship's chaplain mumbled prayers over those already gone to meet their maker. The loblolly boys and the surgeon's mates brought in the latest casualties.

If she saw the midshipman with the filthy face arrive and whisper in the surgeon's ear, or noted the quick alarmed look aimed at her, she gave it no heed for it was brief; the man was too busy amputating a leg.

On deck, Lieutenant Palmer sensed the diminution in the rate of fire all around him, small but significant. It seemed odd to consult his watch but in doing so he realised this fight had been in progress for well over two hours and it was obvious that his guns crew would be tiring. Did that apply to the French or did they have full complements of men? Perhaps fresh from port they even had an excess, which they could carry on sorties that were of short duration. If they did, then they could relieve tired gun crews with fresh bodies.

Palmer had been twenty years at sea, yet this was his first experience of battle and he wondered if he was up to the standard required to do what was necessary. The other thought was just as troubling: would he keep fighting in order to save his own reputation, sacrificing men's lives so he could claim to have conducted a proper contest?

Very apparent and impossible to gainsay was the plain fact that HMS *Semele* was not going to be able to break off the fight. What was left aloft would not draw any wind, which in any case was still foul. To come about required new canvas aloft and he reckoned that would be fatal. To take men off the guns would reduce his rate of fire even more, while the number he might lose in rigging being shot through with chain and bar did not bear thinking about. That was before the enemy guessed what was being attempted and sent case shot into the same area.

It left him nothing more than to stay and pound it out, hoping the French would tire before *Semele*. That showed no sign of being a present possibility and Palmer knew if he was wrong about the prospects the butcher's bill on board what was now his ship would grow and grow. Could he, in all conscience, take responsibility for that?

'All officers to the quarterdeck,' he commanded.

This sent a fourteen-year-old midshipman running off to effect the delivery. It took time for him to get round, more for them to gather from their stations and his first words were to make sure they knew that Barclay was no more. If it seemed odd to be holding a conference on a deck that had seen their senior officer killed and was still exposed to enemy fire, no one mentioned it as Palmer outlined the situation.

'So, gentlemen, I ask you for your opinion on what we must do.'

The smoke-blackened faces before him showed varying degrees of reaction, ranging from shock to surprise, for the question would not have been posed if Palmer was determined to continue fighting. He knew that, which had him say a few words more.

'I know the ultimate decision rests with myself, but I am not prepared to act without your backing. Can we continue this fight with any prospect of being able to defeat the enemy? I repeat that we lack enough intact canvas to provide steerage way and what we will lose if we seek to alter that.'

Just then a blast of case shot swept across the foredeck, sending many of the men working the 18-pounders spinning away screaming, while their mates looked on in stunned inactivity until reality intruded and they rushed to take the wounded below to the surgeon. Two bodies were left; there was no time to worry about the already dead.

'We must strike our colours,' Palmer said.

If it sounded harsh it was because his throat lacked fluid, not because he was either angry or heartbroken. Those before him nodded, some immediately, the marine captain the last.

'Then, gentlemen, I suggest you find anything you have of value to keep about your person, for it will be needed in captivity.'

'The crew?' asked the third lieutenant.

'Will have time to do likewise before the enemy comes for my sword.'

The midshipman messenger was behind the assembly, his eyes beginning to wet with tears that would soon produce streaks on his face. The only answer to his misery was activity.

'The private signal book, fetch it – a sack, as well as a lead weight. Gentlemen, go to your divisions and give the order to cease firing. Then join me in what was Captain Barclay's cabin.'

Then he hauled out his sword for the last act it would perform before he was relieved of it, stepping to the mast and slashing at the halyards holding aloft the battle flag of his ship. Cut through, it fluttered down as the guns close by fell silent. It took several minutes for the enemy to do likewise and when they did the sound that floated across the water was not one to lift the spirits, being loud cheering.

The only other noise was of the private signal book splashing into the sea.

'Jesus, they've struck!' shouted Tucker, as they saw the Union Flag disappear into the rapidly clearing smoke, a cry that brought howls from his mates.

John Pearce was just as stunned; this he had not expected and it presented him with a dilemma. If *Semele* were now a French prize, Hotham's order to Ralph Barclay would be redundant. It also seemed to him to obviate any need to continue on to Naples, much as he was longing to do so. The quartet he commanded were still looking at the scene unfolding before them, four vessels in various states of damage, but what would they say if he ordered them to just proceed on as though nothing had occurred?

His duty was plain; Hotham needed to be told of this loss and quickly, which might afford him a chance, if he moved swiftly enough, to reverse it. He owed a duty to the service as well as to the crew of HMS *Semele* that transcended his private desires or his hatred of the man who commanded her. So it was with a heavy heart that he issued his orders.

'Tucker, get that sail aloft at the double.'

'Back to Leghorn, Your Honour?'

'As fast as this wind will carry us.'

Which will not be at the pace with which we got this far, Pearce thought, as he sank back into his seat in the stern, and it would be laboured tacking and wearing sailing into the wind.

* * *

Down below the sound of battle had been muted by the sheer quantity of timber, only the occasional bang as a French ball struck Semele's hull causing a brief lifting of the head. It was the lack of juddering from their own cannon that alerted those dealing with the wounded to the fact that the fighting had ceased and that did not tell them if it pointed to victory or defeat. That only came with the arrival of Palmer, who delivered it with gravitas.

'You must make preparations for capture,' he told the assembly.

'I can only do that when the wounded have been attended to, Mr Palmer.'

'Of course. I will send a midshipman and you may instruct him as to your needs.' He then turned to Emily. 'I am Lieutenant Nesbit Palmer, madam. I have been given to understand that you are Captain Barclay's wife.'

'That is so.'

The man blinked, no doubt wondering, Emily surmised, why that fact had been kept a secret. About to provide an explanation that would cover her sudden and peculiar arrival, one she had mentally concocted when shut up in her cabin, his next words stopped her dead.

'Then it is my painful duty, Mrs Barclay, to tell you that your husband has suffered a gallant death while commanding his ship.'

'Death?'

What a range of emotions coursed through her mind in a millisecond, some enough to make her feel deeply ashamed.

'He was on deck when it happened and no officer could have done more than he. I can also assure you he felt no pain.'

'He was not wounded, then?'

'No.' Palmer hesitated, coughed, looked embarrassed and then continued. 'What occurred was a most unpleasant event and the loss was immediate, so I had your husband laid out in his cabin, which is being put to rights as we speak.'

'Then I must go and pray for him.'

'That would, I think, be unwise and troubling.'

'Mr Palmer, as you will see, this apron I am wearing is covered in blood. I have stood here these last hours as men wounded, some horribly, have been brought in to be treated and many have succumbed even as I spoke with them. It means I am no wallflower, sir.'

'I accept what you say, Mrs Barclay, but—'

'Is his condition so terrible that you think I will faint?'

'No, madam, but you see the fatal wound suffered by your husband was the loss of his head. Sadly that cannot be found to be rejoined with his trunk.'

Emily had to suppress the thought that then entered her mind: her husband was always metaphorically losing his head, so it was an ironic way to for him to die. Close to mirth she had to drop her head to hide her features and she was fighting to control them when Palmer added, 'I am having him prepared for a burial at sea. Once he is sewn into canvas, I would suggest that would be an appropriate time to say your prayers. The cabin bulkheads will be put back in place so you can enjoy some privacy with which to mourn. Now, if you will excuse me, I have much to do before our captors come aboard.'

'Of course,' she whispered, head still bowed.

'My condolences once more, madam.'

Emily went back to work, bandaging the arm of a fellow who had taken a ball from case shot in the upper arm. He had heard the whole exchange and, added to that, from his recumbent position he had seen how the woman nursing him had found it necessary to supress amusement. Not that he would say anything now, but it would be a mystery to relate to his mates.

'Beggin' your pardon, ma'am, but if we has struck as Mr Palmer says, then I need to get to where I stow my possessions. If I don't, them French sods will pinch anything they find.'

Emily tore at the ends of the bandage with her teeth to create the means for a knot, tying it quickly. 'There you are, you may go.'

'A sad day, ma'am.'

'Indeed,' came the reply, from a woman inwardly unsure if that was the truth.

'Can I suggest, Mrs Barclay,' the surgeon said, 'your work is done here. If we are to meet our captors it would be unbecoming that you should do so in such a bloodstained condition.'

'I would see such garb as a mark of honour.'

'Which it truly is. But decorum?'

'When my work is complete.'

'As you wish.'

Palmer was on deck when the senior French officer came aboard followed by a strong party of armed men, his sword held flat in his hand, subjected to a surprised look as the captain took in his uniform coat, obviously that of a lieutenant. Then his hat came off and he bowed.

'*Capitaine de Vaisseau*, Louis-Jean-Nicolas LeJollie.'

'Lieutenant Nesbit Palmer, First Lieutenant of HMS *Semele*.'

'*Le capitaine?*'

'*Mort*,' Palmer replied, employing one of the few words of French he felt safe to use.

'*Une tragedie, n'est-ce pas, mais la chance de la guerre.*'

'I do not speak your language, monsieur.'

'Sword, you keep.'

'Thank you, er . . . *merci*. May I introduce you to my officers?'

The mutual lack of comprehension only increased as that was carried out; names were provided and LeJollie muttered to each a few words of encouragement, which mostly seemed to allude to their being gallant. What else he was imparting was a mystery. Finally LeJollie turned to one of his own men, who stepped forward with a folded tricolour flag. As he turned back to face Palmer he looked suitably sad.

'*C'est necessaire, monsieur.*' A sharp order had it attached to the sliced-through halyards, now swinging in the wind, and the French sailor fashioned two swift knots before hauling it aloft slightly, just enough for the flag of Great Britain to be tied on below, the two raised aloft together to an outburst of cheering from the frigates that were now within hailing distance.

Emily, now that all that could be done was over, had come to her resurrected cabin to find Gherson rifling through her possessions. When she admonished him he just sneered. 'Happen you'll need looking after now, Miss Nose-in-the-air.'

'It will be your neck in the air if you do not get out.'

The sneer turned to a bitter laugh. 'And who is going to haul on the rope now, that turd Pearce?'

'Get out,' she yelled, loud enough to bring Devenow out of the main cabin. Not the sharpest of men he blinked a couple of times before it dawned on him what was going on.

'Sling your hook, Gherson.'

'You can't order me about.'

A fist came up and he closed to tower over the clerk. 'Can I not?'

The way the clerk sauntered off troubled Emily, smacking as it did of his endemic arrogance, but she could not linger on that.

'Devenow, I require water with which to wash and the privacy to do so, but first, well you know what I must do.'

'He held you in high regard, Mrs Barclay.' It was a lie and both knew it. But this was no time to nail the fact as he stood aside to indicate that she should pass through the door he had used to enter. 'I will see if the galley fire has been lit.'

Entering the main cabin she saw the bundle of canvas on the floor. The outline was vaguely human and she supposed Palmer must have had this begun before he came to tell her the news. The cabin had been put to rights down to the embroidered cushions being replaced on the casement lockers. Emily took one and put in on the floor, then knelt on it, clasping her hands in prayer, for if she had come to despise Ralph Barclay it was her duty as a Christian to pray for his salvation.

Back on deck, LeJollie had made a move to go to that very place, but a word from Palmer, even in English, stopped him. The stilted discussion that followed took time but eventually the Frenchman understood that the late captain's wife was on board and as of this moment probably alone with his body. Time for her to grieve would be seen as a kindness.

LeJollie shrugged; there was much to do, the cabin could wait and courtesy demanded he go below and commiserate with the wounded, with whom he would exchange a few words of comfort. If he now served the navy of the Revolution LeJollie had, at one time, been an officer of King Louis and he still abided to the norms of that service.

Palmer went with him as the muster books were passed over to his inferiors; the French would need a list of those they had taken prisoner.

CHAPTER TWENTY-THREE

By the time night fell, HMS *Semele* was under tow from *Minerve*. LeJollie had decided that to remain in the same location and effect repairs would risk him being discovered by a British Fleet he suspected was at sea. Prior to moving, the crew of the 74 had been broken up, to be sent to one of the French frigates and replaced by a prize crew drawn from the enemy squadron.

A body of men had been held back: Palmer, the master, as well as the other standing officers with their mates, plus the one favour granted by the Frenchman, that Emily Barclay should continue to occupy the main cabin even after her husband was buried. The lieutenant he put in charge of the prize, as well as one other officer, would use the wardroom.

There had been one unpleasant moment when the crew were being shifted into the waiting boats. Cornelius Gherson had sought to take with him a locked chest containing Ralph Barclay's papers, only to be stopped by a Frenchman who demanded to examine the contents. Gherson had thrown something close to a screaming fit, which got him a well-deserved clip round the ear from a French officer. That had brought Palmer to the gangway to find out what was happening.

The complaint, that these were private papers and correspondence in his charge cut no ice. The chest was taken from him, as well as the key he carried in his coat pocket. It was then sent back to what was described as the rightful owner, namely the late captain's wife. Gifted to her, she showed little initial interest.

For Nesbit Palmer it was a strange sensation to be aboard his ship, yet with nothing to do but convey orders to those left behind and they were few. Much time was spent with the surgeon and the chaplain in the former tiny quarters to avoid too much contact with his captors.

His only outright duties were to visit those recovering from their wounds and accompany the carpenter as he traversed his interior walkway to establish damage to the hull. That done and being satisfied, the carpenter was now busy repairing wounded timber, as if the ship was not a capture.

The gunner was updating his records so that he could account properly for what he had remaining in the way of powder and shot, while the purser likewise counted his stores, for they would have a money value to the enemy, while to him, their loss could presage bankruptcy. The cook was still aboard, for everyone – prize crew included – had to be fed.

With everyone convinced she was deep in grief, Emily was left alone to brood and to seek to work out what the future held. She, too, was a captive and having been in such a situation before it held little terror. Courtesies were extended to captains and their wives that were not given to other officers, and certainly not the men, and she knew that part of her duties would be to alleviate their conditions if at all possible.

The body had been removed at her request – again done willingly on the assumption it was too upsetting to share the cabin with – but in reality she saw it as a malign presence, for death had not removed the malice of her husband, but somehow seemed to increase it.

Devenow had been left behind to care for her and was in constant attendance, being something of a trial in that role, seeking to ingratiate himself by endless enquiries as to her feelings and her needs. Since she knew him to be an endemic drunkard his sobriety was remarkable. It was he who brought her dinner to a table he had set, putting on the polished mahogany board crystal glass, silver cutlery and a decanter of wine, all served with deep humility.

Following on from the meal she finally opened the chest and began to examine the contents: Ralph Barclay's orders as well as various communications with fellow naval officers on the subject of their treatment following on from the Glorious First of June. Family letters she did not read, they being from his rather silly sisters and thus would be full of local and dull gossip.

There were numerous missives from Ommaney and Druce, oddly addressed to Gherson, detailing various transactions and investments, as well as updates on prize matters still in dispute. A book listed an account of her husband's holdings, not least in 3% Government Consols, the whole adding up to a sizeable sum of money and given there was no will the conclusion dawned that unless there was one in London she would quite naturally inherit.

The prospect set off a train of thought that she fought to keep sensible, but within those reflections, quite naturally figuring large, was the person of the man she loved. Odd that she cried when it became obvious that all the difficulties under which they had laboured were now no more. Quite possibly the death of Ralph Barclay was going to provide for them both a life of which they could only have previously dreamt.

Pearce was ruminating too, and the cause was that which he had thought on previously: why had *Semele* been on that course when he had expected at the very best to find her in Naples? Such reflections under a sliver of moon and starlight, in the middle of the Mediterranean, taking a turn on watch while others slept allowed for rife speculation only broken by the need to swing the single sail and alter the rudder to change tack.

Also quick to resurface were his previous conundrums: how to confound Ralph Barclay, how to extract revenge on Hotham for his deceitful plan that could have seen him killed, neither without major hurdles that required jumping to get anywhere at all. Then there was Emily's pregnancy and the agony that their child, because of her senseless morality, might end up being raised by a man he despised.

Would Barclay agree to accept the child? He might just to save face, so the thinking took ever increasingly lurid turns as the ramifications of such a scenario played out in an increasingly fevered mind, not least in the imagined kidnap he would undertake to gain possession of his own flesh and blood. Double relief came when his time on watch was up, sleep being quick to take him to more pleasant dreams.

They buried Ralph Barclay at dawn with the full honours due to his rank, a full complement of French officers, LeJollie in particular, attending. The sewn canvas cover had been weighted with a 32-pounder cannonball, though one tradition could not be implemented; there being no head they could not put the thread through the nose, a way of ensuring the victim was dead.

It was brought on deck by *Semele*'s warrant officers on a board, both covered with the flag of his country and, at Emily's request, with his sword laying on his chest. Lined up by the gangway the chaplain intoned the Anglican service of burial while the French behaved with exemplary courtesy by standing heads uncovered throughout.

Naturally, Emily was the chief mourner and if she could not manage the full widow's weeds she had found enough black cloth of a porous nature to fashion a cowl that hid her features. Every eye was on her for a second as the chaplain completed his obsequies and pronounced the final words.

'And now, with God's grace for his salvation, we commit the body of Captain Ralph Barclay to the deep.'

The board was raised at the rear and as the canvas slipped off to land in the sea with an audible splash, every man aboard bar the bosun, who was of the Methodist persuasion, Frenchmen included, crossed themselves. LeJollie, hat in hand, approached Emily to offer his condolences, his handsome face lighting up in a rather inappropriate way when she replied to him in his own language.

Palmer was next, followed by the men who had acted as pall-bearers, each looking keenly at a veil that completely hid her face. If they had expected sobs there were none, but that was seen not as disrespect to the dead but a quality of steadfastness that made them proud. Then she addressed LeJollie in French to say that she had laid out in the cabin a small repast with wine and it would please her if he and his officers would join her late husband's men.

In truth, everything she had, wine included, was no longer her property to dispense: it belonged to France, or at least the men who had just won their victory. But in LeJollie she was dealing with a man who would never consider telling her so and he acceded with good grace.

It was not an occasion of long duration; the French were anxious to get back to their vessels in what was a war zone, while Palmer and his subordinates had an English habit of discomfort in such a setting. By the time the bell tolled for the start of the morning watch Emily was alone once more but the squadron of frigates was not.

HMS *Semele* had been on course for Corsica and so, it turned out, was the French Fleet, which appeared on the horizon on what must have been a previously arranged rendezvous. The tow was passed from *Minerve* to another, smaller frigate, as were the crew of *Semele*, and soon they parted company with the enemy fleet bearing away to the north-east while the towed 74 held to a more northerly course.

It came as something of a surprise to find the fleet still anchored off Leghorn. Pearce had suspected he would only touch there to find out the course Hotham had taken to intercept the

French, top up his water and biscuit then head off in search. The sight of their pinnace approaching had men lining the deck of *Britannia*, and by the time Pearce had got aboard and made his way aft to the admiral's quarters the whole ship, thanks to Tucker and his mates, was abuzz with the news of the loss of HMS *Semele*.

In the end, John Pearce's report was made to Admiral Sir Hyde Parker, he having come back to the Med with six more sail of the line including HMS *Victory*, Hotham declining to meet with him and deputing the man now his second in command to hear the bad news. Parker was a big man, with a bit of a belly on him, full cheeks and a prominent nose. Like most naval officers his face showed the ravages of wind and weather, made more obvious by the snow-white of his wig.

He and Pearce had crossed swords before. He had been Captain of the Fleet under Hood, in effect the executive officer to Lord Hood's C-in-C. Parker saw this lieutenant as entirely unsuited to the service of which he was a part merely for the way he had acquired his rank. Pearce had compounded that in the past by his refusal to abide by the convention that lieutenants were expected to cringe in the company of an admiral and grovel when faced with a fleet commander.

'You will oblige me by stating the fact without embellishment.'

The tone of superiority grated, but Pearce let it pass. There was no cause to prick this man's pride so he related what he had seen, which in truth was not much.

'Well,' Parker growled, obviously less than satisfied. 'Would you say that Captain Barclay fought his ship well?'

The standard reply would have been to praise the man and

imply he had done everything in his power to avoid defeat. The thought of flattering Barclay was anathema but it was not that which made him avoid that which was expected of him, just a desire not to embellish the paucity of what he knew.

'I was in a pinnace, sir, which you will know is very close to the level of the sea. I saw that HMS *Semele* fought for a long time, over two hours by my watch, but as to how well she was handled I am in ignorance.'

'Where is she now?'

'How would I know, sir? I set my course for Leghorn as soon as she struck her colours.'

'You would not have considered it your duty to see where she was taken?'

The reply had a note of irascibility. 'There is only one place they can take her and that is Toulon.'

'Towed or under her own canvas? It makes a difference, and is something an officer could be expected to know.'

'Well I do not, and I have no intention of making up facts of which I have no knowledge.'

'On another subject, I am told you have contrived to sell a pair of French merchantmen and their cargoes without going through the Prize Court.'

'It was the right thing to do under the circumstances.'

'It was very much not the case, and I must tell you that should it prove true, both yourself and Lieutenant Digby will be brought before a court to account for your disreputable actions.'

'No doubt,' Pearce snapped, 'one set up by Admiral Hotham and staffed with officers of his own choosing.'

'Who else would do it?' Parker asked, too surprised by either the tone or the vehemence of the response to remind him of his place or his manners.

'Anyone would do, if we are to have justice. You may tell Hotham that I welcome a court martial and so will Henry Digby, for there we will air certain facts and have entered in the record matters that I doubt the admiral would wish to see the light of day, given they border on criminality.'

'You're mad,' Parker responded, very much taken aback.

'Then ask him, sir, about what orders were issued for HMS *Flirt* to proceed to the Gulf of Ambracia, there to confront a villain called Mehmet Pasha. I state that he hoped that one or both of us would not survive but we did and we took two valuable prizes. And when you relate to him what I have just said please tell him, too, that he will get his eighth as I promised. Neither Digby nor I would stoop to the notion of failing to satisfy his greed.'

'How dare you, sir.'

'I do dare and I challenge Admiral Hotham to bring on his court, where he might find that matters historical come back to haunt him too. And if he demurs, mention the name of Ralph Barclay who, even if he is a prisoner, has the power to cause trouble. Now, sir, I have made my report and unless you wish to detain me for the remarks I have just made I would be obliged to be dismissed.'

'You'll be dismissed from the service if I have my way, Pearce.'

'So be it, for my redress lies in the Inns of Court in London, not here in the Mediterranean.'

'Marines!' The shout brought two lobsters rushing in. 'Lock this man up, now.'

The pair made to grab Pearce but he fended them off by quick acquiescence and, small ditty bag in hand, he was escorted across the deck and down below to the barred cell in which those who had committed crimes were held. There was a small barrel provided on which to sit but very little space to move, and as he sat there he wondered if it had been wise to state so obviously his intention to make Hotham pay for his misdeeds. It never did to forewarn an enemy.

He was vaguely aware of the activity above his head; even bare feet make a sound if there are enough of them. He was wondering what it portended when the master at arms, who had locked the door behind him, appeared jangling his ring of keys. Selecting one he unlocked the door and stood aside.

'You're free to go.'

'On whose orders?'

'What odds does that make, sir?'

'It matters to me.'

'Mine came from the premier, who desires that you vacate the ship as we are in the process of weighing.'

Had the order come from a higher authority? It was good to speculate but there was no point in asking the ship's gaoler, he would not know. Picking up the ditty bag, which had very little of his actual possessions, just enough for the duty he had been engaged, he walked free and made for the entry port to seek a boat.

Normally he would have been required to plead but on this occasion one was provided with alacrity. He walked down the gangway to find the pinnace still in the water but with different men on board and no longer under sail. Looking around the anchorage he saw the whole fleet was preparing to depart and above his head HMS *Britannia*'s signal gun banged out. When he was far enough off he saw flags flying up and down with ships' numbers displayed and messages telling them to get a move on.

'Take me to HMS *Agamemnon*.'

'Orders were to put you ashore, Your Honour,' replied the leading hand.

'Which you can do once I have my dunnage, which is aboard Captain Nelson's ship. I can scarce do without it, can I?'

The man did not reply but he did murmur words to his fellow oarsmen as the pinnace changed direction to make for the side of *Agamemnon*. The gangway was gone and the entry port closed so Pearce was obliged to use the man ropes and clamber up the battens that lined the side. He was greeted by Dick Farmiloe wondering what he was about, as well as a deck full of men working to get the ship to sea.

'I need to get to the wardroom and get my things.'

'Then you best shift for we are about to pluck our anchor.'

Pearce dashed down the companionway two at a time, which meant men coming up had to shift to avoid him. He was calling to the wardroom stewards to lend a hand long before he got to the door. A surly bunch by nature, it required hassle to get help, he on one rope handle and one of the stewards on the other. By the time they came on deck Nelson had taken up his place on the quarterdeck.

A wave got a raised hat – clearly the captain had been told what was happening. Now he needed hands to loop his chest onto a line that could be dropped down to the pinnace. That provided he looked over the side to guide it down, only to see there was no boat waiting to receive it; the men from *Britannia* were gone and in an anchorage full of boats he was unsure which one was his. Added to which he wondered, even if he could identify it, whether a shout would have any effect.

Although far from being the complete naval officer, Pearce knew that this was not the moment to ask Nelson for a replacement. The yards were full of topmen loosing canvas, while from down below he could hear the stamp and go of the men on the capstan, as well as more faintly the cries as the soaking cable was hauled in to be looped round the bitts. She was being hauled over her anchor and the men ready to secure it were waiting.

The best he could do was stay out of everyone's way and wait till *Agamemnon* was under sail. It would be a big favour to ask that a boat take him back to Leghorn, and it would mean a hell of a haul for whoever undertook it to catch up with their ship out at sea, but ask he must.

'Mr Pearce, I am deeply reluctant to oblige you.'

Nelson troubled, with his height and build, looked more like a concerned schoolboy than a post-captain with decades of seniority, and the man to whom he was reacting could understand why. So, judging by the looks Pearce was getting, could Nelson's officers.

'I must wait in Leghorn for HMS *Flirt*, sir, in the hope that she will call in there.'

The conversation had to be abated; HMS *Agamemnon* was required to manoeuvre to take her place in the van squadron to the rear of HMS *Royal Sovereign*, commanded by Rear Admiral Samuel Goodall. He was on the poop of his first rate to see the act properly executed and by the time that was completed Nelson's attitude had changed.

'I have the solution, Mr Pearce. *Flirt* will surely first make for San Fiorenzo Bay, since it was from there you sailed. Even if she does touch at Leghorn her clear duty is to rejoin the fleet wherever we are, so I suggest that you would be best staying with us.'

'Sir, I am far from sure.'

'Mr Pearce, we are, it is to be hoped, sailing to fight the French, fleet against fleet. How can you even suggest a course of action that would cause you to miss such an event? No, you must stay aboard with us and come the contest we will find for you a role in which you can share in our glory.'

Even if Pearce had wanted to dispute that, there was little point. Leghorn was fast receding over *Agamemnon*'s stern.

CHAPTER TWENTY-FOUR

Having sent out every brig and sloop in the fleet, Hotham had a fair chance of finding the enemy. Early intelligence had hinted at an attempt to retake from the British the island of Corsica – Toulon still harboured enough anti-republicans willing to provide information on the military activities of their revolutionary enemies – but that quickly tended to be out of date. Only later was it established that the fleet weighed without the transports carrying the required troops.

For Rear Admiral Pierre Martin, the French commander, with the proposed Corsican invasion in abeyance, the cruise was not going to be one in which he sought his foes or a fleet action. Too many of the men he led were not sailors and thus were lacking in experience. This sortie provided a chance to work them up into crews that he hoped could be relied on in battle.

Extensive training had been carried out in Toulon but there was no substitute for actual sea time, where work aloft and exercising the guns was carried out on swaying masts or a rising and falling deck, not flat calm water. The pity was that with as much powder and shot as he could carry, to actually fire the guns posed a risk; the discharge of one cannon would be audible for miles around, a broadside would carry ten times further and Martin knew the enemy were scouring the sea for a hint of his presence.

Having parted from the captured *Semele*, Martin headed for the Île St Marguerite, off the town of Cannes, which provided a good anchorage and time to rearrange matters on what was a fighting body in a state of flux. Certain officers were removed, others promoted, while the crews were reorganised by watches and duties to encourage greater efficiency. Within sight of the mainland coast he felt relatively secure, only to discover his assumption was mistaken.

HMS *Moselle* had strayed further than their orders really allowed, not that the man in command would be chastised for such elasticity. The sight of the sloop, which immediately put up her helm and raced away with flags flying at the masthead, sent alarm bells ringing through the French fleet, for it implied that Hotham was not far over the horizon. Martin ordered that they weigh immediately for Toulon, but it was then that lack of experience told; it took an interminable time to get to sea and even longer to form up in any sort of order, the whole hampered by light winds that made movement difficult.

Common sense told the Frenchman his ships needed sea room in which to manoeuvre; to hug the coast was risky, given he might be driven into an unsuitable anchorage in which he could be trapped. It was therefore on a southerly course that the first sightings of his enemies were made, and quite naturally Martin signalled for a change of course. From their tops, if they could not really read the signal sent up on the mast of *Britannia*, it took no great deduction to guess what it said.

'Enemy in sight,' Nelson muttered with some satisfaction. 'General chase to the north-west.'

'A bit of wind would help,' John Pearce opined as the orders to comply were carried out.

'Then we must pray for one,' Nelson replied in a deeply serious tone of voice, replicated in his expression, which got a blank look from Pearce, he being a man not much given to supplication either human or divine. 'And it will serve, for I am convinced God hates a Frenchman as much as I do.'

The fact that a passenger was on the quarterdeck said something about *Agamemnon* as well as the man who commanded her. To more inflexible captains it would have been seen as slack; indeed almost everything that happened on the 64-gunner could be termed that by those who lacked the ability to see the efficiency with which tasks were carried out. The vessel came about on her new course with little in the way of bawled orders; the crew knew what they were about and what was required. They were going to their various stations before anyone even spoke.

While Pearce found himself at ease with Horatio Nelson, he did have a problem with the man's deep faith as well as his convictions, not least the one just expressed. The views he held on such matters had been formed from reading Rousseau and Voltaire, as well as the likes of the Scottish philosopher David Hume.

The Sage of Caledonia was a man much admired and spoken of fondly by John's father Adam, who had known the philosopher well. Hume held that if God did exist – and he was sceptical, if careful, in open expression of the notion that he might not exist at all – there was no reason to think him proficient.

Holy indifference was what could be attested to; for all the spouting of the religious as to there being a divinity, as well as the supposed omnipresence and omnipotence of same, John Pearce had observed that it was a deity utterly unconcerned by the fate of its followers. Those who fervently prayed were just as likely to be struck down as the agnostic and revolution or not, there would be men on the French warships praying to the same God, sure that he was predisposed to smite any Briton who crossed their path.

If there had been initial excitement, matters soon settled into the usual ennui of slow and sometimes no action at all. In such light airs, closing with the enemy was going to be difficult while to overhaul them completely prior to their reaching safety might be impossible. For all that, the chase must go on for, as Nelson kept reminding everyone, they were on the wing and who could tell what chance would provide. That was a way of putting the situation with which his agnostic passenger could agree.

The weather changed abruptly over the course of the night, with sudden squalls that kept the crew awake, for it required much work to hold both the course and speed, as well as their station on their consorts, while at the same time ensuring no damage. Sails had to be reefed and loosened in pitch-dark weather, often to avoid the strain on groaning masts and straining yards, while constant attention was required on the rigging to ensure nothing carried away.

In this the British fared better than the French. Dawn showed one of the enemy line of battle ships, identified as *Mercure* 74, had lost her main topmast and was in the process of parting company under a towing frigate. The temptation to chase one vessel was quite rightly set aside in favour of a possible fleet action.

Daylight also showed the gap had closed and there was now a freshening breeze: if Hotham commanded ships suffering from much wear and tear he also had men serving him, right down to the meanest waister, who knew their trade, and indeed it was the lack of that efficiency in the enemy that provided the change in circumstances for which everyone was hoping.

Ça Ira 80, in a general change of course for the entire French fleet, collided with the same-sized vessel ahead of her in the rear squadron. *Victoire* sailed on seemingly unscathed but *Ça Ira* suffered much more, severely damaging her main and fore topmasts. This caused her to fall off her course and lose speed.

Captain Thomas Fremantle, in command of the 38-gun frigate HMS *Inconstant*, closer to the enemy than any of Hotham's capital ships, closed immediately and took station on the *Ça Ira*'s quarter to pour several broadsides into her, an act eagerly applauded on the quarterdeck of *Agamemnon*.

The favourable situation for Fremantle soon deteriorated as the French frigate *Vestale* ranged alongside to pour fire into an enemy fully engaged seeking to disable the line of battle ship. Fremantle broke off the action temporarily and that allowed *Vestale* to get a cable to *Ça Ira* in order to take her in tow. With his opposition frigate occupied in that task, Fremantle tacked to cross the stern of the French 80-gunner and poured a deadly broadside through her deadlights.

Inconstant suffered for that. The crew of the *Ça Ira* had cleared the wreckage of those fallen topmasts and could now man their cannon. With her greater firepower and at near to point-blank range the French shot swept across the deck of the British frigate, carrying much away in the case of rigging and surely spilling a great deal of blood.

More telling was the shot that hit between the waterline and the hammock nettings to smash the scantlings at a point low enough to bring a risk of foundering, damage so severe that *Inconstant* was obliged to swiftly bear away, using the wind to raise the wounded hull clear of the water.

John Pearce observed all this with increasing clarity, a fact that applied to everyone aboard *Agamemnon*, for she was coming up on the Frenchmen hand over fist, the air of anticipation along the decks almost physical in its intensity. Lighter in terms of weight of shot, the rate of fire from the well-worked-up crew made up for any shortfall in metal and *Agamemnon* poured salvo after salvo into the much larger vessel.

A passenger he might be but Pearce was not one to remain idle. He was perfectly willing to carry any orders Nelson gave to whichever part of the ship they required to be directed, mostly to divisional lieutenants to tell them to adjust their aim and concentrate on some particular part of the target vessel. Having never been in a ship of the line in battle, the noise, smoke and seeming general turmoil confused him; it took time to see that for all the seeming chaos Nelson's men were working as a complete and orderly unit.

Having been below decks he missed the arrival of HMS *Captain* 74, come to assist *Agamemnon* in disabling the *Ça Ira*. But the rear elements of Admiral Martin's fleet had worn to come to the aid of their struggling comrades and wisdom dictated that discretion be the better part of valour. Nelson was a warrior but he was not a fool and soon he and *Captain* were dropping back to rejoin the main British line, leaving a pair of their fellow 74s to exchange desultory fire with the enemy rear at long distance.

'Yonder, Mr Pearce!' Nelson cried, pointing to a towering first rate closing in on *Ça Ira*, 'there is their behemoth *Sans Culotte*. Triple-decked, one hundred and twenty guns and a crew of over a thousand men as well as a commanding admiral's flag. What a prize she would be.'

'Might I suggest it would be one to share, sir? If she carries twice the guns and of a larger calibre . . . ?'

'Indeed, but I cannot deny I am tempted. It would be a sarcophagus in Westminster Abbey for the fellow who gave his life to capture her.'

'Is any capture worth a life?'

'What is life, Mr Pearce, compared to immortality?'

Nelson's eyes were shining as he said those words, while the man on the receiving end was stunned to realise he meant every word. It was something he raised that night with Dick Farmiloe.

'He does mean it, John. You will have seen him these last few days as he rarely is. I have never known a man so given to maladies as Nelson, yet the merest hint of action and all his ills fall away. His doctor talks of animal spirits but I believe he has a real wish to be a hero. That is what so drives him and it provides a cure.'

That thought was in Pearce's mind the following morning as the dawn revealed that the towing vessel had been changed to the 74-gun *Censeur*. But it also exposed the fact that there was no sign of the mighty *Sans Culotte*. Clearly it had become detached from the rest of the fleet during the hours of darkness, while *Ça Ira* and her consort, naturally sailing more slowly, were becoming isolated from their comrades by a margin that made them very vulnerable.

'So they are without a commanding admiral now?' Pearce said in a half question, referring to the fact that *Sans Culotte* had not reappeared.

Nelson shook his head. 'Perhaps not. The madmen in Paris passed a law that commanded any admiral in a battle to move his flag to a frigate, I presume so they could avoid capture. I think if you were to go aloft with a glass you would observe that Admiral Martin's flag is flying in one of his smaller vessels.'

'I'll settle for the notion without the proof.'

'Flagship signalling,' came the cry from aloft.

Hotham's fleet had the weather gage and he obviously discerned there was an advantage to be gained. Flags flew on *Britannia* ordering forward *Captain* as well as *Bedford*, another 74, to close and engage. That made Nelson glum and he sent his own signal in an attempt to join with them, his request denied. So he became a frustrated spectator to a hard-pounding artillery duel as the two Frenchmen battled it out.

Even Pearce could see that Hotham had the right of it; to put a third vessel into a fight of the nature of that which they were watching risked the British ships firing on each other and the men on *Ça Ira* and her consort were giving a good account of themselves. Hotham finally called off that pair and replaced them with another pair of 74s.

The damage to the French ships was terrible; they were becoming close to defenceless, but it seemed relief was on the way as Martin sent forward another 74, *Duquesne*, to back up their efforts and to confront the two British 74s, *Illustrious* and *Courageux*.

The wind, brisk at dawn, had now fallen away to almost

nothing, hampering all three vessels in their attempt at manoeuvre. This left the frigate *Lowestoffe*, near to being becalmed and unable to get clear, at the mercy of the slowly approaching *Duquesne*. Those watching as the 32-gunner was mauled feared for much loss of life but the man in command, Benjamin Hallowell had confounded French hopes for a massacre by sending every man aboard below. Then the Neapolitan *Minerva*, coming between *Duquesne* and *Lowestoffe* became the object of the sustained enemy fire.

Victoire and *Tonnant* eventually managed to join *Duquesne* and exchange gunnery with the British vessels, which brought ragged cheer from the decks of *Ça Ira* and *Censeur*. That died as it became plain their comrades were not coming to their rescue but were instead intent on making their escape by getting to windward of the enemy.

The order came to the rest of the French fleet, presumably from Admiral Martin, to set a course northward for Toulon. At that very moment the crippled French vessels that had fought so hard to avoid defeat struck their tricolour flags.

Nelson was already giving orders that would bring on a renewed chase when the flags at *Britannia*'s masthead killed off the notion. To say that he was stunned by this was an understatement; Nelson actually wondered out loud what Hotham was thinking of, for to him it was a case of 'there is the enemy, and our task is to close and destroy them.'

'Mr Farmiloe, my barge.'

If anyone wondered why Nelson wanted his barge at this stage they did not raise the question; it was off the ship and in the water, it being a dangerous article to have on board in battle. If feet-thick scantlings could be reduced to deadly splinters, how much more lethal would be a flimsy ship's boat?

As nimble as one of his own topmen, the captain of *Agamemnon* was in his boat and being rowed with some speed towards the flagship and he was not alone. Rear Admiral Samuel Goodall was also, it was reported, on the way to see Hotham, and Pearce was left in no doubt what the question would be, this from the rest of the *Agamemnon*'s officers.

'Why are we not pursuing the enemy?' Nelson reported on his return, accurate as it transpired, which left everyone waiting for Hotham's reply. 'He feels our van squadron has suffered too much, *Illustrious* particularly, to which Sam Goodall nearly had an apoplexy. And then, would you credit it, Hotham actually said that having taken two enemy vessels we have done very well.'

There was no doubting what Nelson thought of that statement; disgust was too mild a word for the expression on his face and the mood did not improve when Hotham ordered the fleet to head for La Spezia Bay, the badly damaged *Illustrious* being towed, which meant he had no intention of even following the French the next day.

It was almost in the nature of damnation when *Illustrious* suffered her fate; bad weather returned overnight and that had allowed water through her smashed gun ports. Her captain was obliged to change course to save the ship, only to be driven on to the shore by the increasingly foul weather. In the end the crew and stores were brought off but the ship could not be saved and the hull had to be burnt.

'A meagre return, Mr Pearce,' was Nelson's mordant comment. 'Two Frenchmen taken and two of our own lost. It is not a tale that will read as valorous in the *Gazette*.'

Pearce was no longer thinking of fleet actions and possible burial in Westminster Abbey. He was concentrating more on getting back to Naples to both see Emily and to collect his Pelicans for a return to their ship.

Michael, Charlie and Rufus were in the Adriatic, the Chevalier having arranged their journey to Brindisi by the rapid Royal Mail coach, where they found Henry Digby much recovered and near fit to resume his duties. Naturally Michael O'Hagan was required to relate to him what had happened in Naples, which if it got much shaking of the head engendered little else.

For Digby his listening was not an invitation to a discussion or a revelation of his opinion on the matter, especially given he heartily disapproved of the liaison. Then there was the man telling the tale; O'Hagan might be held in high regard by John Pearce but to Digby he was lower deck and not of a standing enough to be engaged in speculation with his commanding officer. O'Hagan was thanked and told to return to his duties.

Edward Grey was a different kettle of fish; even if he was a lobster he was an officer and the so-called abduction of Captain Barclay's wife was much ruminated upon. Could it be called that when it was a husband reclaiming his spouse? Grey had assumed much in the way of work while Pearce was absent.

With Digby still in convalescence, he had negotiated with the British traders, selling their two French merchantmen and their cargoes, albeit every move was reported to his superior. The bulk of the French crews had elected to take employment locally while sale of both hulls and cargo had been carried out without haste. Because of that they had secured for the crew of

HMS *Flirt* a sum of money greater than had been anticipated.

Given the men had been told by John Pearce there would be an immediate distribution of money, Digby risked near mutiny when he insisted he needed permission from the C-in-C to comply with that promise. In his sickbed he had much time to reflect and had worked out that he would need to temper the promises he made to Pearce in the immediate aftermath of the fight in which he had been wounded. He had started out with a career: given their success he might have a much enhanced one now.

So it was with a disgruntled crew that he came back aboard and weighed, his first task to return to rejoin the fleet. Digby was glad that Emily Barclay was no longer in Naples. Regardless of how that had been brought about, he had no need to call there.

The lady in question had been able to enjoy the cabin on *Semele* until the captured 74 finally entered Toulon Roads to much cheering and celebratory cannon fire, having taken shelter in the Rade de Gourjean on the way as an insurance against falling in with the British Fleet. For the same reason Admiral Martin had fallen back on the anchorage around Hyères Islands, which also prevented him from being blockaded in Toulon.

The courtesy that had been given to her up till that point did not abate; she was the recent widow of a fellow sailor, albeit an enemy. The French navy having suffered less from the Terror than other branches, there were still officers in the service whose code demanded she be treated as an honoured guest.

Emily was given rooms in the Admiralty building, while arrangements were made to ship *Semele*'s officers to an inland fortress prison. The wounded were treated at the hospital in a fashion in no way inferior to that which they would have received in Haslar, a couple expiring but most surviving to join the rest of the men.

They were to be put to work repairing some of the damage done to the port when Lord Hood abandoned the place amid much deliberate destruction. It was seen as entirely proper that the late captain's wife should take not only an interest in their welfare but argue for better conditions and treatment.

The saddest part of that, every time she visited them, was an inability to answer the recurring question posed. Every one of the crew wanted to know how long they would be in captivity.

CHAPTER TWENTY-FIVE

Even if he was low in rank compared to the men he observed, John Pearce could sense that the attitude of those who called upon Sir William Hotham had altered. His opposite number, safely anchored in a hard-to-assault anchorage, would be claiming, if not a victory, certainly a stand-off.

In addition, the mood of the fleet was a topic of much discussion in the wardroom of *Agamemnon* and it was generally held to be a depressed one, especially when the captured French officers spoke of the naval base of Toulon being close to open revolt prior to their sailing, the troops designated for Corsica held back to keep order. How could they not have beaten such an enemy?

Lord Hood was often mentioned, the implication being that as a more active sea officer, Sam Hood would have made a better fist of what was being called The Naval Battle of Genoa. Hotham's star had waned and Dick Farmiloe was sure that certain client officers of his were now wondering if they had hitched their cart to the wrong horse.

Those who did not see him as their patron were even less likely to praise him and that would mean letters flying back home. These would question the leadership of the fleet from those known to be less well in favour of his appointment as C-in-C. It was tempting to seek to penetrate the bulkheads that cut Hotham off and wonder if he noticed the changed atmosphere.

In truth, Pearce, as he waited day after day to see the admiral, cared only in how that affected him. He needed to travel to Naples, a destination he was sure would be denied but he could claim he needed to get back to HMS *Flirt* in order to ensure that her commander had recovered. He could also make sure the disposal of hulls and cargo, even if it was officially frowned upon, was being properly attended to.

The difficulty was in making such a claim; Hotham would not see him and Toomey, whom he managed to beard more easily, given he was exposed in his exterior office, refused to either discuss the matter or pass the request on to the admiral. This left the supplicant at a stand, for as of this moment, having run out of money, he lacked the means to make the journey privately.

His troubles were compounded when Hotham moved back to San Fiorenzo Bay; he had even less chance of a private journey from such a remote location, now more crowded than ever since Hotham had received even more reinforcements under Rear Admiral Linzee, led by the 98-gun *Windsor Castle*.

When, after several frustrating weeks, Nelson was sent cruising, Pearce felt it best to go with him and *Agamemnon* headed out to the north seeking any indication of an enemy presence. Given the state of affairs in Toulon, added to the fact that two of Martin's 74's as well as the captured *Semele* were in the base for repairs, it seemed unlikely that they would encounter any French ships.

Thus it came as a real surprise when the topsails of not one warship, but a fleet of seventeen of the line, were sighted on a southerly course. Martin had come out with his whole complement of battle-ready ships and was heading for San Fiorenzo Bay, no doubt in the hope of effecting a surprise on an inferior fleet. Nelson was of the opinion that the French were in ignorance of the recent arrivals from home.

'So our task,' he informed the quarterdeck, as HMS *Agamemnon* swung smoothly round to head south, 'is to lead them into a den, which they will find full of lions.'

Nelson might command the smallest line of battle ship in the fleet but she was, by some measure, the swiftest. Thus it required guile to appear as if she was in flight while never showing her true rate of sailing. There was no doubt Martin had taken the bait; his ships were crowding on sail and there was no attempt at restraining the lead vessels desperate to close.

Agamemnon had several lookouts aloft, one of whom had the task of seeking the first hint of the clouds that ringed the Corsican mountains. When the call came to say they were in sight, Nelson had the main deck cannon manned and fired, not at the enemy and with no round shot either, for they were out of range, but merely to alert Hotham to what he would as yet be unable to see.

As a standing order, and it had been that under Hood, the Mediterranean Fleet anchored on single cables and kept normal watches, while every captain was obliged to either be aboard – not hard since there were few temptations on the island – or so close to his command that he could weigh at speed, and the fleet did so now.

By the time *Agamemnon* was hull up the largest of the warships were already leaving San Fiorenzo Bay, led by *Victory*, her copper bottom newly scraped clean in the Portsmouth dockyard, which stood in stark comparison to the fouled hulls of the vessels who had been in the warm waters of the Med for two years. The 100-gunner had the capability to close with the enemy most quickly and at the sight of her emerging, Nelson put up his helm to take part in what he hoped would be an oncoming battle.

Martin did not react immediately, but as *Victory* was followed out of the bay by six three-decker line of battle ships, he must have realised he risked being outgunned. Even more of a surprise would be the number of 74s in their wake, which had him outnumbered by seventeen to twenty-two capital ships. In short order, Martin ordered his fleet to wear and flee.

'The wind will dictate his course,' Nelson insisted, 'and from where it is blowing precludes Toulon as a destination.'

Such a factor was of much interest to John Pearce. He had found aboard Nelson's ship lessons to be learnt and ones not previously gifted to him in the smaller vessels on which he had generally sailed. He observed keenly the way the hierarchy of command worked with a crew made up of greater numbers than those of which had personally had charge, while the quality of the captain was a revelation.

Nelson could talk to his men in a manner few of his rank could replicate. He could appear to be as one with them without the least hint of condescension, able to share a joke and even to endure some very mild ribbing. No man aboard was in ignorance of either their duty or their captain's aim and what was remarkable was the way they wholeheartedly responded. In short, HMS *Agamemnon* was a happy ship as well as an effective one.

At least it was until Nelson requested permission to act independently. He desired to outstrip the rearmost Frenchmen and possibly by his action bring the whole entity to battle. The request was denied: Hotham declined to release his greyhound to snare a running French hare. *Agamemnon* was to be tied to the pace of *Victory*.

A chase that had begun in the morning looked set to last all day. With a decent breeze both fleets were eating up the sea miles, covering the short distance between Corsica and the southern French shore at a lick. Having consulted his charts, Nelson's master was of the opinion that Gourjean was Martin's destination, for that would avoid the need for an alteration of course and subsequent loss of speed.

'And if we can drive him from that?'

'The next anchorage along the coast is at Fréjus, sir. Deep inshore water and an arc of bay that he can use to form a line. That would be hard to break.'

'But break it we must and will,' Nelson replied, 'that is if we cannot prevent the swine from getting there in the first place.'

He had only just come back on the deck having been in his cabin writing letters, something of which he was a ferocious proponent. In this Nelson was far from singular; all naval officers corresponded at length with home, family, fellow naval comrades and, without fail, politicians, often a local Member of Parliament. This was how they promulgated their views, praised some of their fellows and damned others in what was a very competitive environment.

Public displays of mutual regard often hid deeply conflicting views; admirals lobbied, lied and grovelled to get lucrative commands while the captains beneath them either sought to elevate themselves or diminish others, depending on their personal relationships, and purely for their own advantage.

Pearce had no doubt at all that Nelson had just dashed off letters to several folk, couched in appropriate language, questioning the abilities of the admiral who had just refused him permission to make use of the superior speed of his ship, which in essence questioned his ability as a commander. Never mind they would not be read immediately: they were a quotidian account and had value because of that.

HMS *Victory* was now in company, as was *Culloden*, captained by the irascible Thomas Troubridge. But night was falling and under a cloudy sky it was possible the enemy could escape, which to the way of thinking aboard *Agamemnon* compounded Hotham's obvious error, this driven home when dawn showed no sign of the enemy.

They had changed course, but before the decks had been swabbed the sloop HMS *Flèche* appeared on the horizon. In a seemingly never-ending set of signals, close to one letter at a time, they informed Admiral Mann aboard *Victory* that the enemy was just over the horizon. They had sighted Martin south of the Hyères Islands and by crowding on sail they found the enemy now on a due-west heading, for what the master had reckoned to be their intended destination.

Close inshore there was a lack of wind and that allowed *Victory*, *Culloden* and *Agamemnon* to close with *Alcide*, the rearmost French 74 and to give her a severe drubbing. Martin had no choice but to seek to save his consort and his rear swung round to engage. The trio of British warships now found themselves trading gunfire with superior enemy forces and that would continue until the rest of the fleet caught up.

'Hard-pounding.'

That was Nelson's comment on an artillery duel in which the larger ships took most of the brunt, with *Agamemnon* doing her best to draw off the opposition by use of her ability to manoeuvre even in light airs. *Culloden* suffered greatly in her rigging while *Victory* was near to being dismasted, so ferocious was the enemy fire. But throughout the fight *Alcide* was suffering the most, and bearing down on the enemy fleet was the van squadron of the British fleet, headed by Sam Goodall in HMS *Princess Royal*.

When *Alcide* struck her tricolour, Admiral Martin decided the risk of continuing to fight was too great and he signalled a withdrawal. Two brave French frigate captains sought to take *Alcide* in tow, only to be severely mauled for their efforts by the lower-deck 32-pounders of HMS *Victory*.

Admiral Goodall sailed past the vessels so recently engaged with his hat raised in salute. To his rear Pearce could see the rest of the fleet, *Britannia* to the fore, bearing down on an enemy once more in total flight. By the time they got abreast of *Alcide* a blaze had broken out and was consuming the forepeak. *Agamemnon* was too close for comfort when the fire reached the powder room and the ship exploded, sending bits of wood both into the air and sideways.

As was common, the fighting ships had their boats in the water. They were immediately sent to rescue the crew of the rapidly sinking French warship. The fight would continue under Goodall and if he could hold Martin up with the rest of the fleet closing, it looked as though a stunning victory might be on the cards.

The French admiral was not about to hang about and risk destruction; he was now making for Fréjus Bay where, if he could form a line with the shore at his back, he would present a formidable obstacle. Anchored, the firing platform would be steady and by central control the target could be directed in a more destructive way by the combined concentration of shot on single targets.

'Flag signalling, sir,' called the midshipman who held the book. 'General order to all ships. Cease firing and rejoin flag.'

'He's mad,' Nelson exploded. 'We have them by the throat.'

'More flags, sir, a repeat of the same order.'

In essence it had little effect on *Agamemnon*. The 64-gunner had done her job and so had *Victory* and *Culloden*, now occupied in carrying out repairs, this while their boats picked up survivors from the now sunken *Alcide*. It was later reported that Sam Goodall, in frustration, had kicked his hat all over the quarterdeck of *Princess Royal* when the order was relayed to him.

Hotham had to be obeyed; he was in command and that left no option that did not include a court martial. As ordered, the fleet retreated to San Fiorenzo where it quickly became common gossip that Hotham was claiming once more he had done well. Few agreed and now what had been a slight air of depressed wonder turned into open condemnation of a man seen as too weak for the task he had been given.

Pearce was again at his door seeking and being refused entry, and that lasted until the arrival of HMS *Flirt*, at which point he felt his whole life to be changed.

* * *

As Michael O'Hagan described it nothing could have been done – he was one against too many – so the best he could have hoped for was that, beaten to a pulp, he would be taken aboard the 74 along with Emily. Given he had manhandled Barclay, his fate then would have been certain: the bastard would have probably strung him up but not before he had severely lacerated his back with the cat.

'Still, John-boy, it is for sure I feel ashamed of myself.'

'Not as much as I do.'

Pearce found it hard to contain his fury, not so much at his friend as at his own impotence. He had not acted quickly enough in the matter of getting back to Naples and Emily had paid the price. Even worse, he had sat watching *Semele* fight and be taken – when he now knew she must have been aboard – and had done nothing to prevent it.

Had he voiced such thoughts Pearce would have been told the truth: he too would be a captive if he had sought to effect the outcome, and really the question was obvious. What was he going to do now? His first thought had been that the French would not keep captive a woman, until he realised that as the wife of the captain, Emily would be seen as part and parcel of the whole. She had been a prisoner before when HMS *Brilliant* had been captured and taken into Toulon.

'It is a sobering thought, Henry, that the man I despise has lost two battles and forfeited two ships in a very short time.'

Digby did not reply immediately, given he was really seeking to hide his anathema to the whole idea of the illicit liaison. Nor had he looked forward to seeing Pearce alone in his cabin, which was why he had not greeted him when he came aboard, happy to let him hear the bad news from his Irishman.

'Given the navy often seem to value gallantry as much as success, John, he could be praised for his latest loss. Even you had to report that *Semele* fought long and hard. And remember Barclay commanded her at the Glorious First under Howe, so his reputation must stand pretty high.'

'Of a man who violently abducts a woman.'

'She is his wife!'

Pearce had to clam up then; Digby, quite apart from his obvious prejudices, knew nothing of the offer Emily had made to return to the marital fold on certain conditions. Best he change the subject and in thinking on that he hit on an idea, not that he was open with Henry Digby.

'We must discuss how we are going to make Hotham sweat.'

'Ah!' That stalling expression got Digby a keen look, one that insisted he elaborate. 'I had a great deal of time to think in my convalescence, John.'

'And?'

'For all my anger I cannot see how to make the admiral admit that he took part in a conspiracy deliberately designed to bring about harm.'

'Toomey was as much a part of things as Hotham and he is shocked that we have returned successful, much as he tried to bluff it out. I'm sure I scared the creature enough to make him wonder for his future.'

'That, if I may say so, is a very tenuous basis on which to proceed, besides which, you have not even alluded to how you might accomplish anything.'

'My notion was to force a court martial in which the matter would have to be aired.'

Digby frowned. 'For you or for me?'

'I admit you would be better than I, given my reputation does not stand very high. But if it has to be me, well, let us do it. If we both make the same accusation, one as a defendant, the other as a witness—'

The hand held up to stop his talking achieved its purpose, but it was the palpable look of doubt on Digby's face that really struck Pearce most.

'We are together in this, Henry.'

'Ah!'

'That is the second time you have used that expression, though I fear this time it does not lack much in the way of clarity.'

'Hotham is the C-in-C, John, akin to God in this part of the world.'

'Devil more like, a devious sod who hoped we would all be killed.'

'You cannot know that with absolute certainty.'

'I admit my demise would have served, so you will forgive me if I look upon matters with a little more cynicism than you seem to now display. You saw the orders we were given and you were as party to the verbal lies as I was.'

'Which will be denied.'

'Meaning?'

Digby shifted uncomfortably and the lack of eye contact was telling. 'I cannot go against the service, John.'

'And that is the result of lying in a bed and thinking for near a month?'

'It is the result of a long and hard look at the problem, which I see as intractable. I do wish to assure you that I will hold to my promise of financial aid, so you may pursue the case upon which you are so set, but on the other matter I must remain aloof.'

Pearce's response was sour, both in the words and the taste it produced in his mouth. 'And what will you say if you are called as a witness in that?'

'You must understand, John, I cannot actually take part in any action you bring against a fellow officer, post-captain or vice admiral, and that extends to giving you possession of the written orders I received.'

'It would risk your career?'

If Digby was stung, and he should have been, he hid it well, coming out with a strong rebuttal. 'I have to tell you that is as important to me as your causes are to you.'

'Which is why you declined to keep a promise I made regarding the distribution of prize money?'

'It seemed politic to let the C-in-C oversee that if he thought it wise, so I passed over the draft given to me by the Brindisi traders, to be drawn on a Genoese banking house.'

'And will he?' Pearce asked, adding, 'I do have a personal interest in this.'

'He did not favour me with an opinion.'

'And you did not demand one?'

'No.'

'How many solemn undertakings broken does that add up to? I know you are given to nightly prayers, Henry. I hope this evening you can do so without examining and finding wanting your conscience.'

'I will not have you speak to me in that fashion. Please recall I am your superior officer.'

Pearce stood up; even being bent near double under the low deck beams did nothing to dent his venom.

'I shall speak to you in any fashion I wish, even in public, and invite you to court martial me. If I know one thing about you, Henry, it is that you will not tell a lie having sworn on the Bible, for you fear God more than you fear the likes of Hotham. And do not doubt that the questions you will be asked will force from you that which you should be providing voluntarily. Now, if you will forgive me I have to go and see the man you cannot stand to bring to justice.'

'I have not given you permission to leave the ship.'

'What would you have me do, stay and breathe in the stench of hypocrisy? Say your prayers and ask God for forgiveness, just don't ever ask me for the same.'

CHAPTER TWENTY-SIX

Pearce was fuming as he boated across to HMS *Britannia*. If Digby would not even pass over the orders he had been given regarding Mehmet Pasha he had little with which to proceed. The lack of the written evidence was as much a dent to his hopes as the man's reneging on their agreement to bring Hotham down.

The notion of continuing to serve on HMS *Flirt* was impossible; he knew he had a temper uncontrollable enough to strike Digby and he had been close to that in his cabin. Do that and he would get a court martial all right, it would just be one in which he would be unable to make a case that would expose any wrongdoing.

The time the crossing took allowed him to calm down somewhat and then to examine his recent actions, not least the harsh words he had employed. On reflection he was unsure that had been wise for he had probably turned someone possibly biddable into an outright antagonist. Digby would avoid trouble by refusing to appear if there was a court martial, and the only one who could force him to do so had every reason to avoid his presence.

He was outside Hotham's cabin once more, still being denied entry, as a steady stream of senior officers came and went, which gave him time to examine what it was he needed to do next and that naturally centred on Emily Barclay. It was little comfort to think that she would now be incarcerated with her husband and that quite possibly they were now reconciled.

Could he do the same as Ralph Barclay and abduct her, or at least persuade her that her future lay with him so she would leave voluntarily? There were two ways of looking at what he could only presume to be her present circumstances and his hopes might be the complete opposite of what she was feeling.

Would exposure to the habits of Ralph Barclay horrify her as much as they had done in the past? He could not believe the man would change his ways and nothing proved that more than the way he had kidnapped her. Not that such imaginings produced a solution as to what he was going to do about it. She was in Toulon, he was on the deck of Hotham's flagship and if the great cabin door opened and shut, and it did frequently, it was not to admit him.

'Mr Pearce,' Nelson had exited the cabin, the door promptly shut once he was through. 'Am I to assume that you are waiting to see Admiral Hotham?'

'I'm very much at the back of the queue, sir.'

Nelson dropped his voice. 'Take it as a blessing, for the atmosphere within is far from rosy. I have just had to deny a request from our commander to make certain changes to my log.'

'To what purpose?'

Nelson indicated they were too close for comfort and that they should walk away.

'Sir William feels that I have not given enough appreciation to the damage sustained by both *Victory* and *Culloden* in the recent action.'

'Or lack of action, if I recall your mood on the day, sir.'

'Aye, I felt it wanting and was unwise enough to let that be overheard by my officers and no doubt half the crew.' Nelson looked slightly downcast as he continued. 'Shows a want of proper behaviour.'

'I am inclined to believe you voiced a common view. Even I reckoned the order not to pursue to be mistaken.'

A sharp jerk of the head indicated the place from which he had just emerged.

'I had to be circumspect in there, but how I was tempted to back up Admiral Goodall.'

Now it was Pearce's turn to glance at the same doorway before giving Nelson a look riddled with curiosity. The voice dropped even more, obliging Pearce to lean forward and bend his head to hear.

'Got quite heated between them, I am given to understand.' That could only have come from Sam Goodall; Hotham would never have told Nelson of anything that had occurred with another flag officer. 'Damn near told our C-in-C he was not fit to command the fleet.'

'And your opinion, sir?'

'Counts for little, but it is a rum do when Sir William feels the need to seek that my logs back up his version of events. And in that I suspect I am not alone.'

'It does sound fairly desperate.'

'I think you know I do not stand very high in his favour.'

'Which to my mind shows a lack of sound judgement.'

Nelson took the compliment without a blush; Pearce reckoned it was because he thought it the plain truth. He was a man sure of his abilities and equally convinced that destiny held in store for him something remarkable.

'He invited his flag officers to dine, Pearce, and they all declined– Hyde Parker, Linzee, Goodall and Mann. What does that tell you?'

'They have lost confidence in him, perhaps.'

'There can be no other explanation and they will have penned that opinion to be sent back to London, of which Sir William must be aware. Even those captains he reckons his supporters are seeking to distance themselves from him now.'

He's finished, thought Pearce, which was what Nelson was telling him, not plainly, but in so many words and that took him back immediately to his own concerns. Hotham diminished might be easier to deal with than the same man flushed with fighting success.

'Remarkable thing is, he does not seem to be able to see where he failed.' Nelson sighed, as if he had some sympathy for Hotham, and perhaps he did for he was not of a malicious nature. 'Either that or he is capable of deep artifice.'

Pearce replied in a mordant tone, 'That I can attest to.'

Given he added no more, Nelson was left to wonder, but not for long. 'Well, I must be off, but I did not enquire of you. What is it you seek from Sir William?'

'To talk to him, no more.'

'Well, when you do—'

'*If* I do, sir. He has shown a remarkable reluctance to indulge me.'

'I was about to say you may find him somewhat diminished.'

Pearce raised his hat as Nelson made his farewells but those last words left him thinking. From the gist of what he had just heard Hotham's tenure of command could not last. If his inferior admirals told London they had lost faith in him he would be replaced and no amount of political pressure from his patron, the Duke of Portland, would be able to gainsay that.

To Pearce it was nothing more than just deserts and that had nothing to do with his own relations with the man. He had been gifted two opportunities to destroy the French Mediterranean Fleet, or at least inflict serious damage, and it mattered not that he had failed, it mattered he had not tried and that would be what his peers held in contempt.

The people of Britain had an almost biblical faith in their navy and none were more convinced of its merits than those who served within its vessels. They had a tradition of victory going back to the Armada and if they had lost the odd battle they had never lost a war. Mention the American colonies and they would point the finger at redcoats, not themselves for they had trounced the French allies of the insurgent Americans at the Battle of the Saintes.

Because of that, the officers of the service lived in fear of disgrace and the fate of Admiral Byng loomed large, Pearce suspected, in their imaginings. He had been shot by firing squad on his own flagship's quarterdeck a year after his perceived failure off Minorca in the year '56.

That must serve as a stark warning to the ambitious men who now commanded the nation's fleets and sought glory. All would have been serving in a junior capacity, as lieutenants and newly promoted captains possibly, when Byng was executed. The question suddenly exercising John Pearce was obvious: did Hotham have cause to fear a similar fate now?

His mind in something of a ferment he made his way to the wardroom and requested paper, ink and a quill, writing quickly and then sealing that which he had composed before making his way back to Hotham's doorway, where without ceremony he barged in on Toomey. The clerk was about to protest when Pearce spoke to shut him up.

'Feeling secure, Toomey, are you? Can't be comfortable serving a fellow whose tenure of command is hanging by a thread?' Toomey waved a dismissive hand, but Pearce was not to be put off. 'How long do you give him, six weeks? Time for the reports to get back to Whitehall and be acted upon. Then he will be out of a job and so, my friend, will you.'

'Have you been drinking?'

'No, but you might want to take a glass to steady your nerves. I have just come from HMS *Flirt*, where Lieutenant Digby and I have been exchanging notes. While I was there we examined the orders given to us prior to our voyage to confront Mehmet Pasha.'

'If you wish to question those you must ask the man who wrote them out.'

'Digby will say at the court martial they bear no relation to what he was told verbally.'

'What court martial?' Toomey hooted. 'For that, Admiral Hotham would have to agree to let one sit.'

'And no doubt he would choose the men to pass judgement.'

'He would appoint competent officers, certainly.'

'Who would not be the same officers chosen by the man who will succeed him.'

That struck a chord. Pearce was working on the assumption that Toomey was no fool. If anyone knew the mood of the fleet it would be he, and that would also tell him how tenuous his master's hold on this command might be. The clerk would be loyal, that was to be expected, but right of this moment he would be a dunce not to be examining the possibility of shifting his seat to another berth, which, if not simple, was possible given the depth of his experience.

The point Pearce was making did not have to be elaborated upon; any C-in-C succeeding Hotham would have no wish to defend his reputation, quite the reverse in fact. It would be in the man's interest to make his predecessor look incompetent and that would be true even if there was no personal animus involved.

'I have here in my hand a letter to Mr Lucknor, my lawyer.'

'The name is unknown to me,' Toomey protested, with a lack of conviction that encouraged John Pearce; the man was getting uncomfortable.

'Odd, given he will have in his files a communication from you, which I suspect might be in a hand identifiable as your own, supposedly from Toby Burns.'

'Stuff and nonsense.'

'I wonder what Toby Burns will say at this court martial. Digby shall certainly ensure he is called to explain a series of matters in order to clarify how far Admiral Hotham is prepared to go in certain areas. Indeed, he may be shown the letter he is purported to have written, to then be asked if he recognises it.'

There was so much supposition and bluff in what Pearce was accusing Toomey of to make him nervous. He had no proof that what he had just implied was true and now he was about to wander into the realms of pure fantasy but, looking at Toomey, he could see the sweat slipping out from underneath his clerk's wig, so felt encouraged.

'Such evidence, combined with what I shall say about the mission to the Gulf of Ambracia, especially regarding your part in the inventions by which I was seduced into participating, will make interesting listening to a board of enquiry staffed by officers with no need to protect certain reputations. Or, I might add, certain accomplices.'

Pearce waved the letter. 'You may wonder what this says.'

'Why would I?'

'You sound a trifle short of breath, Mr Toomey. Perhaps a glass of wine will settle you. No? Then let me tell you what I have said to Mr Lucknor. I require that he hand over to anyone sent by Sir William Hotham the fair copy of Captain Barclay's court martial. I have also agreed with Mr Digby that he will destroy the orders he received for the Gulf of Ambracia as well as the copy we made. He undertakes to bring no case on that matter and neither will I.'

Toomey sat in silence, but he did take off his wig and produce a handkerchief with which he wiped his head. Next he sought to loosen his stock, given his neck was damp as well.

'What do you want, Pearce?'

'I want to talk to Hotham and you are the man to tell him that to do so makes sense.'

'You overrate my importance.'

'If I do, I have no doubt of your ability to lay out in plain terms the threat Digby, Burns and I present to his future well-being. Odd that I was thinking of Admiral Byng only a short while ago and the fact that he suffered, for what? A failure to press home an attack on Minorca, was it not?'

The handkerchief was employed again, though Pearce reckoned Toomey was cogitating on his own fate, not that of Hotham.

'I will be in the wardroom, Mr Toomey. Might I suggest you appraise Admiral Hotham of my desire to see him?'

The desire to be a fly on the bulkhead wall was strong. Pearce had no doubt Toomey would pass on what he had said, albeit in a manner more soothing than that which he had employed. He could hardly be said to know Hotham intimately but he came across as man who would not welcome bad news, and what his clerk would have to get across to him was very bad indeed.

Of course, if Hotham sent for Digby he was sunk; that particular bit of bluff was a very fragile thread indeed. He had to hope the whole added up to a scenario the admiral would reckon he would be well advised to avoid. As of this moment he must know he had troubles enough to contend with.

To add to that, what was being threatened made no sense, for the only purpose of the letter from Pearce to Lucknor had to be in search of some compromise and one only Hotham could grant. In possession of those court martial papers, as well as Digby's orders, the man was safe on that flank.

'A request from the admiral's clerk, Mr Pearce. He would be obliged if you would join him on the forepeak.'

'Thank you,' Pearce said, as the midshipman's head disappeared.

Toomey was waiting for him and given the direction of the wind it seemed an appropriate spot, given it was not far from the heads and the odour of their use.

'I have arranged for you to see Sir William.'

'Splendid.'

'However, I must warn you against addressing him in a like manner to the way you spoke with me. He is a man of some position and deserves to be treated as such.'

Pearce was tempted to take issue with the word 'deserves' but decided to let it pass.

'I have pointed out to the admiral that you want something from him in return for the letter you spoke of.'

'I never doubted you would smoke it, Mr Toomey.'

'I insist you stick to whatever bargain it is you seek. Threaten him directly, mention a word regarding his position and it will act against your purpose. He will not allow himself to be trifled with.'

'I agree.'

'Then I ask that you return to the wardroom and wait. I will send for you again when he is ready to receive you.'

'It must have been an interesting interview you had with him.'

The reply was snapped, evidence of deep irritation. '"Interesting" is not a word I would use, sir! Now may I have the letter?'

'When the bargain is fixed, Mr Toomey, and that means in stone.'

'You would dare to doubt Sir William's word?'

'I would be a fool to accept it. Now please inform the admiral that my patience is not inexhaustible.'

The summons came within the ringing of the watch bells and when he entered Toomey followed him, no doubt to ensure Pearce kept his word. Hotham had his back to the door, staring out of the casements, and it was clear he was intent on avoiding any sort of eye contact.

'Well?'

'I believe Mr Toomey has availed you of certain facts?' No reply but a nod from the clerk. 'In order to complete the business, I require a ship and an offer for Admiral Pierre Martin.'

'What kind of offer?' Hotham demanded, in a tone of voice that indicated he was surprised.

'In the recent actions we have taken a number of French officers from those vessels we have captured or sunk.'

Pearce stopped then, feeling a slight wave of embarrassment wash over him. His intention had been to propose an exchange, the French officers for those captured on HMS *Semele*, the former being much more numerous. Captivity for a naval officer was worse than just incarceration: separated from promotions their career would possibly never recover.

That Ralph Barclay would be one of those who would benefit had to be accepted, for with him in the exchange would come Emily and a chance for him to seek to persuade her to once more break with her husband. It was a mad thing to be about but the whole matter was going nowhere as long as she was held in Toulon.

'I sense you wish to propose an exchange, which is not unknown.'

The feeling of shame, for Pearce, had to do with the nature of those he wished to get free. But for every officer taken by the British there were a hundred lower deckhands and added to those were the many wounded in what had been fierce fighting. Could he, with his background and beliefs, forget about them?

'You are also holding on a transport vessel several hundred common French seamen.'

Hotham had replied at first as though he sensed a bargain easy to accept. Those words altered that and it also had him spin round to face Pearce. 'You are not seriously suggesting I exchange them too?'

'In doing so you will recover the crew of HMS *Semele*, which is no small matter given the fleet is short on hands. The prisoners you have to feed, which is a strain on the resources of your command and getting rid of them makes sense unless you intend to ship them back to England.'

'Martin gets the best of it.'

'Does he? I believe we have been told by the prisoners that Toulon was in a state of ferment before Admiral Martin departed, due to a shortage of food and poor conditions. Has that changed and will a whole load more mouths to feed be welcome? Perhaps by sending back the men taken in both actions we will be inducing a bacillus that will foment mutiny and thus destroy the French Fleet as a fighting force.'

Hotham's head dropped in a way that indicated he was considering the idea, which in many respects made sense. It was a strain on the provisioning of the fleet, as well as the personnel employed, guarding and feeding so many French prisoners and no one could chastise him for acting to alleviate such a burden. Then there was the fact that Pearce was banking on. Unrest in Toulon might save him, given the chances of another fight with the French was unlikely, Martin having retired there.

'No one can be sure of that,' Toomey insisted.

'No. But that is my bargain. The letter and the exchange. Meet it or turn it down.'

'I am made curious as to why you are proposing this.'

'And for me, Mr Toomey, you can remain so.'

Would they guess that Emily Barclay was the prize Pearce sought? They had no idea she had been on *Semele* but it was not too much of a leap to make the connection. If anyone would get there it would be the clever Irish clerk, who was now looking at Pearce in a questioning way.

Hotham turned back to look out of the casements. 'Please allow me to consider it.'

CHAPTER TWENTY-SEVEN

Toulon was a place made known to the eye long before arrival, surrounded as it was by high hills close to being mountainous. In addition it was a locale Pearce knew well, for he had been sent to the port first by Lord Hood as an emissary to find out if the rumours of a Royalist coup were correct and he had been there during the siege. When he thought on that he was given to recollect how many times Sam Hood had misused him, even if the thought now made him smile.

The transport vessel *Marchmont* was packed with French prisoners, many bearing wounds, common seamen who had been held in conditions far from ideal in a Mediterranean summer, confined below decks all through the day and only allowed to take the air in batches once the sun had gone down. The officers were packed into a makeshift wardroom and scarcely better accommodated, though they had fared better, being allowed occasionally to go ashore to the town of San Fiorenzo.

At this moment the passengers had no idea where they were headed, and for two very good reasons. First, Admiral Martin had to accept the offer of an exchange and there was no guarantee he would do so, in which case *Marchmont* was to make for home. Second, the men below decks were bound to be a disgruntled lot, poorly fed, obliged to drink Corsican well water, and according to what their captors had been told, mutinous by nature.

'Do you think they will respect the flag?' asked Loach, captain of the transport.

'If they don't it will be the last you will see of me.'

'You can joke about that, Mr Pearce?'

'Gallows humour, sir, which is all that will serve in such circumstances. I have no reason to think they will fire upon me but you never know.'

Loach looked up at the flag of his nation on his masthead as well as that on the two frigates escorting them, HMS *Brilliant* and Captain Fremantle in *Inconstant*. The former vessel had been an object of some curiosity in the two-day journey. The elusive Toby Burns was aboard her but so too was Taberly, which precluded a visit just to scare the wits out of Emily's spineless nephew.

'Two frigates coming out, sir,' called a lookout.

'Best signal *Inconstant* to heave to as we do,' Pearce said. 'We don't want an accidental fight.'

Loach was very much under the Pearce's orders, a fact made plain by the C-in-C himself and he was nervous. He had been told the nature of the voyage and he knew if it went badly wrong he would be as much a prisoner as the men he had been tasked to look after for many a week. So close to France and required to stick their necks into the lions' den, the chances of keeping his freedom were remote. When he wished John Pearce success it was heartfelt and genuine.

The cutter was in the water waiting for him to board, with his Pelicans as the crew, these extracted from Digby by another order from Hotham who, having accepted the proposal, had taken to it with enthusiasm, no doubt hoping that with these men landed, Toulon would become unstable enough to revolt and give him a much needed boost.

'Haul away, lads,' Pearce commanded.

The oars dipped to take him from the side. The portholes of the transport had been sealed but there had to be enough gaps for a pressed eye to pick out some of the surrounding features of high hills and deep-green forest. Certainly the officers would be clamouring to be given a view, but that was for Loach to deal with. He stood with his hand on the staff holding the white truce flag to send a message that he came to parley. Looking back he could see the two frigates had taken up station as required alongside *Marchmont*.

The ability to speak French had been the cause of much of the activities in which Pearce had been involved and now it was a more priceless asset than ever. Within hailing distance of the first French frigate he called to relate the nature of his mission, really no more than a request to be taken to meet Admiral Martin.

The captain who responded insisted he delay and that held until he had two boats full of musket-bearing marines in the water. They took up station on either side of the cutter, this while the French warship raised sail to get, with its consort, closer to the trio of British vessels. They also had truce flags at their mastheads, but to ensure caution the frigates had opened their gun ports and run out their cannon.

'If our Frenchmen are going to ignore our white flag, Michael, now is the time they will do it.'

'And where, I must ask, will that leave us?'

'Possibly in a dungeon.'

'Sure, you do have a love of the steep tub,' was the very softly spoken response.

'Just row slowly, friend.'

It was a long haul; the outer roads of Toulon consisted of a deep and wide bay so to make the actual harbour entrance required they travel a fair distance. On both sides of the arched mole, once they made it, crowds had gathered to watch this apparition, some merely curious, others gesturing rudely.

'I'd be minded to give some of that back,' Charlie Taverner called.

'And me,' said Rufus.

'What for? You don't understand it.'

'Yes we do,' Charlie insisted. 'Some things don't need words.'

'A few less words from you sometimes might serve, Charlie, such as those you used to fire up all those seamen in Leghorn, where my name is now mud.'

'I explained that, did I not?' he protested. 'How was I to know it would get out of hand?'

'Let's worry about this place, John-boy,' Michael hissed, 'and not what's in the past.'

'Which was you so drunk you had no idea what I was talking about when I queried you.'

Michael grinned. 'Innocent as a lamb, then.'

'A wolf in sheep's clothing, maybe.'

In the harbour Pearce took the tiller to steer the boat towards the building that housed the French naval HQ, now lined with officers and knots of curious bystanders. This time Pearce raised his hat in greeting and again stood to touch and stretch out the white flag, calling out that he brought a message from Admiral Sir William Hotham to be given to Admiral Martin and that sent a young lieutenant scurrying off.

Alongside he asked permission to alight and that was granted, but as he got onto dry land the group before him stood back to form a silent semicircle until finally one officer stepped forward and introduced himself as *Capitaine de Vaisseau* Louis-Jean-Nicolas LeJollie.

'Lieutenant John Pearce, monsieur,' Pearce replied in French.

'Am I allowed to enquire as to your reason for being here in Toulon?'

'That is for Admiral Martin to disseminate once he has been informed.'

As he said that, Pearce lifted his head to look at the building that housed the French command. In doing so he saw, at a long floor-to-ceiling window, the figure and anxious face of Emily Barclay, which caused his heart to miss a beat. LeJollie turned to follow his gaze and then remarked.

'The poor woman.'

'Why poor, monsieur?'

'You would not know, of course. Her husband, the captain of your *Semele*, was killed in the action in which I took her.'

'Killed?'

'I am told one of our bar shot came in low and took off his head, which I fear ended up in the sea.'

Pearce could not respond for a moment. That news changed so much it was hard to encompass it all. 'Barclay,' he croaked.

'That is the lady's name, monsieur.' LeJollie produced a wry smile. 'While one has pity for her loss, one must also say that young as she is, as well as beautiful, I do not think she will stay long a widow. And she does have his child on the way, by which she can remember her husband.'

Pierre Martin must have wondered if Pearce was witless, so slow was he to respond to the admiral's questions when he was finally led into his presence. How could he begin to explain how tumultuous his thoughts were as he stumbled through the message Hotham had composed, full of high-flown sentiments regarding the sufferings that would be inflicted on Martin's fellow countrymen by either extended incarceration on a ship or a long voyage back to captivity in Britain, especially those bearing battle wounds?

'In exchange, we ask for the return of the officers and crew of HMS *Semele* and, of course, the captain's wife.'

Martin had a big round face and that broke into a smile. 'I do not think my officers will welcome the last part of your request. Madame Barclay has made a deep impression on many of them.'

'In what way?' Pearce bridled, jealously.

'Monsieur, if you know of her you will also know she is a rare flower. Added to that she has been most concerned for the well-being of the men you seek to free.'

Martin ceased to smile and frowned. 'You do realise, monsieur, that if I do not agree, I cannot permit you, having brought the men I have lost so close to their homeland, to sail them away again without I seek a rescue.'

'Admiral Hotham accepted that risk on the grounds that he sees you as an honourable man. He also knows that the honour of the French navy is as it was under a different system of government. But I must also add that our escorts have orders to fight if they must and the vessel carrying the prisoners would thus be in peril of wayward shot.'

Martin could make of that what he would; was it a threat or just a genuine assessment? He sat back in his chair, hand on chin, eyes locked onto Pearce as if trying to see if what he had relayed from Hotham was the truth or mere hyperbole. His visitor leant forward, pulling from his pocket a list of the prisoners he had carried to Toulon, of necessity a long one formed of dozens of sheets of paper.

'The one detailing the captured officers is on top, the common seamen wounded is the last.'

Martin picked up the first; the rest would be mere numbers but the names of his officers would be known to him. The perusal induced a sigh. 'Since you say you have brought the wounded I assume those I do not see to be dead?'

'Sadly, yes. They were buried with full honours on Corsica according to the Catholic rite.'

Pearce had been aware of a fellow standing by the double doors throughout, who reminded him in his manner, if not his appearance, of Toomey. He was so very much a clerk.

Martin gestured to him. 'Please take the lieutenant and provide for him some refreshments.'

'My boat crew?'

'They, too, will be looked after. I will look over this proposal and I assure you that Admiral Hotham is correct. I would not sully the name of my service by acting in an inappropriate manner that risks useless loss of life.'

'Would it be possible to see Captain Barclay's widow?' Pearce felt like a complete scrub as he added, 'I knew her husband well and would wish to offer my condolences for her loss.'

'How can I deny such a request?'

Emily did not fly into his arms when he entered her apartment; instead she stood biting her lower lip, with a glance at the man who had shown him in.

'Monsieur, I wonder if Mrs Barclay and I could be left alone?'

A dry stick of a fellow, very much an indoor man, Martin's factotum was yet a Frenchman. The request got a lifted and telling eyebrow, before he bowed and departed, his knowing smile hidden because he had his back to the couple. She was in Pearce's arms the minute the door was closed.

'Why, in the name of all that is holy, are you crying, Emily?'

'I'm so happy, yet I feel ashamed, too, that I rejoice in being a widow.'

'Given we are going to have a great deal of time together, it is my fond hope that one day I will understand.'

Pearce did not seek to linger, staying enough time to exchange kisses and embraces and to put his hand on her belly, seeking for a kick from their child. He feared to remain longer than was appropriate, not wishing to complicate his mission, which might impact on her. He had no idea if Martin was going to agree to the exchange, which would mean him pleading for Emily's release on the grounds of her widowhood and condition. That could not be seen to have a personal motive.

He checked that his Pelicans had been taken care of, happy to see them tucking into a fish soup that they complained reeked of garlic before he was taken to what had to be the officers' mess and fed, joined there by LeJollie who gave him an account of the action against *Semele*. It seemed politic to keep hidden that he had been close by in a pinnace. Eventually Martin's factotum appeared and led him back to the man himself.

'Monsieur, I have to tell you that your ship's officers were sent to an inland fortress. I will request their return but that may take some time. I require that you take my word that once they are back in Toulon they will be passed on to one of the frigates patrolling off the port under a flag of truce.'

'The men?'

'You will disembark my sailors then embark your own, if you agree.'

'I am bound to ask about the captain's wife?'

'Let me just say I will miss the occasional sight of her.' He laughed then. 'But I sense some will weep.'

'We must be circumspect, John'

These were almost the first words Emily said to him when she and the small amount of luggage she had were brought aboard the now empty *Marchmont*. With that, having enquired as to where she would be accommodated until they rejoined the fleet – Loach gave up his cabin – she made her way there.

The crew of *Semele* were paraded on to the quay, Pearce ticking their names off a muster roll, a copy of the copy kept aboard the flagship for the purposes of pay. Just as Admiral Martin had seen the gaps in the list he had been given, Pearce had to mark them on his, Ralph Barclay's name first, mentally totalling the high price

Semele had paid in that fight. Martin had provided a list of officers who would be freed later.

The warrants and the purser were afforded the temporary wardroom, which they pronounced a disgrace, as did the arriving crew, and both groups began to immediately clean the ship with vinegar, cursing as they did the filthy habits of the French.

Charlie and Rufus had served on Barclay's 74, before and during the Glorious First, not happily, but they knew faces and names and were busy reacquainting themselves with old shipmates. That evaporated as Devenow appeared because one of the last acts they had committed was to belt the bully round the ear with a marlin spike.

'I was Captain Barclay's servant,' the brute complained, obviously demanding superior treatment to the rest of the crew.

'Well you're not now,' Pearce replied, harshly. 'So follow the others.'

The man was known to him too, and not fondly, for his time aboard *Brilliant*. That also applied to Cornelius Gherson who had to stop and stare when he saw who it was supervising the loading, only moving when given a sharp order to do so or be left behind. He assumed airs even more grating than Devenow.

'Is Mrs Barclay to be freed as well?'

'What business is that of yours?'

'I need to speak with her on some very important matters.'

'I will pass on the message but from what I recall I doubt she'll want to speak with you.'

Gherson produced a sly grin. 'Then she won't find out what I know.'

'Which is?"

'For her ears, Pearce, not yours.'

'Mr Loach, put this piece of vermin in the cable tier so he may learn some manners regarding the correct way to address an officer.'

'Damn you, Pearce.'

'Belay that, have your bosun make up a cat o' nine tails, and a good skin-stripping one at that.'

Gherson positively scooted up the gangway, nearly the last to go aboard, with Pearce yelling after him that he should keep quiet regarding anything he knew about the late captain; really he meant the man's widow and himself.

When Emily said 'circumspect' she meant it. If John Pearce was invited to enter the cabin it was always with Loach and getting her alone was near impossible. But a Mediterranean evening sunset virtually demanded a late promenade and finally he was able to converse with her in private on the poop, right by the taffrail and facing out to sea, though not at what could be called an intimate distance and in carefully controlled voices.

'You must see, John, why such behaviour as I have demonstrated must be maintained.'

'Forgive me if I do not,' he growled.

'Being a widow imposes on me certain standards of behaviour.'

'Is that what I am being obliged to suffer? And what standards do you mean?'

The explanation was lengthy and depressing to the man listening. She would, as soon as she could, be obliged to wear black, the right clothing for her situation. Her husband's death had wiped clean a slate that had caused her no end of worry but now she could return to England and her family without a stain on her reputation, there to bear her child and look forward to the day they could be together.

'Which is when?'

'I feel at least a year is required before I could be seen to be thinking of a second marriage.'

'A year!'

'And prior to any nuptials there would need to be a decent period of courtship.'

'Emily!'

'Keep your voice down, John.' Her voice softened and he could see even in her profile an understanding smile. 'Naturally, if a discreet chance to be together presents itself, we will take it, but it is bound to be a rare event.'

'I cannot believe that such a crumb is all I can look forward to.'

'What would you have me do, John, lose one husband and immediately betroth myself to another?'

'What I would have you do is forget Frome and your family and come and live with me well away from fear of their prejudices. I feel I have the right to remind you that you are carrying my child, which, in a year plus your courtship period will be damn near talking.'

'Do you have to use such language?'

'I do.'

'I did not wish to allude to this so soon, but the child will have to be born a Barclay, I'm afraid. To christen it otherwise would be like flying an adulterous flag.'

'And if I don't want my son or daughter christened?'

'How can you think of such a thing? No, the child will be

named Barclay until a time we are wed and he or she can take your name. I will, of course, consult with you over what the Christian names will be.'

'For which I heartily thank you,'

'I cannot see you are making this easy for me,' Emily protested, aware of the irony in his tone. 'But what I propose is for the best. For my reputation and your own as well as the future of our unborn child. Do you want the world to know how our offspring was conceived?'

'I don't care what the world knows.'

'Well I do, and I regard it as somewhat selfish if you seek to burden our child with a stigma before it is even born.' The voice softened. 'Our future happiness may be delayed, John, but it will be comfortable. In the cabin is a chest containing my husband's papers and I must tell you I see no testament.'

'Which means?'

'That lacking one somewhere else I am going to be left in very comfortable circumstances and that, of course, will, when we are wed, include you. We shall have a home and all the creature comforts we require without worrying about money.'

'Ralph Barclay's money, Emily.'

'And if it's mine now? We will have the means to be happy.'

Emily enthused then, about the kind of house they would live in, a country one close to her family, people he would come to love as much as she. And there would be more children to grow and surround their perfect life. He could give up the navy and live the life of a country gentlemen, while she could become a lady the locality would hold in respect.

The sun was going down, turning the sky orange and in her

reverie of their shared future Emily did not see his expression. The picture she painted was not being received with unalloyed joy by a lover who was being told he would be required to wait a very long time before they could enjoy the intimacy he had come to treasure.

'And if I were to say to you the life of a country gentlemen does not appeal?'

'John, how can it not when our life together will be perfect?'

To discover more great books and to
place an order visit our website at
allisonandbusby.com

Don't forget to sign up to our free newsletter at
allisonandbusby.com/newsletter
for latest releases, events and exclusive offers

f Allison & Busby Books
@AllisonandBusby

You can also call us on
020 7580 1080
for orders, queries
and reading recommendations